The
LioN
—— and the ——
UnicorN

The
LioN
and the
UnicorN

Andrian the Ruthless

Lauren,

Make History Happen.

♡ Helena V

Helena Vor

Library of Congress Control Number: 2013915805
ISBN: Hardcover   978-1-4836-9277-7
                  Softcover   978-1-4836-9276-0
                  Ebook   978-1-4836-9278-4

Rev. date: 09/10/2013

To order additional copies of this book, contact:
Xlibris LLC
1-888-795-4274
www.Xlibris.com
Orders@Xlibris.com
139999

I dedicate this book to my Grandfather Tony who passed shortly before the book was released. Better have a copy sent to Heaven! To the rest of my family for their patience with my excessive obsession with the Middle Ages. To my dear sweet Robert Seamonster-Bagel for being my rock while I have pursued my dream. To my friends Akilah, Joy, and Mary for believing in me. To my friends and neighbors, Bella, Josh, Bahni, and Skarlett for helping keep me focused and taking me to Disneyland and Vegas when I need a break. To Frosty, who enjoyed dinner and theatre when first I dreamt this whole thing up. To countless other people who have helped me make this dream a reality. So many thanks are due to all!!!

"The devil is not as black as he is painted."
—Dante Alighieri, The Divine Comedy

Chapter One

A shadow cloaked in turbulent blue clutched a burning torch. Under a hood embroidered with gold, two ferocious black eyes penetrated the smoky darkness. Reflections of angry flames danced within the droplets of sweat beaded in his beard. The phantom hulked from atop a steed, raging against its master's control as a fiend clutching its last breath. As the midnight stallion pawed the ground, a swift tug of the reins silenced its desperation.

Royal soldiers hardened from a prolonged campaign accompanied the dark rider, though none of the hooligans dared ride sword's length from the grim specter. Even as the company waited high above the river of fire, Andrian the Ruthless hid in shadow. While the villeins in the glen scrambled to rescue each other from the disintegrating town, the soldiers swayed on their feet and waited for orders to march forth or to turn away.

Dismayed by the boldness of the general's actions, the night breeze tore at his cape; the face of the gold-crowned angel of death glowed with light. Andrian the Ruthless leaned forward on his stallion as small silhouettes fled eastward. He raised his arm and signaled for all but two of his remaining soldiers to join the assault. At the bottom of the hillock, five men armed with sticks and rocks tied on ropes fell before the swords of three dozen trained brigands.

Widows and orphans shouted to a heap of brave men slowly eaten by fire. Pulling her hair and wailing, a woman fell upon the corpse of her husband and was taken up in a swift red crackle. Andrian the Ruthless turned his face away.

A mounted knight cantered up the hill toward the dark prince. Though he had seen but two more than the prince's twenty-four winters, inexorable war had carved lines in his face. As the knight's horse hesitated near to the stallion of perdition, he dismounted.

With a turn of his lip and a nod, the prince acknowledged his vassal. "Pleasant evening, what say you?"

The knight swallowed as he entered into the prince's shadow. A single nod he gave in return.

The prince frowned at the knight. "Where is Sir Armand? I told him to give me the damage report."

The knight crossed himself. "Milord, he's been murdered." He handed the prince a bloodstained scrap of tunic. "The people barricaded themselves in the parish church . . . they hold Sir Idwal's brother hostage."

The prince glared at the glowing town. "How many women and children within?"

The knight swallowed, "Nineteen, my lord prince."

Andrian the Ruthless grimaced.

"What'd you want us to do?"

Looking down, he thrust his flaming torch at the knight. "Burn it to the ground." He bared his teeth and the knight's eyes became two full moons.

"But Sir Idwal's brother . . ."

"He's already dead!" The prince jabbed his finger toward the church.

Torch in hand, he bowed. "Yes, Yer 'ighness." He winced as he looked up at the prince's unwavering glare.

"Move, you fool." The prince shooed the man with his boot.

The knight crept away, as a dog kicked in disobedience.

The knight mounted his horse once again and rode down the slope of dried grass toward those who awaited their lord's command. The torch glittered from the prince's vantage point as the rider gained distance from his ruler. The prince's black eyes followed the spark of light until the smoldering red of the town consumed it.

The breeze carried the screams of the innocent long after they burned within the holy edifice. "We seek vengeance." Eerie hisses mixed with the sizzling of the skeletal wood fence beams littering the ground around the ruthless prince. Hot winds carried white wisps of the dead past Andrian the Ruthless. He exhaled and raised his eyes to what should have been a twinkling night sky. Though he lingered a league from the town, smoke veiled the heavens. Ash rained upon him, and he opened his bejeweled hand to catch flakes of his enemies. He rubbed his fingers together and wiped his hand on his cloak.

"Come, let us move out," Prince Andrian hissed to his midnight stallion. With a nudge from his heels, the demon mount reared and bolted toward the village of ghostly cinders.

No children clashed sticks in mock swordplay, no blacksmith clanked hammer on anvil, no maidens kissed lads for a smile, and no one drank ale at the Winking Horse Inn. The sound of embers popping, the breeze whistling through the skeletal dwellings, and the grunts of mercenaries overturning rubble burned the prince's soul.

Andrian the Ruthless paraded past his scavengers with the air of a scorpion. Soldiers clutched cloths over their faces to hinder the stench of the flesh, and gagged as they discovered one carcass after another within the wreckage of the town. Bile tingled the back of the prince's throat, and as he inhaled deeply, he closed his eyes and pictured his father's proud gaze when he returned home from the Holy Land. Nine years fighting the Ayyubid Dynasty opened the young man's eyes to his passion for military glory. Lauded by the belligerents as their Norman Alexander, Prince Andrian came home a Christian hero and had earned the high distinction of general of the Armies of Briton. With that honor, he claimed for himself the most powerful military force in the Western world. Andrian's blade carved greatness in the walls of Jerusalem as he would carve greatness in the mind of every traitor to his father's crown.

"This isn't *greatness*, Your Majesty!"

His fantasy shattered, the prince halted his horse. "Who *spoke* such words?" He unsheathed his sword and pointed it toward the nearest band of vultures. The soldiers looked at each other and shrugged. Andrian the Ruthless roared, "I POSED A QUESTION THAT DEMANDS AN ANSWER . . . NOW ONE OF YOU MUST ANSWER OR ALL OF YOU SHALL DIE!"

A knight carrying a bundle stepped forward from the glowing blackness. "T'is I who've insulted thee, my prince."

Andrian the Ruthless leapt from his stallion, sword trembling in his hand. He stalked up to the malefactor, but stopped as the knight revealed a girl in his cloak.

"She's *dead*, milord."

The prince lifted her face to the last light of the fire. "I can *see* that," he growled.

"There are others here, children . . . and women. You sent them to their deaths because you fancied a *bonfire* would avenge the death of a knight." The knight embraced the dead child. "Our code demands we protect the innocent. This child was no murderer."

Andrian the Ruthless snarled at him, "You try my patience . . . your tongue would not be so bold if I did not value your father's services." The prince turned around, glaring at the men now gathering around in morbid curiosity.

The knight clutched the girl closer. "Show some mercy for *once* in your life, Your Highness." He kissed the child's hair. "It wouldn't make you *less* of a man."

Andrian the Ruthless raised his sword to the knight's exposed throat. "Mercy is for the *craven*, not for cutthroats like *me*."

The knight swallowed against the sharp blade nicking his throat. None of the soldiers approached as he held the knight at bay. The captive knight looked up at his lord, the whites of his eyes vivid against the pitch and hellfire. Panic swelled his ribcage in heaving breaths, and the little girl who dangled from his arms slipped. Before she struck the ground, the prince abandoned his sword to catch her.

With the child cradled in one arm, the prince slipped his boot under the blade of his sword and flipped it back into his hand. Prince Andrian frowned; the child felt light and frail as one-hundred-year-old parchment.

The soldiers backed away, mumbling to each other.

"Bury the dead." The prince kicked a silver bauble into a smoldering daub and wattle hut, and strode off with the girl leaning against him, her head upon his armored shoulder.

The knight stroked his neck and then glanced at his bloodied fingertips. Turning around to the gaping men, he choked, "You heard what His Highness said." Without another word, the crowd dispersed to search for carnage.

Prince Andrian carried his burden toward the graveyard nearest the scorched church. The unnatural red glow from the ambient firelight in the town made the hair on the prince's neck stand on end. Black smoke still puffed from within the collapsed stone walls of the church, and as the prince entered the garden of stones flecked with dewy lichen, he inhaled sharply. Between the shards of stone, red eyes glared at him.

"Who goes there?" He lifted his sword toward the image, though the only response was a barely audible growl not unlike a dog's. His hands began to sweat. "This is a place of rest," he announced as his hand shook with the heft of the sword. The two red orbs blinked out, one by one. He let out a swift groan as he shoved his blade into the hardened soil beside him.

Prince Andrian pulled his gauntlet off with his teeth, spit it to the ground, and wiped his forehead with the back of his hand. Glancing back at the now empty church, he tore his cape from his shoulder, placed it on the ground, and then draped the girl across the fur. He retrieved his gauntlet, and removing the second gauntlet, pulled both through his belt for safekeeping. With a dagger he drew from his boot, he began to dig a shallow grave. Toward the prince, whimpering drifted. He stopped scratching the soil and cocked his head. Rising halfway to his feet, he scanned the yard for any further disturbances. The wind had stilled inside the yard and the prince felt his heart *lub-dub* in his ears.

"Who is in my presence? State your business." The prince stood at full height with his hand slowly reaching toward his embedded hand and a half sword.

A young child in a blackened nightdress rose from behind a tombstone shaped like a cross beaming in the sun. The prince left his sword and approached the waif. She cowered as his shadow fell across her. Prince Andrian crouched beside the girl not more than seven winters old.

"What is your name?" he susurrated.

The child muttered, though she struggled to open her scabbed lips and mouth.

"Did you say your name was *Kieran?*"

She nodded with a whimper.

"Do you know who *I* am?"

She shrugged and cowered as he leaned in toward her.

"Does this *hurt?*" He brushed her scarred jaw.

She winced and large tears fell from her eyes. She tried to talk again but the prince placed his finger over his mouth.

"It *might* make the swelling worse." He stood and grasped the child's tiny hand in his. "Come with me."

She followed him back to the unburied body. With a scream in her throat, Kieran threw her arms around the lifeless child. Prince Andrian shifted his weight from one foot to the other while the child wept and kissed her face.

The prince placed his hand awkwardly on Kieran's back. She looked up and wiped her nose. She pointed to herself and the body, and held her hands to her chest.

"She was your sister?"

Kieran nodded.

The prince clumsily stroked her blonde hair. "Rest assured she sleeps in eternal peace." Prince Andrian withdrew his hand quickly as the girl stood.

Kieran went to the hole the prince had started digging and clawed at the dirt.

He shrugged and knelt beside her. While he used his quillon to cut through the overgrown roots of nearby trees and harder clots of dirt, Kieran used her dress to move the extracted dirt from the entrance of the hole. It took far less time for the man and the child working together to remove enough soil to bury the body. The prince lowered the dead girl into the grave with his cloak and shifted her until she lay as though she may wake at any moment. Flat on his stomach, he reached in and placed two coins on her eyes. Kieran handed the prince the broken end of a tombstone to push dirt down into the grave while she sprinkled handfuls of dirt on her sister as a baker tops off a masterpiece with sugar.

While Kieran plucked a few flowers that survived the now extinguished flames, Prince Andrian constructed a crude cross from two branches he found lying beside the church. Kneeling, Prince Andrian leaned his head on the hilt of his sword while Kieran prayed for her sister. After the prayer, Prince Andrian kissed the hilt of his sword, withdrew the blade from the soil, and stood. "What was her name?"

In addition to garbling her sister's name, she pulled something glimmering from around her own neck. Prince Andrian ran his hand down the blade of his sword, and then smeared the blood on the cross. "*Requiescat in pace*, Gwyneth." He sheathed his sword. With one hand, Kieran nudged the prince, the other hand dangled a brass chain before him.

He held out his uninjured hand as she entwined the delicate necklace around his fingers. Kieran's eyes glistened. The small girl pointed at the necklace and then at the man who had discovered her in the darkness. She tried to say something, but held her hand to her cheek with a grimace instead.

Prince Andrian knelt beside her as she beckoned for him to do so, then she retrieved the necklace and unclasped it with inept fingers. She placed it around his neck and clasped it once again. The child patted her chest and then patted his chest. He swallowed the lump in his throat and stood up. Kieran's eyes met his, and the black curtains to his soul drew back for a moment and he smiled. Prince Andrian ran his fingers through his hair and cleared his throat. "I wish to take you back to camp with me. You would not live without shelter or someone to watch over you." He reached out and tenderly swept her scorched hair back from her disfigured cheek.

Kieran grasped his slashed hand and traced the open wound. Then she tore part of her destroyed dress, wrapped it around the injury, and then kissed it. She slurred another sentence, and though Prince Andrian understood none of it this time, he smiled again. Hand in hand, they walked through the rubble toward the camp.

Through ghostly buildings, over a bloody road, and past wooden posts resembling charred bones, the pair walked in silence. Kieran's eyes widened as they passed the remnants of her home. She and the prince meandered around the dwellings of the dead. The prince felt his ribcage murmur with every creak and groan as timbers snapped and walls crumbed. He raised his sword and pointed at every noise. Faces appeared in the steam. Faces and eyes glowering. Teeth and face and eyes. Andrian blinked a few times as a black shape hunched over by the corpse of a horse, halfway skeletonized and blackened. Kieran had stopped to pick a flower that had survived the ravaging and the prince cleared his throat. She skipped to his side again and grasped his dripping wet hand.

Prince Andrian had shortened his long strides for the foundling child. What would his soldiers think if they realized he was holding hands with a little girl? Tender feelings did not cause him to keep his hand in hers, he insisted to himself. He would dump her somewhere when he had the chance and walk away. He would not concern himself with her fate after he returned to his stronghold in Eddington. She was useless and weak and simply a casualty of war. He looked down at the straw-haired stray and scowled to himself. She stopped and picked up another flower and looked up to hand it to him. He placed it in his belt. She smiled.

Kieran spied the campfires before the prince did, and she pulled at his hand. Through the thickness of the debris, the glowing of the warm fires awaited his return.

He shook his finger as he looked down into her blue eyes. "I know that it is *easy* for a wee child to be lost in the tumult of rowdy men wandering about." He hesitated and added, "I do *not* want to lose you in the confusion."

The girl nodded at him and walked on his left side the rest of the trek to the military encampment. She released his hand for a moment to wipe some blood from her nose. The burning stars from the sky still scorched her face, it seemed.

Soldiers stood at attention as Andrian the Ruthless sauntered into the perimeters. Kieran stared at the ground after the soldiers' mouths dropped while she walked by them. Kieran leaned closer to her protector as the men buzzed. Andrian the Ruthless glared at those who sneered at the detainee, her angelic face melted like a candle on one side. She snuggled against the prince.

"*Où est le médecin?*" Andrian the Ruthless hollered at a group of his soldiers gathered about some injured companions. In unison, they pointed toward a small tent, gray like the smoke that had surged through the glen earlier that evening.

He stormed over to the shelter and threw the curtain door to the side. Kieran tramped behind him. The physician whirled around at the sudden intrusion, and as he recognized his lord, he bowed and kissed the prince's ringed hand.

"Are you *wounded,* milord?" He looked up at the dried blood in the prince's hair.

"It is nothing." He gingerly touched a slight burn on his scalp from falling embers. "However, I have here someone who *has* had a terrible misfortune." He looked to his left side, but the girl had vanished. He lifted his cape and chuckled; she had concealed herself in his sapphire drapery.

The physician covered his mouth. "My God, sire, she's *ruined!*"

The prince felt the child clamber back into his clothes and quaver behind him. Without warning, his fist shot out at the surgeon, who collided with a table laden with surgical instruments.

"How *dare* you articulate such a lie!" Andrian the Ruthless stormed over to the fallen medic, grabbed his shirt, picked him up, and stood him on his feet. The man shielded his face with his shriveled arms. "I *demand* you help ease her suffering!" Odhran lowered his defense, and the prince slapped him. "*That* blow was for cowardice."

The physician bowed, and then with trembling hands picked up his disturbed implements.

While shaking his head, Prince Andrian gathered up a few woolen blankets that lay about the tent. He set them in a pile and then folded them out as a makeshift bed.

"Come, Kieran, sit here and rest."

The child sat down on the heap with a sigh. In the flickering light within the tent, Kieran analyzed her savior. The darkness out in the murdered town had cloaked the sun-bronzed man like a wild animal in the thicket. Bruises encircled his copper eyes. His mouth, a thin line within his ebony beard, frowned with discord. His ebony mane, half of it pulled into an untidy braid, fell to his mid-back. He hulked over when pacing much of the time, though when he stood still his frame lengthened and he stood as tall as the time-worn sarsens near her home. Through his battle shredded tunic, his body twisted with muscles starved for meat and hardened with use. The lionlike prince snarled as he glared at the physician.

Gold and silver rings and bracelets, all inlaid with colored stones, graced his calloused fingers and heavy-metal-scarred wrists. Scarlet, cerulean, emerald, and violet, the gems projected a rainbow across the tent as he ran his fingers through his hair. The soft tinkling of the metal reminded her of the bells on the sheep her neighbor kept at home.

The sword, which the prince caressed at his side, boasted silver and gold pictographs and words foreign to many educated men. Along the length of the scabbard, massive sapphires in various shades of indigo cast stars in Kieran's liquid eyes. As the prince slunk back and forth within the enclosure, her gaze followed his wealth with hypnotic veneration.

"*Kieran?*" Prince Andrian grasped the child's shoulder.

She looked up at him and muttered a few indecipherable sentences. Prince Andrian squinted. Kieran sighed and sat straight.

"I apologize for having difficulty understanding you." The prince pointed to Odhran. "This man is my personal physician, and I trust him to take care of your painful injury. Perhaps when you heal, we shall enjoy conversation." The prince's eyes softened as he crouched by her. "I shall return in a short time to make sure you are comfortable for the night." He touched the child's hair delicately.

Kieran bowed her head and pooched out her lip.

Andrian the Ruthless drew near Odhran, hissed in his ear something that made him cringe, patted his back rather harshly, turned, and left.

Chapter Two

The prince's tent stood on the edge of the encampment amidst plundered furniture and weaponry. He pulled back the drapes of silvery blue and coiled gold rope and sat upon a bed covered with rich fabrics and furs. The prince leaned his head in his hands with a groan.

Something stirred in the coverlets beneath him. He jumped to his feet, sword drawn on the offending lump. A woman sat up and smiled at him.

"Put that away, Andrian. You'll likely kill someone with it."

Andrian dropped his weapon on the ground. "You scared the *soul* out of me."

The woman fluffed her hair. "You *haven't* a soul, Andrian."

Andrian bit his lip. "You know that is *not* true, woman." Prince Andrian sat beside her. "What are you *doing* here, Farida?"

She shrugged, pulled her hair forward, and braided it.

He kissed her cheek and laid himself across her lap. "I have had a *brutal* day. Give me what I want from you."

"Not *tonight*, Andrian." She stroked his black locks.

He sat up quickly and frowned. "Why not, do I not *deserve* love from you?"

Farida pulled him toward her. "Your father has been interested in your whereabouts." She cuffed his face a couple times and smirked.

Andrian kissed her hand and stood to pace the tent. He wrenched the rings from his fingers. Clutched in his hand, the jewels clinked together like tiny bells. He yanked off his bracelets and hurled all in an open wooden box as he passed it. "Did he tell you to bring me home?"

She sighed. "He thinks lowly of me. I am not even allowed to enter the keep." Andrian kicked a chest full of money, several weapons of increasing lethality, and three separate piles of clothes. Farida smirked as Andrian's foot caught in a broken box. Whilst he shook his leg and cursed, Farida beckoned him with her finger. He hobbled to her and lifted his leg onto the bed. "Have you finished with your raving yet?" She pulled his foot free, shook the box upside down, and shoved his leg off the bed.

"Why *did* you come so far for mere gossip then *?*"

Farida slid from his bed and filled the box with trinkets the prince had kicked about. "I came for more than *one* purpose."

Andrian rolled his eyes. "My Farida, how you torment me." He swirled his cape, tore it from the golden clasps on his shoulders, and hurled it to the ground with a snort. "You are still my subject, you know, even if you hold my heart captive."

Farida slammed the filled box on the bed. "Oh stop being so *arrogant.* You haven't the keys to the kingdom just yet. You still have Julian in your way." Andrian leapt toward her and seized her from behind. Farida reached behind herself and grabbed his hair. "Oh, let me *go*, you *jealous* little boy."

"*Who says he is in my way?*" Andrian ran his hands along her arms.

"Why, I saw the king command Julian to send an army for you."

He spun her around. "When?"

She smiled and kissed his forehead. "Relax. Julian is a coward. You've no true competition . . . *yet.*" She wiggled his nose with her finger and smirked.

Andrian groaned and nuzzled against her cheek. "Why must you be *such* a *chat sauvage?*" He released her and picked up his sword from the floor. "You *will* wait for me?" He opened the curtain to his tent halfway to leave, and looked over his shoulder at her.

"*Perhaps.*"

Andrian the Ruthless growled and muttered a few choice insults in her general direction. Head lowered, he exited the tent.

Farida called after him, "Later then?"

The prince tossed his hair, and as he kicked a stone across the blackened soil, it hit a jug of alcohol. A nearby fire flared from the fuel, and as Prince Andrian watched it sputter, he punched the air.

* * *

Prince Andrian returned to the medical tent, his chest seething and jaw set to break. Before he threw open the door flap, he straightened his stance and smoothed his hair. The young girl looked up at the prince from her makeshift bed and greeted him with a squeak. She had doubted his return to her, but as he crouched by her side to examine her face, her heart lifted.

The prince's personal physician approached Andrian the Ruthless and his patient.

"How will she fare? Will she heal well?" The prince rose to his feet and eclipsed the man.

Odhran bowed and kissed the prince's hand several times. "Might I speak about the child in *private?* I don't long to disturb her with the news."

The prince opened the curtain for the man and pointed open-palmed to the night. The physician exited with his head bowed.

Odhran turned around and clasped his hands together, visibly trembling before the dark-eyed prince as they stood in the firelight. "There's not *much* I can do for her—I mean about the *scarring* later. She won't be marriageable. She mightn't even survive the *week* if the wound's poisoned. The salve should help of course, but have little hope in her recovery, Milord Prince."

Andrian the Ruthless wiped his hand over his mouth and nodded. "You tell me that I *should* have let her die?"

Odhran nodded with a shrug.

The prince pursed his lips and turned away from his physician. The campfires glowed as evil eyes about the hillside. A cold breeze punctuated by bursts of heat billowed through his robes and upended his soul. Prince Andrian fondled the bronze chain around his neck. Odhran wrung his hands while the prince's eyes darted to and fro in the red light; his blackening eyes hardened to stone as the wind sprinkled ash upon his shoulders.

"Milord? What'll I do about the girl? She can't be left *alone* for long, and I don't want to be *her* guardian." He approached the prince and whispered, "Perhaps it'd be wise if you *abandoned* her somewhere on the way to Eddington. Nobody'd *ever* know about it."

Andrian the Ruthless whipped around and clutched the man by the throat. "How *dare* you even think it." He squeezed Odhran's throat and shook him. "How must I care for the child?" he said as he snarled in his face.

The physician, gawking at the prince, remained silent.

"Answer me, you *damned* fool!" The prince squeezed harder.

Choking, he grasped at the prince's gauntlet and garbled. Andrian the Ruthless opened his hand and Odhran crumpled to the ground.

After several seconds of gasping and failed swallowing, the physician uttered little more than a peep.

The prince yanked Odhran to his feet by his tunic as a small child does her doll. "If she perishes, I shall consider your *inaction* to be treason and I will *personally* cut you in half. Do you *understand?*"

The flustered physician flapped his hands about. "I'll tell you *all* I know about her condition and give you bandages and the like. I *beg* you, sire, you don't have the *skill* to heal her."

Prince Andrian bared his incisors, seemingly sharper than usual. "It seems like you believe me to be an *inadequate* guardian."

Odhran shook his head. "Not at all . . . I'm merely expressing concern for *you*, my liege . . . I fear you've taken a *lost cause* to be worthy of your devotion."

Movement caught the prince's eye, so he glanced back toward the tent. The child stood outside in nothing but a long tunic, her arms wrapped around her torso as her teeth chattered.

"Kieran, what on *earth* are you doing out of bed? You shall catch your *death* in this weather."

Kieran muttered as Prince Andrian shuffled her back inside the tent. She pointed to her face and said what seemed to be that it felt much better.

Prince Andrian caressed the child's sweaty hair. "Kieran, *please* rest for now. You cannot wander about in your condition." She crossed her arms, but he remained firm. "Sleep, for tomorrow we ride. I need you to be well rested for I cannot stop along the way. It is *imperative* you obey me."

Kieran's face fell and she flopped on the makeshift bed. Odhran entered the tent and gave the child a sneer before he looked over at his lord. "Sire? Perhaps she might sleep *elsewhere* tonight. I've many men who have *graver* injuries than this creature, and they'd do well inside where it's warm and inviting."

The prince raised his eyebrow and rolled his tongue in his mouth. "Are you *commanding* me to take this child from your sight?"

Odhran's eyes pooled fear. "N-nay, milord."

Prince Andrian told Kieran to wait outside for him. When his eyes flashed, she obeyed. Through the flickering of the oil lamps in the tent, Kieran watched a shadowy Andrian the Ruthless draw his sword and slash Odhran's torso. She jumped backward as blood splashed against the inside of the tent. The physician fell in a heap and the prince muttered a few extra insults as he kicked him thrice.

Kieran covered her eyes as Prince Andrian exited the tent. "He *deserved* it." He wiped his blade on the scorched grass and sheathed it. "Come, you shall stay with *me* tonight."

Kieran uncovered her eyes and glanced at the dead man's foot peeking out from under the drapery. She grasped Prince Andrian's hand tightly as they plodded to the royal tent. She stopped and gazed in wonder at all the loot Prince Andrian had acquired during his last siege. Mountains of gold, silver, weapons, and other oddities, many of which Kieran had never known to exist in such quantities, littered the ground. She tried to tell him something about the collection but stopped as a woman exited the tent with a pleasant skip.

"Farida, why are you *still* here?" Andrian unsheathed his sword and used it to pick up a filthy cloak lying outside the silvery drapes. He wrinkled his nose as he heaved it to the side.

"I thought I *told* you, Andrian, I came for a *purpose*. You didn't even wait around for me to tell you. You lumbered away before I had *any* chance to explain myself." Farida glanced over at Kieran.

"*Lumbered*, did I?" Andrian squinted at her.

"*Who's she?*" Farida pointed at the young girl.

Prince Andrian put his arm around the child. "*Je vous présente Kieran.*"

Kieran stared at the woman with embarrassment, for the weather called for more clothing than she wore.

Farida laughed. "What is she, my *replacement?*"

Prince Andrian glared at her. "She is an orphan, and until I make arrangements for her, she is my ward."

Farida approached the girl. "Don't tell me you're to *sleep* with us."

She nodded and garbled a sound of defiance.

Farida chortled and leaned over. "Child, this tent is for royalty. You can sleep outside—with the *dogs*."

Several hounds barked at that instant, and Kieran looked up at her guardian with her starry blue eyes. Prince Andrian smiled at her, and then his eyes blackened at Farida. "If you *insist* on anyone sleeping with *les chiens*, it shall be *you* who find their company agreeable."

Farida stomped up to the prince, grabbed a fistful of his tunic, and jabbed her finger at his face. "You *threaten* me like that once more and you'll *never* sire another infant again—is that clear?"

Prince Andrian leaned his forehead down against hers and pushed forcefully. "If you think that is *frightening* . . . I . . . *what* did you say?"

Farida smirked.

Andrian stumbled backward, his lips too dry to speak for a moment. He covered his gaping mouth and whispered, "Who *else* knows about this?"

"That *girl* beside you."

Prince Andrian looked over at his ward. "You *can* keep a secret, can you not?"

Kieran patted Prince Andrian's arm and nodded.

Farida grasped her lover's hands. "I've *wanted* to tell you. I've wanted to tell you for the last *two* months, but you've been away. I thought you'd *forgotten* me."

Andrian wrapped his arms around Farida. *"Never."* He kissed her fully. "I never *stop* thinking about you." He leaned his head on her shoulder. *"Je t'adore.* I would do *anything* for you." He nuzzled against her neck.

Farida repeated, *"Anything?"* When Andrian nodded next to her, she rubbed his back. "Then let's go home again. Let's go back to where we belong."

Andrian pulled away. "Anything . . . but *that.*"

Farida sighed. "You'll *regret* being king, Andrian. You're not *meant* to have the throne."

Andrian's lip twitched.

Farida stroked his hair and kissed his cheek softly. "A great soldier you are, a great leader, but with blades and bows, not pens and words."

Andrian lowered his eyes, "I will *not* relinquish my power. Not for *you* or anyone else."

"You're a *wicked* man, Andrian. As *cold* and *heartless* as they come, you are." Farida unhooked a clasp on his tunic and ran her fingers over his collarbone. "But I love you *still.*" She kissed him, and he smiled. "Do what you will, but I won't have any part of your evil reign."

Andrian picked her up into his arms. "Then I shall *kidnap* you and hold you hostage in my chambers until you *agree* to be my queen."

Farida slapped his cheek lightly. "We'll see about *that,* you brute."

"Come, Kieran. It is time to sleep." Andrian brought Farida into the tent, and Kieran chased at his heels.

* * *

Kieran slept soundly through the night on a pile of blankets folded upon the straw-covered ground. When dawn trickled in through the cracks in the fabric, she turned on her side and gazed at the prince entwined with Farida. Prince Andrian's face lost its hard edges when he lay still and calm with slumber.

Farida stirred a little and snuggled closer to Andrian. Opening his eyes, he glanced down at her. *"C'est le matin déjà?"*

Farida placed her hand over his mouth. *"Quiet,* I wish to sleep more."

Andrian garbled, "You know we have not the *luxury* today."

Farida kissed his neck. "If you *don't* shut it, I'll *shut it for you.*"

Andrian groaned and stretched. "How shall you do that?"

Farida tossed a blanket over his head. "Now 'tis night and you'll sleep." She laid her head on his chest and stroked his stomach.

"That will not work *today,* Farida." Andrian removed the coverlet and tossed it toward their feet.

Farida yawned and sat up. Kieran did not pretend to sleep; she gaped at the woman beside the prince. She averted her eyes in shame for her nakedness.

"Andrian, your *invalid* has awakened." Farida reached over him and grabbed a dress beside him.

Prince Andrian turned his head and smiled as Kieran pretended to pick strings from her blanket. "Farida, she is *no* invalid. *Tu es cruelle,* did you ever notice that?"

Farida smiled at him. "Speaking of cruel, I'm not the one who murdered all her family and most of her village. *That's* cruel."

"Details," he muttered, and sat up. He yawned and stretched. "Oh, woman, you make me so *angry* sometimes." He scratched his head, and smiled at Kieran. "Do not mind Farida, she is just a *bit* off in the morning."

"Don't you mean *always?*" She patted Andrian on the chest. "My, you've gotten quite *scrawny* as of late." Farida gasped, "Your ribs are showing. You'll regret not eating soon. I want my son to have a father alive when he's born."

Andrian kissed her cheek. "I despise gruel. Makes me retch."

Farida dressed, and Prince Andrian pulled on a robe and then got out of his cot. He stretched once again, and Farida collected his clothes for him. "Andrian, will you *please* let me mend your tunic?" She lifted it up and stared at Kieran through several huge holes.

Prince Andrian seized it from her and examined it. "Aye, many a battle *this* tunic has seen." He wiggled his fingers through a hole on the side. *"Still,* it brings me luck."

Farida rolled her eyes. "The *only* reason the Celts have run from you is your *foul* clothes."

Prince Andrian raised his eyebrow and Kieran snorted. The prince pointed at Farida. "Laugh all you wish, woman, but it will be *I* who laughs last."

"He who laughs last thinks *slow-est*." She smirked as he mimicked her. Farida picked up a box that had fallen over and returned its contents to it. "Andrian, you're so idle. I don't know how many *times* I've cleaned up your mess. Indeed *this'll* be the last."

Prince Andrian collapsed onto his cot once again and yawned. "You have said that before, and here you are cleaning again." He waved his hand above him. "Please tell me then *why* you continue to tidy my living quarters."

Farida walked over to him and disheveled his hair. "I do it because you're *incapable* of doing anything useful."

Andrian grabbed Farida and pulled her to sit beside him. "I do *nothing* worth merit?" He traced her jawline and neck.

Farida eyed him. "Well, *almost* nothing." She kissed him quickly and stood once again.

Prince Andrian sighed and leaned back on the blankets. "You *enjoy* tormenting me." He rubbed his hands together and looked over at Kieran. "Have you any hunger this morning?"

Kieran leapt to her feet like a vivacious hare.

The prince looked over at Farida. "Would you mind showing Kieran where she might relieve herself, and while *you* disappear I shall dress."

"Come, Kieran, the prince must not be so *cruel* and force us to watch him dress. We might *never* survive the sight." Farida herded the child from the tent and turned around. "I thought I might say ha-ha-ha. I have had the *last* laugh."

"*Fiche le camp!* Get lost!" Prince Andrian threw a garter at her.

By the time the prince had dressed, Kieran's stomach gurgled impressively. Kieran placed her head in her hands and sighed. Andrian wished to shave, but Kieran's stomach wound itself like a cobra inside her.

Farida sighed. "Any *day*, Andrian. There isn't a man in this *country* that wouldn't kill for your face." She pulled her hair. "It looks like Kieran is about to pass into the next life."

Prince Andrian felt his face with his hand. "All right, let us have our *petit dejeuner*."

Farida moaned, "It's too *late* for breakfast." She pointed at the sun. "See that? It's *midday*. You took so bloody long to make yourself *presentable* that I will be readying myself for *bed* in a short while."

Prince Andrian wiped the soap from his knife and looked up at her. "You may go *without* me for your meal, but then you might be the main course with my army."

Farida whispered, "You're *lucky* I don't leave you for a forester."

"No matter, I've *scores* of women to replace you."

Clenching her teeth, Farida sat beside him and felt his cheek. "You were *right* when you asked for me to get you this knife. *Sharp* as can be it is." She picked it up and ran her finger along the blade. "Be careful it doesn't *slip* the next time you decide to shave, my lord prince."

He snatched it from her and sheathed it. "Do I sense *jealousy?*"

"Never." Farida plucked the grass beside her.

Prince Andrian wiped his hands on a cloth. "You *know* my feelings about you. I only tease."

Farida caressed her belly. "None of their comfort is as mine, right?"

Prince Andrian wrapped his arm around her. "None of them hold my favor as you, Farida." He kissed her cheek.

Farida watched Kieran poking a locust with a stick and sighed. "*Why* don't you let me come with you when you march like I did in the Holy Land?"

Prince Andrian stood up. "Let us *not* talk about the past. Let us find something to eat."

Kieran heard the word "eat" and somersaulted to her feet.

Farida lagged behind them. When the prince turned around to ask her to walk beside him, she shooed him ahead without her. Her hunger had left, she insisted. Prince Andrian walked away from her while muttering to himself. Kieran hopped beside him and swung her new stick at any of the soldiers who dared stare at her.

The whole time Prince Andrian ate his meal, he thought about Farida and how hurt she had been at his infidelity. He knew he must tell her how he felt about her lack of understanding, but it was terribly unpleasant to bring up. He must try to make amends with her. He stabbed a bean with the tip of his knife and peeled the skin off it as though it were a cloak-wearing insect.

Kieran hummed as she demolished her food, and did not notice the prince's melancholic stabbing of his meat and beans. She ate as much as her little belly could take, and though it hurt to chew, the ability to fill herself for the first time in her life felt glorious.

Prince Andrian picked up his plate and scraped its contents onto the dirt in front of his Alaunts. The two dogs scrapped with each other over a bone and one ran off, tail like a war-torn banner behind her, while the other licked a fresh wound on his paw. Kieran tried to give her bone to the losing dog, but Andrian shook his head and placed his hand out, palm up. "He knows you not. Best let me give him the bone." Kieran handed Prince Andrian the bone and he tossed it toward the Alaunt. The dog grabbed it and began to gnaw, his raggedy tail thumping with each *crunch-crunch.*

"After supper we shall head to Eddington for a respite while I find you a new home." Prince Andrian reached across the table and plucked another bone from a now-absent soldier's plate. He hurled it toward a few Alaunts tied by a tree and laughed as they fought for it greedily.

Kieran sighed and lowered her head.

Prince Andrian stabbed at a peach with his knife and sliced it in half. "It is how things must be, my child. I am not able to care for you the way you need." He removed the pit and stood up. "Would you like to give my horse a treat?"

Kieran lit up and nodded. The prince handed her the two halves of the peach and she smiled. He helped her off the bench and led her toward a blossoming tree where a great black stallion with feathered pasterns stood, head bowed to munch grasses. His tail, a branch the color of pitch, swung back and forth as flies buzzed about him.

Kieran approached the stallion with her peach-carrying hands out flat. Prince Andrian followed behind to encourage her. The stallion raised his head and stared at Kieran, his ears twitching in a circular motion, his nose flaring at the girl. Kieran muttered to the horse and reached toward him with the peaches. Prince Andrian smiled and the horse tossed his head and knocked the peaches out of her hands. They fell to the dirt with a splat and Kieran leapt back at the sudden move. The horse whinnied as though he were laughing at Kieran. The little girl turned and looked at the prince, and he smiled and pointed to the peaches. The stallion bared his teeth, tossed his head, stomped his foot, and snorted. The prince sighed and went to pick up the fruit. "It is not your fault, Kieran. My horse is a bit of a jester."

He put one half peach in her hand again and he held the other. The stallion looked from his master to the girl and back again and allowed the prince to give him the fruit. He chomped it in one swift bite, but ignored Kieran.

"See here, she has a gift for you."

The stallion tossed his head and Kieran backed away.

Prince Andrian picked up Kieran and held her before him by one arm around her middle. The stallion snorted and cautiously took the peach. The prince put Kieran back down and at that moment the stallion whinnied and nibbled on Kieran's hair. She uttered a laugh and the stallion snickered at her.

"Ah, you have made a friend, *ma chère*." Prince Andrian patted Kieran on the shoulder and the stallion snorted and went back to his grassy snack.

Prince Andrian grabbed Kieran's hand and led her back to the royal tent to pack up and leave. Outside the tent, Kieran waited for the prince. She tried to lift up a large iron shield, but it merely dragged in the dirt. She let it fall and turned her attention toward some pewter chalices on a pile of clothes. They were heavier than she expected and smelled musty like an old boot. Prince Andrian exited his tent and scratched his head. "Farida is gone. She must have left to bathe. Will you help me pack then, Kieran?"

She nodded and handed him the chalice.

The prince grimaced. "Spoils of war for my father." He turned the chalice over in his hands. "The man I took this from was clutching it in his hand as he was at his meal. He had an arrow lodged in the back of his skull." He dropped the chalice and twisted his mouth. "Last supper *indeed.*"

Kieran frowned, picked up the chalice, and placed it back where she found it. The prince led her inside the tent and bade her fold clothes neatly, and showed her in which chests they belonged, which would later be loaded onto wagons nearby.

When three hours of packing had passed, Andrian worried about Farida. She habitually said goodbye and embraced him before she left for her home in Pershore. He called for his guard to search for her, but a missing horse, a note, and a single pansy confirmed her absence.

After the prince read the note, he ripped it up and threw it into the wind.

"What'd it say, Milord?" a knight asked.

Andrian the Ruthless clenched his jaw. "She *left* me."

Chapter Three

Andrian the Ruthless growled and bit his fist. "It is not possible that she left me! How could she after revealing her condition?" He kicked his sword and it rolled with a clang toward his tent. He lifted his straw and feather pillow and grabbed a small box underneath. Opening it, he shook his head. Apparently, she had stolen his gold as well as a horse. "At least she could have asked me. I would have denied her nothing." He slammed the box shut.

Prince Andrian decided that Farida would wait for him in Pershore. After all, she would expect him to apologize to her for his trespass. She would expect gifts. Hereafter, he determined, Farida must never leave his sight.

The prince dropped shields beside the wheel of the wagon he loaded. Kieran followed him and put down a tiny golden box. Kieran wandered back to the tent for the prince's clothes.

Lost in thought, Prince Andrian stared at the glimmering weapons stacked like a bundle of sticks in the wagon. He might as well carry Farida wherever he went so she might never find herself in trouble. He stopped staring at a pole ax and retrieved the shields from the dirt. He tore his cape on one splintered end and shook his head. Farida must be safe or he would never forgive himself. He lifted some armor and scooted it beside the shields at the head of the wagon, all the while hoping he would not lose his grip and smash his foot. The way the day had gone, he would be lucky to survive the ride home. He would probably end up in a ditch as the result of his stallion throwing a shoe.

Making a desperate whine, Kieran tugged on his half-tattered cape.

"Kieran! Why are you under my feet? I could have crushed you with this armor, and you would have needed a *priest* and not a physician!"

Kieran gesticulated and pointed toward the woods.

"What are you trying to tell me?"

She pretended to have a bow and arrow and lunged at Prince Andrian's sword.

He restrained her as he peered into the woods through which he had strolled so freely the previous night. A flash of sun glinted off an arrow aimed at him. Witnesses watched Prince Andrian react instantaneously. However, he imagined his response came in a painful stupor. The arrow sang toward the young man; he threw Kieran to the side, unsheathed his sword, and slashed it clean from the air. It took him a second to realize what had actually happened.

"AMBUSH!" the prince hollered, and a dozen more arrows flew in his general direction, followed by at least a hundred foot soldiers. He could not dodge all of them, so he grabbed a tray from the wagon and used it as a shield.

Kieran lay prostrate while covering her face.

Andrian threw the tray aside and yelled, "Come with me, child. Get up!" Prince Andrian hauled her by the forearm to her feet. Five hefty soldiers charged at the prince, but he could not guard the child as well as defend his own life. Kieran stood frozen to the ground as she watched the prince ram his blade through the soldiers. *"Run, Kieran! Run away!"*

Kieran wanted to flee, but she could not feel her legs beneath her.

Two of the men seemed fixated on killing Andrian the Ruthless, and like frenzied dogs sliced at him with steel teeth. Prince Andrian felt the bite of one of the young men's swords in his side, and he staggered. The prince turned to see Kieran standing as a deer with wide eyes, and screamed at her, "RUN, KIERAN, NOW!" While Prince Andrian turned toward the child, one of the men catapulted himself upon the prince and knocked him to the dirt with a *whump.*

Kieran could not believe her eyes! One moment she stood beside the prince and the next Andrian thrashed on the ground, bloodied and desperate. She could do nothing but watch with morose enthrallment. The young man fell off the prince in a spasmodic heave, and once Andrian slaughtered the first man, the second roared with anguish and tried to finish Andrian the Ruthless. Never had Kieran seen a man inexorably stab at another.

A gaping hole in the prince's side oozed. Kieran told her feet to move either to Prince Andrian or away from the battle. Transfixed, she watched the two venomous snakes twisting and biting, slashing and hissing. For what seemed an interminable amount of time, the prince held his own against the soldier, but he slowed as he punched and scratched at the man's face. Kieran looked around for help, but no one could spare a glance toward the fallen prince, let alone spare his sword. Dust rose up around the camp and the sound of metal on metal on wood on bone rumbled all around her.

A sharp cry crackled through the thunder of the battlefield. The two men locked in the deadly tussle stopped moving. Kieran could see Prince Andrian breathing where he lay. Kieran's feet decided to work again, and she ran over to her savior.

Kieran crouched beside the prince and tugged at the corpse of the monolithic red-bearded man. Prince Andrian looked over at her. "Leave me here and hide. You will not be *safe* by my side in the open." Kieran shook her head and tried to speak, but he swallowed and whispered, "Do as I say. You can *hide*, for you are small." He rolled the heavy man off of him, but he could not rise to his feet. "Kieran, save yourself."

Kieran made an angry face and sat by him.

"Damn your foolishness." Prince Andrian felt lightheaded. "Please, do as I say."

Kieran crossed her arms.

Though the battle raged on, it traveled away from the semiconscious prince and the stubborn little girl. Several women had hidden nearby it seemed, for they materialized from the dust clouds onto the open field. A stout blonde-haired woman crept toward Kieran and tried to grab her. She kicked and bucked as the woman begged her to come with her. Kieran grabbed onto Prince Andrian's tunic and refused to let go.

The blonde woman crouched down and lifted the young man's tunic, exposing a knife wound along his side. "Yeh won't be livin' much longer if yeh stays 'ere. Let me get yeh 'elp." She motioned for a couple other women to help her with the fallen soldier. As they lifted him, he made a cry of pain, and blood drooled onto the blonde woman's yellow dress. "Oh, 'e's 'urt *bad*. What's yer name soldier?"

Prince Andrian only gurgled deep in his throat.

"Well, no matter. We'll get yeh safe now. Don't yeh worry none." The woman watched the child follow him, and she asked her his name. The child gesticulated and whimpered. The blonde woman shook her head, "Lotta 'elp the both of yeh. Can't get a word from neither."

The woman and her consorts heaved the prince toward the woods, and Kieran followed, her fist clutching his sleeve. Within the shaded forest, a wagon carrying three wounded knights waited. The women received help lifting the soldier from a rather hardy man who called himself James. James recognized the brother of his lord and liege and dragged him with great force by the collar into the wagon. The prince groaned as he collided with an armored leg.

Prince Andrian lay sprawled on the wood, and the rest of the trip to the hospice blurred before him. The wagon bounced intolerably, horses snorted, the woman nagged the driver named James, and Kieran wept at his neck as she snuggled into him. Prince Andrian's ears buzzed and his eyes darkened into a tunnel with flashes of light until he saw and heard no more.

Lavender, hot mead, and roasting pheasant floated about the prince as he felt his arms and legs tingle with sensation. In the dim lamplight, he saw the blonde woman and the ruddy-complexioned man named James. He wondered as his eyes focused if the fog of awakening had clouded his vision or if they had sedated him.

"Yeh made it, soldier. It be a *miracle*, but yeh just about got yerself through the worst part." The blonde woman carried a young boy in her arms as she leaned over him, and Kieran stood beside her.

"*Kieran,*" he squeaked.

Kieran bent over the prince and kissed his face several times. She pointed to her wounds. "They're much better."

Prince Andrian's jaw dropped. "You speak!" His voice seemed strained with the lack of use, and no matter how he tried to clear the phlegm from his throat he sounded as if he had not yet reached manhood.

Kieran smiled. "They fixed me . . . and they're much nicer than that ugly Odhran was." Prince Andrian laughed and then began to cough violently. Kieran placed her hand in his and whispered, "You don't sound so well, Andrian. I *hope* you get better."

At the sound of his name, the blonde woman stepped backward and sat on the nearest object she could, another patient. When he shrieked, she leapt off him and bounced from an invisible force that kept her from coming near Andrian the Ruthless.

"Yeh *can't* be that foul man. Yeh just *can't.*"

James went about his business and paid no heed to the royal menace lying wounded on the cot. A red-haired girl following James around seemed more interested as she frequently stopped and stared at him while she walked by with dressings for other wounded soldiers.

Clutching his side, Prince Andrian eased into a sitting position. "What is your name?"

"Selma," she responded with a grimace.

"*Merci beaucoup,* Selma."

"Yer not *really* Andrian the Ruthless, are yeh?" She approached him again, guardedly.

He smiled. "I *am*." He opened up the dressing on his side.

She pointed her finger at him. "But yer so *young*, and yer too pretty."

Prince Andrian roved his fingers over his wound gingerly. "*Pretty*, am I?" Stitches closed the swollen gash, which leaked yellow fluid. "Do I *truly* look pretty?"

Selma frowned. "Yer as pretty as God makes 'em, but 'e forgot the 'eart that s'pose to go with yer body. Must've slipped 'is mind."

"That's not *true*. Andrian saved me from a bunch of mean soldiers, and he wanted to take me home but those monsters attacked us and . . ." Kieran sighed. "And it's *my* fault he's been hurt."

"*Nonsense*, Kieran." Prince Andrian replaced the bandage on his side with gentility. "The fault is mine. I should have had men scouting the area. I was *distracted*." He laughed. "My distraction must have cost me many good soldiers, and I nearly lost my *own* life."

"How can yeh find it so *easy* to laugh?" She looked over at James, who pursed his lips and shook his head at her. "I'm sorry, I should be glad to 'ave nobility in me 'ome."

Prince Andrian shrugged. "Whether you are glad or *horrified*, I am still here in your home. I am here because you were kind to a wounded soldier." He scratched his cheek covered in course black hair. "I pity you for looking upon me." He accepted another of Kieran's embraces, though he winced when she squeezed. "If it is not *too* much trouble, may I have something to wet my mouth?"

The young red-haired girl brought over a cup of hot mead for the prince and leaned toward him. He looked up at her, and she frowned. She put her hand on his forehead and looked into his eyes. She handed him the cup, and as he consumed it, they continued to stare at each other. As she retrieved the cup, she lowered her eyes.

"What is wrong, child?" Prince Andrian caught the red-haired girl by the hand before she left his side.

She recoiled at his touch.

Prince Andrian released her.

The girl whispered, "Be careful, Milord," then left to attend the other patients.

Kieran furrowed her brow. "Odd girl."

Prince Andrian stared after the child as she followed James around. He shrugged.

Kieran leaned toward the prince. "I've no idea what happened to Farida. I asked other soldiers, and they haven't seen her at all."

"Did yeh lose someone?" Selma asked as she straightened the coverlets on an empty bed.

Prince Andrian ran his fingers through his hair, so sticky with sweat that his nails caught in it. "As a matter of fact, I *did*. My wife has gone missing. I hope she is safe."

Selma looked intrigued. "Yer *wife*, yeh say. I didn't know *another* royal up 'n' disappeared."

Prince Andrian raised his eyebrow. "Another?"

Selma smoothed her dress, "Me 'usband is Lord Julian's vassal, and 'e gets a *lotta* gossip about yeh. There's talk yeh went back to Jerusalem after it was taken back, and the king don't know what to do. Rewards're posted fer information on yer whereabouts." She smiled coyly, "Yer a lot dif'rent than I woulda thought. Ev'ryone will be interested in this."

"No one need know where I am." Prince Andrian wiggled his feet as the tingling dissipated. "I have been attacked and am in a weakened state. The last thing I need is another attack while I am in recovery."

Selma leaned over. "There be gossip 'bout town." She smiled. "Nothin' gets us peasant folk more heated than the life 'n' times of yer majesty the prince of high places and his dragon steed."

Prince Andrian cleared his throat. "Writing a *chanson de geste*, are we?"

Selma chuckled. "Many are sung now."

"Good heavens." The prince rolled his eyes.

Selma motioned for the red-haired girl to bring the prince more mead. She filled his cup and insisted he drink. "Will help yeh recover, it will."

The prince drank a few sips and sighed.

"So yer wife is missin'. Never knew yeh was a married man." She chuckled. "After that fiasco with that princess whats-'er-name . . . yeh know, the one with the fish mouth." She pouted her lips and squinted.

Prince Andrian's mouth thinned as Kieran laughed.

"Well, then I *must* straighten several things out so that you might spread *more* vicious rumors. Now that you know my wife is *not* royalty, and I will admit that she is not even nobility. She is the daughter of an Ayyubide and a Templar. She was abandoned as a small girl in the great desert of the pharaohs."

"Ooh, a long way from 'ome to be lost, yer wife." Selma set her son down on the ground and sat by the prince and Kieran. "So yeh met the woman as yeh were burnin' a village down?" She smirked. "Or perhaps yeh kidnapped 'er and 'eld 'er fer ransom?"

Prince Andrian watched Selma playing with her bodice. He swallowed. "No. I met her in Damietta. When I was seventeen, I wanted to—" He turned and looked at Kieran, who engrossed herself in his story. "I wanted to find myself lost in a woman's arms. I had been in the Holy Land two years already and had seen men fall and I simply wanted to forget everything."

"Fascinatin'. So yeh bought 'er for the night? And . . . what, then yeh fell in love with 'er?" Selma pulled her hair up and twisted it into a bun.

Prince Andrian turned scarlet at her gesture. "Oh, no, I did not mean I *bought* her company . . . Is it hot in here?"

Kieran laughed and covered her mouth.

"Yeh *did* pay 'er fer love, yeh can't deny it. *I* see yeh blushin'." She pointed at him and bit her lip.

Prince Andrian struggled to keep a straight face. "No, I did not. Not *really* anyway. I actually offered, but when she found out who I was she said she would . . . you *know* . . . not *deny* me anything if I asked her."

Selma snorted with laughter. "The prince can't even *buy* 'imself a lady friend."

Prince Andrian's brow furrowed. "Madame, I would bet if I showed enough gold, even *you* would accept me."

Selma shrugged. "Reward fer information is 10,000 crowns, Milord. Can yeh beat that?"

At that, Prince Andrian laughed. "I am sure I could not."

Kieran sighed. "*Any*way, what happened next?"

"Well, I spent a whole week with her in Damietta, and I truly enjoyed myself. It was a freedom that I had *never* known before."

Selma smiled. "What freedom might that've been, if yeh don't mind me askin'?"

Prince Andrian scratched his beard. "I was not a prince to anyone any longer. I was merely a soldier who decided to abandon his post for a week of recklessness." He sighed. "But it caught up with me."

"How?"

"She *robbed* me, if you can believe that." He ran his fingers through his mane. "She had the *nerve* to con me. Took every silver piece I had in my possession and walked away one morning. I was *furious* and embarrassed. I was in a *great* deal of trouble."

"What kind of trouble?" Kieran sat closer.

He shrugged. "My father always hated extending credit to me . . . I have abused his generosity on many occasions." He rubbed his eyes. "I owe the king so much gold that he has sent me to seize valuables to repay the royal treasury."

Kieran nodded. "Was that what you had around your tent?"

Prince Andrian nodded. "It is a shame I have depleted our resources to the extent that I must force the innocent to pay in my stead."

Both Kieran and Selma shook their heads.

"Well, 'ow did yeh fall in love after she took yer purse?" Selma stretched. "I thought yeh woulda strung 'er up." She smiled. "Especially after the king needs ev'ry half pence yeh get."

Prince Andrian smiled. "Unfortunately, she had tricked *another* poor lonely soul nearby. He did not have the guts to say anything to her. He must have been more *desperate* than me—I asked him where she ran off to, he told me, and I tracked her down."

Both Kieran and Selma sat wide-eyed.

"I *never* got my money back."

"Why not?" Kieran demanded.

Prince Andrian smiled. "She told me that she owed a small fortune to a man who cheats with dice, but she could not prove it. She promised she would give me my money back if I could get rid of that man for good." He scratched his head. "I suppose I was her hired thug."

"So yeh assisted 'er?"

He nodded. "When she brought me to him, he pestered us for more money and he proceeded to handle her inappropriately." He rolled his tongue in his mouth. "I killed him for that offense."

Kieran hooted, "You *loved* her."

Prince Andrian nodded. "Farida was shocked that after I dumped his body I told her that the money was a gift. She told me that if I were *not* a prince she would love me. I told her that if she were *not* a whore I would love her."

Kieran sighed. "So what *happened?*"

"Farida told me that she is not a whore, and I told her that I am not a prince. We spent another week together and constantly made love."

Selma and Kieran leaned on their elbows and sighed.

"Yer a war hero I hear too. Did yeh leave 'er behind when you gutted all those soldiers?" Selma twisted her finger in her hair.

Prince Andrian sighed. "Ehhh well, I did end up in the thick of fights many a time, by accident mostly, but the soldiers seemed to listen to me, and I had myself a new job." He scratched his beard. "Farida was not fond of my being a soldier." He smirked. "Every time I would go to battle she would tell me she was going to leave me, and then when I came to find her in my battered and bruised states she took care of me."

Selma and Kieran heaved another great sigh. The little red-haired girl had also stopped cleaning laundry to listen.

"An audience, I see." The prince sat up straight.

"Go on then, tell us more." Selma shooed the red-haired girl back to work.

"After we retreated and agreed on peace in Jerusalem, I knew it was time for me to return. For once in my life I had received accolades from my peers." The prince sighed. "I have not long been home from war and yet I find myself still at war."

"So you brought her home and got married and lived happily ever after." Selma sat up.

Andrian frowned. "Well, I wish that were so." He spun a ring on his finger. "The church does not recognize my marriage to a heathen." He clenched his fist. "Nor does my father."

Kieran sighed. "So how come you got married even though you knew it wouldn't be good?"

Prince Andrian smiled. "Many strange and beautiful things have happened in the Holy Land." He scratched his scalp. "I brought her home to meet my family and all my father could say was, 'Leave the spoils of war outside, shall we?'" The prince mocked a stern face.

Selma smiled. "Well, this is all be new to me. The girls at the well're gonna love this, straight from the devil 'imself." She paused. "Not that yer the devil."

Prince Andrian sighed. "She is gone now. I know not where. I do hope she does not return home without me."

Selma chuckled. "She will be wantin' more of her true love, I reckin."

Prince Andrian turned red.

"Gold, I mean, 'ighness." Selma chuckled.

Prince Andrian shrugged. "It is true that as my wife I allow her to take what she needs from me. However, this time she has something much more valuable than gold." He whispered, "She is carrying my *heir*. Nothing can happen to them."

Kieran looked over at Selma, who placed her hands on Prince Andrian's cot.

"Do yeh think she be 'urt er captured? I mean, there be a lot o' fightin' out there. I'm not *tryin'* to frighten yeh . . . but she *could* be in trouble, and yer in *no* condition to go and look fer 'er." Selma patted the prince's hand.

"I shall be fine, Selma." He sighed. "Weak or no, I *must* leave. I cannot imagine what she must feel since she has not seen me for so long." Prince Andrian raised himself from his bed and staggered. "I believe I can ride well enough."

Kieran smiled up at him. "Let's go and find Farida."

He pulled a black cloak over his breeches and decided against anything tight, for his healing wounds pained him greatly. Someone had recovered his sword to his surprise, and he threw it over his shoulder, leaving his belt behind.

Selma kissed the prince's hand as he bid her farewell. "When yeh come back fer yer belt, bring some gold." She winked at Prince Andrian.

He smiled and nodded once. As he mounted a sorrel stallion that belonged to some dead soldier, he sighed. "I miss my steed. I wonder if he made it through the battle."

Kieran climbed onto the animal with him and looked up into Prince Andrian's bronze eyes. "We'll find Farida, you'll see."

He smiled and kicked the horse, and it took off at full gallop. The wind blew his sweat dry, and for the first time in the month he had laid injured, Prince Andrian felt cool and not scorching hot. The fresh air smelling of new blooms and grasses soothed him. The sun tightened his skin and he began to glow bronze once again instead of the maggot yellow that he had been turning in the darkness of the hut.

"Where will we find Farida?" Kieran looked up as they traveled northwest.

"If she lives, she may be in our home in Pershore. She *might* be there." He gritted his teeth and whispered, "For the love of all that is holy, *please* be there."

Chapter Four

For hours, the man and child trotted in silence toward Prince Andrian's cottage in Pershore. Silence had fallen upon the two, not from boredom or anxiety, but from wonder. Spring fairies had touched the land, for white petals blossomed from branches above them, sprinkling down on them like lofty snowflakes as they passed below. Along the woods ahead were deer gamboling, fawns tumbling upon each other, does looking on the bucks as though engaged in gossip. Pink horn-shaped penstemon sprouted from the ground in droves; bees hummed about them happily. Great fields of blue and purple bluebells drowned out the meadow grasses, and even the horse of the fallen knight turned to look at the spectacle. Stripes of white, magenta, violet, and pink delphinium paved a path toward the hidden cottage at the edge of Tiddesley Wood.

As prince and his ward entered the wood, ribbons of white light fell upon them through the forest canopy. Bluebells carpeted the forest floor, punctuated by thickets concealing hares that were known only by the *reh-reh-reh* of their teeth gnawing through thick flower stems. The cottage ahead was rather small and fitted against two thick plum trees, the dark purple fruit draping down like the grapevines of giants. The cottage itself had a roof of straw and wood poles, and birds nested in the eaves, not fearful of the master who had returned. They peeped at each other with high-pitched *eah-eahs*. Flat stones separated by wooden beams made up the walls stripped by weather. The mud plaster that served as insulation had begun to chip away. The prince rolled off the borrowed horse and grabbed Kieran to set her down. She spun around slowly, taking in the peaceful surroundings that only existed in bedtime tales. Prince Andrian felt the walls and sighed. More work to be done.

Prince Andrian opened the tied stick door with a creak. "Farida? Where *are* you?"

Kieran ran around the house several times and came back to him. "She's not here."

Prince Andrian sat on a stack of wood by the front door. "She *must* be safe. I will not rest until I find her."

"Well then, get off your lazy bum and *look* for me!" a voice called from behind them.

He stood and turned around. Farida held the reins of his black stallion. "Why did you not *answer* me when I called?"

"I didn't feel like it. I've been trying to get your *idiot cow* for days. He'd *finally* got to trusting me, and I thought if I responded to you he'd *bolt*." She brought the horse to her husband, who raised himself to his feet with a grunt. "Why're you making that *intolerable* face? And why do you look as if you were thrown from the white cliffs and feasted upon by gulls?"

As he grabbed the stallion's reins, she clinched him around the waist. "Ah, *careful*, Farida, *c'est un blessure grave!*"

Kieran held out a plum she had collected from the ground, and the black stallion ate it greedily. She took the reins from the prince, and he hobbled toward the house.

"You're damaged, Andrian. Why didn't you *say* something?" Farida rushed to him.

He held his hand up. "I want none of your pity. It is not *that* bad."

She lifted his cloak. Several shallow stab wounds and a large purple gash marked him like a crude map; all of his injuries sewn closed like the outlines of townships. "My God, Andrian! Were you attacked?"

"No, I thought a scar here and there would look ravishing on me— of course I was attacked!" He plopped on his straw and feather bed and looked up at her. "It was an ambush. I feared for *your* safety, and I neglected to send scouts." His eyes narrowed. "I nearly died because of you, *salope*."

Farida sat beside him. "Well, I'm glad you're here *now*. I'm sorry for leaving you. I was *angry*." She coddled him, but he pulled away.

"Leave me be for now. I feel unloving." He closed his eyes.

Farida stood up. "I'll make us supper, if anybody's hungry. I know *I* am."

Kieran hopped about, but Prince Andrian just mumbled sleepily and did not respond further. They decided to leave him be and go about their business until their lord awoke.

* * *

The following morning, Prince Andrian awoke not to the sun glimmering through the hole in the thatch above him, but to low talking outside his door curtain. Too tired to sit up, he opened his eyes and listened. Farida sounded angry with a man, whose tone of voice seemed insistent. He had better force the unwanted visitor to shove off or flash a bit of steel in his face. The second thought sounded unappealing, as he felt too weak to duel with anyone at that moment. Prince Andrian sat up and stretched. What a waste of a pleasant dream. He sighed and threw off the bearskin that had kept him warm. As he raised himself to his feet, his legs nearly gave out. He needed his sword more as a crutch than as a weapon.

He staggered into the only other room in the hut and snarled as a strange man stood with Farida. "Who are you? State your name."

The man smirked at him. "Who're *you* to demand anything from me?"

"Be careful how you talk to my husband." Farida jolted the man's arm.

"That's right. You might find your head on a spear if you make him angry." Kieran raised her fists. "I could beat you up. Come on." She hopped around, feigning punches. "You're soft in the middle."

Andrian the Ruthless grabbed his hand-and-a-half from its resting place near the door and unsheathed it. He pointed it at the man. "I politely asked you a question. State your name and your business, or leave us be."

"You call your request polite?" The man put his finger on the tip of the blade and then slapped it away. "You'd not attack me."

Andrian the Ruthless snarled, "Try me, *salaud*. I have killed men for merely having poor hygiene."

As the prince raised his weapon to the man's throat, Farida said, "Wait!"

Prince Andrian lowered his weapon and turned to her. "Who is this man to you that you should beg for his life?"

The man turned to Farida. "Who's this *buffoon*?"

Farida looked at Andrian. "My brother, after all this time he's *very* protective."

Prince Andrian lowered his sword and leaned on it. "I apologize for my rudeness. I am sure if I told you my name, you would know to whom you speak."

"Ah, I'm sure you're the man who I've been sent to murder for marrying my sister."

Farida made an awkward face, and Prince Andrian dropped his sword and folded his arms across his chest.

The man raised his eyebrow. "Looks a bit disheveled for the likes of my sister." His eyes scanned him. "Yes, war torn and bedraggled." He sighed and looked at Farida. "Where did you pick this winner up? A leper colony?"

Prince Andrian's eyes narrowed. "I am the crown prince of this godforsaken country, Andrian Gilbert de Langeais. Be careful, sir, for you speak *traitorous* words."

Farida swooned. "I *love* it when you speak in such a tone. It makes me *shiver.*"

Both Prince Andrian and the man looked at her. *"Right."*

Prince Andrian smiled at the man. "And you are Farida's *brother.* I am sorry, I do not have the pleasure of your name." He held his hand out to the man, who took it fiercely.

"I'm Tormod of North Severn. You'd better *worship* my sister or I'll have words with *you.*" He squeezed the prince's hand hard.

Prince Andrian smiled. *"Vraiment,"* and squeezed his hand back with equal force.

Farida pulled Andrian away from Tormod's grip. "Andrian, why don't you come with me for a moment?" Farida led him to their room and pushed him onto the bed.

Prince Andrian looked up at her. "Why is *he* here?"

Farida whispered, "I have never *met* my brother before. As far as I know he has always been a stonemason in Iberia."

The prince pursed his lips and whispered, "He has delicate hands for a *stonemason.*" His eyes narrowed. "Must have done well to no longer need a chisel and hammer."

Farida nodded. "I don't know how he would ever find me. He never cared before." She bit her lip. "He said he was sent by King Arundel . . . something about recognizing our union."

Prince Andrian darkened. *"Is that so?"* He turned his head toward the other room, his mouth thin and eyes black. He sat up and said rather loudly, "So your family *accepts* that I am your husband and the father of your child?" Prince Andrian reached under his mattress and fumbled for his quillon.

Farida sat beside him and embraced him. Toward the other room she too said loudly, "No, I don't find you terrible, but *he* might. You aren't known as being tender and gentle."

"Aye. I am known for being *ruthless*." He straightened and slipped the dagger into his belt under his tunic. "I do not think I could have the power I do if everyone called me Andrian the *Spineless*."

"Or Andrian the *Listless*." Farida looked around the room, already a mess since his arrival. She clasped her hand to her mouth to repress a giggle.

Andrian wagged his finger at her. "No, it cannot be *my* fault. I slept since I have been here. There is no *possibility* it was I who made this room *un désordre*." He slipped one boot on, pulled something flashing from the second, and then pulled on the second boot.

Farida rolled her eyes at him. "I would bet you a *thousand* gold crowns you made this home a muddle." She jabbed her finger at the knife.

He grabbed her and pulled her to him. "Really? If I win, then you shall give me *back* the purse you stole a month ago?" He passed her the dagger from the second boot.

"If I win, you'll let it go. I needed that money, and I'm sorry." She slid the dagger down the front of her bodice and smiled.

In the second room, Kieran sighed. "I hope Andrian feels better."

Tormod pulled out a roll of parchment with a broken seal on it. "He's *acting* better, if he ever acted *well* in his life."

Kieran heard Andrian and Farida giggling in the bedroom. "What're they doing?"

"The prince is going to be a father, and it's his *first* I'm guessing." He picked up a rock from the floor and rolled it in his hand. "The first he *knows* about anyway."

Kieran sighed. "I'll *never* be a mother."

Tormod dropped the rock. "Why do you say *that?*"

She shrugged. "I heard someone say that I was *unmarriageable*, which means I'm ugly." She spotted a cloth on the floor and poked at it.

Tormod exhaled.

Kieran frowned. "It's all about how *beautiful* you are. I know it." She picked up the cloth.

Tormod nodded his head toward the drawn curtain. "That *friend* of yours, Andrian . . . well, he's the *most* unmarriageable of the lot."

Kieran twisted the cloth in her hands.

Tormod looked her straight in the eye. "He's an evil cutthroat who murders, rapes, and pillages for fun. He's a *tyrant*. I'd kill him *myself* if the king so commanded." He adjusted a bronze ring on his finger and sighed as he looked toward the other room.

Kieran's face paled as she listened harder to the prince and his wife in the bedroom, now murmuring to each other. Her father had

once called Prince Andrian *"treacherous,"* and the prince had struck him
down in the street with one blow of his sword, or so she had been told.
Her whole town had burned to ash because of that one word. Kieran
shook her head; it could not have been true. Andrian had rescued her
from the rubble. He was kind and gentle to her.

Behind the curtain, Prince Andrian shouted, "How dare you assault
your liege lord?"

At the screams coming from Farida, Tormod flew into the room as
Andrian the Ruthless flipped her onto her back and shook her. "What
are you doing?" he cried and shut the curtain behind him.

Both Andrian and Farida looked up at Tormod, his eyes transfixed
on the prince. Farida patted Andrian's chest. "Don't worry so much,
Tormod. We're just *playing.*"

Tormod's eyes bulged. "Playing? You call yelling and smashing
things *playing?*"

"Aye, we were having a bit of fun." Prince Andrian kissed Farida's
cheek.

Kieran sat patiently on her chair and sighed. They must all three
enjoy playing horsey, for behind the curtain there were an awful lot of
thuds and noises.

Farida exited the bedroom and sat beside Kieran. "Andrian told me
that he's to take you to Eddington for a bit until he can find you a new
home. I hope it doesn't bother you that you must stay with the brute
for a while."

Kieran shook her head politely, but her eyes wandered toward the
bedroom, where the prince and Tormod remained.

Andrian the Ruthless departed the room and strolled through the
front door without glancing at either Kieran or Farida. Several minutes
later, he slunk back in. He went to the bedroom and washed his hands
in the basin.

"What's the matter with Andrian?" Kieran asked.

Farida said nothing and rubbed her belly. The prince knelt beside
them on the ground. His eyes wavered black and Kieran felt coldness
light upon her shoulders like a frosty bird of prey. Once again, his eyes
swirled to brown and he smiled. Farida returned his contrived smile,
but then concentrated once more on her belly massaging.

"Why don't you two go feed the horses for me while I finish up with
Tormod? There is business and I hardly wish to bore you both." Prince
Andrian stood tall and half smiled.

Farida grabbed Kieran by the hand and pulled her outside toward
the horses. Kieran looked at Farida's trembling hand, her nail beds
stained red with the plums she had been eating for breakfast. The

horses stamped their hooves and tossed their heads as Farida and Kieran silently heaped some hay before them.

"I believe I need to work in the garden for a little while." Prince Andrian announced from behind them. "I miss the sun and the sound of birds and insects." Farida turned around and Andrian handed her the parchment that Tormod had been carrying with him. "For you, *ma chère.*" She nodded and slid it in her bosom.

As he left them to the horses, Kieran went to follow him, but Farida grabbed her by the wrist and shook her head. "He needs to be *alone.* He'll come inside when he's finished." Farida nodded her head toward the house. "Help me get supper going."

Kieran grabbed Farida's hand and obeyed.

Farida rinsed a dagger covered in blood in her basin. Kieran eyed the dagger and Farida smiled. "We shall have rabbit stew for supper." She set the dagger down and grabbed a couple scraps of rabbit, skinned and hanging by their back legs above Kieran's eyesight. Farida handed Kieran vegetables to cut while she went outside to start a fire.

Kieran peeked out at Farida and tiptoed into the bedroom. The room was a mess: a bearskin lay folded upon the floor, water puddled by a wooden chest, papers with what looked like maps lay crinkled on one side of the bed. Streams of paint streaked the walls. Red paint. *Dappled* red paint. Kieran covered her mouth and slowly backed out of the room and into Farida.

"Finished with the vegetables?"

Kieran whirled around. "Oh, yes. Yes."

Farida smiled and scraped the vegetables into a pot and tossed in the rabbit. She took the pot outside to cook.

Kieran crept back into the bedroom. She looked above her and saw skins hanging from posts. Some dripped from the ends, dripped *red.* She sighed; the freshly skinned deer was probably not quite ready for stretching. More skins lay in the corner and had been sliced with a sharp tool. Large squares of soft leather lay folded on a small wooden table. Charcoal markings outlined a shape.

"He's a wonderful craftsman."

Kieran gasped and turned around to see Farida.

"Makes his own armor." From the stack of leather she pulled out a half-sewn riding gauntlet. "I told him he ought to abdicate just to sell his work." She handed it to Kieran.

Kieran turned it over in her hands. "Soft."

Farida retrieved the gauntlet and set it back on the table. "Now, come help guard supper before a pack of hungry wolves takes it away."

Kieran obeyed Farida and licked her lips, imagining the delicious stew.

At supper, Farida decided to call Andrian inside from his garden. Kieran snuck toward the rear of the house and looked out the backdoor. The prince sat stroking vegetables in the garden, and as he plucked dead leaves from a long stalk he talked to it. Prince Andrian looked absolutely out of his mind.

Farida walked up to her husband and placed her hands on his shoulders as he knelt. The prince rose to his feet and stood apart from Farida with his hands across his chest. Farida's hands perched on her hips as she shook her head with a grimace. Andrian beckoned for Farida, and they both disappeared down a little gully.

Kieran wished she could hear what they said.

Farida sighed as her husband pulled her along with him. When they arrived at a small creek, they sat on its sandy embankment.

Andrian put his hand on her belly and caressed his child. "Tormod knew my father."

Farida nodded. "I knew he wasn't right." She pulled the parchment out from her bosom and opened it. "This says that it came from the prince regent."

Andrian sighed. "My brother does whatever my father asks of him, cowardly jackal."

"How long before the royal guard comes knocking?"

"Days." Andrian retrieved the parchment from her and sucked his lip. "Three at most." He rolled it up and scratched his head with it. "What a mess in which we have found ourselves."

"What should I do?"

Andrian sighed. "I must take Kieran to Eddington. You must stay here and wait for me to come for you."

"What if they take me?"

Andrian smiled. "I am the one with the price on my head."

Farida grasped his hand and kissed it. "You are a wicked man and will one day die for all you have done."

"For certain my death shall be most spectacular."

Farida leaned over and kissed Andrian on the mouth before she stood up. She reached her hand down toward him, and he grabbed hold of it and rose to his feet as well. She nudged him. "Catch me, if you *can*."

He smiled as she shrieked and ran away. He bellowed behind her, "Do not even *think* of hiding. I know where you live!"

Kieran heard them hollering at each other, and she feared for Farida. Farida ran from him, and he chased her around to the front of the hut. Kieran crept outside and peered around the wall. Farida peeked from behind a tree then charged at him from her hiding place with a bright smile.

Andrian ran away from her and she barreled after him. Andrian hid behind a different tree and clutched his chest with a grimace. Farida found him, but he remained leaning against the tree. Farida stopped her play and embraced him. They sat together under the tree, and he leaned on her, and as she held him in her lap she hummed to him and rocked him. She rubbed his chest and he looked up at her with contentment.

Kieran snuck away from the wall and toward Andrian's garden. Like a hare, she lay low in the vegetation, with hopes she might not be caught sneaking about. Combing through the bushes, she came across something small and shiny. On closer inspection, she realized she had found Tormod's ring. She tried to pick it up, but it was stuck— to a finger! She scraped soil back over it as her heart pounded in her throat.

She felt a hand squeeze her shoulder and she looked up. Andrian the Ruthless had discovered her. "Is this not the most peaceful garden in all of Briton?" He smiled at her and plopped beside her.

"Yes, it's nice. I like the flowers. Do you like flowers?" She twisted her hands together.

Prince Andrian leaned toward her and handed her a columbine. *"J'aime les fleurs."* He watched her eyes darting from him to a large mound of freshly planted onions, and he stroked his beard. "Why, *whatever* is the matter?"

"Oh, I'm just wondering if Tormod's having a safe journey home." Her eyes flitted back to the mound.

Prince Andrian's blackened eyes glinted. "I hope you have enough sense to stay out of trouble." He picked another flower and twirled it between his thumb and forefinger.

Kieran whispered, *"You murdered him."*

"He was an *assassin*." Andrian the Ruthless crushed the flower in his fingers and smelled the remnants. He grinned. "I do not wish to bring you into this dark world in which I live, Kieran." His smile fell as Farida walked by them and went indoors. "This is why we must put you somewhere safe."

Tears in her eyes, Kieran nodded slowly. "My father said that you would be king one day, and this land would be laid to waste."

Prince Andrian caressed her salty cheek with his thumb. "Peace in this land has already ended, my child."

Farida called for her husband from inside the house, and he stood and left Kieran to remain in the garden with her thoughts.

The little blonde child in white crawled toward the mound of dirt and onion plants. She placed Andrian's royal blue columbine on top of the hidden body and gasped as a sudden breeze blew it into the stream.

Chapter Five

Dawn light left a buttery glow upon the hut in the forests of Pershore. The small stream along the east side of Andrian's garden sparkled with a thousand golden coins from the sun. The black stallion stood still as its master saddled him. The little girl, now in a red tunic fitted as a dress, stood by her lord and rubbed her eyes.

Farida opened the lashed stick door and came out wrapped in the bearskin.

Andrian turned at the creak of the door and smiled. "Nearly ready." He slipped his sword into his scabbard, which he had wrapped upon his horse. He pulled on his mail and leather armor and pulled his cloak upon his shoulders, a golden clasp on each leather breastplate held the fur in place. His gauntlets he pulled on and he flexed his fingers to stretch the leather.

"Be careful, my love." Farida pressed her hand to her mouth.

Andrian strode to her and kissed her cheek.

Farida slapped him lightly. "Brute."

He smiled and turned toward his horse. Kieran, still rubbing her eyes, began to yawn. The prince lifted her onto his stallion and then climbed up himself.

Before he could start his horse, Farida yelled, "Wait!"

The prince turned the horse on his heels and trotted him over to the hut.

Farida held up the prince's coronet. "Can't forget who you are today."

He reached down and took the circlet of gold and jewels. "Indeed." He placed the coronet upon his head. He reached down and placed his hand on her face. "Wait for me."

Farida smiled. "Don't I always?"

As the prince and his foundling child trotted out of the woods, Farida's angelic silhouette grew darker. His heart weakened as her warm presence left him on the road.

Birds chirped to each other as they whirled above the riders. The sky was appallingly blue, the sun burned the prince's eyes, the water shone as white as the sands in the desert.

The desert had been like powdered diamonds. Intense heat had burned him deep bronze like the pharaohs on the walls of Alexandria. Water did not trickle from the ground there like it did in Briton. Water was scarce in that baked land. Water was either a vision when the sun was high and his mouth was parched or else it flooded over the great delta, full of serpents with jaws so wide they could snap a boat in half. There, sweat poured from a man's brow as though rain fell directly above him. There, the winds cooked men in their saddles as they rode toward Ra's red orb on the horizon. There, the heat of the day stretched into the night, which felt long as he lay under the ceiling of sparkling jewels and dreamed of home while he minded deadly snakes and deadly scorpions and deadly sandstorms.

Andrian had left for that desert as a boy, his hair short like a soldier of Rome; his face barely showing signs of manhood. He had never seen a soldier fall to a sword. Never had he heard shrieks of pain as steel skewered knights through the gut. The young prince had never once watched a comrade's eyes darken as blood pooled under him. The desert of the pharaohs turned red and Andrian became a man. His hair grew longer with each passing year, and never did he cut it. He let it fly free like the wild men with whom he rode through the dunes. Andrian was a god of war and great kings bowed to his steel. He held his *voulge-guisarme* high and screamed into that scorching desert wind, the roar of his army behind him.

As the castle of King Arundel rose from the ground ahead as white cliffs from the sea, Kieran looked up at Prince Andrian. His eyes sat straight forward, vacant, unblinking, even as the whitewashed towers, so blinding in their radiance, blocked out the light from the sky. A piece of the moon had broken off and collided with the earth, so became the Château de Gilbert.

Prince Andrian cantered through the baileys and ignored the peasants who dove aside to let him pass. Up to the keep he clattered. Many of the king's guard still lingered after dinner. As soon as Prince

Andrian dismounted, a groom took the reins, and the prince reached up and helped Kieran down. The little girl struggled to remain beside the prince as they headed indoors.

The prince shoved open the entry to the great hall with a great bang, and Kieran lagged behind. The prince's footsteps resounded heavily through the halls as he strode toward King Arundel, and Kieran pattered on cat feet. The king came down from his table to meet his son before he approached his throne.

Prince Andrian knelt on one knee and bowed his head before the king, but his father motioned for him to rise. King Arundel embraced his son. When he released him, he held his head in his hands. "Are you hurt terribly? I sent men to find you, and no party knew of your whereabouts."

Prince Andrian tried to speak, but the king squeezed him again.

"I heard it was an ambush. I heard you were shot and stabbed, oh I *heard* such lies. But now, here you are." As the king shook his son, Prince Andrian tried to speak again, but the king hushed him. "Next time, my son, pay *more* attention." He held the prince at arm's length. "Nine years your mother worried about you, and here you are at home in more danger than with those barbarians with whom you kept as intimates."

"They were not barbarians, my king."

King Arundel waved his hand and with his other grasped his son's shoulder again. "It is good to see you again."

Kieran tugged on Prince Andrian's tunic.

"Ah, who have you here?" The king cringed as he saw the child's scarred face, but then he smiled at her, for her eyes were the winter sea.

Prince Andrian introduced Kieran.

She looked up at Andrian and then said quite confidently, "I'm in the gift of my lord prince." She smiled. "You've got a *pretty* castle, Sire."

"Why, *thank* you." The king curled his finger under his nose for a second and then said, "Is she your *ward*, Andrian?"

Prince Andrian nodded once and patted her head. "I found the child alone and injured and decided to help her until I might find arrangements more suited to her needs."

Kieran grabbed his hand and held it to her face. Then she snuggled into his cloak and hid from the king. King Arundel pointed over to the moving cloak behind Andrian.

"Does she do that frequently?"

"*Souvent.*" Prince Andrian nodded and patted the repositioning lump behind himself. "Father, I have an important question to ask you."

The king straightened his son's tunic. "You ask at the wrong time."

Prince Andrian frowned. "Why, you have no idea the question I wish to ask, so how can it be the wrong time?"

The king pointed behind him, and the prince turned around as the hall doors opened to welcome the treasures Andrian the Ruthless had confiscated for the treasury.

The king strode toward the valuables and shook his head. "Is this all you could squeeze out of my subjects?" He picked up a platter of silver. "I thought you told me you had loads of gold and silver."

Prince Andrian lowered his head. "I did . . . but . . ."

The king slammed the platter on the ground. "I heard the word *but*. Do not make excuses for this. You told me you had more than this meager pile I see before me."

Andrian swallowed. "May I at least explain?"

The king laughed. "This treasure will not repay me for your trip to Granada, let alone the cost of your gambling habit or your addiction to women, or even your love of expensive refreshments." Andrian shrank through his father's tirade. King Arundel grabbed his son's shoulder and squeezed lightly. "Now, let us hear that important question."

Kieran poked Andrian in the lower back a couple times, and he stood straight. "I wanted to ask again if," he lowered his head, "if you would recognize my wife."

The king cupped his hand behind his ear. "Speak up, Son. I did not catch that last bit."

Andrian looked up. "Father, I am twenty-four and I am a married man. I wish for you to recognize my wife."

The king began to chuckle. Then others around him snickered. Finally, the hall roared with laughter. The king raised his hand and the noise ceased. "Let me tell you something, my son. I, as well as the rest of this country, will never recognize any marriage to a belligerent you brought home from the crusades as a slave. Do you understand?" He shook the prince's shoulders. "You cannot marry a heathen. This slave of yours is just that, a slave."

The prince pulled away. "She is not a slave. She is my *wife*."

The king shook his head. "Take that dark woman back where you found her and the devil take her."

"See here, Father, you must accept her. She will give me an heir. You cannot deny her."

The king's face clouded over. "When an animal births an unwanted litter, you drown the beasts. It is as simple as *that*, my son." He smiled at Andrian's horror. "I hear it would not be the first time you eliminated undesirable pups."

Prince Andrian clenched his teeth as he fondled the ring upon his finger. "You are merely unenlightened. You never saw what I saw. The world is different than you imagine. *Far different.*"

"Forgive me, but around the world it is the same. Precious metals are commodities, commodities which you have failed to retrieve for me yet again. I asked you to levy *taxes*, not murder women and children."

The prince scowled. "I did not murder them. I responded to a hostage situation. They were casualties that could not be avoided."

"You *murdered* them, Andrian. You burned them *alive.*"

"I did what was necessary."

The king's eyes narrowed. "This is my kingdom and I swore to protect my subjects. I cannot have my own son plundering the land like a drunken Geat on a pilgrimage."

"I am sorry I failed you then, my king." The prince swallowed. "I have been home from war not more than three months and so have not felt like myself. I desire forgiveness."

"I would forgive you if you came home with some holy gold instead of holy ideas of enlightenment." King Arundel sighed. "It is not even I from whom you must beg forgiveness, but the families devastated by your serious lack of morality."

The prince grimaced. "As commander of the great army of Briton, I take full responsibility for the behavior of my men."

"Hero of the Kings of the Desert, you are hereby allowed to ride along with the cavalry but you are not to lead it. Am I clear?" The king straightened and Andrian shriveled. "You are no longer in command of any army, even one made of children or dogs." The king began to smile, and as Andrian lowered his eyes he added, "In fact, my son, because you maliciously razed a town while bearing my colors, you are no longer allowed your armor, your shield, your bow, or your spurs. Your sword you may keep, though if I see you threaten another man as you did before, I shall confiscate that as well." The king cleared his throat. "See what *real* power does, my son? It keeps tyrants from having too much power of their own."

Andrian clenched his fists.

The king caressed Andrian's black hair. "Oh, my child, whenever will you learn your place in this kingdom?"

Andrian raised his eyes but did not meet his father's gaze. He focused on a knot in the oaken door directly behind the king. "What orders have you for your humblest of *squires* then, my king?"

"Take that slave back to the crossroads in Damascus or wherever you bought her and cease shaming your country and your God."

"But I *love* her," Andrian whispered, but King Arundel had already turned his back on his son to greet Lord Julian, entering the throne room with an appallingly huge grin.

Andrian glared at his brother and swirled on his heels. As he proceeded to exit the hall with Kieran, who now held on to the prince's cape as he strutted away, Lord Julian pursued him.

"Andrian?"

The prince turned his face from his brother as he halted. "What is it you want? Surely you wish to laugh at me as everyone else did."

Lord Julian placed his hand on Andrian's shoulder.

Andrian jerked away. "I *despise* you."

"And I, *you*." Lord Julian, hands on hips, smiled. "I come to ask if I might help you put some money in the treasury. I am Prince Regent, and I have several fiefdoms I might tax to aid your cause." He whispered, "I know it was not your fault."

Andrian snarled, "Pity is reserved for the weak in spirit, and charity is for the weak of body. I am neither, so do me no such favors."

Lord Julian whispered, "Andrian, but you are both. You *need* assistance."

Prince Andrian's eyes glimmered. "Do you want to help me?"

Lord Julian nodded, "Of course I do."

Andrian gave him a hearty shove. "Then stay out of my *way*."

Lord Julian glanced over at his father, who shook his head as the prince exited the hall with a snort.

As the prince stormed toward his room, he snapped his fingers and several attendants rushed to their lord's side. He asked one for a bath to be drawn for him and another for fresh clothes. The servants rushed to do their lord's bidding, and several maidservants came toward the prince. He asked them to show Kieran where she would spend the night. Kieran begged to stay with him.

"I will see you *tomorrow*, Kieran. *Dormez-vous*." He smiled as he entered his room. The prince shut the door and Kieran heard the clank of a sword upon the ground. She lowered her head and shuffled behind the maidservants toward her bedroom for the evening.

As Prince Andrian looked up at the ceiling in his room, he began to doubt his love for Farida. Perhaps his father was right. He lusted after Farida and no more. He flipped onto his uninjured side and stared at the wall. *Hero of the Kings of the Desert* his father had called him with mockery. His father was due blame for his years of battle, if anyone. Home in Briton, Andrian's life seemed empty and pathetic. Now with no career as general or even as knight, Prince Andrian had been cornered yet again. King Arundel had even dismissed his son's request to recognize his marriage for the second time. Andrian knew that bribing the church to wed himself to Farida could not work, for his father had overwhelming power in the ecclesiastic realm. King Arundel pleased Pope Gregory IX with his righteousness, and requests granted to the king had clout. One such request had earned Andrian the cold shoulder when it came to his marriage. Besides, she looked like one of the queens carved on the walls of the great tombs in the desert of the never-ending sun. The country would be angrier with him over that fact than his campaigns to take their wealth from them.

He found himself missing Farida, and he grew angry with her for not sleeping beside him. When he had returned from the crusade three months ago, Farida had spent the night with her husband. In the morning, King Arundel had entered the prince's chambers to find his son entwined with her, a smile across his face. Outraged that the prince had invited a devil woman into the castle, King Arundel had her removed at once. Andrian had tried to explain that he had married her, but his father had beaten him and warned him never to bring her back again. Andrian never brought Farida home again, but he took any woman who would accept him to replace her. Soon the king had given up on controlling the love life of his heir. Andrian had told Farida she could stay once again, but she had refused to openly enter the palace walls. On rare occasions she would slip into the castle to spy on his brother for him, but she would come in the dead of night when the guards on watch played knucklebones.

Farida could no longer deny his invitation once she delivered his child. She must then accept his love, because if she did not he would wear her down and he would wear his father down. In the end, the king could not deny who his son chose to be his own heir.

Farida would never enjoy the throne beside Andrian. She came from a long line of people who survived on the edge of life and death. How could she accustom herself to an easy life of "ask and it shall be given"? With Andrian as king, Farida would have anything she wished, and if unable to grant her request, Andrian would cause the country to suffer until she got her way. Andrian could actually taste his desperation for power. *Could* he taste it? Something seemed odd about the flavor in his mouth. He spit into his palm, and blood swirled about in his saliva. He must have bitten his tongue in the night. He wiped the sheet with his spittle and sat up.

Prince Andrian looked down at his wounds and frowned. His concern for the little girl had given him such scars. What a fool he had been for allowing his heart to bleed for an orphan.

The prince left his bed and stood in front of his window. He looked down upon the upper bailey. An angry spirit of fog swirled between the trees and the garden. He shivered and wondered if the recent chill in the air was a bad omen or if he had gone mad.

Though the morning sun had not yet hoisted itself into position above the curtain wall, the prince decided his night of sleep was not to be, and so he dressed himself for the day.

After dressing, he threw open the door to his room and stormed down the hallway in a whirlwind of midnight blue. Upon entering the great hall, the recently promoted steward of the household, Lorcan of Carrickfergus, and an annoying herald accosted him. He tried to avoid them, but Lorcan insisted he read a letter.

"I have no *time* at the moment." Andrian the Ruthless grabbed the parchment and tore it to shreds. He pointed to the bits of paper. "*That* is what I think of your intrusion." He walked away and said loudly, "*Imbeciles.*"

Lorcan froze in place, but the herald pursued the prince. "Milord, I think it *was* important, that letter. I really think you should've *read* it."

Andrian the Ruthless turned around, seized the herald by the tunic, and lifted him off the ground. "People beg for my aid when I am present, not with letters. Anyone who writes to me for assistance does not know how I do things."

The old hop toad's eyes bulged out. "A woman . . . sh-she ins-sisted you read it immediately."

Andrian the Ruthless dropped the man on the ground. "A woman? *What* woman?"

The man coughed hard. "Said it was *urgent* . . . slave woman in a tumble-down shack a short hard ride from here."

"Farida," he said under his breath.

The herald nodded. "And she was full to burst, sire."

Prince Andrian clenched his teeth. He *knew* he should have stayed. He paced in the hall, in the view of all the company. He stomped his foot and then drew his sword. "Damn you for not telling me sooner. *Va au diable!*"

The herald trembled before Andrian the Ruthless. As he raised his sword to strike, King Arundel entered the hall. "What do you think you are doing at this ghastly hour?"

The prince lowered his sword.

"If you had killed him that would have been the *third* time this month I would have needed to find another herald. You forced the last one to eat the message from me because you disagreed with my request, and the one before that you disemboweled because he laughed about your *tooth* infection."

"In front of several French nobles," Prince Andrian sneered.

He approached his son, snatched his sword, and handed it to Lorcan. "I find it to be quite *expensive* to pay the messengers hazardous-duty pay simply because I have a bad-tempered son."

Lorcan looked down and his eyes widened, tugged on the king's robe, and poked him with the hilt of the sword.

Andrian the Ruthless snarled at the man on the ground and looked at his father pitifully. "May I have my weapon back? I fear I have an *urgent* message to attend to."

"I told you that I would confiscate your sword if you brandished it with ill intent again, and look here you have immediately disobeyed me."

Andrian held out his open palm for his possession. "Why else would one brandish one's sword if not for ill intent? It is a *weapon* after all." He raised his eyebrow with expectation, but his father stood still and wrinkled his nose. The prince sighed and rolled his eyes. "I promise no harm shall come to the pitiable fool before me."

King Arundel turned around, Lorcan tossed the hot sword to the king, and the king thrust the hand-and-a-half back to Prince Andrian, who proceeded to lean on the steel like a crutch. Lorcan wiped sweat from his forehead and exhaled.

"Where must you go so soon? You have not even stopped to visit your mother."

Prince Andrian hissed, "Mother can *wait*. I have *many* more important things to do than attend her."

King Arundel struck his son in front of everyone. "Your *brother* would not *dare* deny his presence to his mother and scoff her loving gestures as *you* do."

Prince Andrian clutched his swollen cheek, and his mouth curled into sneer, "She is not his mother."

King Arundel struck him again. "How *dare* you."

The prince felt blood on his lips and grumbled, "My bastard brother can run himself through with a halberd for all I care."

He stalked toward the herald, who raised his hands to his face in the shadow of the prince. Andrian the Ruthless swung his sword and stopped an inch from his throat. The prince leaned over, smiled with his bloody mouth, and whispered, "Boo." The herald wept as his breeches darkened with urine. Andrian the Ruthless forced a laugh. Then as he left the man cowering on the floor with prayers of thanks to God for mercy, Andrian's insides burned.

Andrian the Ruthless heard his father call for him, but he bulled his way through the meandering servants. Someone reached out and grabbed him by the tunic.

"Andrian? Where're you going?" a voice begged.

Prince Andrian looked down. "Kieran, I must go back to Farida. She sent me a letter. I will be back, and then I shall find you a new home."

"What happened to your mouth?" she gasped.

He reached up and touched his bloody lip. "It is nothing."

"Oh." She scooted her foot and twisted her body. "Are you still wearing the necklace?"

Prince Andrian pulled it into view. "I *never* take it off."

Kieran beamed. "You're my friend!"

"*Mon Dieu,* of course I am." Prince Andrian knelt by the girl. "I *will* be back. I promise."

"Don't break your promise. I'll wait for you." She put her arms around his neck, kissed his cheek, and wiped the blood from his mouth with her sleeve.

Prince Andrian looked this way and that as several people stared at the child's affectionate display. "Enough of that nonsense," he whispered and he pulled her from him. "Listen to me. When I make a solemn oath, I *never* break it. *Tu comprends?*"

She nodded.

"So I will swear to you that I shall return . . . and if all goes well, soon you shall have a home. I *swear* it." He took a bracelet from his wrist and handed it to her. "Just so that you believe me, I want you to watch over this. It holds *special* meaning to me. Swear to me you shall keep it safe."

Kieran slipped it on her wrist, and it dangled precariously. "I swear it, Andrian." Kieran could see dark clouds in Prince Andrian's eyes, the storm of lonesome terror that he could not hide even when he grinned. He placed his hand gently on her face. Prince Andrian stood and gave her a peck on the forehead.

Kieran knew he would return.

* * *

Andrian and his midnight stallion flew across the countryside as the blur of a banshee. Like the wings of Pegasus, the prince's cape flapped behind him. His horse touched one hoof for an instant upon the grass, and then remained in the air for a great while before his next hoof lit upon the soil. Villeins stood, their hands blocking their eyes from the sun, as they watched the pair thunder across the horizon. Never before had they seen a heavy warhorse hurl itself so quickly at the bidding of its master.

In Pershore, Andrian hopped from his frothy stallion and tied him to a tree. He pulled over a nearby barrel of water and the stallion shoved in his muzzle to drink. The prince glanced over at the home. It remained as he left it the day before: clean and inviting. He did not see Farida around, but a brown horse pulled at its tether around another tree. He loosed the borrowed horse and slapped its rump. The horse charged away. Andrian opened the door to the home and called for Farida. A raven above him in the trees answered him with a caw. Andrian wandered around the premises with fullness in his chest so great that it blinded him.

Farida sat by the stream, dipping her feet in its cool waters and humming. She greeted her panting husband as he sat beside her. "*Tu es saine et sauve?*" he gasped for air. "You are well?" He placed his hands over his face. "I came as *soon* as I could."

Farida chuckled, "Why, whatever did you *rush* here for?"

Andrian shrugged, "I did not read your letter. It was destroyed— an *accident*. The herald said it was urgent." He gripped his chest as he breathed. "I thought you were *ill*, or worse. I was sure I would find you in dire peril. And *here* you are." He leaned against a tree and threw his hands in the air. "You sit *gladly* enjoying yourself while I come running with such," he closed his eyes tightly, "*concern.*"

Farida hooted, "You should *see* yourself. I write to tell you that your *vegetables* were eaten up by the king's deer last night and you come to me in frenzy!"

Andrian sat up and glared at her. "*That* is what was urgent?"

She pointed at him as she covered her mouth. "I wish you could see your face! It's *intolerable*! I could die tomorrow and the last image would be that *face* of yours. I'd laugh into the next life!"

Andrian squinted at her. "You do *feel* well?"

She stood up. "Of *course.*"

Andrian looked up at her. The sun sparkled around her head like an aureole.

She exhaled casually. "It's *just* about time, I think."

"*Maintenant?*"

"God, I *hope* not now. He's got a little while left before he's ready. But I think perhaps a week, *maybe* two." She took his hand. "I *want* you to come inside with me."

Farida seemed frail to Andrian as she walked in her bare feet along the soft path he had made for them to the creek. He put his arm around her as if any moment she might pass out and fall.

"Andrian, will you lie with me under the stars tonight?" She wrapped her arm around his waist.

"If that is your wish." He glanced about for any enemies he might have led to his wife and their soon-to-be-born child.

"Why're you so restless, Andrian?" She smiled up at him.

"Let me *carry* you, Farida."

She smiled. "I wish to be off my feet *anyhow*." She looked down. "My ankles swell with the weight."

He hoisted her into his arms.

"Aren't I too *heavy* for you, my darling stallion?" She felt his taut forearms.

"Not at all. You are *lighter* than I imagined." He carried her toward their home, and she pushed the door open with the hand that did not stroke his face.

On the bed in their room, Farida sighed and stretched out. "Will you bring me something to drink? My mouth feels as if I've been chewing on feathers."

Andrian left her to bring cold water from the stream. Meanwhile, Farida closed her eyes and fell asleep. When Andrian returned, he set the jug of water by the bed and watched her breathing slowly in her dreams. Nothing seemed more beautiful in the world than Farida.

He reached out and touched her sleeping body. Her skin felt so soft and looked as deep as the bronze statues lining the halls of great kings. He traced her lips with his fingers. Pomegranates he had seen growing in the parched desert were shamed by her mouth. Her hair, so thick and full, he wound around his fingers. It pained him when she tied it back instead of allowing it freedom. He felt his child within her and bent to kiss her belly.

Farida opened her eyes as Andrian kissed her repeatedly. She yawned. "Why didn't you wake me, you sneak? I told you I'm *thirsty*."

He stopped kissing her. "I wanted you to rest. You look *fatiguée*."

"Well, I'm not too tired to drink. I'm parched." Andrian shared a cup of water with Farida and then she leaned over to him and kissed him on the mouth. He returned her kisses and they lay together entwined for a long while enjoying their love. Farida told Andrian that she had felt more exhausted lately, but she rejoiced in his presence, even if his concern for his vegetables had brought him home to her.

Night had lowered her silken veil upon Tiddesley Wood. Andrian carried Farida to the half-eaten vegetable patch. He laid her gently upon a bed of columbines and plunked down beside her. He fingered the shredded vegetation around him and then lay on his back. "It *pains* me to see the damage a deer can do to my precious onions," Andrian chuckled. "I spent so long caring for them, and in an *instant* they go to be fodder for my next quarry."

Farida patted his thigh. "You'll plant more *next* season."

"And they shall be larger and more plentiful than before." He held her hand as they gazed at the night sky. The black and blue swirled cosmos moved about the tiny firelight red and yellow prisms, swelling and receding with each pulse of light.

"Ooh." Farida pointed at a streak of green. "Make a wish, Andrian."

He squeezed Farida's hand. "I wish I knew what the future held for us."

Farida reached up to him and twirled a lock of his hair. "The future is already written, but it is only for the divine to know."

He rolled onto his side. "I was afraid of that."

Farida sighed and combed her fingers through his black curls. "We have our plans, and that is all we can do." She smiled and pulled his hair and let it spring back.

"I am torn inside of me. I must be king one day." He removed his coronet and placed it on the grass above him. "I will lead because the weak hand me their lives, not because I wish it for myself. I rather I never came home from the desert. A disappointment I have become."

"We are born into this world already ourselves." Farida retrieved the coronet and turned it in her hands. "You're a *soldier*, and you're good at it. But . . . you've got your country to run when you're king, and you won't have time for battles and bloodshed." She placed the coronet on his bare chest. She sighed. "You *are* a king, and I a vagrant doomed to grovel at your feet, not share your bed."

Andrian snuggled into her. "I will not be king without my queen beside me."

The lovers kissed each other fondly and embraced as the night deepened into an immeasurable indigo. The moon floated above them, brightening the inky night with ever lighter shades of sapphire and cerulean. Farida reached up toward it. "If I wanted the moon, could I *take* it from the sky?"

Andrian placed his hand on hers as she reached up. "I would *give* it to you."

She smiled at him. "You gave me something far *better* than the moon."

"*Qu'est-ce qui?*" He rubbed her hand as she reached for the white orb in the sky.

She lowered her hand with his and kissed his fingertips. "You gave me your love."

His heart trembled and he leaned over to his lover and kissed her deeply. She threw her arms around him, and they embraced with more passion than they had ever felt before.

"Wherever you go, there I shall be beside you." Andrian took a sapphire ring from his finger and placed it on Farida's finger. She turned the stone inward, and he kissed her. "I will no longer tolerate my father turning his back on you." He swallowed. "I shall turn my back on him. I shall turn my back on this whole wretched kingdom." He hurled his coronet into the woods like a Greek discus.

Farida rubbed the ring on her finger. "I've always wanted to live by the sea."

Andrian smiled. "We *can* live by *la mer*. We can live on the *beach*, and we can build *another* home and love each other the rest of our days."

Farida ran her fingers over Andrian's face. "We can bathe in the sea and swim without anyone to watch. I'd like very much to have a boat to take to the ocean, and we can go fishing and catch our meals."

"Mmmm that sounds *wonderful*." He kissed her and whispered, "*Demain,* let us put our cares behind us and find our new home by the sea."

Farida smiled. "I agree. Let's go away *tomorrow*. No one would miss me anyhow."

"Likewise, *ma chère*."

The lovers fell asleep under the stars, and though the night was cold, they felt not the bitter bite of the wind for their warm hearts sheltered them from the elements.

*   *   *

The dawn shone more brilliantly than Farida had ever seen in her life. The halo of amber light floated through the trees, and the smoldering fire lit the ground around her and Andrian. Twinkles of dewy sunbeams spread their glowing smiles upon all the bushes, and radiant blues and reds shined more vibrantly since the sinister pall of night had risen from the earth.

Andrian lay with his wrist over his eyes, mouth agape, snoring like a dog after a hunt.

Farida poked him. "Andrian?"

He opened his eyes.

"Look at the sun this morning. Isn't it the most *wondrous* sight you'd ever imagine?" She cradled him in her arms as they watched the sky change in kaleidoscopic glory.

He turned around and embraced her. They basked in the morning sun until it climbed to the highest point in the sky.

Andrian finally stood up. "We should ready ourselves to leave; there is a long journey ahead of us today."

Farida stood, and they walked back to the hidden shack, which they would abandon to live in an unconcealed home by the sea.

The lovers packed their belongings together, and before they left, Andrian visited his garden to caress the plants and bless their fruitfulness. While among the foliage, a white rock caught his eye. He bent over, picked it up, and laughed as he held it.

"Farida! Come here!"

Andrian's lover rushed to him. "What is it?" she said breathlessly.

He took her hand and gave her the stone. "I can give you the moon, if only in *miniature*."

Farida grinned and kissed him on the mouth. "It's *beautiful.* Thank you."

Andrian looked over at his horse eating the last of his onions. "*Zut!* Get out of here, you *worthless* animal!" He stamped his foot on the ground.

Farida watched the horse bolt away and said, "Well, you just frightened off any chance we had to go to the sea." She smoothed her hair. "I wonder how he got loose?"

Andrian shrugged. "He likely chewed through his tie. He has never thought to do so before. Such poor luck."

"Don't say that." Farida laughed. "Let me go get him. I'll be back with our ride in a bit." She loped off after the stallion as Andrian rolled his deerskins together.

A sharp cry sounded nearby.

A trapdoor in the pit of his stomach opened up. Andrian dropped the leather and sprinted after the sound. *"Farida!"* he cried. The stallion stood guard over a ditch in the ground. Andrian looked down inside. "It is a good thing my horse was here, I might not have found you for a time." He crouched above the hole.

"Oh . . . then your cow isn't so worthless after all." She laughed painfully. "I had forgotten about this bear trap. Ha. I slipped and fell in. I'm sorry if I frightened you." She pulled her hair from her face.

Andrian lay on his stomach and reached into the darkness. "Grab hold, *ma chère.*" She clutched him and he scooped her into his arms. "By the by, he is *un cheval,* not *une vache.*" He kissed her forehead and carried her toward the home. "I would have corralled the horse. You did not need to chase him."

She laughed as he laid her on the bed. "I don't know what came over me."

Andrian pulled his arms away from her. "Oh, Farida, did you injure yourself?"

"Why?" she asked, and when he showed her the stains on his hands, she gasped.

Andrian watched as blood began to dribble from her like warm gravy. "Farida?" He lifted up her dress so he could see well. "Farida? I think . . . I think it is coming from . . . from . . ."

Farida felt a spasm of pain throughout her body. "Andrian!" she cried out.

"What can I do?" he panicked.

"Andrian! *Help* me!" She wept as she felt the pain again. *"Please!"*

He wiped his sweaty face, smearing blood all over his cheek. "I do not know *how* I can help you." He spread her legs and watched with horror. "How can I help you, tell me?" She screamed and he watched the blood gurgling freely. He felt nauseous and fell onto the floor. "Oh . . . I cannot . . . I *cannot*."

"Yes, you *can*!" she cried.

He shook his head. His ears buzzed loudly, and he smelled a fire in his nose as his world darkened. He leaned over, trying to recover, and he breathed in slowly.

"Don't sit there! Don't leave me to do this alone!" She pushed on her own as her husband sat dazed on the ground. "I love you, Andrian! I *trust* you! Help me!"

Feeling a suction pull him downward, he crawled back to the bed and sat before her as she pushed. His eyes blurred and bile splashed the back of his throat. His sickened stupor muted Farida's screams of pain and horror as he helped birth his son.

"I have *killed* him," he whispered to her. "I am so *sorry*. It is my fault. I should have helped you and not sat on the floor." He cradled the dead child in his arms and rubbed his face against him. "I am so sorry, my son. Oh, forgive my *uselessness*."

Farida groped for Andrian. "I should've forgotten about the stupid horse and stayed with you." After he let her pat his face, he gave her the child. She kissed his lifeless body.

Andrian watched his lover breathing laboriously. "We can always try again for a child . . . when we get to our new home."

Farida pulled his hair and shook her head. "I *can't* go now, Andrian."

"Not *now*, of course," he whispered. He looked at the sheets soaked through with more blood than he ever saw in battle. He felt a knot twist in his chest as the amaranthine stain soaked through the bed; her face paled with every moment. "We can change the mattress tonight, so you need not sleep in discomfort."

"It doesn't *matter* anymore." Farida smiled at Andrian.

"I will give you everything in the heavens if you so desire later, but perhaps a new bed would be *more* appropriate for now." His eyes glistened as he rubbed her nose.

She laughed weakly. "All I want is a kiss to make me touch the sky. Think about the bed *later*."

"That *can* be arranged."

"I love you," she sighed and he kissed her forehead. When he sat up once again, Farida's eyes were empty.

"Farida?" he caressed her cheek. *"Farida?"* He pushed on her. She still stared sightless. He placed his hand over his mouth and shook his head. "Please . . . Farida." He cradled her and her head lolled to the side. "Oh . . . oh no, *please*." He held her to him. "Come back. You *cannot* be gone. No . . . I *love* you. It cannot *be* this way. It cannot . . . oh . . . *Farida*." He moaned and rocked her in his arms while he stroked her hair gently. "It is not fair. I will not *let* you leave me here." He pulled her arms around him as if an embrace might breathe life into her lungs. As he nuzzled her cheek, he became conscious that nothing would help her but allowing her soul to take flight. He swallowed hard and laid her back on the bed. He shut her eyes gently and took her hand and kissed it once for a very long time.

Andrian looked out the door at the dawn. Farida had labored all afternoon and through the night. As he attempted to leave the room, his legs gave out from under him and he fell to the floor. For a moment he lay there, unable to rise; numbness had consumed him. Slowly he felt his arms and legs tingle sensation once again and he propped himself up. So this was what it was like to die. His head whirled as he grabbed onto the bed and stood. Regaining his composure, he forced his feet one after the other to go to his garden.

He spent hours clearing his garden and digging the hole for his family. After his work seemed satisfactory, he went indoors and sat beside his lover for the last time. She was sleeping. He was only having a horrible nightmare and she would sit up and laugh at him. He could almost hear her teasing him about his sorrow. She did not sit up. She lay still and breathless. Andrian looked down at his dead wife and child and grasped his aching chest. Biting his lip until it bled, he put one arm around his son and one around his wife and brought them into the cursed forest.

He carried them toward their final resting place and laid them in the grass side by side. He removed his cloak and swaddled his infant in the blue of a dismal sea. He kissed Farida on the cheek and his son on the forehead, and then he lowered both into the grave. He made sure she held the child to her breast protectively. Then he picked the last of the pansies and carnations from his garden and placed them around her, petals outlining her silhouette. He removed his tunic and covered her face with it so that the soil would not mar her eternal beauty.

He sprinkled dirt into the grave handful by handful. If he shoveled it in, he might hurt her or his son. The whole process took the entire day, from the digging to the last stone he placed on the dirt mound. He did not mark the grave with a standing cross, though he placed seven black stones about the site: one over her head, two over her hands, one over her breast, one over her womb, one over her feet, and the last he placed on top of the mound. He removed his quillon from its sheath and cut both of his hands in turn as deeply as he could bear and walked about the grave, smattering his blood on the black rocks.

He knelt before the tomb, and then, consumed with his grief, wailed as loudly as his soul could bear. He shed no tears; his eyes hurt too badly and his heart ached too deeply. He screamed such pain that birds flew away in silence, his horse bowed his head, squirrels hid their faces, and time stood still.

After he could holler no more, he covered his face and lamented, "I *loved* you." The miserable young man lay beside the grave. Caressing the rocks, he fell asleep.

Chapter Six

For six days and six nights, Andrian lay by the grave and mourned Farida and their child. He felt no hunger or thirst, save for her company. He weakened when he knew that he must rise and live his life.

Andrian dragged his feet as he approached his horse, wandering about near his master, though never looking as if he might bolt away. Andrian's sword carved a line beside him as he trudged to mount his stallion for the journey home. He slowly turned his head for one last look around and then pulled himself into his saddle. As he sheathed his hand-and-a-half by his side, something with sharp nails clawed its way down the back of his throat into his chest. He bent over in defeat.

In most circumstances, Andrian's jet-colored steed would start excitedly when he urged it to go. As Andrian slouched in the saddle, so the horse could not lift his head, and the going seemed sluggish and agonizing. The sound of the hooves on the ground was not a joyful *clop-clop*, but a scratching thud that only came from a lame animal, though the stallion had not twisted his ankle, pulled a muscle, or overextended any ligaments.

The scenery about the young man glowed fresh and colorful; plants smelled of dew so that the nose tingled with their fragrance. Andrian's world consisted of shades of gray, and the only scent that wafted his way was the salt from his stifled tears. Besotted birds chirruped and warbled in fantastic circles higher and higher still above his head, but Andrian heard silence. No birds he saw spinning around, save the vultures whirling above, ogling him with lusty eyes.

As the shattered man crossed a wooden bridge, he looked down at his reflection in the water. Instead of a hearty youth of nearly twenty-five winters, he saw a frail phantom wasted away from his throbbing despair. He saw no leaping fish in the clear waters, only globular mud congealing the true image of its crystal trickle. He watched his tanned skin become pasty and yellow almost before his eyes as he passed the bubbling stream. His eyes grew heavy-lidded and the last he saw of his reflection, he had become a skeletal cur.

In three days' time he had managed to plod into view of the grand castle his father's father had begun. Its pinnacles faded from majesty in the shadows before his eyes. He saw no proud turrets of limestone, no curtain wall as white as a fair maiden's skin, and no garden of sanctity. The image he enjoyed so as he would arrive from long journeys past soured his stomach as he approached it. He had traded love for that tumble-down hunk of rock and mortar. He clenched his teeth as he entered the barbican. The closing bang of the portcullis rocked him in his saddle.

He could not straighten his back with royal pride as his guard stared after him. Someone the size of a prize heifer sat upon his shoulders, though he could not see him there. He did not bother to salute his knights, for he could not shift his eyes from the small patch of dirt three meters in front of him as his horse shuffled like an old man toward its destination.

Instinctively, the stallion halted at the stables, but Andrian did not dismount to go greet his father. Only when a groom took the reins of his horse did reality hit Prince Andrian, and he slid from its back to land with a *plonk* on the ground. He gathered his effects in silence, for his world was hushed, and he made his way to the keep for dinner with his parents.

The prince weaved through the bustle of servants and knights as a colorless blur, blind to everything but his next footstep. As he entered the great hall, his hands refused to carry his belongings and they slipped and hit the floor with such a clatter that the entire room fell silent.

King Arundel looked up at the bang. Andrian stood in the middle of the room and wavered like a stalk of straw missed by a scythe. Never in his life had he seen such a look on his scion as he wore at that moment. The bedraggled Prince Andrian faltered for a moment but then slowly shuffled his boots toward the king with invisible leg irons attached.

Prince Andrian approached his father and collapsed to his knees. He looked up at King Arundel with mirrors. The king placed his hand on Prince Andrian's shoulder, and his heart bubbled into his eyes. King Arundel looked up at his company. "Leave us!" he hollered, his voice echoed throughout the hall like an avalanche.

The hall emptied and only the king and his son remained inside the closed doors. King Arundel heaved the young man to his feet and helped him to the nearest table, for he could not imagine he could walk much further than that.

As the king eased his son onto the bench, Prince Andrian's head fell hard on the wood, no sound uttered at the impact.

"Tell me, my son. Why this *display* when you come into my castle?" He patted him on the back.

The prince mumbled something into the tabletop.

"Speak to *me* and not the *oak*, if you please."

"Dead." Prince Andrian raised his one-hundred-stone head and turned toward his father. To the king's shock, Andrian's mouth fell agape and his glazed eyes looked like a startled horse had brained him.

King Arundel leaned into his face. "Who, my son? Who is dead?"

Andrian shifted his eyes toward a servant who had come in to ask something of the prince, and as the man approached the royal company, he stopped. Prince Andrian looked ready to vomit. The king roared, "Did I not say that we should be left alone for now?" He grabbed the prince by the hair, for he wore no tunic. "Does *this* man look *capable* of holding a conversation with you at the moment?"

Drool dribbled from Prince Andrian's mouth as the king shook him back and forth.

"No, Sire. He looks bloody *awful.*"

King Arundel released his son's hair and he once again collided with the table and remained there. "Leave us for as long as it takes, and I shall call for you when my son has regained his right mind." He paused, "That is, if he ever *had* one to begin with."

The servant bowed to the king and scampered off to tell everyone who had a free ear that Andrian the Ruthless had become a mindless corpse.

King Arundel turned his attention back to his son, who started to slide off the bench. He grabbed his upper arm and hauled him onto his feet. "Let us take a walk, shall we?"

Prince Andrian said nothing, but when his father led him out the door by the arm, he clomped behind obediently. When they reached the upper bailey, the king let the prince fall onto a grassy patch without as much as a sound. Prince Andrian lay on his belly, staring at nothing in particular while his father paced to and fro.

"What is this *madness*, Andrian?" He wheeled around. "Do you *enjoy* being a laughingstock? Shall I confine you to your chambers until you cease your *folly*?" He paced again. "Now, once again, I *ask* you *why* are you moping about as if the world has been destroyed?"

Prince Andrian's glossy eyes turned upward to his father's snarling face. "Because indeed the world *is* destroyed." He lowered his eyes. "I have *nothing* to live for . . . anymore. There is no *reason* to go on."

King Arundel kicked his son hard in the thigh. "What fool idea was put in your head that it mattered whether *you* went on or not? There are duties that cannot be put aside because *you* have had a bad day. I cannot *believe* how selfish you are! You are only a man. And might I add a pathetic excuse for one as well."

Prince Andrian looked up at his father and nodded.

King Arundel continued as he lashed at his son with his boot. "Your whole world, which you say has ended, only ever consisted of death and destruction. You seem to be *incapable* of humility, of compassion. I would highly *doubt* your heart could find a way to love *anyone* but yourself. You are an *absolute* disgrace to my name."

Prince Andrian's chest heaved.

"If only your *brother* were here. Now *there* is a man worthy of my name . . . it is a pity *his* mother was not my wife . . . why, *he* would rule in your stead. A *fine* man he is." He looked down at Andrian, now curling into a ball to hide his shame. "If you were not the crown prince, I would hang you for making me look like an idiot. The *whole* kingdom wants Julian as king, and they wonder why I will not crown him instead of *you*."

Prince Andrian placed his head in his hands and sighed jaggedly.

"Do you *know* why I will not crown Julian? *Do* you?"

"No," Prince Andrian croaked.

"*Answer* me so that I might know I have a *man* child and *not* a mouse!"

"*No,*" Prince Andrian said it louder and felt a sudden gush of anger.

"Now *that* is more like a man. I will *not* crown your brother on principle. He is a *bastard*, and you are not. That is the *only* reason. If it were *not* that way, I *would* have left you on someone's doorstep."

Prince Andrian's eyes flashed black.

"If you *embarrass* me once more," he held up his finger, "my son, I shall take your title *completely* from you, strip you of your clothes, and put you in the stocks. Then you will *know* how I feel when I lay my eyes on you."

"Why don't you simply murder me?" He rose to his feet. "Protect your kingdom from a tyrant."

King Arundel stepped into Prince Andrian's face and poked his bare chest with his sharp fingernail. "You have been a *disgrace* since you were a boy. Your cowardly nature disgusts me. Bullying the other children for pleasure, that was one of your favorite games. To this day, you enjoy playing the part. I cannot trust you to complete any tasks with relative intelligence. If I told you to purchase a stallion for me, you would bring me an ass." King Arundel lifted his son's chin to look at him.

Andrian pulled away from his father. "That is untrue. I have done everything you have asked of me. I am quite capable of discerning an ass from a horse."

King Arundel laughed. "That may only be so because you would send someone other than yourself to do my bidding. Meanwhile your vassals work for you as you enjoy evil pleasures. You are a worthless leader, and I should never trust you to govern this country. It might become Sodom and Gomorrah before my eyes."

"I never asked to be *king*."

"Oh? Then what do you want?"

Andrian lowered his head. "Nothing anymore."

"I am at an impasse with you my son. I know not how to teach you how to behave any longer. I fear you will shatter this kingdom if I allow you to remain here."

Andrian clasped his hands together. "Give me a chance. I will prove that I am up to your standards."

King Arundel stroked Andrian's hair. "I have given you many chances, and you have disappointed me each time." King Arundel pulled his son's hair from his face. "What am I to do with you?"

"Embrace me as you do Julian. Perhaps I would be a better man."

King Arundel frowned. "Embrace you so you might drive a knife in my back? I would do no such thing. You are cunning and dangerous, my son. Even as we speak, archers stand ready to pierce your heart if you decided to turn against me."

Andrian looked up and around the battlemented walls. Indeed the guard stood watching him. The sun glinted off their helmets, and the tips of their arrows sparkled with menace. He turned back toward the king. "I am a prisoner here. Why do I even come home if I am unwanted?"

"You are always welcome here, Andrian, so long as you remain my son and not an assassin." King Arundel smiled. "They are well trained."

Andrian looked up at the nearest archer. "If he missed me and hit you instead, that would be most unfortunate."

King Arundel raised his hand and waved it sideways. The archer raised his bow and aimed at Andrian. "Would you like a demonstration?"

Andrian swallowed as the sun cast the archer's shadow upon him. "No, that will not be necessary."

"Are you afraid for your safety?"

Andrian turned toward his father. "I am no coward."

King Arundel held up two fingers, and the archer aimed toward the king instead. "If he were to shoot me, would you step before the arrow and throw your life away?"

Andrian looked up again and frowned. "I would not."

"Are you certain? I know that your brother would step before me, even though I am an old man."

Andrian glared at the archer as his father raised his hand again. An arrow flew toward the king and the prince stood still. The arrow struck not his father, but an empty barrel to his right.

"Ha, he missed." Andrian pulled the shaft from the wood, snapped it in half, and threw it on the ground.

"I *will* not be surprised if one day I *execute* you for your *ghastly* nature." He hissed, "You have done *nothing* your whole life that warrants continued existence, let *alone* my praise. You did not even move to help me."

Andrian looked up. "He would not have hit you."

"How do you know?"

"I see things you do not. I am a soldier. I know my enemies and I know yours. There is no one here who you must fear."

"Andrian, you have made enemies of those who love you. The next moment you disregard my safety will be the last moment of your life."

"I will die by your hand?"

King Arundel frowned. "If *that* were the way of it, we *all* would be better off."

Prince Andrian's eyes glistened, but he swallowed the salt through the back of his throat and bowed to his father. "I understand *perfectly* well. Good day."

Andrian shuffled away with his head lowered. King Arundel scowled at his son. He merely needed discipline for his actions. Still, the empty look in his eyes disturbed him. He had not witnessed such behavior in Andrian since his sister Jonquille had died before he left for the Holy Land. King Arundel watched the prince kick rocks half-heartedly and began to regret the harsh words he had spoken.

Chapter Seven

After the death of his wife, Andrian the Ruthless spent an entire month in seclusion. Few saw even a glimpse of his pallid figure as he opened his chamber egress to accept hot water for a bath, his meals, or even a letter or two from his vassals. Kieran did not even see him that first month, though she kept busy learning about the inner workings of a castle with Lorcan, who had grown fond of her as she was his granddaughter's age.

The absence of the dark prince's shadow on Briton should have brought peace to the country. King Arundel enlisted Julian as commander of the army in Andrian's stead, but he marched them aimlessly around the countryside. More than one time soldiers were heard to have grumbled for their true general. Upon hearing the mutinous words from his own men, Julian informed his father that he desired his place of nobility more than his position in war.

King Arundel was at a loss for that first month. His son and heir apparent had completely lost his mind. He had come up to his apartment in the keep and knocked, hoping that Andrian would exit with his peacock flourish and shout a few obscenities at him. The king merely knocked and heard silence. King Arundel went so far as to send the prince his ailing mother for tea and biscuits. Andrian remained reticent through all her pleas.

The second month of the prince's confinement truly began to disturb the king, as now the prince would not even open his door for his bath or his meals. King Arundel began to fear that his son had vanished or had died. Sir Idwal brought five large men to unhinge the chamber door so they could check on their lord.

The heavy oak door moved aside, King Arundel knocked on the side of the wall. "Andrian, are you awake, my son?" He tiptoed into the room, past shredded draperies and upended furniture gashed deeply by the prince's sword. Sir Idwal followed the king, and the five men hung back at the entrance.

It was daylight, though the chamber remained dark and haunted. The king motioned for light and one of the stout men brought forth an oil lamp. Even with the spark of light in his hand, the king knocked a standing candelabrum to the ground with a *clang.* He paused for a moment, hoping that his scion would hurl toward him in rage. With not a peep from the prince, the king stepped over the fallen bronze and continued to make his way over the destruction.

At his escritoire, the prince sat, still as a fox on a hunt. He faced the dark wall, his hands flat on top of the wood surface, his body moribund.

King Arundel cleared his throat. "Andrian, are you well? Are you in need of assistance?"

No movement or sound came in response.

Sir Idwal approached. "My liege, we have not seen you for a very long time. Is there something the matter?"

Still, Andrian did nothing.

King Arundel came closer and pulled a chair beside his son, who stared blankly at the wall. The prince was sallow, his eyes glassy, and his mouth dry and cracked. How long had he not eaten? His hair was limp and oily; no baths for quite a time, it seemed. His beard had grown in and gray had begun to grow among the wiry black. The king held his oil lamp up so he could see his son clearer. Streams of tears had drawn trails down his dusty cheeks.

"Andrian, why don't you come to breakfast? I hear they are making your favorite, beef stew with barley." He placed his hand on his son's forearm. No movement and no response.

Sir Idwal crouched down. "My lord, a good meal and a hot bath would do you much good. Why don't you let us help?"

Prince Andrian whispered, "Dead."

King Arundel removed his hand from his son's forearm. "Who is dead, my son?"

"I am," he whispered.

"Nonsense." King Arundel patted his son's shoulder. "You merely need a good meal and a wash. That will make it better." He touched his son's hair. "A nice soak in hot water will relax you. It has not been the best of years for you, but it shall improve."

"Leave me here to rot." Prince Andrian bowed his head.

Sir Idwal put his hands on the prince. "Come, let us take care of you. Cannot have you moping about like a specter."

"Remove yourself from my person." Prince Andrian turned his head sharply and glared at Sir Idwal, who yanked his hands away as though the prince were on fire.

"Now, now, my son, we are here to help you."

Andrian turned to his father. "Help me?" he spat. "HELP ME?" He flew to his feet.

King Arundel leapt back out of his chair, away from his son.

"YOU SENT A MAN TO MURDER ME AND MY WIFE! YOU CALL THAT HELP?"

"I know nothing of that, my son." King Arundel held his hands out. "Please, let us take you to eat and then we shall have a hot bath drawn for you. You can dress in some comfortable clothes and perhaps you would like to visit Kieran."

Andrian the Ruthless stood heaving with his hands clutched tightly into fists. Blood trickled down his arms from cuts in his flesh.

"You are injured, my lord." Sir Idwal reached for the prince, who whipped around and glowered at him.

Andrian the Ruthless clamped his jaw so tightly that he trembled.

Sir Idwal, like the king, raised his open hands. "Let us help you."

"Leave my sight, the pair of you. I have no need for false pity." The prince sat back down on his chair and went back to staring at the small stones lodged in the mortar of his walls.

King Arundel and Sir Idwal slowly backed away from the prince.

As they exited the now open egress, Sir Idwal sighed, "I feel a storm brewing."

"So do I." The king marched away from his son's apartment, the large men and the knight following closely behind him.

Inside the dark room, Andrian the Ruthless let out a lion's roar that echoed throughout the castle.

*   *   *

As the first two months brought silence from Andrian the Ruthless, so the next two months brought wrath upon Briton as an angry Zeus hurled his thunderbolts upon mere mortals. Avoiding the storm cloud rumbling around the prince meant everyone walked ten paces around him, even when in confining hallways. Men died if they did not move quickly enough. Andrian the Ruthless raged about the castle more than he ever had before, and as he smashed everything to make the most intolerable racket he could muster, his eyes bled mercilessly. Only Kieran had tried to reach for him, but he pulled away from her and insisted she should go play with the other children in the castle.

Weeks of weathering the unending storm weakened Queen Mireille, and she became bedridden and ill. Nothing could be done, it seemed, to calm the Titan; everyone simply hunkered down and waited out the wicked cyclone.

At meals, the prince had sat alone at the far end of the table, the king and his consorts at the opposite end, all eating a bite at a time, all never taking their eyes off the prince. Only Kieran dared scoot down to her protector to retrieve the salt cellar.

As she sprinkled salt on her meat, Kieran asked Andrian if they would go visit Farida again soon. Prince Andrian twisted his mouth. "We shall never again see Farida."

Kieran patted him. "Why not?"

Andrian wiped his eyes, "She left this world. Now, never bring her up to me again. I cannot bear the thought of her."

Kieran bowed her head and patted his arm once again. Instead of returning to her seat by the king, she remained by Andrian. For a brief time, the sun peeked through the storm cloud; Andrian grasped the child's hand in his as they ate their meal.

*   *   *

After the months of solitude and the months of rage, the prince had spent the last of the summer petitioning for a place for Kieran to reside. He finally found a home for her if she might take it. A convent of Franciscan sisters would take her in and give her an education. Later, she might wish to become a sister, or she could leave to live her own life. The choice she could make when she felt ready in the future.

Though Kieran wished to stay with the prince and give him some comfort, she decided to get an education and live apart from the turbulent castle that had now earned the epithet "Le Château Noir."

Prince Andrian agreed with her wise decision, and made plans to take her the following week to the convent nearest his brother. If anything happened to her, his brother would inform him. Even though he despised Julian, he admired the man's decency to keep after family business if asked.

* * *

Prince Andrian and his ward, Kieran, made the journey to the Franciscan convent accompanied by minimal guard. He planned to visit Selma Halloran on his way back to Eddington to retrieve his belt and to visit for a little while. She had seemed pleasant enough, and he felt like she might offer some relief from his tragic thoughts.

Kieran hummed a cheery song as they marched along, and twirled a stick in her hand. She glanced up at Prince Andrian as her tunes became louder and more exultant.

"Why have you such joy today?" Prince Andrian asked as he surveyed the landscape for any danger. He did not wish for another ambush; his company might not survive the next onslaught—not that he cared if he survived.

Kieran glowed. "Just tryin' to cheer you up, that's all."

"Hmmm," he said under his breath. He looked down at her for a moment. "I am afraid that humming and carrying on in such a jovial fashion shall do no good."

Kieran poked him with the stick. "You don't want to be happy."

Prince Andrian steered his horse around a ditch. "Oh?"

Kieran patted his hand. "There's a lot to be glad for. You saved my life, and I *love* you."

He blushed. "You know, I do not think any child has said that to me before."

Kieran looked up at him. "You're not *really* a brute, you know. You just pretend to be."

He kicked his heels against the horse's flank, and he charged ahead of the cavalcade. "What makes you *think* I pretend?" The horse cleared a log and after that snorted and tossed its head.

"When you're cruel to people, you've got a funny look on your face." She wrinkled her nose. "It looks like you're gonna cry. I think you should cry, you know. If I got yelled at by my dad I'd cry too."

Andrian snorted.

"Don't you want to feel better?"

Andrian snorted again. "I shall never feel better, so do not insist I try."

She sighed. "Sometimes I wish I weren't going away and I could be your daughter. Maybe you could adopt me?"

He laughed. "Why would you want *me* to be your father?" The stallion leapt over a small creek and whinnied with excitement.

"Because you need someone to cheer you up. We could play games and have loads of fun. You could teach me to read and write . . . I'd study really hard. *Please?*"

Prince Andrian halted before a gated convent. "I am sorry, Kieran, but my life is too complicated for *myself*, let alone to burden you with my troubles. I *like* you too much."

Kieran slouched and nodded. "If it's all right with you, can I write you?"

Prince Andrian dismounted and Kieran vaulted into his arms. "If it makes you feel better about everything, then I shall be delighted to correspond. I must remind you, however, that I am extraordinarily busy and you shall not receive a letter *every* day, but I shall make a great effort to at least write when I have spare time."

Kieran smiled. "Can *I* write all the time?"

Prince Andrian nodded. "I would be grateful for your kindness. So few people in this world have as big a heart as you."

Kieran patted his chest. "*You're* one of them."

He laughed uncomfortably and set her on the grass.

Several nuns came out to greet the visitors, and Prince Andrian took the mother superior to the side. "She is a very good little girl. Please make sure she has everything she needs. As you can see, her face has been badly damaged by a fire, but I *assure* you it has not damaged her spirit."

The mother superior nodded. "She shall receive attention for her healing injuries, and she will receive food and clothing and a good education. We like to give the parting company comfort in that we are quite attentive to young girls' needs. I assure you, she will not feel anything but God's love here."

Prince Andrian placed his hands together and bowed to the nun. "Bless you for doing this." He pulled out a bag of money from his belt and handed it to the nun. "This is a donation for helping my ward. I shall indeed be sending more periodically for the upkeep of your convent in gratitude for your kindness to Kieran."

The purse weighed heavily in the hands of the nun. "You are *most* generous, Milord."

Prince Andrian smiled. "I ask if it is proper if I might write to her while she is here?"

The mother superior nodded. "It is proper. We do, however, make sure she keeps regular hours, so she might not be able to write to you all night and day." She studied his face. "I hope that does not displease you."

He chuckled. "No, Madame, it *pleases* me to see such discipline. I myself should have had more as a boy."

"Andrian, they told me that I share a room with other girls and I'll have many friends and I'm going to learn a lot!" Kieran ran toward Prince Andrian while holding up a small gray rabbit. "And look! They've got pets here too!"

Prince Andrian stroked the rabbit, which recoiled at his touch. "How *charming.*"

"He's scared of strangers, but he'd get used to you if you let him." She kissed the hare and smiled. "He's shy, just like you."

"No, Kieran. I truly think he dislikes me." He reached out to pet the animal again when Kieran begged him to, and it kicked Kieran a couple times and escaped into the woods surrounding the convent.

Kieran guffawed as several girls shrieked and sped after the convict.

"Milord?" a nun asked. "Would you like to visit the grounds?"

Prince Andrian opened his mouth to refuse, but when he saw the look of longing in Kieran's eyes, he sighed. "It is up to this young lady whether she wishes for it."

Kieran hopped up and down. "Yes! Oh, please just this once, for me?" She clung on to his tunic. "Please?"

Prince Andrian raised his hands in defeat. "Aye, you have me for a little while."

Kieran did a cartwheel, and Prince Andrian followed the nun, who in a French accent called herself Sister Claire.

As they reached the gates, Prince Andrian turned to the nun, *"Pardonnez-moi, parlez-vous français?"*

She nodded. *"Oui, monsieur le prince. Je parle français. Pourquoi?"*

Prince Andrian shrugged. *"Pas la raison, je suis curieux, c'est tout."*

They walked in silence through a garden, and Prince Andrian stopped for a moment to take in all of the various vegetables and flowers the convent kept. He stroked the stalks of onions and wiped his eyes.

Sister Claire eyed him. *"Vous vous excusez pour demander, monsieur le prince . . . mais, pourquoi vous pleurez?"*

Prince Andrian looked over at her. *"Je ne pleure pas, mademoiselle."* His face became hard, *"J'aime les oignons. Ils sont mes favorites végétaux."* He told her he did not weep, but since he would bear his heartache alone, he told her that he liked onions and they made him sad. He did not think she would believe him.

Sister Claire smiled. *"Moi aussi."*

Kieran watched the prince stroking the plant life. "Andrian?"

He looked at her. "Aye?"

"What're you saying? I don't understand. You two aren't the only ones here, you know." She put her hands on her hips.

Prince Andrian smiled. "I was merely commenting on the garden. It is quite lovely." It was the truth, he had commented about the onions, and to his surprise Sister Claire liked them as well.

Through the garden flowed a small stream, and several girls diverted its waters into the plant beds. Kieran jumped up and down. "They look like they're having fun!"

Two of the girls looked up at Kieran and snickered at her. Kieran heard them and stuck her tongue out as she grabbed a hold of the prince's cloak. Both girls looked about fourteen or fifteen. Girls meandered about, ranging in age from five or six to seventeen, and most of the older girls seemed to concern themselves with the youngest.

The two jeering girls looked over at Prince Andrian and fell silent. Their eyes followed the prince as he strutted by them, though oblivious to their presence. When the nun walked out of earshot, one girl whispered, "Did you see that . . . *man?*"

Sister Claire led the prince and Kieran to the church cloister, where many girls strolled around and chatted, some even had pets in their arms. Most of them had birds and rabbits, and one even had a small dog. Kieran yanked on the prince's arm. "Oh, Andrian, let me go pet the puppy! Oh, please!"

Prince Andrian nodded, and Kieran rushed to the girl with the dog.

Sister Claire watched Kieran and the girl playing with the puppy, which barked and tumbled with every tickle from the children. She turned to the prince. *"Vous étés de Langeais, n'est pas?"*

The prince nodded. *"Oui, ma famille est de Langeais. Pourquoi?"* Now she wanted to know if he came from Langeais in France. He thought it a peculiar question to ask, but he answered that his family indeed came from that city.

Sister Claire looked over at Kieran, who rolled around on the ground as the puppy licked her face. *"Je suis née en Langeais aussi."*

"Sans mentir?" Prince Andrian raised his eyebrows. She played games with him, for she came from Langeais as well. He felt a little uneasy as to where the conversation was headed, but he had better find out instead of wonder for the rest of his days why she found it important to tell him such information.

She shook her head. *"Sans mentir. Vous vous souvenez-moi?"*

She had asked him if he remembered her. The conversation would end in tragedy; he knew it. Prince Andrian shrugged. *"Je me ne souvenions pas vous. Est-ce que je?"*

Sister Claire sighed. *"Je suis l'amante première de vous."*

Prince Andrian covered his mouth. *"Mon Dieu . . . Vous étés la fille a qui le frère je meurtrit, non?"* So Sister Claire was his first love, though she had since changed her name, and they had come face to face again after a decade. Her brother had attacked him after what he had taken from his sister, and he had killed the boy in self-defense. His murder, of those he had committed outside of the battlefield, had earned his regret long ago. It had truly been an accident. He had fallen from a precipice during their tussle.

The nun nodded. *"Oui, monsieur le prince."*

Prince Andrian shook his head. *"Zut."* He turned toward Sister Claire. *"Ne gardez pas rancune a moi, je demande de vous."*

Sister Claire placed her hand on his shoulder and patted it. "Don't worry, *monsieur le prince,* I've put the past behind me."

Prince Andrian placed the top of her fingers on his forehead. *"Merci."* She had forgiven him for his trespass. He had asked for clemency, and she had granted it freely.

Kieran bounced over to Prince Andrian with the puppy in her arms. "Isn't she cute?" The puppy licked her face and she giggled.

Prince Andrian smiled. "She is sweet."

"Pet her, Andrian; she's got to like you. She's not shy at all!" She held up the sinuous puppy to him.

"I would rather not." He watched the dog wriggling in her hands. It had an endearing face, with an elongated body and stubby legs. Its ears flopped about and one of them turned inside out while it squirmed. He reached out to pet it in hopes that it would not run or bite. He placed his hand on its head and scratched its ears.

Kieran squealed when the puppy slobbered all over his hand. "Oh, she loves you! Isn't she the cutest thing ever?"

"No-no-no," Prince Andrian protested when Kieran handed the dog to him. He held it in front of himself and it began to whine. "What does she want?" he asked. Kieran pushed the dog closer to him, and he cradled it. The strange-looking puppy put its head into his chest and scratched the crown of its head up and down on his tunic. "She is *très mignonne,* now take her back."

A little girl, perhaps two years older than Kieran, took the dog from the prince and smiled. "I'm Shannon. How d'you do?"

The prince smiled. *"Bien, merci."*

Kieran poked Shannon. "That's Prince Andrian . . . he's my friend."

Shannon gasped and curtsied. "Sorry, Your Ruthlessness—I mean Highness. I've forgotten my manners."

Prince Andrian frowned. "It appears we both have, for I had not introduced myself. Perhaps this awkward situation might have been avoided if I had not been thinking about which city to burn next." He smirked. "Where did you say you were from again?"

Shannon's face became a pale stone as she looked at Sister Claire, whose lips pressed together as she folded her hands.

Prince Andrian grinned. "I see my reputation precedes me to all corners of my father's kingdom." He kissed the child's hand. "Forgive me for frightening you. I was merely jesting. I could not help it, for after your comment about me, I found I needed to respond."

Shannon nodded and said, "All right." She whispered to Kieran, "Are you sure he's safe?"

Kieran nodded. "Yes."

Sister Claire cleared her throat. "*Monsieur le prince*, I would ask if it's good to continue about and sightsee, or do you wish to go about your business?"

Prince Andrian scratched his beard in thought. "Well, this evening I really must be leaving for Eddington. I have quite a full schedule the upcoming week—beheadings, meaningless tantrums to throw, fires to light—all those lovely things." He paused. "But I would like to continue on the walk, if you do not mind. I still have time before sundown when I become my most demonic."

"We get the idea." Kieran eyed him.

Shannon looked nauseated and croaked, "I'll just stay here, if it's all right with His Disgrace." She gasped. "I mean His Grace."

Prince Andrian wagged his finger. "Oh that *is* clever. I shall remember that one."

Sister Claire spoke up, "Let's get along, *shall* we?"

Prince Andrian and the two girls plodded along behind the nun as they visited the rest of the convent. The prince did not wish to visit the dorter where the girls slept, because he thought it would be inappropriate for a man to go barging into such an area. They did, however, visit the library.

The room, though modest in size, abounded with books. The prince loathed to leave. He wanted to sit down and read the rest of the day.

"I must come here to visit, if only to sit with Kieran in the library and read." He stroked the shelves of books.

Sister Claire raised her eyebrows. "*Vous lirez?*"

Prince Andrian patted a shelf, "Mademoiselle, I was educated in Alexandria. Of course I can read." He paused. "I am able to read five languages."

Kieran added, "He's gonna write to me when I live here, and I'll write back when I learn to read and write too."

Shannon smiled. "I'll help teach you, if you'd like. I can read."

Kieran bounced up and down, and the puppy, still in Shannon's arms, watched her with raw fascination.

"This next room is the locutorium, where we visit after dinner and between classes." Sister Claire led them down a hallway.

They peeked in, and several girls sat playing games and a few sang songs while dancing in a ring. Kieran looked up at Prince Andrian. "I wish I could sing."

He sighed. "I wish I could as well."

While playing chess, a girl glanced over to the doorway and saw the visitors watching them along with Sister Claire. She nudged the girl across from her and whispered.

Several other girls began to stare at the visitors, and the singing stopped.

"Please continue; I found your singing to be quite lovely." Prince Andrian entered and sat on one of the three chairs in the room.

The girls sat with their mouths open and remained silent.

He folded his hands and leaned forward. "You play chess?"

One girl nodded.

He rubbed his hands together. "Now we are getting somewhere. Will one of you play a game with me?"

They all shook their heads.

Prince Andrian frowned. "Oh, come now. I promise to play fairly."

One girl who was about five strutted over to the prince. "I'll play."

He grinned. "I like this girl; *elle a du cran.* She has guts." He sat by the chessboard, and she sat opposite of him. "What is your name?"

"The Winner."

Prince Andrian chuckled. "Oh, you think so?"

"Yes." The little girl looked up at the man. "Which color d'you wanna be?"

"*Noir.*" He selected his pieces and placed them on the board accordingly.

The little girl cleared her throat. "The queen goes on her *own* color."

"Oh, right." The prince placed his queen on the black square as he switched it with his king. After she too had positioned her pawns, knights, rooks, bishops, and her king and queen, he smiled. "Your move first."

Kieran sat beside the prince, and out of curiosity the rest of the girls moved closer. Sister Jolie stood behind to watch. The girl moved her pawn and announced, "Pawn to king's fourth."

Prince Andrian gaped. "You know what the *moves* are called?" He put his face in his hands. "I am doomed, for I am really quite terrible at this game." He looked through his fingers at the girl. "Be kind to me."

She cackled and said, "Your move next."

He moved the pawn opposite of hers and blocked her. "Forgive me for being inexperienced, though I would have expected an easier game from a girl of your age."

She moved another pawn and grinned.

He moved opposite of her and then she made the queen's knight leap over her pawns and he gasped. He placed a pawn two steps from his queen's rook. Move after move, she avoided his aggressive pieces, and she took both a knight and a bishop.

"Now, I have captured *your* bishop!" he said but she proceeded to place him in check. "Never mind *that* move," he sighed, until he smiled and took her knight with his queen.

In several successive moves, she had captured more pawns, and he had put her in check with his rook. She took his rook, and he snickered.

"Why, *adieu, Monsieur Rook.*" Prince Andrian took his queen and captured her rook. "Check."

She chuckled. "Not for *long*." She moved her bishop to block the queen.

Prince Andrian sighed. "You are quite good at this game." They moved the pieces for a while longer, and then she put his king in check with a pawn. "A bit too good."

The girl frowned when he captured her queen with his own queen. "Check."

She blocked the offending piece.

"I will be surprised if I win," he laughed.

She made the mistake of moving her pawn and he found that a bishop only protected her king. He then took it and chuckled. "Checkmate."

"I don't believe it." She eyed the board. "You *beat* me!"

"Aye, but the only pieces I had left were three pawns, a rook, and a bishop." He smiled. "You are by far a more skilled player than I."

She put out her hand in congratulations. "Who'd I play against?"

He shook her hand. "Prince Andrian Gilbert."

The other girls in the room recoiled, and he looked around with a grimace. One girl inadvertently let out a squeal, and another placed her hands over her mouth.

Kieran grabbed the prince and whispered, *"Bunch of babies."*

He shrugged. "It does not matter much. I only hope they do not give you difficulties during your stay here."

The five-year-old girl stood up as the prince did. "Thanks for playin' against me."

Prince Andrian nodded his head once. "No, thank *you.*"

Sister Claire insisted they continue their walk, for morning had drawn to a close. In accordance to the prince's wishes, they visited the necessarium. With a great scream from several dozen girls, several nuns escorted them from the building to allow the prince to be alone for a while.

Kieran whispered to Shannon, "What's the necessarium for?"

Shannon giggled. "Y'know, when you hear the call of nature . . . you go inside and answer."

"Oh." Kieran chuckled and snuck to the side of the building.

Prince Andrian heard giggling through the wall. He rolled his eyes. He would feel relief when he returned home, away from the throng of sometimes screaming and other times tittering girls. He exited the building and announced that he must return to Eddington.

Sister Claire allowed the prince to say his goodbyes privately, and Kieran looked excited. "I think I'll have fun." Her face fell. "I'll miss you, though."

Andrian embraced the child. "I shall miss you as well. You write to me, agreed?"

She nodded, and she held out her wrist to him. "You almost forgot your bracelet."

He smiled. "It is a gift. I hope it reminds you to write when you are lonely."

She looked at the gold around her wrist, and then kissed Andrian on the cheek. "That's to remind you that you're not alone."

He blushed again and embraced her once more.

Kieran watched her friend and his cavalcade riding away, and she sighed. "He will forget about me." Prince Andrian turned his stallion around, saluted her, and then blew a kiss. Kieran smiled and waved, and then followed the nuns inside the convent to meet the other girls and the rest of the sisters.

Chapter Eight

In the village of Bracknell, Andrian had tasted mercy and love for the first time from strangers. People he had caused to suffer had shown him kindness when he stood before the precipice of death. He stood at that same dark edge again, and he needed love or he would tumble into the abyss with no one to hold him to the earth.

He stumbled across the Halloran home. He recognized the outward appearance from a while ago when he had stayed while healing from his nasty stab wounds. He leaned his ear on the door to listen to the utterances inside. Curious to see if Selma would allow him to visit for a short time, he tapped on the rotted plank.

An old woman answered and looked him up and down.

Finding it quite rude that she should stand gaping and silent, he cleared his throat.

"And who might yeh be? Beggar? Robber? Rich man comin' to take advantage of me daughter's charity?"

Prince Andrian raised his eyebrows. "I am Prince Andrian Gilbert. I was wondering if I might see Madame Halloran. I left her something a while back to keep for me."

The old woman's eyes narrowed. "I can see I'm right on *all* me thoughts. There's no nastier man in the business than the ruthless prince of England."

Prince Andrian grimaced. "Aye, there is no worse devil than myself. However, I have only come to retrieve my possession, and I shall depart if Madame Halloran wishes it so." He made a wicked face and the old woman cowered before him.

The old woman opened the door for him. "I'll be a moment. Me daughter's not home, only 'er son. I'd ask yeh to stay, but I'd as soon as die 'n' meet the devil 'imself. Wait, y'are the devil. My mistake."

Prince Andrian stood in the living room, or so it seemed by the looks of it. The Hallorans owned few possessions, and straw and grasses covered the ground, clearly placed to ease the feet from the soil or perhaps to make the home fit for human habitation. He picked up a homemade bowl and examined it. Whoever lived there or nearby had talent as a potter. The drafty shack reeked of a strange cooking. The odd smell wafted to his nose. The somewhat grassy and sheeplike odor begged him to investigate, but he ignored the urge.

He looked out the backdoor at the old woman, who shook her finger at a boy as she gripped his shoulder with her other hand. He could only imagine what she whispered to him: Be polite, hold your tongue, and do not make him angry—all the things he would warn a child if he stood in her position. It amused Prince Andrian how the child glanced up at her and nodded as she spoke. The prince smirked at her gesture, for he knew everyone took his threats seriously, even children. He frowned, and wondered if the boy thought him a monster as his grandmother did. He shuffled his foot on the floor and the straw piled before him. Just a monster, he imagined, and his own son would have heard the hatred for his father. Prince Andrian clenched his fists.

The woman and child had remained outside so long that Prince Andrian eyed the cooking on the fire again. Perhaps a peek would do no harm. Besides, the prince felt sorrow creeping once again to his eyes and he needed a distraction. Maybe he needed more than dinner. Perhaps he might stay longer.

The old woman caught him prodding the lid, and she chuckled. "Milord, I don't think yeh'd like what yeh find inside."

He looked up at her. "I was only interested in the smell. A bit *unusual,* your meal." She watched as he lifted the lid and made a strange face. "What the devil are you, a witch?" He gazed inside. "*Mon Dieu,* there is something *bizarre* floating about . . . is it the skin of a dragon or something of that nature?"

The old woman dipped a hook into the pot, and the prince backed away several steps. She pulled something green and filmy from inside. "*Try it.*"

He looked at her with a wretched grimace. "What is it?"

She threw it at him, and he dodged it with a loud cry of disgust.

"It's the *laundry,* Yer 'ighness."

The little boy guffawed at the prince's mortified look.

"Aye, that was indeed a laugh. I was merely . . . *pretending* to be frightened." Prince Andrian turned a shade redder than the boy's hair.

The child slapped his knee. "Pretending? That was a *real* scream! Yeh really were scared o' the 'ose in the pot! Ha-ha!"

The old woman watched the prince fiddle with his quillon.

The prince turned and looked out the door. "When do you expect madame to be home?"

The old woman shrugged. "Soon, I suppose. I ne'er know when she finishes 'er business."

Prince Andrian scratched his head. "What business is that?"

The little boy looked up at the prince. "Mama's a *healer*, Milord." He smiled. "Can I get yeh somethin' to eat?"

Prince Andrian glanced over at the pot and shuddered. "If it is a bite of sock or tunic, I would *rather* pass."

The boy guffawed again. "Oh, yer funny. I meant bread 'n' ale! Not sock 'n' mud water!" He roared again and left the room. He returned with a slice of bread and a jug of ale. "It's all we got now, but Mama *might* get us somethin' later."

"Why don't yeh 'ave a seat?" the old woman pointed to a dusty pillow. From the looks of it, something lived within, just waiting for some poor fool to sit down before it took a bite of his posterior.

His mouth straightened as he replied, "I would prefer to stand, if it is all right with you. If it is not, I would *still* prefer to stand." He took a bite of the bread and a swig of the ale.

The little boy giggled again. "Grandmother, 'e's afraid the cushion's gonna get 'im."

"No, I am ruddy well *not* afraid of the cushion. I simply prefer to be on my feet, as I had been riding a horse for so long . . . besides, the cushion looks a bit *questionable* from my standpoint," he said through a mouthful of bread.

The boy bounced over to the cushion. "Y'see, it's not gonna bite yeh. I swear it's safe." He patted the pillow. "It feels really good on yer backside."

Prince Andrian waved his jug of ale. "Then *you* may sit on it." He drank the rest of the liquid and set the empty container on the floor.

Just as the boy relaxed on the cushion, Selma Halloran slogged through the door.

"Mum, there's a visitor fer yeh," the boy cried out.

"There'll be no time to visit today, me darlin' William," she said without looking at who might ask for her companionship. She whirled around, nearly colliding with the prince. She looked up into the prince's desperate eyes, "Oh . . . well, 'ello." She smoothed back her hair. "Didn't fancy yeh'd be 'ere so quick now."

Prince Andrian leaned toward her. "Have you my belt?"

"My, yeh certainly get down to bus'ness, don't yeh." Selma backed away from him and began to clean the room. "I don't, I'm afraid."

He followed behind her as she cleaned. "And why is that?"

She turned around. "It was valuable 'n' I needed food, so I sold it." She slapped a grimy rag on the ground.

He raised his eyebrows. "You sold it for *food?*" He looked over at the little boy as skinny and awkward as a sheared lamb. "How much were you compensated?"

She shrugged. "Fifteen shillings."

The prince held up his hand and wiggled his fingers. "It was worth five times that, Selma." He added, "I assume you were desperate and would have taken anything for it."

She looked away from the prince. "I . . . I gave 'im more than the belt, yer 'ighness."

He looked at the boy, who hung his head and wiped his eyes. "What else did you . . . give him?"

She shook her head and tears flowed without control. "Ne'er mind that."

Prince Andrian saw a purple mark on Selma's neck as she cleaned a wall. She noticed him watching her, and she pulled her hair around the mark.

"What is that?" He pulled her hair away and touched her neck. She cringed and whisked away from him. *"Well?"* He followed her.

"The man beat me. Yeh 'appy now?"

Prince Andrian scowled and placed his arms around her from behind. He leaned against her head and whispered, "Tell me who did this to you, I swear I shall make him pay."

Selma wrenched herself from his arms. "Yeh'll do no such thing. It's somethin' I deal with ev'ry day."

Prince Andrian reached out and unlaced the back of her dress and pulled it off enough to see that the bruising extended down her back. "*Mon Dieu,* why did he do this?"

He stroked her broken skin and she pulled away again. "What's the matter with yeh?" She pulled her dress back over herself and turned around. "Leave me be!"

Selma busied herself around the house and wiped her dress on her face. Defeated, Prince Andrian sat on the pillow. Finally, he spoke. "I never *really* liked that belt anyhow."

Selma restrained a laugh and got back to her scrubbing of the two dishes she owned. "I can't stand bein' so poor. It must be 'eaven to live in a castle with servants 'n' such. Don't go a day without food er clean clothes. Must be right *wonderful.*"

Prince Andrian felt something heavy hit the bottom of his stomach with a slam. He cleared his throat. "I have lived much of my life as a soldier. I know want and I know starvation. However, I can assure you that life in my home today is no holiday either."

She glanced over her shoulder. "Oh . . . *there's* a good lie if I ever 'eard one."

Prince Andrian quietly fidgeted with his robe. "When I was here before, you had beds and furniture. You had food and wine. Why is this home so barren now?"

Selma tossed her hair to the side and turned around. "I had a few soldiers come pounding on my door a month ago. They told me I had to give them my possessions."

Andrian looked up. "On whose command did they confiscate your comfort?"

Selma threw the rag at him. "Yours." She kicked the dust under her feet. "I'm not the only one. This whole village was ransacked. Ev'ry neighbor I've got now suffers more than ever."

Andrian swallowed. "I swear it was not my command."

"Oh no? Then why'd they tell me they got orders from yeh to take ev'rythin' 'cause yeh need to fill the treasury er somethin'?"

Prince Andrian's nostrils flared. "I never told them to come to Bracknell. Not once. I said rich towns that could bear loss. I never wanted to hurt you after your kindness."

Selma smiled. "Thank you so much fer the thought, but yer wishes don't bring my things back. They don't fill me sons' bellies and they certainly don't warm us at night."

Andrian shook his head. "I am sorry. I truly wish I could have known what they did sooner."

"Well, Yer Majesty, now yeh know."

Andrian picked up the cloth and handed it to Selma as she approached him.

"Is there something I can do?"

Selma turned around and placed her hands on her face.

He furrowed his brows and sighed. "I was going to ask you if I might stay, but it seems I am unwelcome. I had better leave now." He stood up and brushed himself off.

Selma continued to weep in silence.

He clumped out the door. As he mounted his horse, he looked back at the home. He truly had no one else to turn for care, and she had rejected him like all the others. He had considered giving her gold for holding his belt for him. Now he could not extend generosity, as her admission deemed it unnecessary. He wanted to replace her belongings, but since she blamed him, the gesture would seem idiotic in the least. He would need to give back all the loss in town to please her.

He started the horse and trotted away from where he thought he might find sanctuary. He had been wrong yet again. Perhaps he was wrong about everything. Perhaps he should knock on Selma's door and beg for her to let him in . . . perhaps he should fall on his own sword and end his misery. Any way he looked at it, no alternative came to mind but to remain the figurehead of evil to every living creature. He could earn no redemption for his faults, for even a poor woman had scorned him. In self-disgust, he lowered his head. No power existed that might grant peace to Andrian after the crippling loss of Farida.

When Andrian arrived at the edge of Bracknell, he pitched his tent and crawled inside to mourn his loss once again. Solitude amplified his grief, but at least he could think whatever he wanted in loneliness. He lay on his cot and looked up at the tassels dangling from the ceiling. He folded his hands over his chest and heaved a ghastly sigh.

As he drifted to sleep in the heat of the afternoon, he dreamt of Farida. He sat by the river and she waded in it, bare down to her waist as far as he could tell. She wanted him to join her, but he felt terrified of the water. She reached out for his hand and tried to grab it, but when he fell in the water he began to drown.

He woke up in a cold sweat, and the world around him was dark. He sat up and rubbed his eyes. The campfires about him glowed as fiercely as his heart ached. He sat up and cracked his back.

He watched the shadows of his guard dancing along the side of his tent. Of course, he thought, they do not dance, they patrol, but it seemed much more interesting to imagine sprites parading back and forth before his royal abode. One shadow came closer and closer, and he wondered who might need him at that ungodly hour.

Selma Halloran poked her head into his tent.

"What the—" he gasped.

"I came to see yeh." She closed the curtain behind herself. "This must seem a bit awkward after this afternoon, but I wanted to tell yeh that I didn't mean to have yeh leave—well I did, but not fer the reason yeh might be thinkin'."

She sat beside him and smiled.

"Ehhh, why are you here then? I must admit I am more than *slightly* confused."

She smiled slyly. "I didn't want James to get all bothered by yer presence. I wanted to be *alone* with yeh."

Prince Andrian raised his eyebrows. "Why on earth would you?"

She silenced him with a breathless kiss, and he froze for a moment. He then smiled and pulled her into bed with him.

Outside the tent, unbeknownst to the prince and his lover, William heard his mother and the prince, and he felt angry and ashamed. He knew his mother had to do those things sometimes, but he wished she would have money and not find it necessary anymore. He skulked off and went on the short trip back to his home, where his father waited for him with his older brother, John.

* * *

Night after night for a week, Selma visited Prince Andrian in his tent, and in the morning Selma left. Every time she went to bed with him he felt some relief, but still he felt empty. She caressed him and held him and tried to comfort him when he talked about his grief, but her tender gestures could not compare to Farida's embraces.

He found the amorous encounters one-sided for the most part, and he once again felt sad isolation creep between him and the woman who lay beside him.

She noticed his distance, and when she asked him why he slept further way, he said nothing.

"Andrian, I've risked ev'rythin' to be with yeh. Why don't yeh at least tell me why yeh can't open up the last door to yer 'eart?" She stroked his chest.

He rolled over on his side and grumbled.

"It 'urts, I c'n see that. But yer gonna go yer whole life alone unless yeh open yer 'eart to *someone*." She leaned over him and looked down at his sad face. "At least tell me why."

He flipped on his back. "You would not understand . . . I just . . . I cannot love any longer. I want to . . . I try to . . . but . . . all the same, there is no room in my heart for any woman but Farida."

"I do understand. I'm sorry I cause yeh conflict. I'll leave yeh from now on."

She stood up, and Prince Andrian grabbed her wrist. "Wait. Come back and lie here with me once more, *s'il vous plaît*."

Selma sat beside him and then lay down and allowed him to hold her.

"If there were anyone I might love beside Farida, I would hope it would be you. I am only sorry my heart has not had enough time." He leaned his face against the back of her head. "Forgive me for hurting you."

Selma turned around and kissed his mouth. "Go back to yer castle with yer fancy belongings and yer lovers waiting fer yeh. Go back to yer riches 'n' servants 'n' family." She kissed him again. "Yeh don't belong with me, 'n' we *both* know it."

She left his arms, dressed, and kissed him goodbye. Her weeping shadow faded in the firelight until she disappeared. He lay in silent thought for the rest of the night. In the morning, he came to the conclusion that he had thrown nothing away since he had not loved her, and therefore he had traveled back to where he had started: deserted and distressed.

* * *

Prince Andrian charged back to Eddington, the guilt over his love affair electrifying his insides through his skin. When his vassals greeted him, he shoved them aside. His thunderstorm built up anger and velocity as he whirled to his room and slammed the door. His thunder echoed throughout the castle as booms and crashes. His lightning struck his bedding once, twice, three times; he upended his mattress and threw his possessions around the room.

Those near enough to the prince's chambers to hear his frustration ran down the stairs as quickly as their legs could take them without falling on their faces. A warning sounded throughout the castle and the king heard that a gale had begun yet again in the prince's room.

King Arundel, accompanied by several knights, did not hesitate to answer the call of panic.

The king knocked on the prince's door, and suddenly the whirlwind ceased.

Prince Andrian opened the door a crack and the eye of the storm glinted out at his father. "What is it you want, my liege?"

The king peered into his son's room, and from what he could see Noah's Ark had decided where to dock after the cessation of the squall. Animal skins lay strewn about in great ragged heaps, the prince's weapons stacked haphazardly before had landed helter-skelter and even jammed themselves into the walls during the tempest; at least a dozen books had blown at random during the gusts of wind. Worst of all, the prince was half-clothed and bleeding because of Hurricane Andrian.

The king forgot his son's question as he saw Andrian's state of being. He looked back at his son and whispered, "What have you done to my castle?"

Andrian the Ruthless pursed his lips in thought. "I have redecorated. It goes with my mood. I thought neat and tidy clashed a bit with furious and depraved, *d'accord?*"

King Arundel opened his mouth to speak, but instead said, "*Harrumph.*"

"I approve as well, Father. Now I agree the clothes are not much in the way of fashionable, but I assure you I am working on that." He tore more of his pants and threw the scrap behind him.

The king pointed in silence, and the prince opened the door.

King Arundel entered and Prince Andrian smiled and clapped his hands together as his father grew more appalled with every second he stayed inside the room. "I made a point of discarding anything that lacks *utmost* value to me—books, clothing made of fine materials, and of course my bedding. I assume you see the logic in the things I have kept. Nothing at all exists in this room intact any longer."

The king began to shake; his hands clenched at his sides.

Prince Andrian serenely glanced about his chambers and tapped his finger on his chin. He threw his hands in the air and cried, "I have forgotten!"

The king glanced over at his son with incredulity.

Prince Andrian strode over to his chair and pulled out his knife. As he started to slash the upholstery, the king shrieked, "THAT IS QUITE ENOUGH!"

The prince smiled to himself and stood up, sheathing his knife.

The king began to weep. "All of your valuable things . . . destroyed . . . discarded . . . ruined. Why?"

Prince Andrian stepped into his father's face. "Because you should think of *me* as one of your most valuable things, and you do this," he waved his hand in glory about the room, "to me." He glared at him. "I mean nothing more to you than this *chair.*" He kicked it violently. "*Ou le livre.*" He shook a poetry book in front of his father's eyes and hurled it against the wall. He picked up a silvery tunic and royal blue hose. "I mean more to you dressed in these," he tossed the clothes to the side, "than wearing the rags I have on now." He tore the rest of his tunic from his chest and released it to the ground. "I am worthless to you, and *you* above anyone else should have love for me."

King Arundel frowned as his son's eyes glistened.

"I am your son, and you treat me as if I am a *mongrel.*" He shouted, "Do you want to know what I think about your rules? About your stupid hatred for me? About your bastard son who you compare me to and make me to be such a pitiful excuse of a man beside?"

The king's mouth fixed in a snarl. "What do you think of it then? Come on, I have not all day to wait for your point. I have better things to do than watch my heir rave mindlessly."

Prince Andrian shook his finger at his father. "That is very good, you want me to lose track of my thoughts. You want me to be humiliated over my behavior."

He lowered his eyes for a second after his son's eyes grew blacker than a starless night. A chill coursed through his body that he had never felt in his life.

"You were *wrong* about me, Father. I am worth something in this world. I am more powerful than my brother because I do not fear my own death, and I do not fear your wrath." He smiled curtly. "*Je suis un mort homme*, Father, and you *made* me that way."

King Arundel shook his head. "You are not a dead man, but you are this close," he held up his fingers as if to pinch the air.

"Do not mock me, Father; I shall bow to your cruelty no longer."

King Arundel placed his hand on his son's shoulder. "You will not bow to cruelty?" He put a vice grip on his son's neck, and he collapsed to the ground, squinting in pain. "Then you will kneel to justice." He looked into the prince's watering eyes. "I see you have already removed your tunic. It shall be easy for you to receive your lashes now." King Arundel hollered, "Guards!"

They stormed into the room.

"Bring him to the lower bailey. I want to teach my son a lesson about destruction of property." He slapped Prince Andrian's face. "And about giving not only his king the respect he deserves, but his father as well."

Prince Andrian howled as four guards restrained him as they dragged him from his room. Servants, curious about the prince's latest tantrum, stood around to watch him pulled down the hallway.

"What are you *looking* at?" he screeched at the servants.

The servants did not respond to his question. The half-dressed prince wailed angry words and twisted in the guards' grip. If any other man had found the king's wrath, the servants would have laughed and jeered. Because Andrian the Ruthless shrieked and hollered, the servants gawked, and many maidservants covered their eyes at his nakedness. His performance could not help but cause not only jaws to drop, but also platters and other household utensils.

All the way through the castle, through the hall, and out to the lower bailey, Andrian the Ruthless hollered, cursed, and thrashed about. He had a demon within him, the whole of the castle muttered, and many wondered if he would have it expelled. The foam spewing from the prince's mouth confirmed it to many onlookers, and they followed the spectacle outdoors, some muttering prayers and holding crosses in plain view of the young man.

The guards threw him to the ground and King Arundel arrived just as the raging fiend had gotten to his feet. The prince dusted himself off and flipped his hair back. He straightened his appearance to give himself some shred of stateliness after what had just occurred. Andrian realized the throng of evil-wishers longed to watch his degradation. As he looked down upon his clothing, he pulled the rest of the rags before himself. The entire crowd laughed silently at his shame.

King Arundel produced a leathery club and stood before his son. "I do this because you need it, Andrian, and *not* out of spite." He made a spinning motion with his finger, and the prince turned his back to his father.

Prince Andrian felt the blow of the club again and again against his bare-skinned back. He felt the bruising of the leather repeatedly, and after a while it became harder to breathe. He felt his knees weakening, and he consciously told his legs not to buckle.

Dozens of people stood around to watch the prince's beating. He felt their cold glares on him, but because his eyes streamed from squinting in pain, he could not see them.

Relentlessly, the king beat his son. Persistently, the prince stood. Although it felt as if his father had crushed every bone in his back, Prince Andrian gritted his teeth and repressed the groans he felt coming to his throat each time his father laid the club across him.

After an interminable amount of time, Prince Andrian could stand no more, and his right leg collapsed under him, and then his left leg. Still, his father beat him. He placed his hands on the ground and breathed sharply. Still his father beat him. He cared no longer whether anyone laughed at his nakedness; he only wished the pain to cease. Then without warning the club found its way to the back of his head and to his face. He felt blood drip from his split lip. His shaking hand he placed to his mouth and wiped away the blood and slaver.

"Have you learned your lesson, Andrian?" The king leaned over toward his rasping son.

"Aye." Prince Andrian spit out a globule of blood.

The king placed his hand out, and the prince waved it away. He sat up with one of his legs at a right angle and placed his hands on his face. He knew that everyone stared at him; he had found his place at the feet of the king, in front of scores of people.

He feared his father's face as he sat crushed, and hoped he might leave him alone. He felt his lip, and it bore an ugly gash. Selma's words came to mind. He was too pretty to be the prince. He could not possibly have beauty now. His father had taken yet something else away from him.

King Arundel crouched by his son. "Are you not going to rise to your feet?"

Without looking at him, the prince shook his head.

"And why, might I ask, are you sitting like a coward?" The king placed his hand on his son's back, bruised and bloodied. The king looked at the crowd. "Your ruthless prince is but a dog to be beaten. Never forget what you have seen here!" The prince cringed and the king dropped the club to the ground. "On your feet, Andrian."

The prince inhaled sharply and King Arundel watched as a few tears escaped from the corners of his eyes. The king removed his cloak and handed it to the young man, who shook his head.

King Arundel tossed the cloak over his son.

Prince Andrian pulled the garment around his shoulders and grumbled.

King Arundel stood up. "That is more like it." When Andrian remained on the dirt still, the king bent over again. "Allow me to help you to your feet."

The prince looked up at the crowd; their heads turned slightly to each other, passing along derisive comments. No pity manifested itself on anyone's face; disgust and horror ruled the populace. "They all hate me," he said under his breath. *"Every single one of them."*

"What was that?" King Arundel leaned over further.

Prince Andrian felt something hard in his mouth, and he pulled it out. He examined it and grimaced. He showed his father. "At least I cannot have a toothache in *this* one."

King Arundel placed his hand on the prince's face and told him to open his mouth, but the prince shook his head. The king grumbled something about still having a sharp tongue, and he waved his hand as if swatting a fly as he stood and walked away.

Prince Andrian staggered to his feet, and his knights rushed to help him. Prince Andrian shoved them to the side with his feeble efforts. "Leave me be." He wobbled back toward the castle, and the same servants who stared at him being dragged outside like a writhing serpent covered their mouths as he passed again.

The prince limped by Lorcan, the steward of the household, and he watched his lord lean on the wall as he climbed the stairs. The prince's back, already scarred from battle, had earned fresh bruises from the incident that afternoon. Prince Andrian's face seemed desolate to Lorcan as he turned the corner. Blood trailed along the wall as he scratched into the limestone. For a moment, the steward felt pity for his young master.

Lorcan began to follow him up the stairs. "Milord? Do you need some assistance?"

Prince Andrian turned toward Lorcan, and a string of bloody slaver slurped from his lip. "Do I look as if I need help?"

Lorcan cringed. "A little bit, maybe." He reached out to the prince and pulled the robe around his torso to hide his nakedness. "I think you need a holiday. Get away from your pain for a while. Relax by the sea. Fresh air does wonders for a man."

The prince furrowed his brow as Lorcan tore his own tunic and dabbed at his bloodied lip. Prince Andrian shooed him away. "Why do you do this for me?"

"I do this for me. I hate the sight of blood. It makes my stomach turn."

The prince squinted at Lorcan, and then turned around to resume his climb to solitude. Prince Andrian entered his room and picked up a bent mirror of polished silver and gemstones. He sat on the floor and inspected his lip; it would need stitches. With a hiccough resembling a sob, he hurled the mirror, which hit the wall and scattered the precious stones across the room. He pulled his hair, curled into a ball, and moaned.

As he rocked back and forth on the floor in his room, the door opened and both Lorcan and a surgeon entered. "My liege, you've got to have your lip sewn. I don't want you to have a nastier scar than you're already doomed to have."

Prince Andrian rocked harder.

"What's the matter with you?" The surgeon looked at Andrian and then at Lorcan, who shrugged.

Prince Andrian shook his head. "I have been *un fou pour les annees*, my good man, *crazy for years.*"

The surgeon approached him and set his tools beside him. "Relax, my lord prince. Let me have a look-see." The prince sat still as the surgeon fingered his lip. "That's pretty bad."

Prince Andrian watched the man readying his sewing kit, and then he began to stitch the open wound. The surgeon gave him advice on how to watch for swelling and to put an ointment on it. Prince Andrian reeled and the words coming from the man's mouth no longer existed to him. He only heard the slipping of the thread in the needle, the rustling of the surgeon's sleeves, and other sounds that normally seem inaudible. Loud noises muted, and the prince felt hypnotized by a strange glow in the corner of the room.

"Milord?" Lorcan snapped his fingers before the prince's glazed-over eyes.

Prince Andrian fell backward on the stone floor, and Lorcan called for help. The yelling and men crowding around him did not exist. The amber glow became the focus of his attention. He turned his head to watch the light bouncing off the walls.

Suddenly he felt cold and wet and the commotion around him came into sharp focus. He cried out as he sat up.

The king held a bucket of water above him.

Prince Andrian looked at his father and said, "She came to me . . ."

"Who, Andrian? Who?" King Arundel shook his son.

"Farida . . . she still loves me." He smiled, and his eyes rolled back into his head and he hit the floor with a *crack*.

* * *

Prince Andrian awoke, though his eyes felt crossed. He tried to lift his head but a sharp stab kept him down. After his eyes focused, he recognized his bedroom, but it had the blessing of cleanliness and he rested in a new bed. Andrian realized someone had cleansed his wounds and dressed him.

"Andrian, are you well now?" a voice whispered.

The prince turned his head to see his mother sitting beside him. She looked frail and tired.

"Mother? What happened?" he croaked.

She stroked his face. "You passed out." She fondled his hair. "You were out of your mind with exhaustion, I think."

Prince Andrian frowned.

Queen Mireille kissed her son's cheek. "Your father went too far. I told him so myself."

Prince Andrian felt his swollen lip. "Father hates me. Everyone does. Perhaps I shall hang myself."

Queen Mireille shook her head. "Do not say such things. I love only you, my son. You are a good boy." She kissed him on the forehead. "Sleep now." She tucked him in bed and turned to leave.

"Wait, Mother."

The queen turned around.

"Am I beyond forgiveness?"

The queen frowned. "Whatever do you mean?"

He sighed. "I mean nothing, of course." He slouched down in the bed and tightened his lips. When the queen patted his hand, he looked up at her. "Can Father ever forgive me for the past?"

She crinkled her eyes. "I am sure you have forgiveness, but you must ask for it, my son."

He bit his lip. "Why does Father like Julian so much?" He swallowed hard. "Why can I do nothing to please him, yet Julian pleases him no matter what he does?"

The queen patted his hand again. "Andrian, nothing you have done causes your father to favor Julian." She sighed. "Though you have made mistakes to be ashamed of, you are a good man. Julian is a good man as well."

Andrian looked up. "Then why does he hate me so if I have done nothing to cause him such disfavor?"

The queen lowered her eyes. "Your father loved Julian's mother more than anything. That is why he favors Julian." She sighed. "He feels *cheated*."

Andrian scowled. "Because I am not Julian's full brother, and that is the only reason?"

Queen Mireille shrugged. "More or less." She kissed his forehead once again. "You shall still be king, and Julian your vassal. Do not worry so, and try to get some rest." The queen left her son alone with jealousy engulfing all of his senses.

Prince Andrian snarled and gripped his sheets. His father had humiliated him before everyone, and when he healed he would punish the kingdom as never before. He would strip the heart and soul from every person who had dared to scorn him. Until he had made every woman weep at his lust, every man cower before his sword, and every child run from his shadow, he would not cease his madness. This time it was war. He promised himself and he promised his mother.

Chapter Nine

True to his word, Andrian the Ruthless brought Briton to its knees. Against his father's command, he took his place once again as general of the Great Army of Briton. Sixty days of sieges brought the attention of not only King Arundel, but also King Haakon IV of Norway, Louis IX of France, Ferdinand III of León, and Alexander II of Scotland. Letters inundated King Arundel about his dangerous son. King Louis wrote an extended letter to his cousin in hopes that King Arundel would see how greatly the prince had affected his own treaties. The ruthless prince chipped away at the years the great countries of Europe had maintained relative amity.

With his head hung, King Arundel sent an envoy to hunt down his heir and to try to make peace with him or else bring him to face punishment.

* * *

No one had recognized how irate Andrian the Ruthless felt that morning. Hungry and frustrated at the lack of provisions, the prince growled as he sat in his tent. Rocking back and forth with unsettled anger, he thought of all servants at fault for his food shortage, the cook should take the blame. Earlier, the rapacious prince had demanded the cook, whom he had kept in service for three years, to find chickens for consumption. He had failed. All of the livestock had disappeared as the soldiers razed the city, but the prince needed an excuse to avoid responsibility for his own failure to secure supplies for his men. The

Mephistophelean prince at last had come to a decision about this pressing matter.

Throwing the cloth door to his royal tent aside, the prince marched out in a flourish to meet with the offending cook. Andrian the Ruthless demanded the guards bring the criminal before him. The guards hauled the unfortunate transgressor toward the prince, grimacing as he leaned upon his freshly sharpened sword.

Seeing the weapon, the frightened cook dropped to his knees. "Your Highness, there's not a *thing* I'm able to do 'bout the food. *Nothing* stands here fit for any use. Please let me *continue* to serve you. I'm sorry that this time I've failed you. Please spare my life with your mercy. I've a wife and four children. They need me. *Please*." His hands shook as he clasped them together as if in prayer. The cook's eyes teared up and his nose dribbled.

Andrian the Ruthless regarded the man with disgust. Cowering before him, the grown man seemed as though he might wet his breeches. The prince's mouth twisted as the man became himself before the king. "Andrian the Cowardly Prince of England," the crowds jeered. Faces glared, snarled, and gnashed their teeth.

"Milord?" a knight said.

Prince Andrian shook the vision from his head and glared down at the man.

The blubbering poltroon seemed very sorry. With an abrupt swipe of the prince's blade, the cook fell dead.

In response to the knights' gaping mouths, Andrian the Ruthless hissed, "I have changed my mind. I no longer feel hungry for *poulet*." He kicked the headless body of the cook and strutted off toward a creek nearby with his sword swinging as a walking stick.

Hunkering down by a fragmented boulder, Prince Andrian sighed. The tyrant prince had become bored of gallivanting off to sack cities and plunder goods. Truthfully, he loved to fight and he loved to have riches, and most especially he loved that women wanted him when he wielded power. Now, something nagging him at the back of his mind made his dominating life feel overwhelmingly trivial. The thrill of his conquests interested him little. He had no friends or family anymore. Either the friends had proved traitorous and he had executed them, or they were his disposable underlings. His family all wished for his demise. Prince Andrian heaved a massive rock into the creek, watched it splash, and frowned. It seemed so long ago that he had lost the only reason he existed. Four years had passed since he knew the joy of love. Sometimes at night he still would look at the glowing moon and his heart would ache.

Loitering by the campsite and out of the megalomaniac's view, a small crowd of knights began to whisper against him with the lead of a knight in green and a knight in yellow. They had sent a young boy to him while they conspired with mistrust. The prince would execute each of them personally if he knew of their plots.

Prince Andrian heard the boy advance toward him and smiled. The boy stood a distance from Andrian the Ruthless, whose back was turned from the camp. The prince raised his hand and beckoned him with a soft voice, *"You may approach me, Son, if you wish. I shall not harm you."*

The boy hesitated, for with all the raucous of the soldiers the prince had heard him. Moreover, the prince knew without a glance over that he addressed a boy and not a man. The tyrant prince frightened him; only evil men had all-seeing eyes in the backs of their heads. Perhaps the prince could speak to the demons.

Prince Andrian noticed that the boy had tried not to move a muscle. "Are you or are you *not* here to distract me from the whining rabble which I lead? Come now; do not be *shy*. Sit with me awhile." The prince pointed to the ground beside him. That time, the boy obeyed.

The boy had not seen more than twelve winters by the look of him. Lean and lanky, and had the gawkiness of a day old calf. His teeth protruded from his upper jaw, a shock of red hair swirled up from his scalp, and infinite freckles spotted his pale skin. He fiddled a bit while sitting by Andrian the Ruthless.

Gazing out at the water, Prince Andrian cleared his throat. "I know your father, boy . . . *good man*. He is damn proud of you for looking after the family by becoming a soldier." The prince turned toward the boy, who sat consumed by his shadow. "Tell me, Son, what name shall I call you by? I fear my *memory* has been giving me difficulties as of late." He glanced over at a jug of wine he had drained earlier.

"I'm William, Milord. William Halloran." The boy sat in tense silence as he watched the prince throwing stones. "My prince?"

"Aye, young William?"

The boy looked up at Prince Andrian with seriousness, and the fear had begun to leave him at the prince's tranquility. "Are you . . . afraid out here? I mean . . . aren't you afraid to die?"

The prince smiled at him with wavering warmth. "What do *you* think, lad?"

William shrugged. "They say you've the courage of a lion and the strength of a bear. You don't fear death for you can't be touched by it. You're like a *god*."

The prince laughed heartily. "Who has been feeding you that *merde?*" Prince Andrian cuffed the boy in the chest.

The boy rubbed his chest with a groan. *"But I know you're afraid of death."*

Prince Andrian patted the boy on the head. "You *are* an astute young man!" His face darkened for a second. "Fear is not the enemy." The prince rolled a smooth stone in his strong hand. "I have found that fear makes you fight for what you believe in. It gives you strength in the heat of battle, and it gives you a reason to go on. Without fear, we all would die needlessly. No man would care to fight for his country or his family. Fear is a good thing when utilized *judiciously.*"

The boy nodded. "Were you afraid of the laundry, I mean when you came to see Mama? Or did you just pretend like you said?"

Prince Andrian chuckled. "I was shocked. It is unusual for a peasant to throw hot clothing at their liege lord."

William shrugged and nodded. "Sometimes I fear my father, but I know he loves me. I just think he's hard on me. Is your father hard on you?"

Prince Andrian frowned and scratched his beard. "All fathers are hard on their sons. It is the sole job of the father to mold his boy into a man."

The boy tapped the ground with his fingers. "May I ask you something about being a man?"

Prince Andrian smirked. *"Ask what you wish."*

Sensing the prince's willingness to listen to the troubles of a lowly soldier's son, William let his thoughts loose. "How come men get whatever they want? I'd like that very much. I never get what I want. No one cares about me. My father sends me to bed without my meals if I tell my sister off for doing wrong. He thinks I'm a *bairn.* He thinks I'll never amount to *anything.* He sent me to war under your command to turn me into a man, yet he still calls me a *boy!* My father also says that my mother loves you, but there's *nothing* he can say to you about what happened. He fears you'll take all we own if we speak against you, though we own *nothing*—which means you'd take our lives."

Prince Andrian put his finger to his lips to silence his rambling. The boy obeyed the prince immediately. "William, is that in *truth* what your father said?"

"Yes, Sire, I don't wish to have you *behead* him though." The boy glanced back toward the camp.

"You have my word; I will not harm *ton père.*" He patted the boy's back, and he positioned his upper body toward some young women drawing water from the river. He licked his lips and then turned back to William. "Pray tell me *what else* he has said."

William gave the prince a black rock, and he threw it high into the air to land in the water with a *plop-goosh.* He smiled at the prince and then he frowned. "Well, he says my sister isn't his, but she's *your* daughter. My sister knows nothing of his thoughts; she thinks you're just royalty and not any man of kin to her." The boy covered his mouth.

Prince Andrian furrowed his brows. "How old is your sister? What does she look like?"

"My sister's but four. She's got hair the color of a raven . . . *like your hair*, Milord. Only . . . I don't know what to think. *Are* you in love with my mother? *Would* you kill my father for her?" William bit his nails.

The prince sat thoughtfully for a time. "I love *no woman*, William . . . yet I love *all women. Tu comprends, garçon?*" The young man shrugged. Prince Andrian looked into the confessor's eyes. "*Do* you *think* that your sister is my child, William?"

"I only know what I saw, Sire."

Prince Andrian's eyes darkened.

The prince scrounged for another rock and threw it into the water. "I am *sorry* you saw your mother betray your father. Believe me, all fault for her wrong is *mine*." The prince picked up one of the sticks that littered the ground beside him and twirled it in his left hand. "*If* you believe that your sister is of my body then bring her to me. I wish to see her for myself."

William watched the stick slash back and forth through the air with the prince's slight flicks of his wrist. "Sire? *Begging* your pardon, but *how'll* I bring her to you? I don't wish for my family to catch me." The boy sulked. He did not want to cause trouble for his parents, but he did not wish to anger Andrian the Ruthless, who was more dangerous by great lengths than his father.

The prince loosed the stick in mid-twirl and it snapped in half as it hit a tree trunk. William gasped. Prince Andrian placed his hand on the crown of William's head. "*Think*, boy. If you tell them that I have sent for her, do you *doubt* they will let you bring her?"

William trembled and stuttered, "I . . . I don't think my parents *w-will* say no, Sire."

Prince Andrian released the boy. "They would not *dare* scoff at my demands." He picked up a sharp rock. "They *know* my power." He slammed the rock on a snail as it passed by. As its guts oozed from the shell, William swallowed hard.

Prince Andrian dug his nails in the dirt and pulled a root up from the tree he sat under. He did not wish for fatherhood at this time in his life. If he accepted this child as his own, he might lose much. He did not want any other claim to the throne, and most especially he did not want the bastard child of another man's wife to be his heir.

He gazed at another woman drawing water from the river. She glanced over at him and put her nose in the air. He scowled at her, though she did not catch his glare. Prince Andrian pulled out his quillon, glanced at William, and became intent on cutting the root he had unearthed with an angry sawing creak.

Prince Andrian thought about his past desire for Selma's comfort. His indiscretions upset him when they got out of hand so that all might know where he had found solace. The fact the woman had not told him of her condition by word of letter embarrassed him far beyond the act he had committed in the first place. She at least could have admitted to him that she had wanted the child. He might have let her keep it if she had sent him information. Now he had no choice in his mind but to abandon the child somewhere and make sure she remained lost.

He wondered if he should even consider her or if he should send a man to *kill her*. Prince Andrian felt hasty about fretting over a girl child, but he did not want the woman to control him by having her daughter use him. He might need to execute the whole family if they attempted to barter the life of his daughter for money, power, or prestige.

He imagined the child in his mind as only the result of a foolish mistake. Prince Andrian had finished cutting the root and he beat the ground with it. A worthless individual, the toddler he could not blame, but the fact that her mother, Selma, had lied disturbed him. It seemed most prudent to dispose of the infant. Aye, unfortunately he *must* kill her.

"My prince?" William asked. He saw the contemplative face he made and twisted grass in his fingers.

"Aye, William? *What* is it?" The prince looked over at the boy again and slammed the root on the ground.

"Sorry, Sire, but I was thinking what'll you *do* with my sister *when* you see her."

Prince Andrian scratched his beard in thought. "I will find out if she is truly my own." He wiped his hand on his chainmail as the dirt from the root had darkened his skin.

"*How'll* you know, sire? I mean, how can you *tell?*" Young William's voice quavered. He did not want anything to happen to his family, and most especially his baby sister. "My mother's been with loads of men . . . I mean, maybe she's not yours."

"*Trust me,* I will be *quite sure* when I see her. I only want to be sure, *c'est tout.*" Prince Andrian threw another heavy rock as if it weighed as little as a loaf of bread. "By the by, what *name* does your sister recognize as her own, William? If you do not mind my asking, does it befit her bloodline?"

"She's called *Sabrina,* my prince. She's *lovely.*" He smiled. "Except when she makes this *evil face* when she doesn't get her way." He stuck his tongue out and waved his hands by his ears.

Prince Andrian ignored the boy's comment. "*Si elle s'appelle est,* then she *must* be a princess." The prince gritted his teeth. She belonged to him, and her mother had no right to keep her to herself. Because her father was the crown prince of England, Selma had committed treason by keeping Sabrina's existence to herself. Sparing her life would make no difference; the prince must control the child. He would never allow outside influence on his power and future sovereignty.

"Prince Andrian? Will you keep her with you if she's *your* daughter? Will I see her *at all?*" He stopped. "I *love* my sister. She's *good.*" William looked up; the prince had gotten to his feet.

Prince Andrian ran his fingers through his black hair. "*Mon petit garçon,* do not fret for your sister. If she is *not* mine, then she will *stay* with you. If she is, she will be raised in my noble house. I would not let *a hair on her head* be harmed." The prince smiled at William with jagged teeth.

William sighed. "I heard something else when I eavesdropped."

Prince Andrian made a strange face and crouched by the boy.

William cringed. "When Sabrina was born, my father shouted at my mother and told her to throw the baby in the water to drown out the evil she represented."

Prince Andrian bit his lip. "Did your mother ever mention taking the child to see me in my home?"

William shook his head. He paused and looked up at the father of his sister with tightened lips as he struggled not to reveal his own sad emotions.

Prince Andrian spared the boy tears of embarrassment. "In two days this rebel force will be crushed, and then you shall bring me Sabrina. *Trust me,* I am in a hurry as much as you to leave this *awful* spit of land." The prince held out his hand for the boy to take hold of. William grasped it, and the prince raised him to his feet. "You must *gain* some weight, boy. You will not win many wars weighing but *eight* stone."

"Yes, Milord."

"Remember, I want to see your sister Sabrina. *Do not forget it.* I will find you if you *do not* bring her to me." Prince Andrian smacked the boy on the back.

"Yes, Sire," William simpered.

"Now run along and *finish your chores.*" Prince Andrian leered as the boy tottered off toward the camp.

Chapter Ten

As soon as the young red-haired boy disappeared from his sight, the prince lurked behind a tree and watched a beautiful maiden filling some water pitchers. He had spied her as he threw rocks into the river with William. Prince Andrian stood still, his heart pounding as he imagined her arms holding him. She seemed not to notice him as he approached her doing her chores. He wondered if she would love him or if stupidity had overrun his mind again. As he watched her bending over to draw the water into jars for drinking, he imagined that she would make a lovely companion for him this afternoon.

Not knowing how else to draw her attention to his presence, he cleared his throat and she glanced over at him. She straightened her back to greet him but did not recognize the man as the feared prince against whom her townsmen defended themselves. She gave him the once-over and beheld a coronet with four *crosses-pattée* and four *fleurs-de-lis* surmounted by an arch. She dropped the jar she held on the ground with a splattering crash.

"Oh, *pardonnez-moi*. Did I frighten you?" The prince walked over to her and held his hand out, but she did not take it. He grimaced at her rudeness. His urge to mate seemed not to bother most women, and if it did he compensated them for their loss of time. Most women wanted to care for their families and they took his money with gratitude. He felt he did them a service in one way or another as they satisfied his need for affection.

She saw the look in the prince's eyes and panicked. "Oh . . . oh no . . . I was just drawing water." She pointed to the river frantically.

"I . . . I apologize . . . I hope you aren't angry." She curtsied to him and then began to pick up the broken shards of clay that used to be the jar.

"Leave that," he suggested.

The woman stopped as suddenly as she started. She slowly rose to her feet. "You're Andrian the *Ruthless,* I presume."

"*Ruthless* . . . that depends on *who* you speak to." He flickered an inebriated grin. "I can also be quite *gentle* as well." The prince beckoned her with his gauntlet-clad hand. "I beg you not to stand so far from me. I shall *not* harm you."

She looked over her shoulder in hopes that someone would stop this monster from shaming her. As she approached him one step at a time, she continued to glance around.

"*Whom* do you search for?" He pulled off his glove and grasped her hand in his.

"I'm not *permitted* to speak my mind in the presence of royalty, Highness." She turned her face from him.

He placed his arm around her. "You *may* speak your mind, though I fear it will not help *your* position any." The prince pulled strands of her dark brown hair from her face. "*Tu es une belle ange.* Beautiful angel."

The woman placed her hands at her sides. "I'm searching for help. I don't *wish* to be your lover, Sire." She chose her words carefully.

"Are you certain, *jeune et belle nymphe?*" he purred as he kissed her cheek.

"I wouldn't *dare* say no to you, Milord. But if it *were* my choice, *then* I'd deny you. I wish for the first man that I know to love me and be my *husband.*"

His eyes darkened. "What are you called, my pure angel?" He leaned into her and kissed her fully.

"My name, what is it?" Breathing heavily in her terror, she gasped at his overwhelming touch.

The stallion corralled the mare toward a boulder. "Aye, your *name.*"

She could not run from him or hide. He turned her face toward him and kissed her again. She pushed him from her. "What'd you *need* my name for? I'm sure you don't *remember* the names of all *your* conquests. What pleasure'll the *knowledge* of my name be for you?" She resisted his advances, but his strength convinced her to let him do what he wished.

"Humor me with your name, my snow white dove," Prince Andrian insisted.

The woman focused on the knife in his left hand. "Genevieve's my name." She saw his eyes flash with an intense blackness and then become riverbed clay once again.

She closed her eyes hoping she would survive the onslaught of passion. To Genevieve's surprise, he tossed the knife to the side and unsheathed his sword. He saw that the maiden had kept an eye on his steel, so he flung the blade to the side as well. "I do not threaten my lovers with any kind of weapon." He opened his cloak and wrapped her arms around him. "There is nothing here that shall hurt you, for I *always* make love unarmed." She reclined on the grass as he knelt before her. She covered her eyes, though his aggression remained subdued.

"Genevieve . . . now this will not hurt much, I *promise* you." After unbuckling his belt, he caressed her. "If you are not tense, then this shall be enjoyable for you as well."

She obeyed him as he placed her arms around him once again. "I wish there might be *something* to say to stop you, Milord."

He faltered for a moment. Prince Andrian's second thoughts could not overpower the lust that drove him, and he continued to undress her. "You will not *regret* my love for you, sweet child." He kissed her neck and breathed into her ear.

"I know I will, because you'd not love me and marry me. Therefore I'll regret lying with you. I'll be shamed in my house and cast out as a whore." She began to weep as he lifted up her dress to take her.

"Do not weep at this, Genevieve. I *promise* I shall go slowly so I do not harm you." He was about to enter her when he heard men behind him. He turned his head. *"Do you mind?"*

"Sire, pardon the intrusion but it's urgent you return to camp. There's some sort of raucous going on. *Truly* it's urgent." The man watched his lord grind his teeth.

"As urgent as this?" He pointed to the maiden and emphasized his lust.

The soldiers looked at each other. *"More urgent."*

Andrian the Ruthless groaned. "If it is that necessary for you to have my presence, then I shall return with you." He tucked himself back in his breeches. He sat up and helped Genevieve cover her bare breasts. She hid her face, for the soldiers had seen her in such a state, and she blushed at the man who had violated her. The prince retrieved his discarded weapons and stood.

Genevieve sighed with immense relief. The prince helped the maiden to her feet. She felt her body wavering where she stood, and he held on to her for a moment so she would not fall. He smiled at her and then turned to the soldiers and scowled.

When his expression turned soft yet again, he whispered, "Shall I take you home, my sweet Genevieve?"

"*Home,* Sire?" She looked at him blankly.

"Why, you live where I target next, merely a *few hundred meters* from my encampment. I might as easily walk you to where you reside as to the river. Or perhaps you shall come back with me, since I am so close to your home, and later we might *finish what we started.*"

She thought his eyes blackened again, but she had herself convinced that his eyes were an unfathomable brown. She knew that she could not escape the desire the prince felt for her. "I'll do your bidding, sire." She paused for a moment and then kissed his bejeweled hand.

Prince Andrian nodded. "Then you shall come back with me to my camp and stay in my tent with me tonight. As a gift for your graciousness, I shall spare your life. And if you accept me as your lover, *your town shall be spared as well.*" He kissed her mouth, and she pretended he had not murdered so many.

The soldiers nudged each other as they sniggered.

After he released her, she nodded in agreement to his proposition.

Prince Andrian grasped her hand in his once again, kissed it, and tugged her behind him as they rushed back to his encampment. Tethered horses surrounded the camp, and loose dogs of a strange lean sort. When the prince walked by them, they whinnied and howled. Genevieve did not know if the animals rejoiced to see him or if his presence appalled them.

As they reached the guards outside the camp, they witnessed the men in an uproar. Several soldiers ran about the fires in naught but their socks and swords, and still others consumed supplies many times their ration. One man looked at the angry face of the prince and called to their attention his arrival. No one listened to him. Andrian the Ruthless roared for them to keep order. Silence followed. Groans of lust from many of the soldiers punctuated the silence as she walked with her captor as a shield.

He led her to his royal tent, a luscious blue and silver drapery, and sat her on his cot. "I apologize for the unruliness of my military; uncontrollable, the lot of them. When I turn my back, they make a *mockery* of me." A banshee raced by the tent with his hands waving in the air, and the prince rolled his eyes. "As I had *but* finished saying." He pointed out the door.

Genevieve looked up at the prince and nodded with a forced smile.

Prince Andrian looked down as he twisted his tunic in his hands. "I shall return shortly. I do not believe it is best here in camp for you to succumb to my love; I would have rather shown you pleasure in the wild grasses by the river. I am sorry." He kissed her cheek and closed the cloth tent entrance behind him.

Genevieve noticed the prince seemed controlled, unlike his mob of an army. As she contemplated what she would give him, she heard Andrian the Ruthless yelling at the top of his voice at a captain of some sort. She would have died of fright if she had to endure such anger.

Sitting among the furs and silk, wool, and feather pillows, she wondered if Andrian the Ruthless had lied to her about his deal to leave her town alone. If he stole her dignity, she felt grateful he allowed her to at least keep her head.

The woman glanced about the royal tent. The skin of a wild beast, striped the color of day and night, lay on his floor. A rug made of a strange-colored weave hung from a post beside the entrance. The blues and reds burned her eyes even when she closed her lids. A beautifully worked saddle, silver and gold inlaid in the tooling, sat in the corner. The prince's body armor in the midst of a polish and oil remained unfinished on a hook. It looked as if he conditioned it himself, for the cloth still hung from one shoulder plate. Awkward compassion consumed her when she discovered drained jugs of wine and ale beside the bed.

Prince Andrian returned to Genevieve after he had run the gamut of his camp and chastised any man with whom he could find any fault. She hid something behind her back when he entered the tent without warning.

He held his hands up. "Relax, I shall not harm you." When she looked away from him, he ran his fingers through his hair and sat upon the cot. "What have you behind your back?" he said as he supported his head in his hands.

"You miss nothing, do you?" She revealed her hands.

He grasped her fist. "A dagger? Did you think you would assassinate me?"

She sat beside him. "I don't know what to do."

He released her fist.

Andrian the Ruthless sat still with his hands in front of himself, palms up and tilted slightly. "Resisting would be a very big mistake, Genevieve."

"My sister . . . she . . . she waits for me to come home. If I don't bring more water this evening, my family will worry about me." She raised the dagger.

His mouth twisted to the side as he folded his hands together. "You will be home tonight, I promise. They need not worry about you."

She pointed the dagger at his throat and sighed. "Being here with you, I worry about me."

Prince Andrian wiped his face of sweat. "I am known for my malevolence, but there is more to me than my public image." He looked at her with glimmering copper eyes.

She pressed the point into his jugular. "I wish for freedom. I wish for you to leave my city be."

His mouth twitched. "I will not promise such a thing to an assassin."

Genevieve pushed the dagger lightly, drawing a trickle of blood.

Prince Andrian swallowed. "Go ahead and end my life."

Her frown deepened.

"Thrust with all your strength and your nightmare will end."

She lowered the dagger slowly. "I cannot kill a man."

Andrian the Ruthless grabbed her wrist and forced the dagger by his throat. "End the suffering of this land. Be their heroine."

She screamed and twisted her arm. "Release me, please!"

Andrian the Ruthless ripped the dagger from her hand and forced himself upon her.

Outside the royal tent, screams of fear and pain broke the rumblings of the men gambling, complaining, and drinking.

Genevieve tensed as she awoke. She shuddered as she sensed an icicle in her heart: Andrian the Ruthless stared at her from behind. She wanted to turn over and make sure that the hideous nightmare remained in her sleep. She felt her bruised neck and whimpered.

Genevieve moved her arm to reach behind her and see if the criminal in her dream became reality. Something grasped her hand, something cold and rough. It was his murderous hand, which had slaughtered many good men fighting for their freedom from his tyranny. That hand held her down and choked her until she could no longer see. That hand now caressed her bare back as though he was her lover and not her destroyer.

"Genevieve?" his strong voice wavered.

"Yes, Milord?" The woman flipped to look upon he who had stolen her decency.

The prince's eyes shadowed in exhaustion, and his youth no longer became him. He looked older than natural, and even his black and shiny hair had lost its luster.

Andrian felt unsure of himself now. Looking upon such beauty gave him an ugly feeling. "Do you think . . ." He reached out and stroked the woman's face. "Is there any way, any possibility that you could . . . forgive me?"

Genevieve inhaled sharply. The fine lines on his forehead drew together in wounded disquiet. Genevieve touched his face. His eyes would burn in her memory for the rest of her life, both in dreams and as she woke. They haunted her in their sadness and in their mania. She began to weep, and he took her hand in his and kissed it repeatedly.

Genevieve sat up. "Please let me go home." She wiped her eyes. "Have mercy, milord."

"Be still." He moved closer to her.

"You *frighten* me!" Genevieve sniffled.

Prince Andrian kissed her cheek gently.

Genevieve shook her head and tried not to scream.

Prince Andrian grabbed the woman and shook her. "Don't you want to save your city?"

She grasped his arms as he jolted her. "Please stop . . . Milord, you're *hurting* me!"

Prince Andrian released her. "I beg your forgiveness."

Genevieve wept harder and reached for her dagger. "Take all of me. Don't make me go back after what you have done!"

She made to stab herself in the breast, and as he grabbed the blade with his hand, blood splashed on her. He wrenched the dagger away and hurled it into his wooden chest, where it remained, wavering with force.

Genevieve hyperventilated and covered her eyes. "Am I to be ransomed? Who'd pay to have me returned unharmed? I don't think anyone has the money to *buy* mercy from you." She cowered with tears in her eyes.

Prince Andrian wrung his bloodied hands.

She held her breath; the prince would kill them all, she knew it.

Prince Andrian caressed her hair, leaving streaks of crimson. "Your town harbors a criminal I must bring to justice."

She removed her hands from her eyes. "Who might that be?"

"Gerard Lafontaine."

Genevieve gasped. "But that's my father."

Prince Andrian chuckled. "You have done well by him to let me have you."

Genevieve sobbed. "What has he done?"

"I want you to tell him to cease his transgressions against my father." Prince Andrian held his bloody hand before himself and turned it slowly as he watched the twin cuts bubble.

She stiffened. "You have my word."

He reached over the bedside, snatched up her clothes, and threw them at her. She caught them and stared. "You have my leave to go." He waved at her and then covered his face with his bleeding hand.

Genevieve could hardly believe that the madman had freed her. "I may go home."

"*Leave*, woman. I have use for you no longer." He looked up at her. "I will keep your town intact, for I will honor my word to you." He bent over and retrieved one of his cloaks. He slipped it over his head and sighed.

Genevieve walked over to the prince, grasped his hand, and kissed it eagerly, "Oh thank you. Thank you."

He snatched his hand away. "Get out of my sight before I change my mind!"

She curtsied to him, and weeping, ran from his tent.

Chapter Eleven

A week had passed since Prince Andrian had spared Gerard Lafontaine and his city of traitors. The army had not yet packed up camp, as the prince had not quite decided upon his next move. The prince knew he needed to get back to William Halloran about his daughter, Sabrina, but he also knew that King Arundel would be furious that Lafontaine had been pardoned.

The worst of everything at the moment, to Prince Andrian, was that the boy had not kept his word to bring the princess to him. Either William had warned his family of his intentions and they wished to make a mockery of him, or the boy had not told them for fear of retribution. No matter what the circumstances, Andrian the Ruthless decided that day he must take some guards with him to hunt down the Hallorans. It would be easy to dispose of the girl once he marched off to war. No one would be suspicious if she were killed by a crossbow during a heated battle.

William and his family lived in Bracknell, and the prince headed south to take his daughter by force. "I will make them pay for keeping her from me," he fumed.

Rallying behind the angry father, several knights agreed that peasants should never deny the mighty prince his right to see his royal child.

Prince Andrian stormed through the town and up to a hut made of rotten timbers and a grass-thatched roof. He rapped on the door, and a woman as old as sin answered. Seeing who called, she dropped to the ground. "Yer most *noble* majesty," she croaked. "Whom d'yeh wish to call upon today at me humble home?"

"Humble is *right*," he gagged. "Madame, I wish to see the master of this—you call *this* a home?"

The soldiers laughed.

The woman did not look at Andrian the Ruthless as he said this; her eyes blazed. "Some've us *aren't* as well to do as others, milord. Forgive our *wretchedness*." The old woman hated this man before her, yet she dared not insult him outright. She knew he could break her feeble body like a sapling in a hailstorm.

"As I was saying *before* I was interrupted, is the master of this . . ." He eyed the men covering their mouths. The prince slicked back his hair. "Is Master James Halloran at home?"

"No, Sire, he's out doing yer dirty work for yeh." The old lady looked up at the prince digging his fingernails in the door.

"I do my *own* dirty work, madame. I *daresay* he would fail me if I had the *foolishness* to command him to do anything of *importance* for me." He sniggered. "If the master is *not* here, then perhaps the lady is. I want something from her." The prince leaned on the doorjamb and it creaked under his weight.

The obstinate woman sneered at him. "Yeh've taken *enough* here, Sire."

"Is *that* so? By law you cannot deny me the right to appropriate what is mine." The prince pushed the crone to the side and entered the shanty. He turned toward the old woman, his cape swirling violently about her. "Where, old witch, are your possessions? I sent Selma gifts after I left years ago. She had clothes and dishes. I gave her furniture and I gave her blankets. I see nothing!"

The old woman bowed her head. "We sold everything to care for the infant."

Whether he did not hear or did not care what the woman had revealed about the child, the evil prince roared, *"Où est l'enfant? Où est William?"*

Cowering at the tone of his voice, she pointed to the backdoor. "The family's in the field, with the sheep. I could call 'em if yeh wish, Sire."

"Aye, and be *quick* about it. I have not all day to loiter in this *filth*." The prince curled his lip. The soldiers drew pictures in the dirt with their swords and giggled about them. Andrian the Ruthless glimpsed the drawings, and finding the subject matter quite tasteless, kicked one of his soldiers to force him to stand at attention once again.

Immediately they scuffed out their pictographs and stood like foul ducks in a row.

The woman shuffled toward the back of the hut and looked out. She waved her wrinkled arm at them. They lay prostrate in the grasses like a family of hares evading a gyrfalcon.

"What is taking them *so damned long*?" Andrian the Ruthless sped over to the woman and grabbed her crooked neck. "Call them *now*," he hissed in her ear.

The old woman's eyes became wide at the prince's sharp teeth near her face. "Selma, come quick!" she gasped to them.

Two young boys and a woman at least ten years the prince's senior rose from the field. A small child stood still behind them. The straw-haired mother turned and picked her up and ran toward the old woman. Panic beset their bodies and they stumbled toward the old woman. Andrian the Ruthless despised feeble trickery. In fact, they might have caused her a violent end if they had refused him the second time.

"I'm sorry, Yer 'ighness," the old woman whispered. He released her, and she rubbed her neck, tears forming in her eyes from both the shock of his grip and the fear of his wrath.

The woman carrying the child arrived first and her two sons followed; the straggler he recognized as William. The boy had not any time to think of an excuse for the awful man had come sooner than he had expected. "Your Highness, I couldn't tell you where, I couldn't bring . . ."

"Shut it," he growled at him. Andrian the Ruthless seized Selma and turned her around. She held a female child in her arms. "Tell me, is this *your* child?"

"Yes." Her ocean blue eyes watered.

"How *old* is she?" he barked at her.

"She's born four spring seasons ago, the year we had such a blessing of rain." She caressed the little girl's lean face.

The prince looked at the child with loathing eyes. "Who sired your baby?" She stood silent. He towered above her, a ghostly mountain lit with the fire of hell.

"The monster standing before me now." She braced for a rebuke, but the prince stared at the child. He gently turned her face to examine her profile. The child, untroubled by his touch, gazed at him. He half expected her to scream with fear.

"She's the spittin' image of yer sister, Milord," a soldier noticed.

"*Fermez la bouche,* twit!" The prince slapped him from behind himself. Immediately calming, he felt the baby's hair. Her mother had pale skin and fair hair, yet this baby had a ruddy complexion and dark hair. The owner of this shack had hair as red as a torch on an autumn night.

"Please, Sire. What 'tis it yeh want of us? Surely we're so poor now there's nothing to take?" Selma watched the prince stroke the face of their daughter. She hoped his knowledge might satisfy him and he would depart.

"May . . . may I hold her?" He stroked the toddler's hair, as course and black as his own locks. Selma reluctantly handed him the child, heavier than she seemed at a glance. Feeling her warmth in his arms, he let a soft smile slip through his stoical expression. He had intended to murder the toddler if he felt he needed to, but now he could not kill the most beautiful creature he had *ever* seen. The girl looked up at him, her tiny fingers in her mouth.

Looking at her child with a longing expression, Selma reached for her, though he blocked her.

"Does she *know* that I am her father?" Prince Andrian held her out in front of him and studied her. The girl stared at him wide-eyed and took her slobbery fingers from her mouth and pointed at him.

"She knows that yer an evil tyrant, and that's all she hears about who y'are. She, like us all, lives in fear of yer wrath." The woman wiped her eyes. "Please, we'll do *anything* yeh wish . . . we'd leave this country if yeh'd only let 'er stay with us. Yeh'll ne'er 'ave another thought of 'er again."

The prince sneered. "You *lied* to this child? She is too young to be corrupted by your *tongue*. And no, I do not wish for you to leave this country. Your husband is my father's vassal. He has sworn fealty to him, and he would pay too great a fine if he were to break his oath."

Prince Andrian caressed the girl, and she spoke. "Mama . . . Mama."

"Please let me care for 'er, Milord. Yeh don't wish such a burden upon yeh. Yer still a *young* man and don't need such problems. I'm 'er mother. If yeh'll please let me 'ave 'er back. I beg yeh . . . if there's any good left in yeh, let 'er be."

The prince ignored her tearful pleas. "What do you call her?" He rocked his daughter in his arms and cooed.

"I'd die before yeh know the name of this wee angel!" Selma moaned.

"I surely hope you do not mean that." Andrian the Ruthless sneered at the woman. The girl seemed unperturbed by her father's gentle rocking motions. He looked down at her. *"Bonjour, ma petite Sabrina."* The girl looked up at the prince in surprise, and he rubbed the bridge of her nose.

"'Ow did yeh . . . No matter, I'll ne'er relinquish 'er to yeh. I won't allow 'er to be twisted by yer evil fer a day, let alone a *lifetime*." Sabrina's mother reached for her yet again.

Sabrina's father turned away. "It is not your choice whether I keep her, for she is of my body as *much* as yours. You have kept her from me all this time, and I believe I will make up for losing her by taking her *home with me*."

"Don't be so pitiless. She's known only me all this time . . . 'Ow can yeh take 'er now?" When Sabrina's mother tried to take her daughter back, the prince's guards stopped her.

"Why do you not wish for me to love this child? She is my *only* offspring and *j'adore la belle princesse*." Prince Andrian kissed the girl on the forehead. Sabrina smiled at her father as he rocked her gently. The black curls upon her head, he caressed. "So beautiful, my child."

The mother raged, "There's *no* good in yeh! 'Ow can yeh believe she'd grow up well?" She grabbed at the prince, but he stepped away from her.

"I have money, Selma. I have power. Most of all, I love this child. I would not have her grow up in refuse as this place of your husband's. I will spare her the pain of poverty. I will spare her the misery of having no food for her belly. She will never be in danger with me." Prince Andrian rubbed Sabrina's back as he clutched her to his chest.

"She's *always* in danger with yeh! Yer a foul and sinister criminal! 'Ow I loathe the day I let yeh dirty my body with yer seed! I spit at yeh and damn yeh to 'ell!" Selma wept in anguish as the prince smiled at their daughter and made the girl smile in return.

"You have given me permission to take her, for you just said you loathe the love that created her. Therefore, you do not wish to retain her. She is *mine* then." Andrian the Ruthless laughed.

As the prince turned to walk out the door, a husky red-haired man entered the house. Filthy and sweaty, James Halloran had come home from his day of labor. "What're you doin' in me house?" Master Halloran had forgotten for an instant that he spoke to the most horrendous of men, and though the prince cradled the child in his arms, James felt bolder than usual.

"Taking home what is rightfully mine. I do hope you do not interfere." Andrian the Ruthless knew that Sabrina's guardian would not dare challenge him.

James stopped the prince with his hands opened. "Now wait a minute. You can't just barge in and steal me daughter!"

Andrian the Ruthless smirked. "She is not *your* daughter. By your wife's own admission, she is the product of my boredom. I fear that you cannot prove that she belongs to you, for you look *nothing* like her."

"Yeah, the princess is the spittin' image of—" the soldier could not finish his sentence, for the prince kicked backward and caught him in the shin with his boot. "Ow!"

Selma pleaded, "Can't yeh 'ave a 'eart? I comforted yeh in yer time o' need. I loved yeh, and I birthed yer child. Can't yeh find the decency to let the past stay buried?" The prince bared his sharp teeth as she continued, "I'm sorry yeh lost yer son, but it's no reason to take me daughter."

Prince Andrian's lip twitched. "How dare you mention my son . . . h-how dare you! You know n-nothing of my pain!"

"I know I 'eld yeh when yeh mourned yer love, and I felt yeh tremble with sorrow. Isn't that enough to grant me the chance to love yer child?"

Prince Andrian looked at the ceiling and clenched his jaw as he tried not to scream at Selma for opening his wound that had still not healed. He regained his composure and looked at her again. "I loved her more deeply than you could *possibly* imagine."

She frowned. Prince Andrian watched Selma pull a cloth from the bosom of her dress. "Yeh left this 'ere when yeh abandoned me. Yeh ne'er told me what it meant, but I saved it anyway."

She then opened the cloth and revealed a round white stone.

She handed it to Andrian, whose jaw twitched involuntarily. *"I would give you the moon,"* he whispered as he fondled it. His eyes quavered, but he clenched his jaw harder. His dark lids glittered as he rolled the stone over in his hand. He looked up at Selma and choked, *"Merci."* A single tear escaped his control and splattered on Sabrina, who looked up at him. She patted his face roughly, and he laughed as he wiped his eyes.

James Halloran looked dumbfounded as the prince nuzzled Sabrina in his arms. Unsure of how to retrieve his daughter, he fiddled with a knife by his side.

"Adieu." Prince Andrian nodded politely at the master of the lean-to and left with the girl safe in his arms.

Inside the hut, the man began to yell at his wife. Suddenly, Selma ran outside to stop the prince. "Wait! Milord!" She flung herself to the ground before his muddy boots. The prince paused and shifted the girl's weight. "My noble prince, if yeh'd but wait and listen."

"What *is* it, Selma? I have not any more time to lollygag with you." Through the prince's severe words, his voice betrayed his grief.

"My prince, please promise me yeh'll always care for 'er. Promise me she'll ne'er grow cold from the lack of fire in the stove or love in yer heart. I want yeh to promise me that yeh'll have 'er best interests in mind. Don't treat 'er as yeh do ev'ryone else. She's special; I know it. Promise me yeh'll always love 'er!" Selma sobbed at his feet. She wrapped her arms around his legs and leaned her head on his metal-covered shins as she wept.

The mournful woman made him uncomfortable, and he shook his legs to escape her embrace. She would not release him until he promised. "You have my *word*, Selma Fair."

Selma stood up and wiped more tears that formed in the corners of Andrian's eyes. "Find peace and embrace it."

Prince Andrian turned away from Selma. The father rocked his daughter in his arms as he strode toward his steed. He looked down as the child stared after her mother. She raised her small hand into the air to say farewell to the only family she had ever known. Her mother returned her wave weakly and then put her hand over her mouth and watched her only daughter leave her before she had a chance to raise her. The prince looked away, locking his jaw.

The prince cradled his daughter in his right arm as he mounted his stallion, and when he had secured his child, he turned the horse around. He saw the mother of his child weeping for her and he frowned. He would not give her back, even though her mother's heart breaks. As soon as he had laid his eyes on Sabrina, he knew that if he parted from her he would lose everything else to grief. The prince sat looking at Selma and nodded his head in thanks. Great tears rolled from her eyes and she nodded back.

The prince's horse cantered away from the hut where Selma had birthed Sabrina, and Prince Andrian did not look back. The mounted guards hovered around their lord; they wished to protect him and his child but they also wished to keep looking at the princess. They all pretended they had not witnessed Andrian the Ruthless admit his heartsickness over a woman, and no one mentioned his tears. They simply made cooing sounds, played peek-a-boo, and wiggled their fingers at her.

For many long hours they marched together, and the child began to fuss. "Mama? Mama?"

"Hush, Sabrina. Mama is not here anymore. I am here. I am your papa. I *am* Papa." Andrian let those words sink into his heart. This girl, born of sin, had become the closest thing to God he had ever known. Holding his daughter to his chest, he kissed her forehead. "Papa is here. No one is ever going to hurt you, *ma chère*. No one can take you from me. *Je t'adore.*"

Sabrina sobbed in Prince Andrian's embrace. Her little arms wrapped around his armored forearm, and she hid her head under his cloak. She missed her mama and brothers. She could not understand why she had to leave. Who was this man, and why did he want to take her away? "Mama! Want Mama!"

Prince Andrian noticed her quivering lip and halted his horse. "We must rest awhile. *Ma fille* is tired and cold." He trotted to a sheltering grove of trees, and his cavalcade followed him. They dismounted, and a soldier lit a fire for warmth. He held his daughter on his lap and rocked her. She shuddered violently with the cold though he protected her in his arms, so Andrian removed his heavy woolen cloak and swaddled her in it. She quickly stopped shivering and proceeded to whine again.

"Tummy hurts." Sabrina pointed to her belly.

"Papa will get you some food. *Tu es affamée*, sweet child. I fear there is not much. I hope you do not mind *rassis pain*." The prince opened his pack and withdrew stale bread and his water bladder from which he desired for her to drink.

Sabrina snatched the bread and shoved as much as she could in her mouth. She grabbed the water from her father, and he tried to help her drink it but she poured it onto herself in her desperation for the coolness inside. She bawled. Patiently, Andrian removed the cloak and wrung it out beside them. Still cold from the moisture, he flung the cloak toward the fire to dry. She trembled again, so he removed his cape and wrapped her in it. This time he felt how bitter the night air was and began to shiver, but he would rather have himself ill from the wind than his baby girl. She sobbed again and he tried to soothe her, but she would not stop.

"What's wrong wit' 'er? Why's she cryin' like tha'?" one soldier asked another with concern. "You'd think she ne'er saw er father b'fore."

"She ne'er 'as, idiot," said another soldier as he slapped the back of his head.

"Hush, my child. I am here. Do not cry," the prince hummed to Sabrina. His voice rarely made music before, and the soldiers became silent as the prince rocked his child and sang this haunting lullaby:

"Je suis le furieux protecteur. Je vais ou je veux. J'y pense, plus je me dis que . . . j'ai la passion de tu! Ou que tu allies . . .

rassurez-vous . . . je serai été à côté de tu! Tu te réfugies dans mon étreinte. Parce que advienne que pourra, tu es ma petite fille."

The soldiers began to get drowsy as their prince comforted his girl. The child smiled and began to get drowsy as well. Soon she fell asleep to his mournfully peaceful voice. Prince Andrian kissed his daughter. *"Dormez-vous, ma chère."* She murmured in her sleep, her fingers once again in her mouth.

The soldiers sat up when the soothing melody had ceased. "Tha' was *so* pretty, sire." They all nodded to each other in agreement.

The prince scooted against a tree to relieve his back from the weight he held close to him. His daughter murmured again and snuggled close to her father. "You are so beautiful, Sabrina. You are *my* baby girl." He kissed her head. "You shall come home with me." He stroked Sabrina's head as he made sure she remained warm in his cape.

"What's the king goin' to say when 'e sees you wit' 'er, my lord?"

Prince Andrian looked at the soldier and grinned. "He will say that he is a fortunate man to have such a wonderful granddaughter." The prince kissed Sabrina again and leaned his head back on the tree in exhaustion. He grumbled to himself and cleared his sore throat. The open air bit at him through his cloak.

"Pardon me, Your 'ighness, but what're you goin' to do wit' her? You know, when you 'ave to fight a war er somethin'?" The soldier approached the prince. He looked upon the sleeping toddler. Then he added, "Ain' she somethin'?" He smiled at her sweet face nestled next to her father's neck.

Prince Andrian looked over at the soldier. "I am the child's guardian, and I protect her by defending my father's kingdom. I am sure there will be someone willing to care for her in my absence."

The soldier nodded. "Of course, Your 'ighness." He smiled at her. "She does look like Jonquille."

The prince caressed Sabrina and sighed. "I miss my sister. Please cease speaking of her. It pains my heart."

"Yes, Milord."

Prince Andrian felt content as the child slept in his arms. Life became precious to him as he realized the small child in his arms needed him to survive. Without her father's care, she would perish. He thought of how the following day they would need to ride hard for his home so his daughter might have more than a crust of bread for a meal. Hot food sounded pleasant to him as well after such a long battle away from home.

Sleep overtook the party of men save Prince Andrian and the soldier sitting beside him. They sat up, on guard for second watch. This time the prince guarded more than his own existence, the life of his daughter as well.

"Where'd you learn to sing, my prince? You ne'er told anyone you 'ave such a beauty-full voice," the guard said.

Prince Andrian whispered so as not to disturb Sabrina. "I have *always* known how to sing. My heart has not had a reason to share it in so very long." He kissed the sleeping girl again. "You *are* my reason, sweet child. You are the reason I *exist*." Sabrina stirred in his arms, and she opened her eyes. "Go back to sleep, *ma chère*."

Sabrina reached up and felt her father's smooth cheek with her slobbery fingers. Then she felt the trim beard around his chin and mouth. His eyes shone with love for her and she feared him no longer. He kissed her small hand as she patted his face repeatedly. His long black hair fell about her as he nuzzled her, and he had deep brown eyes like the puppy her mama had to chase the foxes in the field. She yawned. "Papa." She leaned against her father and inhaled his scent. He smelled like cloves, musk, and perspiration that all together smelled sweet and safe to her. She drifted back to sleep in his arms.

Prince Andrian caressed his daughter and whispered to the soldier, "She called me Papa." He smiled.

"Tha' she did, Sire. Tha' she did."

Prince Andrian leaned his head against the tree once again and listened to the night noises around them. "No one is going to take you away from me. I love you so, my Sabrina."

Prince Andrian did not realize how relaxed he had become until he opened his eyes at dawn. In shock that he had dozed off while on guard duty, the prince looked around himself. Everyone else had awakened. Only Sabrina still snored softly, and he smiled down at her as he stroked her hair. For a moment he thought he had heard seraphim, but as he had come to his senses one of his dream angels had settled in his arms.

"We didn't want to wake you, Milord. You needed your rest." A soldier brought over a bladder full of water and handed it to the prince.

The prince felt a drought in his own throat. He moved his arm slightly to drink the water, and as he gulped down the wetness Sabrina opened her large brown eyes. He stopped. She looked up at him.

"Papa." She licked her lips.

Prince Andrian wagged his finger at her. "This time *I* shall hold the water." She reached at the bladder. He held it in front of her, and she put her mouth on it and swallowed faster than she could handle. She coughed. He patted her back. "Slow down, *ma chère*." He let her drink again, and after three or four attempts Sabrina managed to drink from the water bladder without much difficulty.

"Papa." Sabrina put her hand on his face again. "Papa." Her stomach growled, and she whimpered, "Papa, *tummy hurts*."

Prince Andrian smiled at his daughter and then spoke mellifluously, "I will find something, *ma chère*, but we must go on a long ride today. We are going to go home so you can fill your tummy up with good things."

"Home? Mama?" she squeaked.

"No, Sabrina. *Ne pas Maman*. No more Mama." Prince Andrian felt his gut sink when his child's eyes filled with tears.

"No more Mama. Mama gone." She bowed her head and her stomach howled.

"Will *one* of you bring me something? She is *famished*." The prince rocked his daughter in his arms as she whimpered, "Mama . . . Mama *gone away*." Sabrina wept in her father's arms and chewed on her forefinger as she leaned into her father's chest.

"Hush. Hush, my child. Mama is gone, but Papa will care for you now. Papa is here, *ma fleur*. Papa is here." He rocked the girl in his arms, and she sniffled. He wiped her runny nose with his sleeve, and she swatted his hand away with an annoyed squeak.

One of the soldiers handed the father a large piece of bread, and he thanked him. Sabrina saw the bread, and her stomach growled more violently than before. Prince Andrian ripped the bread into small bites for her, and as soon as he handed them to her, they vanished. When Sabrina finished the bread, her stomach ceased growling. The prince held the water for his daughter, and she drank more down as if she had never been given water in her life.

"Papa," Sabrina whined pitifully.

"We are going home now, my sweet little daffodil. This home is where Papa lives. You have *never* been to where Papa lives." Prince Andrian raised himself to his feet and lifted his daughter into his arms. She seemed wet to him. He felt her. She was definitely wet. She had urinated in her sleep and soaked herself through. He sighed and looked at her. "Sabrina, when you have to go peepee *tell* Papa. You do not want to be soggy. When you have to go, tell me." He put his daughter on the ground, and she wandered over to the horses. The prince picked up his cloak and shook the dust from it. At least it was dry. "Sabrina? Come *here*, my child. Over *here*. That is it, come to Papa."

Sabrina ran around everywhere while the prince tried to get her to stay still so he might change her clothes. She made everyone laugh but Prince Andrian. He did not wish her to become ill on his first day as a father. Sabrina laughed while her Papa chased around after her.

"Sabrina? Sit with me. Come on, over here. *Please*, sweet child. You *need* dry clothes. Come back to Papa. That is good, over here." Prince Andrian ran up to her and swept her off her feet before she could dodge him again.

"No. No. No. No. No," Sabrina muttered.

"You *need* dry clothes. Stay right *here* with me." He struggled to remove her wet clothes, and she wriggled as much as she could to resist the clothes he stuck on her. His lucky tunic worked for the most part, save its size and several unfortunate holes plaguing it. The encampment of soldiers laughed at Sabrina as she flapped her little arms in the sleeves. Prince Andrian figured with some minor adjustments . . . Sabrina twirled in a circle. Her father rolled up the sleeves on her new "dress" as he caught her before she fell on the dirt from vertigo. He added a sash to hold her in the tunic, made from a bit of his cloak already torn from battle. Sabrina looked up at her father, impressed with his efforts to create suitable attire for the child from his clothing.

Sabrina looked up for his giant shadow blocked out the sun. She longed to flee from the dark-haired man, but she felt drawn to him as well, though she had never seen him before in her life except the day before . . . when he took her away from home and Mama.

At that thought, Sabrina wailed once again, "MAMA?"

Prince Andrian frowned. Would she *ever* stop crying for her mother? He picked her up, and her father's scent relaxed her impulse to run and she again felt the soothing touch of the parent she had not known until then. "Sabrina, do not *cry* any longer . . . *please.*" He stroked her head and rocked her in his arms. She sniffled for a little while longer, but soon enough he had calmed her once again and he made to put her down. As soon as one of her feet touched the ground, she howled. He sighed and rocked her longer. The second time, he merely made the motion to set her down and she hollered again. He rolled his eyes. "I do not *believe* this."

The soldiers laughed as they watched the prince carry his child around; no matter what his duty, she insisted he tote her with him everywhere. If he tried to sit, she clutched him around the neck as if he might forget she existed. Whenever he needed both of his hands for anything, he carried her piggyback. Unfortunately for her poor father, she discovered she could place her hands over his eyes so that he could not see where he went. Not only did he not expect to be blinded while extinguishing a fire, as a result of his abrupt incapacitation he managed to not only burn his foot but also catch a blanket and several bags of supplies on fire. Although Sabrina released his sight when she heard her father howling curse words as he tried to put out his scorching foot, she found the fact his boot still smoked appallingly comical. Eventually, Prince Andrian needed to relieve himself, and as he handed her to one of his soldiers so he might urinate in peace, the abandoned pup howled until he returned.

"We must head back to Eddington before she becomes *more* difficult," Prince Andrian sighed, and all agreed with him. With his daughter Sabrina in tow, the prince collected his belongings for the journey home. When the encampment of personal guard became orderly, the prince urged his company to get on the move.

Sabrina found the day fun for the most part, and as her father reassured her that she would have more fun than burning her papa's foot, she smiled and fell asleep on the long, hard ride back to Eddington.

Chapter Twelve

Sabrina having come home to her father did not cease the onslaught upon the kingdom as King Arundel had hoped. Upon meeting his granddaughter for the first time, the king was delighted with her. Over her shyness after a few days, Sabrina became rambunctious and excitable. She wandered about the castle at all hours, and the maidservants who watched her in the prince's absence pulled out their hair and cursed. Only Queen Mireille could keep the child calm. Unlike her father, Sabrina looked forward to tea and biscuits and would sit upon her grandmother's lap while she read to her and sang her songs.

King Arundel fought with his son every time he returned from the countryside. Sabrina would be taken from the room by the maidservants before she would see the king and the prince argue, though she could still hear them shouting. After several such instances, Sabrina ceased coming out to greet her father when he returned home. Sabrina chose to stay with the queen. She had even taken to sleeping in her bed at night.

So busy in his fights with his father, so busy with his armies, and so busy with his personal gains, Prince Andrian searched for his daughter less and less. The maidservants and his mother had been doing a fair job with her. Besides, it was a woman's job to raise a child.

*   *   *

The dark-hearted prince had marched his armies to the ends of the country and ransacked enough riches to last a lifetime. The lands he pillaged abounded with not only natural resources, but many wealthy families also offered their gold and ransomed their properties after he threatened to ravage every one of the noble's wives and daughters if they resisted his demands. None of these men, knowing the violence within the prince, took their chances with his threats. With relief, the nobles saw Andrian the Ruthless march the army of demons away from their castles. Dignity, however precious, lost did not concern the nobles, as they considered their cowardly lives more important than riches.

After bidding goodbye to his latest victims with a victory burning of their crops, Prince Andrian, the most ruthless and most sullen, marched his army home to Eddington. It had been so long since he had slept in his bed and ate food fit for human consumption. Trotting ahead of the army dressed in wasteland blue, he imagined roast peacock, hunks of boar, pheasant soup, bread slathered in butter, salted fish . . . his mouth began to water. His imagination kept his mind occupied on the two-week-long march home. Peaches. Meat pie. Blanc manger. Duck. Bear. The castle rose from the ground. *Oh*, he thought, *but that is no stone wall.* A great stack of bread piled high loomed ahead of him. Cherries. Geese. Lamb chops. Beef. He leapt from his horse and ran to the kitchen and immediately ripped a leg of goose from the dinner awaiting his arrival.

The chefs looked at each other as the prince tore into it like a wolf. "So good," he mumbled as he ate. "Oh my." He snatched a loaf of bread and tore into that as well. He raised it to them and muttered something through his full mouth and left. The chefs shrugged and continued making pastries.

Upon hearing that Andrian had robbed the pantry as he arrived home, King Arundel frowned at his son's lack of self-control. He had asked Andrian to join him for a supper to discuss his conduct yet again, though the kitchen incident would merely need to be added to the list of complaints. The king believed the crown prince suffered from a deplorable excess of power, and the situation had not improved on its own. He must cease the chaos even if it meant more punishment for his son, though he hoped that he would not need extraordinary measures for reining in his increasingly unmanageable heir.

As Prince Andrian entered the great hall, he did not enjoy the harsh and disgruntled look upon his father's face. He bowed before King Arundel's throne but did not look up at him, for he could not bear his ashamed gaze. The silence that followed his genuflection discomfited Prince Andrian.

"My *son*," the king said with finality. He saw the angst in his rebellious scion and decided that heavy-handed words should fall once again that evening. He beckoned to his son. "Come to me, my *ruthless* prince."

Prince Andrian approached his father the king and kissed his ring. He felt his father's anger at the same moment he touched his quivering hand. The never-ending disapproval of King Arundel always discouraged the tyrant prince. Andrian mourned his failure in his father's eyes.

"Join me for supper, my beloved son, we *indeed* have much to discuss." The king placed his shaking fingers on Andrian's forehead and smoothed his son's furrowed brow.

Prince Andrian nodded. "Aye, Your Majesty." After he agreed to his father's invitation, he excused himself to prepare for supper with the king. "I am full of the dust from the road and sweat from riding for days."

King Arundel nodded once.

While his son left with a swirl of his midnight cape, the king sighed and placed his head upon his right hand.

The servants would call supper in an hour, and Andrian hoped time might fly as he dressed. The time did not pass quickly, however, and he felt tormented beyond his own expectations. Pacing back and forth in his bedroom, Prince Andrian grew eager for his father's talk. His restlessness amplified before meetings with the monarch, but as soon as he sat in his propinquity he calmed.

Ever since childhood, Prince Andrian had disappointed his father, and he still enjoyed reminding the young man now and again of it. He had shamed his family somehow by not being like his brother, Julian.

As he grew up, Andrian always heard praise for Julian. If Andrian threw a stone twenty meters, he could bet Julian would throw it five meters further. Whenever Andrian raced his horse, Julian would always beat him. Andrian always fancied girls who found his brother more delightful. Julian bested him at chess, in reading, in mathematics, and he could draw a human far more realistically than Andrian, though Andrian practiced and Julian did not.

Everyone thought Julian a better man than his younger brother.

Julian had charm, he had style, and he had grace. Everyone looked up to him. Andrian only had his sharp tongue, which cost him more friends than earned them.

Repeatedly Andrian's brother entered conversations. Always compared to each other, Andrian came out wanting every time. Andrian had begun to learn how to ignore his brother's favoritism, and to do so he had made a name for himself so far apart from Julian that no one in his family wanted to admit that Andrian, now nicknamed Ruthless, was of any relation. A foundling leper child could find more favor in his family than he could.

No matter what Andrian did, he could not make his father proud of him. No matter what Julian did, his father always boasted about him.

King Arundel had labeled Andrian, *"A humiliation to my line."* After a while, Andrian, already a failure, could do no good, for his every fault magnified itself to absurdity. At least when castigated his father actually spoke to him.

A servant knocked once upon the prince's door. The young heir threw it open with such force that it caused the unprepared servant to shriek. The prince stood staring at the man with surprise. The servant flapped his hands continually as he squealed.

"Oh shut up *you!*" Andrian the Ruthless slapped him with his leather glove. "What a *twit*," he mumbled to himself as he left the servant covering his mouth, straining to keep himself silent.

In the great hall, King Arundel awaited his son's arrival to share his evening meal with him. Through the heavy doors, Prince Andrian strutted. The king shook his head with disbelief.

"*Bon soir*, Father." Prince Andrian bowed ostentatiously.

"Sit down, my little *peacock*." King Arundel rolled his eyes at his son.

"*Aye*, Father." The prince frowned at his comment. He drew himself a chair and sat quietly. Yet again, whenever Andrian exuded any pride his father would crush him with demeaning words. "Will Mother and my daughter be joining us this evening?"

King Arundel shook his head. "An early evening for them, I am afraid. Perhaps tomorrow, my son."

Prince Andrian sighed. "Perhaps."

The servants entered the chamber with the food, and as the king and the prince washed their hands in the appointed basins, silence reigned except for the noise of the dishes placed upon the table. Prince Andrian had not eaten more than gruel in a month save for his earlier theft, and all of the delicious smells drove his hunger to insanity. As a maiden served the prince, he felt his empty belly punch his insides, though he did not give in until his father began eating first.

Prince Andrian relished every bite of the sustenance he rarely enjoyed. King Arundel nibbled the food before him with a silent frown. It disturbed Andrian to see the king stare at him with such unease, and the prince sat up straight as he awaited his father's comments, which still did not come forth.

Prince Andrian wondered how the king might jab him in the heart at the meal. How much longer would his father ignore his son's feelings? Did he expect he should act as though he never lost his family or his father's love? Should he smile, when inside he wept and cowered in guilt? Perhaps his father wished for an apology, as though all pain might vanish with forgiveness.

"Have you been eating much lately?" King Arundel looked up from his roast duck.

The prince ceased chewing and swallowed. "I have eaten little since last I have been home. Why do you ask?" He took another large bite.

King Arundel shrugged. "Last you were here you had bulk and seemed healthy. Now . . ." He pushed a bowl of fruit toward him. "You look half-starved."

The prince eyed the fruit and saliva poured from his mouth. "I am so hungry most of the time, but I have little provisions. You ceased the funds for my armies and I have been forced to use the land to feed my men."

"I hear you have been raiding towns for their supplies as well." He pushed the fruit closer to his son. "Eat, boy. Your eyes cannot be larger than your stomach the way your clothes hang from your skeleton."

Prince Andrian began to eat fresh cherries, and he spat the pits into an empty bowl beside him. He spied a fine-looking young maiden who gazed at him as she gathered used tableware. She blushed when he smiled and caught her eye. With the way she bit her lip and looked away from his stare, he knew he had a friend for the night already. He felt terrified when he slept alone at night, though no one who lived knew such a thing about him. Thank God he had the ability to convince women to sleep beside him. Grinning, he held out his goblet for her to refill with wine, and as she took it from him, he rubbed his fingers on her hand. She gasped and her arm acquired goose bumps. He winked at her, and she flushed red once again.

King Arundel slammed his chalice on the hard wood of the table. Anyone else would have shrieked, but Prince Andrian merely turned his head and drawled, *"Aye, Father?"*

The king felt it disgraceful how his heir behaved in such a rude manner, especially at the table. He could respect Andrian's youth and lustful feelings, but it was one thing to be in the bedroom and quite another to display such sinful desires in a place of royal community.

Prince Andrian shrugged at the lack of vocal response to his question, so he continued to eat his cherries. He sucked on them and grinned as he did so. He needed her; his desperation ate him from the soles of his boots to the coronet on his head. His grave loneliness had amassed in his chest for the past week. He dreaded the coldness of his loss far more than the coldness of steel. At least when a warm body snuggled beside him, he might imagine love and he felt less despondent.

As the maiden giggled silently at the prince, King Arundel sighed. "Andrian, if you would be so *kind* as to recall your manners at my table?" The king nodded his head at the prince's feet.

The prince spit a cherry pit into the bowl and dragged his boots from the top of the table. "Aye, Father."

King Arundel shook his head. "Do you recall why I placed you as commander of my largest and most skilled army?"

Prince Andrian nodded. "I remember you wished for me to have renewed respect for my power and to use it to protect the kingdom." He smiled. "I have been the greatest general Europe has known in two centuries."

King Arundel sighed. "I thought if I surrounded you with good men you might follow their lead and control my subjects with wisdom and show them you have authority. I had hoped you would gain respect and love for your watchful eye."

Here he goes, the prince thought. His father would drop him until nothing remained but an ignored memory of a haunted young man.

"Instead of my knights assisting you with your behavior, you corrupted them into an army of mercenaries. You are known throughout the land as a murderer and tyrant. I gave you the power to bring criminals to justice, and you open your arms to them as a shepherd welcomes his sheep." He frowned. "I asked you to bring a known criminal to me, Gerard Lafontaine, so I might try him for treason, and you failed. Not only has he continued to spread malicious lies, his village also backs his tongue by withholding their taxes due to me. I cannot allow that."

Prince Andrian grimaced. "I promised someone I would not harm him."

King Arundel sighed. "My request outweighs begging for mercy from anyone." He frowned. "This must be the fifteenth order I have given that has collapsed underneath you. Why is it so difficult to follow through with your duties?"

Prince Andrian bit his lip. "I gave her my word. Is that not honorable to keep one's word?"

"It is indeed noble to keep one's word, but why not keep your word to me? I am your father after all. Besides, what debt could you owe this person that demands more than the treasury?"

"She spared my life, Father."

"Having your physical needs met is hardly saving your life."

Prince Andrian snorted. "That was not the way of it."

"But it had something to do with it. I am no fool."

Prince Andrian grabbed a handful of cherries and stuffed them in his mouth.

The king growled with frustration. "What has happened with you, Son? You have become even more careless, reckless, and dare I say it, *murderous!* You seem to care little for those around you. And the people you have any care at all toward, it is only to use certain *talents* of theirs!" The king glared at the maiden whom the prince found so attractive.

"Did you *never* realize I always have been so, Father?" Prince Andrian spat the stripped pits at the bowl like a succession of stones. He looked at his father with feigned conceit. "I am a warrior. I am a blood-letting, steel swinging, bone-crushing fiend of a man. I will never bow to the words of small men like you do." He smirked. "You are my king and I am your subordinate. *All kings fall at the hands of their subjects.*"

The king's eyes bulged as his son stroked his beard. "I do not know how long you have imagined yourself *the son of the devil,* but I do know that your behavior is absolutely *unacceptable!* I will never tolerate such ruthless abandonment of the law and disrespect for your king and country!" King Arundel dug his yellowing fingernails into the table while Andrian nibbled another cherry and hummed. "Oh, my boy, you are sinking to new depths every day you walk this earth!" He smoothed his frizzy beard. "I have no alternative with you, Andrian. It pains me to say this, but if you *refuse* to cease your dark armies from marching through the good in this world," he picked up his knife, "I shall consider . . . no, I shall *have* a new heir to my throne!"

Prince Andrian spat another cherry out and missed the bowl entirely. "You cannot be *serious,* Father!" He scooted his chair back and leaned forward, his hands clasping the edge of the table. His father had finally put his foot down! More than anything, Andrian had misjudged how long it would take his father to do so.

King Arundel leaned forward. "I *am* quite serious." The king jabbed the knife in the wood and it wavered with a hum.

Prince Andrian slapped his hand across the wood and then placed it on his forehead. "After all I have done for your kingdom? I have all but ceased civil unrest everywhere I go."

The king raised his voice. "You have caused *utter chaos* every time you stroll into a town! You need not even brandish a sword and they scatter as ants in the rain! I cannot look the other way as you abuse your power with joy!" King Arundel sighed. "It is a *travesty* that you should not be punished severely for your crimes!" The king pointed his bony finger at his son. "Mark my words, Andrian, if you do not calm yourself I will not allow you *any* freedoms . . . and you will be escorted in all places you go. I do not care if you need to relieve yourself or make love to a woman, I *will* have a man to watch your every move!"

"That is *not* just, Your Majesty!" The prince looked down. He ran his fingers through his wild hair.

"Watch your tone of voice with me, Andrian!" the king warned him.

"Aye, Father." Prince Andrian knew he must sit this chastisement through. He must remain in control of himself, for one more outburst might cost him his crown. Only his crown gave the country reason to accept him, but without the gold behind the madness he might only find laughter and open scorn. No one dared laugh in his face now, but if his father denied him claim to the throne all would spit in his face and mock his pain. They must *never* mock his pain.

The king stroked his long beard as his son's jaw twitched. "Do you *know* what is unfair? It is unfair that you should leave your baby here alone to be looked after by whoever is in the castle who has a spare moment. It is *unfair* that she asks for her mother and yet she cannot even see her father. It is *unfair* that you should cause your mother and me such *grief*. You *are* the reason your mother has taken ill, Son. It is your *evil* that has made her so weak and sad." King Arundel frowned at his autocratic son.

Prince Andrian's eyes widened and liquefied. "But . . . Mother *always* tells me I am such a good boy, and that she is so *glad* that I am her son! She *always* embraces me and kisses me fondly! Since when has *Mother* thought evil of me?" Queen Mireille had always gone out of her way to show Andrian tenderness, and the news that she might only cater to him out of pity caused his heart to drool in his throat.

King Arundel grunted at his son. "Your mother shows kindness to you because she believes you are good deep inside. How deep, we do not know! Andrian, you are completely destroying yourself . . . and your name."

Prince Andrian disbelieved his father's complete denial of his goodness. "It is *wrong* to bring Mother into our arguments about me. You turn me into this *vicious* and *uncaring* creature before all . . . and she does *not* think that of me!" Prince Andrian's mouth contorted with frustration at his father's misunderstanding and his own disbelief. "I *can* love, and I have! I have feelings and *can* be merciful! Because no one knows how I am within does not mean that I am *wicked throughout my whole body.*" The prince clenched his fists. "Perhaps no one has asked me of my feelings and that is why I am labeled as a *heartless brute.*"

King Arundel laughed at his son. "You, my son, are *quite* the actor. You say you have loved, but *where* is the proof?" He twirled his beard. "A man who is capable of love is capable of compassion, and I see no mercy when you have men punished severely for minor offenses."

Prince Andrian cried out, "Where is there compassion for *me*? Where is the mercy allotted for *me*? No one told me they felt sorrow when I felt pain! No one embraced me when inside I ached so badly that I went to *throw myself from the tower*!" Prince Andrian watched his father's eyes glinting with confusion as he pointed in the citadel's general direction. "You *never* cared for me! You never give me *any* words of kindness or understanding! My *suffering* is no concern to you!" Prince Andrian began to tremble. "For all this time I have been scavenging for a scrap of affection and you offered no consolation but everyone would be better off if I were *dead*!" Prince Andrian's lip quivered and he forced his eyes to the ground.

King Arundel stood and leaned over. "Then let us ask how you feel to be this *fiend* that everyone cowers before. No one can be in your presence without being frightened that you will put him or her to death. Is *that* what your goal is? To inspire terror in *every living thing* on God's earth, that no one dare love you for fear of being murdered?" The king stared unblinkingly at his son. "That is why there is no mercy or compassion for you. You give none *yourself.*"

"I *am* a fearful enemy, and I am proud to be a man that *everyone* cowers before. Since no one knows me and will never give me a chance to prove my character, I never worry about losing friends. It makes my job much less difficult." Prince Andrian straightened himself. He could not lose his argument.

The king snorted. "What *job* do you believe you have, Prince? Whatever *sickness in your head* tells you that the butchering of innocent men and women is an acceptable occupation? God have mercy on your soul the day you *realize* the serious mistakes you have made and *pay* for them." King Arundel raised his hand as if he had forgotten some bit of vital information. "Oh, and by the way, you *are* a vicious fiend. You may ask anyone, though I hardly think they will tell you the truth. They will tell you what you want to hear, of course. Even *I* have difficulty telling you anything but what you wish to hear." He smiled falsely, sat, and folded his long bony fingers on the table before him.

Prince Andrian bit his lip and closed his eyes as he repressed a stream of curses aimed, at least in his mind, toward his father. He calmed himself, opened his black eyes, and retorted, "I am *not* as terrible as everyone makes me to be. I do not see *demonic behavior*. I see a man willing to extend his reach of power for a kingdom awaiting expansion. I see a man who desperately wants his father to say that he is proud of his son for *any* job well done."

"You are *not as terrible*, you say. That is humorous to me. I see *no* love in anyone's eyes for you. No friends by your side. In case you noticed not, your own Sabrina calls for her *mother* and not her father. *Not as terrible?*"

"No, Father, I am *not* as terrible." Prince Andrian twisted a golden ring on his left index finger. "I love my child. If I could not love, then why does she recognize me as her guardian?" Prince Andrian could see the skepticism forming a cloud around his father. "She is merely *confused* at the recent events in her life and that is why she has been upset."

King Arundel smirked. "I believe *you* are the one who is confused about your disreputable behavior. You are a *wicked* young man who has done naught but evil your whole existence."

"I *have* done some good, Father, I *have*." Prince Andrian swallowed the lump forming in his throat.

The king snarled, "Have you looked at your reflection as of late? Take a *good look* and study yourself. If you are honest, you will loathe who you see staring back at you. A sick and contemptible man in *all* eyes, you will *never* find love and happiness in anything if you believe the only way to be content is through the shedding of innocent blood."

The prince frowned bitterly. "I have looked at myself. You do not accept my goodness because I am not the way you wish me to be." He grimaced. "I also find no *joy* in killing; it is merely an unfortunate effect of my duties." He ran his fingers through his hair. "As for the lack of love in my life, I *have* been loved but it destroyed me. I am the man before you because I suffer in my loneliness." He wiped his eyes. "I asked you long ago for you to recognize my wife and you dismissed me. I told her that I could not be her husband openly because you hated me enough to deny me even her affections. You showed me no mercy out of spite."

King Arundel slammed his hand on the table. "*Have you lost your mind?* Not a maiden alive would take you as her husband willingly! There is not a woman within *ten thousand leagues* who would bed you because she loved you! I see the women who keep your nightly company. They wish for power and your riches." He tossed his hands in the air. "You could be *anyone* to them and they would look at you as the same: a man who gives them what they want and they need give nothing in return but their bodies. No, Son. No woman would want you as her husband. Of *that* I am sure."

"You are wrong! My wife wanted me more than she wanted anyone else! You cheated me out of happiness because *you* do not love *me*!"

King Arundel hooted. "I saved you from foolishness. You are not even a man, so how can you be a husband?"

"I am a man! I am twenty-six years old, in case you did not notice!" He pulled his tunic open. "I have more hair on my chest than Julian does!"

King Arundel chuckled. "Having the body of a man does not make you a man." He sighed. "No woman wants you as her companion if you holler and stomp your feet every time you are denied your way. She would do as well to marry a five-year-old child."

"I do not believe that less than a *thousand* maidens would wish me to be their husband!" Prince Andrian snatched a baguette from the table and pointed to the lovely maiden as she cleaned up the mess he had made with the cherries. "I bet *she* would be my wife." The prince caught the girl's eye and he laughed as he stroked the bread, causing her to gasp as she restrained her own laughter.

King Arundel rolled his eyes at his son. "How many times have I told you to mind your manners while we are eating?"

Prince Andrian ceased his bread fondling. "I do not know, Father. I am unable to count that high." He smirked. "You must remember that *Julian* is far more skilled in mathematics than I."

King Arundel gave the prince a sigh and shook his head. "We shall leave your jealousy of Julian out of this discussion." The king knew the situation would only escalate if he allowed his son to slash his elder brother's reputation. "Your mother, as I had said earlier, is feeling terribly ill. She had wished to visit with you today. Do *try* to be a good little boy and upset her not." He wagged his finger at his son. "A man cares for his family, especially his wife. I do not wish her to die of a broken heart and leave her husband sad and very much alone."

Prince Andrian stood and leaned toward the king with a scowl. "I *know* that she will leave you behind, Father, but you forget that she is my *mother,* and she will be leaving *me* behind as well." This time, Prince Andrian's snarl betrayed his eyes, bloated with pain.

King Arundel grimaced. "You have already left her, my son. To her, you are already *gone*." The king stood, and as Prince Andrian bowed, a tear trickled down his cheek.

Chapter Thirteen

Prince Andrian turned to see his ailing mother, who preferred to remain in her room alone to the kingdom. The lustful maiden saw that Prince Andrian had left and she snuck out behind him. He heard her following and turned around. She looked as if she wished to speak to him. The prince grasped her hand and pulled her to him. After a moment of passionate kissing, he whispered, "I will see you in my chambers soon." She nodded, and he let her go. He ran up the stairway to visit his mother, leaving the girl with a cat's smile across her face.

Prince Andrian had many things to think about that evening as he ran up the flight of stairs. He had always listened to his father's advice and absorbed the knowledge he had shared with him at all times. Unfortunately, the young prince did not always take each bit of wisdom to heart, and furthermore, put it into practice. He retained his devil-may-care attitude from his early youth because everyone brutalized his heart. He could never make anyone love him, so what did it matter if he took any advice anyhow? It would just make his father right, and he would never live his humiliation down.

Winded as he arrived before his mother's bedroom door, he stood around to catch his breath. After several minutes of gargling gasps, he felt the air rush back into his lungs, and he tapped four or five times on the solid oaken egress. He waited patiently for an answer, and since none came, he knocked yet again. He wondered to himself what his mother did within her room that she would not hear his rapping on her chamber door.

"Mother?" He leaned on the door.

He heard a shuffling around inside and a stumbling toward the entrance. The door creaked open and the sallow face of the queen appeared with her hollow eyes.

"Mother, it is I. May I come in to see you for a short while?" Prince Andrian's voice switched to a soft tone when the queen appeared. Normally his voice was deep and ferociously melodious, but his voice had raised a complete octave and sweetly resonated from him. He did not realize that this only occurred around his mother. His family thought it obvious, but they never said a word about his change.

The queen blinked at her son a few times and then mumbled, "Oh, aye, Love, come in." She opened the door wide, and he entered the room with excessive caution, for his mother hobbled before him.

"What is the matter, Mother?" Prince Andrian asked tentatively.

Queen Mireille turned around, nearly falling over, and her son caught her. "Oh dear, this leg of mine." She smiled up at her only son and patted his arm. Noticing his taut muscles, she squeezed his left bicep. "You *are* a stout young lad, you are."

"Aye, Mother." He ignored her comment. "Why do you not sit down? I shall make a *nice* place for you to rest." The queen nodded, and Prince Andrian pulled a comfortable chair for her and selected the softest cushions to put upon it.

"Thank you, my dear child. It is *very* sweet of you to think of me. I *always knew* you were a good boy. You take after your grandfather, who always thought of his mother." The queen looked at her son with tears in her eyes. "I love you so; I wish you would stay home for a spell. I miss your handsome face while you are away." Queen Mireille patted her son's cheek as he helped her into the seat.

"I would stay home, Mother, but I must defend our way of life. I indeed miss you, but duty calls elsewhere so *often.*" The prince swept his billowing robes aside to sit in the chair by his forlorn mother.

"Ah, I *remember.* You lead your father's armies . . . I *knew* that giving you that power would drive you out from under my wing." She straightened her dress and then looked up at her prince. "Tell me, Andrian, have you thought of *other duties* besides making war? I have not heard if you have found a fair lady to marry yet."

Prince Andrian patted his mother's hand and shook his head. "Father had but finished informing me that I am an unmarriageable brute."

The queen frowned. "I am *sure* there are many beautiful and kind maidens to love you out in this world."

Prince Andrian sighed. "Many fair maidens live among us, which is something I am sure of. But alas, I have not found *une femme* who would love me for *all* I am just yet."

Queen Mireille gasped. "But, Andrian, *surely* there have been women who have loved you thus far!" She grasped his hand and shook it, causing his rings to jingle merrily. "What about that young girl . . . what was her name?"

"*Quelle jeune fille*, Mother?" Prince Andrian had known scores of young girls.

The queen tapped each of his jewels with her long fingernail. "The pretty young lady you wished your father would allow you to marry. The girl you met on your crusade . . . Oh, what *was* her name? I do not recall any longer."

"Oh . . . you speak of Farida. I knew her for four years. I . . . I am still from tip to toe in love with her." The queen's eyes widened and he paused for a moment. "*Elle . . . elle est morte*, Mother." His pretense showed unconcern, though his mother knew his soul had torn.

"You *never* told me. How did she die, my son?"

Prince Andrian grimaced. "Giving birth to *mon fils*. He . . . he was stillborn." Prince Andrian looked away and wiggled his feet. "There was *nothing* I could do for her. It is the way of things sometimes." The prince gritted his teeth; he must not show weakness. His mother needed to recover from her illness; weeping would make things worse for both that evening.

The queen placed her hand on her son's face. He looked distant. Prince Andrian breathed in and out forcefully. He talked of Farida only to himself anymore, and he struggled with the decision to reveal his pain. He swallowed and decided it might be time to release some of his inner strife. "Mother, I never knew how much a woman's love could make me forget how much of a failure I am. She alone held me to comfort me because she enjoyed sharing her life. I never had to ask her, she just knew I needed to be touched and held." He put his head in his hands. "When I lost her, my world was destroyed. *Je ne pense pas* . . . I cannot think anymore. I cannot feel my own body. It is as if I have died and my soul left my corpse behind to walk about alone." He looked up at her. "When will my suffering cease? Will it ever end this torment I endure?"

"It is not your fault, Andrian. It is as you say. The way of things can be cruel, and you lose those you love all the time." Queen Mireille smiled knowingly. "I believe the sorrow will one day cease for you. At first, the loss will be unbearable, but in time you will find peace and you will find another woman's love to be just as satisfying."

Prince Andrian shook his head. "How could that ever be since no other woman will give me a chance? I could no more kindle love in a fair heart as jump in the air and fly like a bird."

Queen Mireille stroked her son's black hair. "Time, my son, it takes time."

"Time? I cannot wait for love that shall never come. I cannot entertain such thoughts. I know who I am to all. I am a figure of despotism and hated for everything I do. I could give a woman *un fleur* as a gesture of adoration and she would step on it just to spite me." He sighed. "There truly is no hope for such a creature as I."

Queen Mireille removed a necklace she wore and placed it in her son's hand. "When you find a woman who makes your heart soar and your body turn to flame, I wish for you to give her my necklace."

"Mother, I cannot . . ."

She closed his fist around it. "Yes, you can. I have enough faith in you to give this in trust that you shall fall in love again. Tell her that it was mine, and she shall see how much she means to you."

"And what if she refuses?"

"Trust your mother. She would not refuse you if given this." She kissed his forehead.

"She would be honored to be in your favoritism that you would offer her your mother's necklace." She winked. "Besides, how could anyone resist your persuasion? You have a gift for being quite convincing, or so I have heard."

He blushed. *"Merci beaucoup."* He pocketed the jeweled necklace and then sighed. "Along the lines of my lifestyle, I have many concerns about the past year. I know that I risk my safety *every time* I go to war, and I do see the chances I take on a regular basis." Andrian thought of his recent trip to the tower and the urge to leap from it. "My health has been poor as of late, and it bothers me to leave home when I have *ma fille* waiting for me to return."

The queen rubbed her son's nose. "I know that you have not felt well, and it worries me that you have not taken a respite from your quest to *expand* your future kingdom. I have quite enjoyed your daughter. She is dear to me."

Andrian scrunched his face. "Do not burden yourself with her if you are unwell."

"When I heard you had left for war yet again, I was sorrowful for the child." She sighed. "She is no burden, but she cries much for her mother. Why do you not bring the child's mother to live with us? She *might* make an acceptable wife for you as she is the *only one* your daughter truly longs for."

Prince Andrian frowned. "I *cannot* marry Sabrina's mother."

The queen brushed a bit of fluff from her son's tunic. "You have no love for her?"

The prince shook his head. "It would make no difference if I did. Selma is married already to one of father's vassals . . . You may remember him, James Halloran?"

The queen nodded. "He is a good man. Why did you do such a thing to his wife?"

Prince Andrian scowled. "Because I could . . . and because *je suis un corbeau*." He sighed. "She was the only woman who took me into her arms when I was wounded and needed care. When I broke her heart, she denied me my child. I had made a mistake, but it was a wonderful one it seems."

Queen Mireille smirked and patted her son's arm. "You are no crow. A fox perhaps."

He shrugged. "No matter, Sabrina is here and she needs a mother."

"She does."

Prince Andrian slicked back his wild hair and grumbled with frustration. "I have thought *many times* about finding a suitable mother for my baby, but I feel as if I will never find a woman worthy to hold my child in her arms, and no woman would find me worthy to be her husband." He groaned. "So you see I am at an impasse."

Queen Mireille frowned. "Not quite, Love. You *are* worthy to be loved, and whoever loves you will *surely* love your daughter." She patted his leg. "Do not make Sabrina suffer because *you* refuse to believe in yourself."

The prince looked up at his mother and grasped her hand. "I heard Sabrina crying at night for her mother when I first brought her home. Not once did she ask for me. *Ne jamais.* I feel as if I must right all my wrongs, and furthermore beg Sabrina to *one day* forgive me for the evil I have done to her. For that I would be *grateful.*" Prince Andrian lowered his eyes. "But I have too much shame to ask for Selma to come and see our baby after the *dreadful* thing I did to her." He fiddled with the necklace in his pocket and waited for his mother's response. He knew that Selma had given him so much, and he had stolen his only gift to her out of anger.

The queen asked about the circumstances in which Sabrina had come to live with them. Prince Andrian frowned but enlightened the queen with his story, beginning with meeting the child's brother and ending with how they had spent the long night and day going home. Andrian felt his heart sink at his mother's tears. Even his mother felt sorrow over his stupidity. He could not make wise decisions when given a chance.

Queen Mireille dabbed her eyes with a handkerchief she pulled from her pocket and sniffled. "The child weeps for her mother because she is *afraid*. I cannot understand why you took her away so suddenly. She is not only upset, she is also *greatly disturbed* at the fact that the only comfort she had ever known is no longer present in her life." The queen stroked her son's leg.

Prince Andrian nodded his head. "I see that Sabrina runs from me so *much*. It seems as if she does not wish to come out and greet me. I ask her to come to me, and she hides like a deer in spring. Even when I had to go to war for this last time, she did not even wish me *bon chance*." He nodded again. "Perhaps you are correct; I am no comfort to her." He looked at his mother as if she might help him with this problem of his, but she seemed unsure as well. "Mother, all I want to do is love and nurture my daughter, and I seem to be ill-adapted to doing so."

"She is unable to be nurtured and loved by you because you cannot give such care to yourself." Queen Mireille sighed. "Perhaps you might *still* consider bringing the child's mother to visit. At least she will have some sense of comfort when she sees her again." The queen pulled at a string on her sleeve. "Perhaps you might write a letter apologizing for your rashness. Who knows? Perhaps she might give you advice."

"Mother, I *know* that it was difficult for Sabrina to leave her mother, but she is *so much more likely* to have a fulfilling life with me here. Her mother is tremendously deprived. They had no bed for her . . . I could not *stand* my child living in such reduced conditions when she might one day be a queen. I do wish that she might see her mother, but alas, I have already burned that bridge as I crossed it." Prince Andrian scratched his beard in thought. He looked at his mother's pensive look and exhaled. "I am sorry that I have wronged everyone so many times, and I am sure that the evil shall catch up to me someday. I think I quite deserve such hatred."

Queen Mireille grasped her son's twiddling hands. "I would rather you admit to guilt and accept the burden of asking forgiveness than roll over and give up." She thought for a moment as she caressed her son's rough fingers. "My son, why did you *truly* go after your daughter?" She watched his expression become more intense. "Did you wish to be her father as *soon* as you came to the realization that you were of such importance to her? Or is it truly your fear of the usurping of your throne that drove you to seek the truth? I will not be *angry* with you whatever your answer shall be. I only wish for you to begin the journey of awareness at least."

Prince Andrian ran his fingers through his tangled jet locks again and grimaced. "Mother, I did *not* wish to be a father at first. *C'est la vérité*. I also did not want some woman who I barely knew to have any claim to share my throne when father dies. That is *also* the truth." He covered his face. "In fact, I had planned on killing Sabrina if she were my own, but as I saw the child I could not think of *anything* but protecting her innocence. The instinct to nurture and love my daughter was so great that I knew I would lose my sanity if I turned my back on her to those peasants who had begun to raise her." He stopped for a moment as the words tumbled out without considerable thought. "I had already lost my son, and I thought perhaps it was another chance to do well. It seems as if I have been mistaken. Forgive me, I find that happening more and more often."

The queen smiled at her son as he rubbed his tired eyes. "Surely you realize that being the father of a little girl has many challenges attached. The girl *needs a mother*. She needs a female influence, whether she is a baby or being given in marriage. She will feel it emotionally if she lacks that womanly company in her life." Queen Mireille patted her son's thigh. "I also wonder *how* you plan to raise her if your main goal in life is *to draw and quarter every man who crosses your path with a look that displeases you*." The queen squeezed his hand. "Surely the child will not follow you to battle?"

Prince Andrian sighed. "I do not wish to burden anyone unnecessarily."

Queen Mireille laughed. "You have caused Sabrina and her mother much grief by separating them so violently. Why not give Selma back her child and simply visit them when you wish? That would be the least burdensome choice in my opinion."

Prince Andrian bit his lip. "I will keep my daughter for her own good, and with honesty, mine as well. I will raise her with or without a wife—not because I do *not* love her, but because I cannot bear to see her back at that filth in which she was born. I keep my word to you, I will never give her up no matter what the circumstances. I love her more than *ma vie*."

Queen Mireille nodded. "Indeed." She watched her son fiddling with a bronze chain he seemed to always wear. "It is noble to desire the well-being of your daughter, and by housing her in this grandest of halls you are doing well by her completely, except for the lack of *both* her parents."

Prince Andrian placed his head in his hands. "*D'accord*, Mother." He mumbled something about difficult choices, and his mother tightened her thin lips further.

The queen stroked the prince's hair and hummed a soothing song to him. He relaxed a little and looked up at her. She cooed, "You were such a sweet baby. I do not know why you have *changed* so much these past several years."

"*Vraiment,* Mother?"

She shrugged. "You have, my son, unless you had hidden your soul from me your whole life." She pulled her caressing hand away from the young man as he leapt to his feet and began to pace the room. He bit his lip and the queen heard an ever so faint whimper coming from his throat. "Come, Andrian, do not be *so* upset. I am sorry I have caused you further distress."

The prince stopped his pacing and leaned himself on the back of his chair. "Oh, *Mother* even says I am evil," he moaned aloud. "*Please* tell me the truth. I promise I shall *try* to understand." He sat again and ran his hands through his hair. "Am I *truly* so horrid to you? *Truly un bête du mort?*"

The queen wrung her hands while avoiding his eyes. "I know that the child Kieran fares well to this day." She patted his arm. "It is because of *you* that she lives, Andrian."

Prince Andrian shut his eyes. "It is." He gnawed on his tongue. "It is *because* of me that she was threatened in the first place. If it were not for my stupidity, she would be safe still and she would not be . . ." He stopped as his eyes began to burn. He placed his hands over his face and took a deep jagged breath. "She would not be so *terrible* to look upon."

Queen Mireille sighed. She had heard that the child had endured disfigurement, and she had heard it from the very physician who treated Kieran when she arrived at the castle. Whatever her appearance, Prince Andrian had called her a delightful child and she had become a friend to him more or less. They corresponded through letters, and he always smiled when he found he had received another note. The queen did not believe that anyone's outward appearance represented his or her soul, especially since her only son assumed the form of a fallen angel.

"My dear Andrian, you *did* all you could to assist the girl, and you are *quite* generous to the sisters who took her in." She stroked her son. "Do not dwell on what can *never* be changed. *Please.*"

"Aye, Mother."

"That wisdom should be applied to Farida. If you loved her as you say you did, honor her. Do all good in her name. I see your pain even through that little grin." She tickled his chin. "I beg you to weep for her. The pain will subside when you shed tears of sorrow."

Prince Andrian protested, "I must be terribly frail if I feel like weeping every moment of the day."

Queen Mireille smoothed his hair. "Andrian, cherish her love in your memory. Embrace her time with you and be prepared to mourn for a while. Be understanding of your emotions. Let yourself feel sorrow. If you do not, if you resist the tears, you shall end up worse than when you buried her. Beware of that, my son."

He nodded.

The queen sighed. "Why not rest tonight, and tomorrow decide on what needs are *most* important for Sabrina. Remember, she *needs* a mother."

The prince stood. "Aye. *Ce soir* I *shall* rest, and perhaps tomorrow I will be in a fit state to make amends *and* care for my child."

Queen Mireille beckoned for her son to bend over toward her. She kissed his cheek and smiled. "I shall see you tomorrow."

He smiled and nodded. "Aye." As the prince left his mother sitting in her comfortable seat, he shut her door.

Walking toward his own room, Prince Andrian thought about how many mistakes he had made recently. Why did he feel the need to perpetuate more problems by causing his daughter unnecessary heartache? He passed a guard on his right, who genuflected. He opened the door to his chambers and sighed. The maiden did not come to him as he had insisted. He sighed and flopped onto his bed, face down. "Rejected again," he muttered to himself.

Meanwhile, Sabrina wandered the castle alone. The maiden who the prince had ordered to watch her had fallen asleep, and Sabrina had taken that opportunity to sneak away to explore. Her new home interested Sabrina. She had only ever lived in a small shack and slept on the floor, and furthermore had only ever eaten stale bread and meat if she were lucky. She had only ever known terrible physical discomfort until she met her father. Despite all of her former misfortune, she had also only ever known love and kindness. Because Prince Andrian was her father, he had a nice big home, a huge bed from which to throw pillows and leap, and she had lots of good food to eat if she wanted. Because Prince Andrian was her father, she now knew of sorrow and fear. She missed her mama and her brothers. Her sister she never knew. She had gone away before she was born, and she only ever heard Mama cry about her little girl swallowed by the night. She had not been able to understand how someone could disappear and never come home until she met her father.

Wandering up and down the corridors unguarded and undisturbed, Sabrina, tiny in body, went unnoticed for nearly two hours. Prince Andrian had no idea that his only child shuffled about in the dark without protection, and thought nothing of her safety.

Up a staircase that giants built, Sabrina crawled. The stairs seemed too big to climb one foot over the other, so she wormed up. When finally she reached the summit, she threw her hands in the air in triumph. A thick door appeared to her left and it lay ajar. Her eyebrow rose in curiosity and she snuck toward it. The dark wooden door felt heavy even for a grown man, but Sabrina managed to slip through to the shadows within.

Along the walls in the circular room, the prince had stacked various books and charts. Small dots spread about on massive maps littered the three tables shoved before the only window in the chamber.

Upon closer inspection, Sabrina giggled at the ink spots. She thought they made funny pictures, and she found a feathery pen and proceeded to connect the dots together. When she tired of the odd maps, Sabrina dropped the quill and the jar of ink on the floor, which shattered and stained the red carpeting.

Sabrina had never seen so many odd things before. A big golden thing had a tube with glass on the ends and a stand that looked like a horse. She looked through it and saw a bright light. With a gasp, she jumped backward and fell upon a pile of books, and with another gasp she stood back on her feet and hid beneath one of the tables.

While under the table, she spied more books, each with funny drawings inside. After she opened each of the books, she laughed at each page. One page in the thickest book showed two naked people in a garden: a man and a woman and a snake. Sabrina laughed at that picture hardest of all. She liked that large book. She wished she could carry it back to her bedroom, but she could not pick it up, so she ripped out her favorite pages and shoved them in her dress. She crawled out from under the table with a box that she found under more books.

She tried to open the box, but it stuck when she scratched at it. She felt the outside but she could find no way to force it open. The box felt light enough for her to take back to bed, so she placed it where she would not forget it.

A roar echoed from down below in the castle; instinctively, Sabrina crouched low and covered her mouth. She recognized the voice as her father's, and she wondered if he was mad with her. She knew good girls never ran away, but her papa seemed so busy that she never saw him. Another howl sounded, and Sabrina felt torn between finding more things in the room and going to see her papa. He sounded really mad, so she decided to stay hidden.

"Calm down, Son! She is a four-year-old child! She cannot have gone very far!" King Arundel cried to the distressed prince.

The prince had never truly considered murdering a woman with his bare hands before that moment. "You fell *asleep* while *watching* my . . . my . . . *my baby?*" Andrian the Ruthless shrieked when the maiden nodded apologetically. "*So foolish!*" He drew his sword and pointed it at the woman, who dropped to her knees.

"Andrian, hold your sword to you. *This* is not the time to administer a judgment. We *must* find your daughter." King Arundel stood in his robe, his hair a briar patch of tangles. He had braided and tied his long white beard, but even that looked ridiculous.

Through all the commotion, Prince Andrian just wanted to blame the maiden for all of his wretched choices. The maiden had no fault in Sabrina's behavior; she snuck about as her father had done in his youth. He knew he should not blame her for his own neglect as well. He should have taken her to bed with him, only then could he know her whereabouts. At that moment he *knew* the girl must have a mother.

Prince Andrian's bestial outburst had woken Queen Mireille from her slumber, and she too emerged from her boudoir half clothed and half awake. "What is going on?" she yawned.

"It appears as if our son has misplaced his daughter," King Arundel sighed.

"I did not *misplace* her, *cette salope abandoned* her!" The veins on the prince's neck bulged out.

The maiden lay prostrate before the prince and repeatedly begged his forgiveness. At the maiden's pleas, the prince paced back and forth and shook his head.

"*Shut her up before I shut her up for good!*" Andrian the Ruthless stopped and stomped his foot.

Queen Mireille hushed the maiden and picked her up off the floor.

King Arundel placed his hand on his son's shoulder. "You must go and look for Sabrina. If you wish, I shall send some men to search as well."

The prince yanked himself away from the king and sheathed his sword. "This is my fault. I should never have trusted *anyone* with my baby but *me*." He pointed to the maiden. "If as much as a *scratch* has happened itself upon the fair child, you will happen yourself *on the block before my sword.*" The prince punched a hole in the mortared wall beside him. "You have my *word* that shall be." The maiden began to weep, and Andrian the Ruthless sneered at her. "I despise cowards, be they men *or* women."

King Arundel watched his son stalk off to find his baby and shook his head. The queen embraced the maiden, who wept anew. "He'll put me to death. I *know* it. I di'nt mean to sleep. I'm *sorry.*"

King Arundel placed his firm hand on the maiden's head. "I pardon you from that fate. My son *cannot* harm you."

The maiden kissed the king's hand. *"Bless yeh . . . bless yeh, sire."*

Since the shrieking had stopped, Sabrina thought that whatever had made her papa mad had gone away. Therefore, she continued to poke at the different things within the room. She smashed several objects and felt guilty, so she piled books and papers over the mess. She thought that her father would never notice the broken things, and smiled. She sat on the floor, pulled several maps in front of her, and began to doodle on them with a new feather pen and pot of ink.

"SABRINA? WHERE ARE YOU? ANSWER ME!" the prince called for his child, but he had walked in the wrong direction from her hiding spot and his voice did not reach her.

Following their lord, several guards called out in vain to the princess as well. At nearly two in the morning, Prince Andrian had become frantic and weary. Fighting back tears of panic, he struck anything in his path to help keep from weeping.

"Damn that *putain . . . Damn her . . .,*" Andrian the Ruthless muttered as he thought about the reckless babysitter.

Sabrina finally felt tired, and as she laid her head on the floor, she fell asleep. She had slept in the dirt at home and the castle floor seemed good as her bed for the night. She dreamt of her mother, who wept for her child. She saw her father wearing white in her dream, in the middle of a bunch of people. Many people threw things, shouted and hollered, but he did not say anything. She called for him, but he did not see her. A large man picked her up and carried her away from Papa, who could not hold her; his hands had ropes around them. He wept, "Sabrina . . . Sabrina . . ."

"Sabrina?"

She woke up with a jump, and Prince Andrian crouched above her.

"Papa!" Sabrina cried and sat up.

"I have *found* your hiding spot." Andrian picked his daughter up to cradle her in his arms. He kissed her many times, and Sabrina felt warm and safe.

"Papa." She leaned her head on his chest.

The prince looked around the room, in disarray, and laughed. Relieved that he found his princess safe, Andrian the Ruthless forgot his anger at the incapable maiden and kissed his child again. "What were you doing in here?"

Sabrina cackled and put her fingers in her mouth while glancing about the room.

Andrian saw her wily look and held her closer. "The apple never falls far from the tree, I see."

Sabrina nestled into her father's arms, but then remembered the box she had placed to the side. "*Mine.*" She reached out toward the table, and Andrian looked toward her gaze.

"*Where* did you find that?"

Sabrina pointed to the table and smiled. "Mine."

Andrian shook his head. "I am sorry, my love, you cannot have that."

She pouted and leaned her face into the prince's neck.

With one arm Andrian held his girl, and with the other he picked up the box. "I have been looking for this for *years.*"

Andrian and his daughter headed back to his room to go to bed with his child in tow. Sabrina snuggled into his coverlets. Andrian tucked his child in, flopped beside her, and passed out.

Chapter Fourteen

Winchester, a city to the south of Eddington, had great wealth and a large cathedral filled with riches for the man most willing to take on the burden of guilt. The prince had never felt guilty about gaining money—at least, he had not felt remorse until recently. For the past seven months since he spoke to his mother, Andrian thought he might go mad for he had begun to regret his actions on many occasions. Queen Mireille had somehow instilled in him a conscience, and it sat on his shoulder a reliable nuisance.

His jealousy of Julian had escalated and he felt rancorous to extreme levels every time he heard his name uttered. During Advent, Julian had finally convinced his brother to join him and the king for mass. Before the sacrament of communion, the king had pointed out that Julian always took communion. Prince Andrian felt shame, because unlike this instance he usually avoided reconciliation. When the prince had gone to receive the sacrament, he looked at his father, spit the host on the floor, and crushed it with his boot. In fear of the wrath of God, the parish forced his immediate removal from the mass, and Pope Gregory IX had signed the prince's excommunication immediately after receiving the petition from King Arundel. Prince Andrian regretted his mistake later for he had oftentimes enjoyed sitting in church. After that incident, all churchgoers shunned him. Worse still, the church threatened him that he could not beg for alms if ever he needed them.

Prince Andrian had found his impulses ranged far from his usual control, and on numerous occasions he had not only crossed the boundary of respect for his father, the king, but he had also taken to yelling and cursing at the clergy at the parish church he had formerly attended. On each occasion, King Arundel chastised and beat him, but he laughed at the punishment at the time. Afterward, he felt remorse cast over himself. He felt worse still, because he could no longer attend reconciliation and it might have helped relieve his anger.

Nobles tittered that the prince had been possessed by the devil and his imps, and therefore he ought to be given an exorcism. They convinced the parish priest of it, but Rome specifically denied the request. Apparently, Andrian Gilbert, Crown Prince of Briton, Duke of Langeais, Lord of the Isle of Wight, and Viscount of someplace Andrian had never heard of, was merely "Practicing his role as actor in a church play where the part of the devil needed rehearsing." To such a retort, the prince cackled, his father glared.

Of all of the trespasses Andrian the Ruthless had committed, he felt the guiltiest over his own claim to his daughter. On the one hand he felt foolish for wishing that he had not mistreated her mother, but on the other hand he thought he had done his child a favor by taking her home with him whether Selma had wished it or not.

Prince Andrian had in past grinned in pleasure with thoughts about how *everyone* feared him; now for most of these last few weeks the thought of hatred from *all* embittered him. He longed for a friend who did not fear him so, a man to drink with and laugh about the inanities of life. Likewise, he wanted a woman to love him for his being and not for anything else. The woman would enjoy his company above all else. She would find his personality engaging, they would share the same desires, and they would love each other as if the two were one body, mind, and soul. Love ends in tragedy, he had reminded himself for so long, and he had resisted love with all of his might for several years. But recently the urge to settle down had flared, and he found himself becoming enraged at his inability to show tenderness toward potential mates. He found himself terrified to find a woman who adored him only to lose her as he had Farida.

He felt troubled inwardly, depressed, and morose. Outwardly, however, he grew more violent, more drunken, and more passionate. To help him forget his sorry state of being, the miserable prince drank burning ale so powerful that other men would pass out from its potency. The prince would consume it like water and it made him ill. He had monstrous headaches every morning, and another tankard of the liquid amusement seemed the only cure to the ills he endured. He could do nothing to avoid the fact he needed to abuse the ale to get through the day. He became mercurial if he did not drink enough, though he honestly felt it did not help his demeanor to ingest the poison.

Prince Andrian found himself disregarding reality more so as his moodiness reached its summit. As a result of his illness, the prince had become amnesic. Important events he might recall with no trouble slipped his mind only an hour or two after transpiring.

One such nebulous day as he swung through his madness, he rampaged throughout his *own* encampment. Anybody in his line of attack, he killed. His soldiers had thought he was trying to make a point with them; he wanted to inspire fear, and it worked. But the prince had just imbibed too much of his fiery ale. Pacing to and fro through the camp with threats, he challenged any and every man to take a stab at him. Anyone who acknowledged his intimidation, he destroyed with his sword. He had awoken the next day next to two women, his discarded clothes lay drenched in blood. Memories of that day he had little of, and only knew what his trusted knight, Sir Idwal, had revealed to him.

Thinking on these increasing problems with raw obsession, Prince Andrian had taken to working off his pent-up energy by beating trees with his sword where none of his soldiers could watch him in his fury and no one might be injured. In the small forest near his camp, Prince Andrian withdrew his blade to demolish any tree he could find. Broken trees from the previous day had already dried. He took a deep breath and tried to concentrate on relaxing, but the more still he forced himself to be, the more hate flowed through his body. He opened his eyes, his sword vibrated before him.

With all of his rage, he roared and swiped his blade at the defenseless trees. *Chop, creak, smash!* He howled in misery and anguish. He kicked the fallen branches, picked them up, and hurled them. "I HATE THIS PLACE! I HATE MY LIFE! I HATE EVERYONE! WHY DO I GO ON? WHY . . . CAN . . . I . . . NOT . . . FEEL . . . HAPPY?" the prince wailed. He felt genuine hatred for himself, and he knew that peace could not come until he died. "WHY AM I SUCH A COWARD? I SHOULD GET IT OVER WITH! END IT ALL! STOP THIS PAIN I FEEL EVERY DAY I WAKE UP!" He hollered so much and so long that he made himself hoarse. No comfort embraced his soul. Nothing came to help pass the anguish that ate him alive. His nothingness had become *everything*.

He dropped his sword on the ground and collapsed with it. Leaning his head in his hands, he moaned, "I wish you were here . . . God, I miss you." He embraced himself and whispered, "Help me, I am frightened." His voice trailed off. When he felt no comforting touch, he bounded to his feet and roared as he butted his head against a tree several times in a row. He ceased his head battering and leaned on the bark for a while and then embraced the trunk. "Why did you die? Why?" He coughed and sputtered blood from his mouth.

Walking back toward the encampment, the prince wanted to weep but he felt furious at that thought. If he wept, that meant he *was* a pathetic man. Contrary to his mother's beliefs, he did not believe weeping was an acceptable alternative to his problems. Bottling his rage contaminated his body and he became very ill. Queasiness washed through his corporal being, and he staggered as he entered the royal tent.

He collapsed on his cot, nearly fainting with unbearable nausea. His vision blurred as a massive pain exploded in his skull. Weakly he reached for his jug of mead by his bed and consumed most of it in a few breaths. His hands shook so violently that he could not place the jug back on the stone beside him, and it slipped from his hand and fell on the ground with a loud *smash*. He placed his hands over his light-sensitive eyes, which he *knew* had gouged themselves out of his head. He groaned with each throb in his forehead. He closed his eyes and felt as if he could see flashing even when he obstructed his vision. A buzzing rang through his ears as if he had shoved his head in water and inhaled. He turned over on his side and passed out.

Prince Andrian opened his eyes to darkness. He ripped himself from his position. A residual shape looking like his left side marked the coverlets in sweat. As he stood up, his body swirled around though he stood still. He sat down again. For at least an hour, he tried to muster enough courage to face his men after his nonexistence. He must live again, he decided as he rose to his feet, stumbled over to the cloth door, and peeked outside.

The soldiers seemed unaffected at his extended oblivion; in fact, they behaved themselves and did not run amok. He put his sword on his belt, threw the door open, and swaggered over to the nearest soldier. "You, what day is it today?" He grasped the soldier's shoulder and squeezed. The soldier could tell that his prince leaned his weight on him to disguise his weakness with aggression.

"It's Tuesday, Sire," the soldier answered.

"Tuesday," Prince Andrian muttered. He had last remembered Thursday evening. He had been ill for six days! His foolishness had left his men alone without command. "Aye, of course . . . Tuesday. *I* knew that." He scanned the camp. "Who is in charge here?"

"Why, *you* are, Sire." The soldier frowned.

Prince Andrian rolled his eyes at the man. "*Je ne suis pas stupide.* I have been ill for near on a week. *How* could I have been in charge?"

"I just say what I am told, Sire," the soldier whispered.

Prince Andrian glanced around with a scowl. *Who had I left in charge?* He collapsed by the soldier's fire. "Will you fetch me a drink and a blanket?" the prince purred to him, an unusual feat for the roaring lion.

"Yes, my liege." The soldier left to bring his lord some comforts.

"I hate being so tired." The prince muttered angry comments to himself as he waited for the soldier to return to him. He rubbed his eyes, swollen from sleep. He looked to have lost a fistfight with a giant. The prince's mouth stuck with dried-up saliva, and no matter how he tried to lick his lips to moisten them, his tongue felt equally swollen and dry.

"Here, my prince." The soldier handed him his blanket and a fresh tankard of ale.

"*Merci.*" The prince did not look up at the soldier, who shook the gratefulness from his lord's voice out of his head.

"You're most welcome, Sire."

Prince Andrian took a swig of the ale and set it down. He attempted to wrap the blanket around himself, but failed. Exhausted, he gave up.

"Let me help you, Sire."

The prince let the man cover him with the blanket. "*Je répète, merci.*"

"It is only my job." The soldier shrugged.

The prince looked at the kind soldier. "It is not in your job description to be my slave; I am quite sure of that."

The soldier handed the prince his ale again. "I do it because I've sworn fealty to you, and I believe that if you feel comfort, then we'll all be comforted. I don't wish for you to be so ill."

"Nor do I," a voice boomed behind them. A man yanked the ale away from the prince, took a gulp, and threw it into the fire.

"Who do you think you are?" Andrian the Ruthless leapt to his feet, almost falling backward.

Several groups of somewhat cheerful soldiers ceased their conversations and turned around in curiosity.

"Easy, Highness. You do not want to fight me now." The cloaked man grasped the prince's collar violently and took a whiff. "Have you been drinking, Your Excellency? Father will be angry." He released the prince.

Andrian the Ruthless drew his hand-and-a-half clumsily, and though his eyes focused inefficiently, he slashed at the man. Catching the prince's arm, he twisted it, causing him to yelp and drop his sword. The man held the prince at bay by pulling his face back by the hair. "Bring this man a tub and water!" the mysterious man roared at some bystanders.

"Let me go, and I will refrain from ripping your throat out!" Prince Andrian threatened halfheartedly.

"I hardly think you may tell *me* what to do, Andrian. You are in no condition to give orders around here." The man shook the prince, who winced with a fresh headache.

Soldiers dragged a tub of water before the man, and the prince struggled. "What are you doing? Release me!" Andrian the Ruthless thrashed about, desperate to loosen the stranger's grip.

"Time to sober up, my boy." Wrenching the prince's arm, he dunked him face first into the freezing water.

"Aaaah!" Prince Andrian shrieked as the man let him up again. He spit out a mouthful of water and cursed.

"Watch your mouth, Your Majesty." The stranger slapped the prince's face hard. Several soldiers jumped where they stood in surprise at the stranger's nerve.

"How dare you strike me!" Prince Andrian clenched his teeth.

"I do not think you get my point, Milord!" The dark-cloaked man plunged Prince Andrian's face into the tub again, but that time he held him longer.

Andrian the Ruthless writhed, and the man held him longer still. The man pulled the prince up, his eyes blackened with furious mortification.

"*Qui étés-vous?* Whoever you are, you will curse this day. Never meddle with me. I am too much of a man for you when I get angry," Prince Andrian vaunted.

"Cool off!" The man shoved him into the water again.

The prince squirmed and bubbles filled the tub. He came to the surface and wretched. Water leaked out of his mouth; his eyes rolled back into his head.

"Do you think he has had enough?" The man laughed at the enervated prince. They all shook their heads. "No? Once more then!" The stranger picked up Andrian the Ruthless and dumped him into the tub.

He yelped with shock. Coughing, he tried to escape, but the man shoved him into the water with his hands on his shoulders. As he resurfaced, he gargled, "Stop! Desist! Quit your hassling!" The prince sat up in the water and frantically tried to catch his breath.

The man roared at him, "Do you yield, Your Highness?"

"In your dreams!" He gagged on the water in his lungs.

"You do not know when the game has been won, do you? I always knew that was a weakness of yours, Andrian!"

The man went to dunk him again, but the prince whined, *"J'abandonne."*

"What is this? I cannot hear you. If you do not speak up, I cannot tell if you want to be dunked again!" The man cackled like an overfed crow.

"J'abandonne." The prince's lip quivered as he glanced around at the staring soldiers.

"So we can hear you, whelp!" He grabbed the prince and forced him under.

As the Andrian the Ruthless brought his head above the surface, he spat the last of the water in his mouth. "J'ABANDONNE!" His voice could be heard throughout the whole camp. He shivered in the water though he felt more ashamed than cold.

"That is more like it."

The stranger pulled Andrian the Ruthless out of the tub, and he fell on his hands and knees, coughing and spitting. His nose oozed from the water in his sinuses, and he gagged on it. Vomit burned his throat but he swallowed it, to his own disgust. The man kicked him in the backside, and he landed face first into the mud before him. He lay there, unsure of what to do in his predicament. Should he stand and face his attacker, or should he wallow in the filth with hopes that no one might point and laugh? If not bathed in mud, everyone would have seen that the prince glowed redder than when his father had beaten him before his servants. He spit sludge from his open mouth and groaned.

"Come on, *you.*" The strange man grabbed the prince by the tunic and hauled him to his feet. He forced him to walk before him with his sword drawn in caution, and when the prince stumbled, he kicked his back to keep him moving.

Andrian the Ruthless scowled at the men jeering as he marched by. "Just you wait, *I know your faces.*" He pointed his jeweled finger at each of them.

"That is no way to speak to *anyone!*" The stranger smacked the back of the prince's head with his gauntlet. "You need to learn manners, boy! Apologize to your comrades in arms!"

Though the prince felt a searing pain in his scalp, he roared, "I will never do such a thing! They are my *servants!*" He booted mud in their general direction.

"You will be judged, Andrian, by the way you treat your vassals! Now apologize and we can get back to the matter at hand." The man pulled the prince's hair, and he shrieked from the open wound and fell to his knees. "To be humble is a great asset, Boy!"

"*Pardonnez-moi,*" the prince said with his head bowed.

"We are learning! That is *fantastic!* You are not such an old dog, so you might learn new tricks." The stranger jerked the prince to his feet. "Now, *move!*"

Andrian the Ruthless, beaten along by the strange man in the hooded cloak, wanted to turn and destroy his captor, but he thought better of it. "You are making a *fool* out of me," he murmured to him from the side of his mouth.

"You have made *yourself* the fool, young Andrian. Now keep marching. You shall enter my tent and sit down to *listen* to me." The man propelled him into a large tent, and several of the prince's own knights followed.

"What are *they* doing here?" he croaked as he collapsed into a chair.

"They wish to help you as I do."

"Come off it." The prince stood up, but his knees buckled. He groaned on the hard ground. "Who are you to tell me what to do?"

The hooded stranger pulled off his disguise, and the prince covered his face. "Your elder brother tells you what to do." The man picked Prince Andrian up by the arm and plunked him in the chair again.

"Why are you here, Julian?" the prince complained.

"*Father* sent me." He eyed his younger brother.

"For what purpose did he send you?"

"*To remove you from power.*"

"*Quoi?*" Prince Andrian wrung his hands and grimaced.

"Since you did not quit abusing your rights as the heir apparent, you *will* be forced to hand over the crown to *me.*" Andrian's brother folded his arms and glared at him.

"Why? I have only brought Father riches and land and servants." The prince knew why Julian threatened him, but he thought if he gave some sort of justification for his behavior he might earn another chance.

"You have given him more than that. You have brought shame to your house and all who think of you are chilled at your name. They call you Andrian the Ruthless. I do not expect you know *why* that is, do you?" Andrian's brother pulled a chair next to him.

"It is because I am the fiercest man that *ever* lived," he bragged while he twisted his fingers together and gazed at the floor.

"No, because you are unfair . . . and it rhymes with toothless, which is what *you* will be if I catch you committing atrocities again. I will *personally* be the one who ties you up and gives you the lashing of your life." Julian leaned toward his brother.

"You would not *dare!*"

"Would I not? I just bested you in front of your armies. You have forgotten what Father wanted you to do for him. You fail him as we speak, yet you act as though it is not your fault. Father wants you to step down. He cannot defend your behavior to our people any longer."

Andrian shook his head. "Father promised me another chance. He *promised.*"

The angry older brother pulled a letter from his belt and slapped it into the hand of Prince Andrian. The prince opened it, and as he read he scowled and ripped it up into the tiniest shreds possible. He threw them casually, and the lackluster confetti fluttered to the dirt. Prince Andrian bit his lip, and his knights grimaced with condescension.

"Do you believe me *now*, Andrian?"

"Aye." The prince glowered at Julian.

"These men here are *loyal* to you, and they wish to keep your toes in line. They *will* report to me if you begin to stray too far from righteousness for your own good." He gave his younger brother a smile. "I *do not* wish to have your crown, Andrian, if that is what you are thinking. It is your right by birth. But I *will* gladly accept it if you *continue* to harm innocent people for amusement. I cannot stand back and watch them perish under the boot of a tyrant. I hope you understand the seriousness of your errors." He placed his hand on his brother's shoulder.

The prince pulled away. "I will *give* you my crown if you believe yourself a better man than me." Prince Andrian clenched his jaw.

"What would you do that for? I am no better a man than you." Lord Julian's voice softened, but the prince did not hear it.

"Making a *fool* of me before my army was a big mistake, Brother. A very *serious* mistake." Andrian the Ruthless clamped his shaking fists together. "All my life I have stood in your shadow with my head lowered in shame. Father made me into a worthless creature because I am not the man you are." He grimaced. "We shall see who has power now, you or I."

"What are you, *mad?*"

Prince Andrian's eyes had flashed a demonic black. "Why do you not press your luck? I will send my armies after you and the king himself. He will not think me so weak then." Prince Andrian's nails had dug into the palms of his hands and blood began to stain his fingertips. His mouth twitched.

His words took a moment to sink in, but when their severity penetrated Julian's mind, his jaw dropped. "You are talking *treason*, Brother."

"*Et alors?* So I am." Prince Andrian wiped the fresh blood on his tunic.

"With regret, I must inform the king of your threats, and I pray you find sanity . . . because if you do not it is a terrible waste to hang a *good man* for such an impulsive tongue."

"Since when have you ever thought me a good man?"

"I never thought you to be anything else."

Andrian's eyes turned to ice. "You lie to me." He looked at the knights and each one shook his head and turned his back.

After a sad silence, Julian added, "I shall care for your daughter, for she will need a stable home to stay in while you are being tried, and . . . then if you are found guilty, well, I do not know what to say, Brother." Lord Julian's face paled the full moon, but Andrian's face caused a lunar eclipse.

Andrian the Ruthless bared his teeth. "Tell Father to watch for me. I will be at his doorstep within a fortnight." The prince stood before Julian and scowled. "My child will *never* see me hanged. I would fall upon my own sword before she watches her father publicly humiliated." He patted the weapon by his right side.

"I would hate to tell your child that her father died unnecessarily. I hope you do not resist the guard when they come to arrest you for high treason to the crown. That would not fare well in your trial. God have mercy on you, my brother." He turned around, shaking his head.

"Nay, I hope your God shows *you* mercy for sending *ton frère*, your *only* brother, to his death." Prince Andrian's voice cracked and Julian paused in the doorway for a moment, his head lowered. And not knowing what else to say, he left.

The prince followed him and they parted, each with a great burden in his heart.

Prince Andrian watched his brother walking away, his face in his hands. *"Weeping?"* The prince laughed inside. "What kind of coward would be king if I died?" A bitter emotion welled within him, but repressing it, he kicked at the ground. "I have better things to do than weep like a *little girl*." Immediately he felt the necklace he wore around his neck, rubbed the bronze trinket between his fingers, and sighed. "What have I done?"

He had not thought of the little girl who had given him the necklace in so long, though he never removed her gift. As he shuffled toward his royal tent, the image of the child, Kieran, edged its way into his mind. She told him that he looked sick the last he had seen her. In truth, he had felt deathly ill. He always felt ill now. Not all the riches and power on earth could give him happiness. Farida no longer eased his suffering with her tender touch.

"I want to be free of these burdens," he sniffled, though no tears fell from his eyes. "Let death strike me now." He waited in the clearing for a bolt of lightning, but nothing happened. He raised his hands to the sky. "Send me where you will, for surely *this* is my punishment!" He used his complete lung capacity to shout, "IF THERE IS A GOD, THEN LET US END IT!"

Lord Julian heard his brother's cries of sorrow as he walked away from the camp. He wanted to return to him and give him hope. He longed to convince him that if he had made a mistake he should not die over stubborn pride. "Why can he not ask for help? Why must he deny his illness and remain in his gloom?"

Sir Idwal had come to help Julian confront his brother. He too heard the prince's wailing torment. "Julian, shall we go back and *try* to dissuade Andrian's plot?"

Lord Julian stopped walking and pondered that question. "You *know* my brother. Do you *truly* believe that he will listen to us?"

"No."

Julian frowned. "You, of course, are correct." He placed his right hand on his hip. "I wish there was a way to save him from his own stupidity without killing him."

Through the trees, Prince Andrian moaned. No one could forgive him now. Julian would insist on execution simply because he hated Andrian. The prince leaned on a moss-covered tree and sank to the ground. So many serious mistakes he had made, and this was the worst yet. Prince Andrian drew his sword and twisted it in the soil before him.

From where he sat, Prince Andrian could see the torches from his brother's cavalcade float along in a line like military fireflies. "He is leaving to inform Father of my betrayal, and I have but days to run before I am apprehended and executed." He dropped his sword and placed his head in his hands. "I am done for."

Lord Julian mounted his sorrel stallion and sat for a moment as he waited for his escort of four hardy knights. A knight dressed in black approached his lord. "Sir Garland, have you located Prince Andrian?" Lord Julian placed his helmet on his head.

Sir Garland nodded. "Yes, but he is not acting as I had assumed he would in this situation."

Lord Julian raised his eyebrow. "What is he doing, I ask you?"

"Fleeing."

"*Really.*" Lord Julian turned his head toward the encampment.

"Shall we pursue him?" Sir Garland's horse reared with excitement.

Lord Julian rolled his tongue in his mouth and then turned to his vassal. "Nay, let the coward go. The king's men will accost him soon enough."

"Sire?" Sir Garland controlled his horse.

Lord Julian smirked. "Send a brigade to follow him but do not engage. I want my brother alive and his whereabouts known to me." He waved at the man. "That is all."

"Yes, Sire." Sir Garland nodded respectfully and charged away from his lord.

Chapter Fifteen

Abandoning the trek to Winchester seemed quite wise at the moment to Prince Andrian. His brother had expected him to turn and fight, but he knew better than to stand his ground so near to home. His brother's men were tailing him, he knew that much for certain, but he allowed them to follow.

Marching toward Selsey, the prince's mind swam with guilt and betrayal. Andrian the Ruthless had led a long march before, but barring his time spent in the desert of the pharaohs, this would be the longest war campaign he had *ever* conducted. He would march as long as it would take before the armed guard gave up on him. Prince Andrian marched far southeast for a good reason: his father had sent his armed guard and they would not expect him to march to the sea. His knights on patrol had seen the blue-clad brigade from a distance, and the prince did not wish to become entrapped with them in a landlocked battle. Ships bound for Sweden waited for him and his men along the coast, if only he might arrive before the royal guard. King Arundel's personal troops had a reputation for mercilessness, and in dealing with the ruthless prince they would hardly give his safety a thought as they arrested him. They would try to block his escape by any means necessary. Because Andrian's threats had endangered the king, he would find it surprising if they did not put his mouth out of commission before his trial.

He imagined that the unit sent by his brother following close behind his own army consisted of bounty hunters dispatched for the enormous price on his head. He wondered if he would return unharmed, or if he had become their target for assassination and his head would be worth its weight in gold. After what happened to him a bit over a week ago with his own brother, Lord Julian of Sussex, Andrian believed his own men cared not whether he perished.

When the soldiers came to arrest him, he knew he would fight them to no end even if it meant his immediate execution; even if he fought his own armies, he would die standing. He would accept humiliation no longer. As he saw the approaching city, he readied himself to pillage and burn it. Nothing could stop him from fulfilling his lust for destruction. He would raise hell before his father's troops sent him there.

Andrian the Ruthless felt jittery as he entered the city, and he ordered his men to take anything, rape anyone, and burn the rest to the ground. Many of his men frowned, but the majority rubbed their hands together. He let Hell's demons loose on the city, but did not relish the sounds of screaming and hollering. Hearing the crashing of windows and the crackling of deadly flames no longer excited him.

Men ran with goods about the prince but did not join them. He shuffled his feet and pulled on his clothing as the wind carried to him every sound of terror. Remorse for the dying pierced his swollen heart with spasmodic thumps. His burning soul became hopeless. It did not matter if the soldiers took him into custody anymore. He would resist so that someone could extinguish his worthless light. Even Hell seemed better than the torment he constantly endured.

Within the flames that danced around the skeletal structures, he thought he saw Farida. Feeling discarded by life and out of his mind with grief, he walked toward the image that wanted him to hold her. As the heat became unbearable, he realized only a fiery mirage beckoned to him, and his leaden soul melted into the hardness of the ground.

Again he saw her image running through the flames as though she wished for him to chase her. For a time he did, but when she vanished, the loss felt even greater than before. He moaned her name pitifully. He cried for her to hold him, though he tried to convince himself that he had gone mad. She had died, and she could no longer love him.

The image teased him, and she motioned him to follow her. He could almost hear her sweet whispers, but as he drew nearer to her the soft voice became the hissing embers of the destroyed buildings.

He shuffled along the path of flames that his wife's fire ghost left him, though he knew very well his imagination played tricks with his heart. He muttered to the spirit, and if his soldiers heard him they assumed he was drunk.

"I wish for peace," Andrian said to the flames of Farida. He touched her arm, the smoldering beam of a house, and felt no heat on his flesh though his skin blistered.

The fire spirit led him to a cobbled road and stopped. When she disappeared, Andrian asked Farida not to leave him alone, and he added, "I am frightened." He looked around at once, realizing he had said that aloud and how foolish it must have sounded. The words somehow soothed him, so he said them again under his breath. *"Help me, I am frightened."*

At that moment, he noticed that hundreds of beautiful red flowers lined the road. He bent to pluck one from the earth and inhaled its fragrance. "Farida," he sighed and twirled it in his fingers. Then he dropped it; he must look the fool, playing with posies.

With anger, he turned around to walk back to the town and take his share of the loot, but he spun toward the road once more. He felt a nudge from behind, and thinking someone had followed him, he began to withdraw his sword from its scabbard, looked over his shoulder, and found no one there. He scratched his head, dropped his sword to sheath, and continued on his travel up the pebbly way. As he strolled further from the chaos, an old church, ornate in essence, sat amid the simplicity of the countryside.

The church building defied the bounds of earth as it reached toward the heavens. An abundance of ribs and piers shored up the immense weight of the stone roof, and among the many dozens of flying buttresses, carved statues peered knowingly down upon him. Angels with smiles and frowns abandoned their heavenly posts to settle by the stone saints, who moved when the prince did not look directly at them. Three spires pointed at the sun high above him, and he strained his eyes to see the tips, gilded as though Icarus had taken a bucket of the sun's rays and dribbled them over the pinnacles from on high before he plummeted to his death.

Prince Andrian did not think of the riches held in the sacristy, he merely wished to go inside to take a look around. He entered the front doors and closed them behind himself softly. The church was silent, and stillness settled within him as well. The air was cool, and as he stood in marvel at the woodwork above him, the sweat from the fires outside trickled down his neck and chest and then disappeared.

Glancing around the church, Prince Andrian ran his hands over the ornamented tympanums, capitals, and moldings. Each carved panel bore a scene of importance, for the detail flowed as if chipped from stone by the hand of the divine. Thousands of candles lit the long nave in the front of the church. The light danced about the walls and flickered in his eyes; human figures danced in the colored light, playing beyond his sight. The vision did not disturb him, for he felt an unearthly ease in his body, and since he entered the parish church, he did not reach for his sword again.

As the prince approached the gilded altar surrounded by a cluster of long and short white candles, he recognized the figure on the crucifix above him. It was who his father had always mentioned. It was Jesus Christ, his Savior. Prince Andrian wanted to go toward the figure and look upon the wooden Messiah. No guards stood about the art, and it confounded him that no one objected to the prince of darkness entering here, as if they did not care whether he treaded his muddy soul upon sacred ground.

Prince Andrian approached the figure and felt a heavy pressing upon his shoulders that dropped him to his knees. As he knelt, he felt a finger prod his soul. Tears began to flow that he could not stop, for the fingers extracted a great plug from his body. He did not wish to weep, but the more he fought the floodwaters, the more they poured from him. He caterwauled as out gushed the pain of his blackened soul. He covered his face and fell upon the floor, prostrate before the Christ. He moaned as he regretted his evils, and he wished that his suffering would end. His emotional river paralyzed his consciousness, and he heaved spasmodically as regret burned his tongue as he bellowed.

Coming out of hiding, a priest had heard the lamentations of the prince. He approached the young man weeping upon the floor, and soon realized the terror known as Andrian the Ruthless had come to mourn. Though this sight would seem unusual to anyone else, the priest did not find the works of God to be below saving the seemingly irredeemable. The young man clawed at the floor and pulled on his clothes as he wept.

Putting his hand upon the shoulder of the sorrowful man, he whispered, "Andrian?" The priest knelt beside the prince, who moaned every bit as bitterly as a half hour before, and patted him again. "Andrian?"

The prince grasped the hem of the priest's robe, causing his heart to palpitate in momentary terror. Through the sniffling tears, Prince Andrian whispered, "Please, is there *nothing* you can do? I feel so lost." The prince shuddered. "Please help me. I want to be loved. I want *forgiveness.*" He clutched the priest's robes and wept into them. "Please, I beg of you, help me. Call upon your God and make me whole again. I want compassion . . . I *implore* you."

The priest enveloped the prince in his arms, and Andrian cowered, a frightened child. "Andrian, *you* have called upon God and asked for his mercy. I do not need to ask for you. Your faith has saved you. I will hear your sins if it will make you serene. I shall sit here for as long as you deem it worthwhile."

"The Lord has mercy on my soul. I rejoice in the fact that a single man has compassion for such a wretched spirit! One man to hear my sorrows is more than I have had all my life."

The priest pitied the prince and helped him to his feet.

"I lost the only person on earth who loved me. This emptiness gnaws at my soul like an ill rat, and I have no comfort." He put his face in his hands and trembled as the pain continued to purge itself. "*Nobody* loves me, not even my family. They all want me to die . . . my father said *everybody* would be happier."

The priest smiled at him with love. "You are *mistaken*, Andrian. You are loved. The Lord Jesus has loved you since the day you were born, and I too love you."

The priest felt no shame in counting himself a friend of the tyrant prince. It relieved him to see the prince come before God and beg forgiveness. God could overshadow any evil that man could purge, and indeed the most cursed of men had come before him on bended knee with tears in his eyes.

Andrian had difficulty understanding the priest's words. His friends and acquaintances at present consisted of lying and murderous criminals. The priest acknowledged that good people could love him. God gave him the chance to find peace in his heart and relief from his burdens. Few called themselves the acquaintance of the foulest creature to walk the earth, let alone did anyone embrace him as a brother. The prince smiled through his still flooding tears and asked the priest his name.

"I am Father Dallan," he introduced himself. Before the prince could tell the priest his name, the priest laughed. "I *know* who *you* are."

"I am sorry; I had not introduced myself properly." Prince Andrian hung his head.

"Do not feel shame for being overwhelmed with the goodness of God. There is no reason to apologize for this." Father Dallan embraced the prince again. "Do you wish to tell me *anything* besides the fact that your troops at this very moment are burning the city in which I live to the ground?"

"I wish to tell you so much; it would take years to explain it all. I shall call off my soldiers. It is wrong to cause such chaos in this city, or any at that. I shall return to speak with you as soon as possible if you will hear me," Prince Andrian said.

"Of *course* I shall listen. Please feel welcome in this church and any you shall feel drawn to." Father Dallan patted the prince's back and smiled.

Prince Andrian did not wish to leave this sanctuary, but he must stop his troops before they caused more damage than forgivable.

With a sudden feeling of dread, he exited the church and saw the town in bedlam. Guards in royal blue questioned several men. Horror rumbled through Prince Andrian's body like an earthquake; he knew these men. As they caught sight of him, the guards pointed in his direction. A dozen or more rushed up to him and stood, swords drawn.

"Prince Andrian Gilbert de Langeais?" a large man roared.

"Aye, c'est moi." The prince lowered his head.

"You are under arrest for high treason! Do *not* resist us or we have the authority to *gut* you!" The men raised their swords to his face, ready for what the ruthless prince could unleash.

The prince shook his head and withdrew his sword from its sheath with caution, dropped his most prized possession onto the dirt, and placed his hands before himself, open palmed. Two of the largest guards grabbed his arms, twisted them behind his back, and roped his hands together. He winced at their brutality but said nothing.

The priest heard the commotion outside and rushed from the holy edifice. He witnessed the men tying the prince up and ran to see him. *"Andrian!"*

The prince looked up to see his friend by his side. *"Adieu,* Father Dallan. It was nice to have *someone* care for me. I have committed a terrible crime and am to be tried and executed." Prince Andrian's eyes leaked. "I am so sorry."

Father Dallan felt the man cower with fear that he had obviously never felt in his life. He grabbed Andrian's shoulder. "What crime have you committed that *demands* your death?"

"High treason!" A guard shoved the prince forward. "He will be dead soon, this one!" he cackled at the prince and shoved him once more.

"I will see you again before your trial, I *promise* you, Andrian." The priest grasped his shoulder once more.

"Father Dallan," Prince Andrian grumbled. "I need a favor."

"What is it you request?"

"I have a daughter in Eddington. Make sure she is all right during my trial and execution. I do not wish for her to see me die that way. I could not bear it." Prince Andrian sniffled. "Please watch over her.

She will be going with my brother, Lord Julian Robert de Langeais, to his home in Sussex." Prince Andrian's heart thumped in his chest as he imagined his little girl fearing for her father's return and hearing that he would never return home for her again. The prince looked into Father Dallan's eyes and begged, *"Pray for me."*

The priest nodded, and the guards shoved him into a wagon so that they could transport their prisoner to his death. The back of the wagon lowered with its burden. Father Dallan wiped his own eyes and he knew that he must prepare himself for coming to the prince's counsel and preparing him for his last rites.

Chapter Sixteen

Shackled and bound in the back of a wagon, Prince Andrian's journey back to Eddington became a nullifying nightmare. He knew that not only did his reputation give his jailers apprehension, it also gave them a right, in their minds, to relentlessly harass him. He tolerated the snide remarks and rude laughter, he put up with the lack of comfort and hot stuffy confinement, he also accepted that a breathless herring flipped within him, but he could not endure the restless thoughts spinning in his mind and plummeting into his already nauseated stomach.

Within his cage, Prince Andrian became a zoological spectacle. He was but an injured lion. Spectators pointed and laughed. Nobody shed a tear for him and nobody gave a damn if he were on his way to his execution. The dangerous animal glared out at the crowd and growled. His eyes swept the faces with cunning and craft. His glittering eyes had not burned in ire but in grief, and the glare but his remorse. The crowd rejoiced in the predator's capture. Cheers and hoots and screams of laughter echoed in his ears. He wished he could escape.

He wondered if Sabrina would grow up hearing stories about his wickedness and believe that he did not love her because of his cruelty. He roared with grief for his little girl would never understand that her papa did something bad, and even though he felt sorry he had to die for it.

When familiar homes whisked by his cage, the prince knew they had reached Eddington. People he had grown up seeing—like John the Baker with his cakes sitting out, Frederick the Butcher's son and his foreign meats—all hurled refuse at him as he passed by them. John used to give Andrian and his sister a taste of his latest recipes when he was very young. Frederick, not much older than he was himself, had loved Andrian's dog and often would have a cutlet waiting for him. Andrian leaned his head upon the wooden crate and sighed.

Soon after arriving, the guard would lock him in his father's donjon until the trial and perhaps until his execution as well. As they wheeled through town, the taunting of his subjects grew louder. People on all sides threw produce and rocks and anything else they could find at the imprisoned animal. The villagers laughed when his armed guard did not defend him. They simply ducked when the projectiles flew at him.

As they approached the forbidding gates of the castle Prince Andrian had called home, the tower guard drew near the prison wagon. The wagon slowed in front of the portcullis, and two brawny men in black, each lugging what looked to him like jagged halberds, began a conversation with the jailers.

Prince Andrian sighed as the darkly clad men informed the wagon drivers that King Arundel expected them and they would receive their reward that evening. One man rapped on the wagon and chuckled. The drivers asked where the prisoner should stay, and the black-cloaked men offered to take him in custody from there.

The door to the wagon opened and the prince squinted. He sat still, awaiting the guard to drag him out from the gloom. He peered through a crack in the side of the wall. Many onlookers had come to watch their tyrannical prince's humiliation. Hundreds of hagglers shoved toward him. Soldiers stood in a line, their halberds crossed together to discourage the peasants from forcing their way through to harm the beast.

Andrian glanced at all the faces he could see from his enclosure. None of the subjects' eyes filled with pity; not a man, woman, or child looked sorrowful, and all of the villeins cursed his name, pitched rocks, and spat toward him.

The two enormous black-cloaked men reached in, grabbed Prince Andrian around the upper arms, and hauled him out. The crowd cheered as their prince emerged browbeaten and exhausted with emotional excess. A few children slipped through the legs of the guards and ran up to their oppressor.

A young boy, perhaps five winters old, punched the prince in the groin and kicked him in the shins. Another boy about the same age beat the prince in the back several times with a stick after tearing at his cloak. Other children threw small rocks at him, hitting him in the face. He could not raise his arms to protect himself, for the guards had bound his hands behind his back. Blood filled his mouth, and he spat out the sticky salt as another child shoved him along as if she wanted him to hurry to his execution.

Prince Andrian turned his head as another rock sailed toward him; instead of blinding him, it bruised his jaw. He deserved it, he thought. He deserved every curse, every stone, every curse directed by the people he abused. His hair stuck to the sides of his face with sweat and oozing blood. He looked like he felt inside.

"Yer gonna die like a dog!"

"Go to Hell!"

"You killed my papa! I hope you *burn* good!"

"Hope they break yer neck in a *thousand* pieces!"

"I hate you!"

"I hate you!"

"I HATE YOU!"

At the last unbearable statement screamed at the prince, the frenzied crowd pressed on the guards. Many villeins wedged through and made to attack Prince Andrian. Fortunately, the guards surrounded him in a circle and pointed their swords out so that any more rushing at their lord would result in the offenders running *themselves* through.

The final gates to the castle opened for the prince and his company, and they edged through. His parched throat and mouth became unbearable as the prince caught one of his guards gulping water from a bladder. When the guard saw the prince licking his lips, he swallowed the water faster and wiped his mouth. Prince Andrian began to weep, and the crowd and several of the guards laughed.

A young girl watched with horror as the guards jeered at the prince, calling him a pitiful excuse for a noble, and they turned their backs when Prince Andrian apologized through his flooding tears. Faint with thirst and hunger, the prince collapsed on the ground. The girl let out a cry and rushed toward him. The guards kicked their lord and mocked his tears when he did not defend himself. All the while, Prince Andrian bled as he accepted the blows.

The girl elbowed her way into the midst of the abusive guards and threw herself on top of Prince Andrian. "Leave him alone! Don't you kick him! Give him some water!"

The guards jeered, "Look at tha'! A li'l girl comes to save Andrian the Ruthless from his self!"

The child caressed the bloody forehead of her lord and smiled at him. He gazed at her beautiful fiery hair. He recognized the little angel; she had been at the Halloran home when he lay injured.

"Worry not, Milord. You're all right. Get up and walk." She pulled on him and tried to help him to his feet.

"I *cannot* get up. I am so tired, child." He nudged her away. "Leave me."

"*Never*," she said as she snatched a bladder of water from one of the guards and opened it for the prince. She shoved it toward him. "Drink." He did gratefully, and she wiped the blood from his face with her dress. "Poor thing." When he finished, she threw the bladder to the side and tugged on him again. "Get up, Milord. Up . . . *up-up.*"

Prince Andrian found he had just enough strength to raise himself to his feet. The red-haired girl smiled at him, and he felt himself smile back as she kissed his hand, though his eyes filled with tears. "I will find you later, child."

The guards yelled at him to keep moving, and he obeyed when they beat him on the back.

He looked back at the girl who was the only person present who had shown mercy. "You will be rewarded."

The girl followed him toward the gate. "I don't need a reward."

Prince Andrian struggled to release himself. He turned to the guard. "Let me speak with the girl." They would not stop, but the prince used all his strength to dig his feet in the ground as they tore at him. "Why do you show such kindness to me?"

The girl leapt through the men and tugged on the prince's tunic.

Into his ear, she whispered, "Have hope."

His eyes widened. "What do you want?"

She turned his face to hers and looked into his eyes. She kissed his bloody cheek softly and slipped something into his belt. He looked down and then nodded.

He turned around to walk once again, and as he entered the final gate, he glanced back toward the girl, who vanished back into the crowd like a specter into fog.

The guards dragged Prince Andrian up several flights of stairs leading to his father's hall. Each step toward his doom felt agonizing yet strangely humbling. As he fell into the presence of King Arundel, he hit the floor with a hollow clang. Prince Andrian looked up at his father with miserable degradation, and the king looked down upon him with offended disappointment. The prince wanted to say something to his father, but as he opened his mouth the word "silence" echoed like a thunderclap. He bowed his head in resignation.

"My son, you have been accused of speaking against not only your father, but also against the crown that you swore fealty to. There are many witnesses to attest to the allegation of high treason, and *several* are present within this very chamber."

Prince Andrian nodded his head, not daring to look up at his father again.

"You have *also* been accused of numerous atrocities, including rape, murder, heresy, and pillaging towns under your own banner. *What* do you offer in your own defense against these very *serious* claims?" King Arundel sneered at his son, who glanced up at him with scarlet eyes.

Prince Andrian muttered, "I *have* no defense."

King Arundel barked at his son, "So you *admit* your guilt?"

"*I do.*" Prince Andrian began to weep silently.

King Arundel paused for a moment at his son's blatant admission. "You have not *denied* these charges, nor come to your *own* defense; therefore, I have *no* choice but to offer my *verdict.*"

Prince Andrian's guard untied his bonds and brought shackles instead of the feeble rope. They placed the tight-fitting cuffs on his wrists, and the prince cried out in pain. Prince Andrian's eyes pleaded with his father, who hesitated with his verdict.

He knew he must decide, so with regret the king looked directly at his son and whispered, *"Death by beheading."*

Prince Andrian did not say a word but wept at his father's callous glare. He tried to speak, but his voice failed him.

Several knights approached the king, and one in blue whispered into his ear. For what seemed like an eternity, King Arundel nodded to the knight and turned back toward his son. "However, I *will* grant you a stay of execution so you might find adequate counsel. Putting a man to death *immediately* if there are no witnesses in his defense is unfair, as it had just been pointed out to me, even though in this case I would most certainly wish to relinquish any of your rights because there are many hundreds of testimonies *against* you and there is not one man *for* you."

Prince Andrian sighed as the knight in blue, Sir Idwal, gave him one meaningful nod of his head.

"You have but *one* fortnight." The king turned his back away from his son, and the guards hauled the silent prince away to the donjon.

*   *   *

Lord Julian of Sussex had heard the news that the royal guard had captured his brother. Even though he believed that the guard could apprehend the crown prince, the fact that he came without so much as a clash of steel upon steel disturbed him. Lord Julian had heard information that Prince Andrian had shed tears before a crowd of hundreds of witnesses while apologizing for his behavior. The ruthless prince of hell never begged for compassion from anyone, and the news stirred Julian's heart.

Lord Julian remembered his word to his younger brother, and the very day he heard of the capture he left to care for Princess Sabrina. He told his wife, Margrethe, and their two young children that he would bring Andrian's baby home for care during the trial, with the stipulation that no one tell her why her father remained absent. The responsibility of telling Sabrina in the future that King Arundel executed her father for treason burdened his heart. He did not look forward to taking her away from her grandparents either.

*　　*　　*

Her grandparents fussed over Sabrina so much lately, and it bothered her. Where had her papa gone? Why did the servants pat her head and say things like, *poor child, darling little girl, daughter of a monster,* and *who will care for her when he's gone?* All of the commotion about the castle frightened her, and her papa had not given her kisses in forever. She wanted her mother still, but the feeling that she wanted her papa grew desperate within her.

In the midst of the disorder, many strange people that Sabrina had never met before called attention to themselves. One such person was a tall man with short hair and a kind voice that reminded her of her papa in a strange way. He called himself Julian and he wanted to take her to another place away from Papa for a long time. She did not like that thought at all, and every time the Julian person wanted to pick her up and hold her she screamed for her papa to come back, and escaped from him. Sabrina had discovered the easiest way to resist the man was to hide from him.

*　　*　　*

Lord Julian had stayed in his father's home for only two days, but he sensed the electricity in the air. He heard the murmurs behind closed doors, saw the looks upon the faces of the servants, both sad and glad, and he watched the queen fall further into despair and illness. He did not visit his brother in the donjon for fear he would not forgive him for being the rat and also for fear that his brother might ask him to plead on his behalf.

On the mark of the first week of Andrian's fortnight postponement of conviction, Julian had noticed a priest visiting the king and offering his services for his son. Lord Julian did not know that Prince Andrian had asked for a religious man as counsel and it vexed him. Prince Andrian had been accused of heresy, so why would he seek a man so devoted to orthodox beliefs as his one and only witness?

Lord Julian decided he would ask the priest about his devotion to his accused brother. When King Arundel granted the priest permission to not only give Prince Andrian his counsel but his comfort as well, Julian took that opportunity to confront the man of God about his intentions.

Someone had told Father Dallan the way to the donjon, but he found himself losing his way in the large establishment. "Now, if I remember *correctly*," he said aloud, "Andrian is being held *that* way." He sighed as he turned in circles. "Oh my, now I *truly* am lost."

Lord Julian came up behind the priest. "I was wondering if you could help me, Father."

Father Dallan clasped his hand over his heart. "You gave me a fright, Milord." He turned around. "I am afraid I can't even help *myself*. I am terribly lost, and ashamed to say I can't even find my friend in captivity."

Lord Julian ushered the priest with his hands. "Follow me, Father."

"Thank you, Sir." Father Dallan followed the man toward the donjon and marveled at the impressive home of the king.

"I am sorry, but I have not introduced myself. I am Lord Julian Robert de Langeais, the *brother* of Prince Andrian." Lord Julian held out his hand, and the priest took it.

"I am simply Father Dallan. I have no use for long-winded titles." He laughed at Lord Julian's strange face and continued, "I have come to give your brother my counsel and a gift."

Lord Julian nearly tripped on his own feet as they ascended the stairs. "A *gift*, you say? Well, as long as it is not a means for his *escape*, I am sure it is perfectly acceptable for him to receive within the walls of his cell."

Father Dallan laughed. "It is a means of escape *figuratively* speaking, though I daresay *not* a threat to his punishment."

"What is it then?"

They had arrived at the cell, and Prince Andrian looked up to see his brother and the priest before him. Father Dallan handed the prince a package, and he clutched it to his chest as he thanked the priest. As he opened it, Father Dallan answered Julian's question, "It is the *Word of God*."

Julian scratched his head; his younger brother seemed different from when they last argued.

Father Dallan asked the prince how he felt, and Andrian cradled the book and said, *"Bien, merci."* Julian became more confused, and Andrian saw his brother's look. "How is *ma jonquille?*"

Julian stared at his brother, unshaven, unclean, and unhappy. "Hmm? What did you say, Andrian?"

"I asked if Sabrina was doing well. I miss my baby daffodil." Prince Andrian frowned.

Julian sighed. "Sabrina is giving me trouble. She will not come to me—nay, she *refuses* to. She wants her papa to sleep with her at night, but I cannot tell her *why* he cannot."

Prince Andrian jumped up. "Bring her to me. Bring her to me, *please.*" He placed the book on his makeshift bed and stood before his brother, his hands gripping the bars of his cell. "I *need* my child. Please *let* me visit with her. I want to kiss her and tell her that I love her."

Lord Julian glanced over at Father Dallan, who made no hint of opinion whatsoever. "My brother, you *know* that it is not wise to bring Sabrina into the light this way. She is too *young.*"

"Let me say *goodbye* then. Allow her to receive my blessing." Prince Andrian pressed his face against the bars as his brother's face remained stoical. "Let me *see* her! If I die without a farewell . . . if it comes to *that* . . . oh, *what* do I do?" No sympathy ebbed in his brother's eyes. He shook the bars. "Do not *deny* me my child! I *beg* you, have mercy on me! Have *mercy!*" He sank to the floor in tears and leaned his head on the bars. *"Mon Dieu,* what *have* I done to her? *What have I done?*" He looked up at his brother. *"Please."* And then he wiped his eyes. "Give us *both* mercy."

Lord Julian looked at Father Dallan, who watched the prince's flood of emotions over his daughter. "Bring him his child. If he longs for her so and is denied, it may make this punishment worse than it should be."

Lord Julian scoffed, "The punishment is for treason and it *should* be terrible."

Father Dallan shook his head at Lord Julian. "I meant the punishment for *you.*"

Lord Julian stared at the priest and then at Andrian, who leaned his face in his hands, his back against the cot. "The prince *is* guilty of his crimes and therefore is to be *punished.* I daresay that execution *would* be appropriate, though I do not think it is up to *me.*"

"You would have your own *brother* put to death over his crimes? Are you sure he will *not* be cleared of his guilt?"

"Quite sure, Father. I was *present* when he threatened the king. I am aware of *many* of his escapades with women, the burning of *innocents,*

and his *faithless* life." Lord Julian looked over at Prince Andrian, who glanced up at him with a grimace. "His daughter Sabrina, for instance, is the product of *uncontrollable* lust. He slept with the wife of the king's vassal. Tell me *that* problem is not a terrible crime in itself. James Halloran deserves compensation in the *least*."

"*You are a bastard as well,*" Prince Andrian muttered.

Lord Julian's eyes fell upon his younger brother. "How *dare* you bring that fact into this conversation."

Prince Andrian stood to his feet and leaned on the bars of his cell. "Dare not mention my daughter in such a tone again." He sighed. "You do not know my life, and how could you? I have been alone to fend for my well-being since I was young." He stared into his brother's eyes. "I was abandoned, a child soldier in a sea of dust and blood."

Lord Julian gnawed on his tongue.

"You would have given up *long* before I did."

"That is just a rationalization to commit inexcusable crimes."

Prince Andrian growled, "I do not *pretend* to be innocent. I am merely pointing out that I have suffered enough without your opinions. You know that it is *Sabrina* who is the heir apparent."

Lord Julian sneered, "It is *unfair* that you should place that *curse* upon her."

"What curse would that be *exactly*? The one where she is given *her* rights or takes *yours*?" Prince Andrian glared at his brother, who remained silent.

Father Dallan watched Lord Julian's face contort. "You do know if the king *denounces* his rightful heir and gives *you* the crown the reason you dislike Sabrina would be irrelevant."

Lord Julian frowned.

Prince Andrian sighed. "Why *do* you dislike Sabrina so much? *Is* it jealousy? Do you wish for the crown as much as I did, yet have *falsely* displayed righteousness in order to gain *favor*?" He raised his eyebrow at Lord Julian.

Lord Julian shook his head. "I do not wish for *her* right to be disputed as mine was so *often*." He placed his hand through the bars and onto his brother's shoulder. "And I wish for her *father* to crown her, not her *uncle*."

Prince Andrian scoffed, "If you wish for me to live to see my daughter a queen, then *why* did you judge me so harshly and *now* avoid defending me to our father?"

Lord Julian looked down. "I *know* you too well, Andrian. You are *crafty*, and will turn the tables on me in the trial. You will find *some* way to shift the blame and escape the consequences of your actions." He shook his head. "I cannot let you weasel away from justice to any *further* extent. It is in God's hands now." At Prince Andrian's teary-eyed look, Julian added, "I wish it were *not* so, but you will *surely* be put to death. I cannot see *how* you will be found innocent now, save a miracle. I am sorry, my brother. I *truly* am."

Prince Andrian smiled. "Wait a minute. You say if I am *found* innocent?"

Lord Julian shrugged. "My mistake. There is no *if*—you shall be convicted."

The prince's mind churned like the rapids in the Thames. "Julian, *will* you ask Father if he would be willing to revert to the practice of trial by ordeal?"

Lord Julian's mouth dropped. "That has not been the way of justice in a very *long* time! Why would you even *consider* it?"

Prince Andrian stood tall. "Because then it *would* be a miracle if I was found innocent, and it would *prove* to all that I am a good man who *is* worthy of life."

"Trial by ordeal is a sure way to get you *killed.* It is a snare! Few have *ever* been found anything but guilty; you *know* this, do you not?" Lord Julian thought his brother had lost the remainder of his faculties.

"Aye. The history of guilty verdicts, I *am* familiar with, but that is *why* I wish for the king to sentence me by the results. Let it be my last request." Prince Andrian sat on the cot.

Lord Julian began to laugh. "My brother, why do you not simply *ask* for a pardon? He *is* your father, you realize?"

Prince Andrian rocked forward. "Father would feel blessed to execute me. Besides, a pardon for treason is improper. My release would cause an absolute *uproar* in the country." The prince scratched his untidy beard. "No, Julian, I stand by my request. If it is God's will, then I shall be *exonerated.* If I *must* perish for my crimes, then so be it."

Father Dallan nodded. "With your faith, no matter the circumstances you will be found *innocent,* whether in the trial or in your death. You *will* be forgiven, Andrian."

Lord Julian tapped the bars. "I assume you are ready for death then, my brother? For if you do not plead for a pardon you will *surely* die."

"Then die I shall." Prince Andrian smiled. "It shall be most *spectacular.*"

Lord Julian shrugged. "I shall tell Father of your request. And what of the child Sabrina? Surely you will not *still* insist on visitation in these conditions?"

Prince Andrian lay back on the bed. "*Still* I insist."

Lord Julian bowed to his brother, "As you wish, Your Highness," and left his presence.

Father Dallan felt uncertain the prince asking for a heinous trial was prudent, but the prince had nothing to lose. All he could do was pray for his soul. The prince turned his head toward the priest and grinned.

"*Why* do you smile, Andrian?"

He began to laugh. "I smile because there *is* no hope for me and still you sit here beside me as *mon ami,* my friend."

"Andrian, there is little hope for any of us, and Christ Jesus remains our friend. That is why I believe there *is* some hope for you."

Prince Andrian scratched his scalp. "*À demain?* I shall see you tomorrow?"

"Yes, you surely will see me tomorrow. For this day's remainder, read the book I have brought you. I believe it will be your light in this dark time for you."

Prince Andrian nodded. "*Merci.* You have been helpful to me and I feel blessed to have met you."

Father Dallan smiled. "I feel blessed to have met you as well, though many would consider that to be a curse."

Prince Andrian smiled. "Perhaps one day others will find my company worthy as well."

"I'm sure of it."

Chapter Seventeen

Lord Julian searched everywhere for the daughter his brother requested. Sabrina, the cleverest of children he had known, had hidden yet again. She had not concealed herself in the pantry, had not obscured herself in the hall, had not secreted herself in the lower bailey or upper bailey, and she had certainly not buried herself in any of the beds. Before he ripped out his hair, he found her.

"Sabrina? Why are you in the chapel? I was looking *all over* for you!"

The princess looked up at her uncle. "Not *looking* hard 'nuff."

Father Dallan cleared his throat. "I invited her to visit with me for a while. She is *quite* a smart little girl." Sabrina leapt up on a chair beside the priest and stuck her tongue out at her uncle.

Lord Julian sighed. "I am to take her to Sussex with me during the trial, and if Andrian is *cleared*, then she shall come back here to Eddington. If of course he is to have the fate I *believe* he shall receive . . . well, I shall become her guardian until she marries."

Sabrina rocked back and forth on the chair. "Where's *Papa?* I *wanna* see Papa!"

Lord Julian bent over. "I will take you to see your father *tomorrow*. I am sorry that you will come and live with me for a while, but it is your father's wish."

Sabrina leaned toward her uncle. "See Papa *now*."

"No, you shall *not* see your father now. You are to see him *tomorrow*, and that is *final*."

Sabrina sneered, "You *not* Papa. Papa wants me *here*. I am not *going* to you and far away."

"Your father *said* to come with me, and there is *no* way you will *stay* here *and* be sad."

Sabrina climbed off of the chair and stood before her uncle, who then knelt. She placed her hands on her hips. "Papa needs me, and he is in *trouble. Papa needs kisses.* Wanna see him *now.*"

Julian wagged his finger at her. "You are *incorrigible,* Sabrina, just like your father. Be careful it does not lead you to the same *fate* one day."

Sabrina's eye teamed with tears. "Papa *not* gonna die! Can't die *now!* Won't *let* him!"

Lord Julian fell on his backside. "*Who* said your father was *going* to die? He is only *away* for a while."

Sabrina stomped her feet. "I *seen* it! He *can't* die, no-no!" She punched her uncle. "No *die* now! You a *liar!* He gonna die if I no more here!"

Lord Julian sat with his mouth agape. "*How* did you see your father die?"

"I sleep and see him in trouble. He's sad and cries and says '*Sabrina!*'" She clasped her hands to her chest.

Lord Julian bowed his head. "Sabrina, you *must* come home with me. Your father *is* in trouble, and you may never see him again. I do not *want* to make this hard on you, but I really do not desire to tell you why he may never see you again."

Father Dallan motioned for Lord Julian to have a word with him, and told Sabrina to dust the benches while he and Uncle Julian talked. Sabrina nodded fervently. While they turned their backs, Sabrina dusted for a little while but then crept away from them. She wanted to see her Papa, whether her uncle or the priest wanted her to or not.

Lord Julian mentioned to Father Dallan that he would take Sabrina the following day to visit Andrian, and turned to see how she fared. "I do not *believe* it!"

"What?" Father Dallan looked behind Lord Julian.

"She is gone *again!*"

Father Dallan laughed. "You had better find her, though I think that it is obvious where she has gone."

Lord Julian smiled. "*Indeed.*"

*　　*　　*

Prince Andrian lay in his bed, looking up at the marred stone roof to his cell, and wondered if he would ever see the carved wooden ceiling to his room again. He positioned his hands behind his head and placed his feet on the wall. He sighed, and scratching his beard, imagined that he would soon attend his trial. He had a few days left, and he would stand in front of his kingdom to face the charges to which he could only plead guilty.

He rolled onto his side, faced the wall, and his heart raced. What if his father *denied* his request for the trial by ordeal? How soon would he know if his own father *truly* sentenced him to death? Would he shame himself more by asking for a pardon? Was begging below him? Would he break down before the hundreds at his trial or completely lose it? Would he *ever* see his daughter again?

Would he ever see his daughter, sweet innocent Sabrina, *ever again?* Oh *how* it tormented him that he could not hold her in his arms. He cradled his pillow and stroked it. He remembered her toothy smile in his mind, and how she made him look the fool before his men when at first he took her to his home. He did not mind now if she made him look foolish, for fatherhood had saved his soul from complete desolation. No matter what happened in a week's time, he found comfort knowing that he had always wanted the best for Sabrina.

He caressed the pillow and kissed it. "My little Sabrina," he thought. "I wish your papa were not so wretched. I have abandoned you, though I wish I did not. I wish you knew that I never meant for any of this to happen." He laid his head into the pillow and wept bitter tears. "Poor Sabrina . . . poor Sabrina . . . poor belle jonquille," he wept to himself.

Prince Andrian lay on his back as he sobbed and covered his face with the pillow. "Oh, God, I *promise* if you save me . . . if you wish to spare my life, I *promise* I shall do *everything* in my power to right all of my wrongs. I would sell all I own to change this fate of mine. I would do *anything*. I would accept *torture* if I can live to raise my little girl." He moaned, "Please, I *beg* you, dear God, let me *live* . . . let me live to protect my child. I am so *sorry* for all of my evils. *Forgive* me, Lord. I *beg* you to forgive me."

Prince Andrian heard no reply to his prayer, but he felt a stirring within his body. More tears poured from his eyes. More emotions flooded his heart. He cried out in a loud roar. He could not bear to leave his child alone in the world without her papa to hold her to him. He would die alone and unloved, unloved except for his little girl who barely knew him, and who would grow up believing that her father had been a vicious and evil man who stole her away from her mama. And he might never have the chance to apologize to Sabrina for that wrong and have her understand his pleas.

It hurt to cry, though Andrian could not stop. He had made so many terrible mistakes in his life, and now that he regretted them, he would not pay for them—his daughter would. Julian, who surely had left already with her, would take her in, and she would probably grow old with only faint memories of her papa. Perhaps she would forget him altogether. Or perhaps she would have gruesome nightmares of him, if she could imagine the horrors he had done to so many good people.

He placed the pillow by his feet and slicked his tears through his hair. He felt his face, unshaven and rough. He had not changed his clothes, nor bathed in over a week. He knew he looked unkempt. He had not eaten all day, and even if he had food shoved into his cell, he probably could not have eaten anyhow.

Prince Andrian wanted company in the darkness of the room, but not the way he had longed for company. He did not imagine physical pleasure; he merely wanted comfort, coddling, and the promise that he would survive. He doubted that if he did live he would ever find love again in the arms of a woman, for who could believe he wanted more than anything to change his life for the better?

No one believed in him anymore. His father and the kingdom despised him, and every last man, woman, and child had spat and cursed him. Everyone hated him except one girl. Reaching into his breeches, he retrieved a shred of deerskin. Upon the scrap, no words the girl had written, though a crude drawing of a cat with a smattering of red ink marked its surface. He sighed and put his hand behind his head. *"Freedom and courage."* He frowned, set the skin on his belly, and put his other hand behind his head. He closed his eyes. The girl's eyes glowed in his mind. Something seemed strange about her, though he could not place why he felt so.

Andrian squinted. The girl had not truly been a child. She had looked about twelve or perhaps thirteen. Perhaps she could befriend his daughter. Sabrina needed a caretaker.

He yawned. "If I should get out of this mess, I promise, child, I shall seek you out and reward you for your loyalty." He grasped the deerskin in his hand and fell asleep.

Andrian walked in a field and people smiled at him . . . everyone loved him. He laughed and held an infant boy. He tossed him in the air. The baby giggled as his father kissed him. The infant looked up at his father and spoke, "Why did you ruin everything, Papa? *Why? Why? Why?*"

Prince Andrian woke with a start. The infant's voice had sounded like the clanging of metal. He glanced over toward the doorway, but no one stood there. He groaned and looked up. The faintest glimmer of light cracked through the walls above him. Another night had passed, and now he had but six days until his final sentencing.

Once again the prince heard the strange clanking of metal on metal and he sat up, looking around. He saw no reason for the sound, so he lay back down. *Clink, clank, ponk.* What made that odd noise? He stood up, and lo, he spied the reason: Sabrina had hidden by his cell and thrashed something against the bars.

He could not withhold his cry of joy. "What are you *doing* in here, *ma chère?*"

She looked up. "*Papa.*"

"Aye, Papa is here. Oh, my little *Sabrina.* Why have you come now?" He crouched by her and reached through the bars for her. "Oh, I *wish* that I might hold you to me."

Sabrina reached for her father. "Papa, come out now, Papa." She shoved her body at the bars to try to slide through. "Papa, don't *hide* now . . . come home."

Prince Andrian could not keep himself from weeping for his child. "S-Sabrina . . . Papa . . . Papa c-cannot go home *anymore.* You must be . . . you must be *strong* n-now. I cannot be here for y-you *anymore.*"

"No. You come *now.* I *want* you to. *Yes.* You come to be outside. We can *play* now." Sabrina grabbed her father's hand and tugged on him as if she might pull him magically through the bars to freedom.

"Find Julian, Sabrina, he should care for you from now on. You *will* be all right with him. He is a *nice* man." He reached and caressed her.

"So is *Papa.* You good and nice too." She clanged the object in her hand against the bars again. "You come out now. No more sad-sad."

Prince Andrian reached through further onto the other side of the bars, and drawing Sabrina as close to his face as possible, he looked her in the eyes and whispered, "Papa loves you so *very* much. Do not *ever* forget that, no matter what *anyone* says." He kissed her forehead through the bars.

When her papa could not hug her as he always did, Sabrina knew something bad would happen. He had stuck himself in there, and she did not understand why. "Papa, *please* come out. *Please.*" She jumped up and down in place and moaned.

Prince Andrian kissed her forehead once more and told her to behave for her uncle. When he said that, Sabrina knew her papa would never hold her again. She reached as far as she could through the bars and grabbed him around the neck and kissed his scruffy face over and over. "I love you, Papa." She stopped kissing him and felt his face. Tears dribbled down his cheeks and he seemed pricklier than she remembered, but she knew her papa. He just looked unhappy and he looked sick too. She kissed him on the nose and said once more that she loved him, and held out the object she had clanged around.

"What *is* that, *ma jonquille?*" He held out his hand. As she dropped it, he laughed. "You have the keys to this cell."

"Come out, Papa," Sabrina beckoned him.

He shook his head. "I am sorry, but I am not *allowed,* even *with* the keys. I did something *bad,* and I am in trouble. I am so *sorry, ma jeune fille.*" He kissed her again and told her to give the keys back to the guard.

"*No,* Papa, no-no."

"*Aye,* take them back, sweet Sabrina. Go on . . ."

Sabrina lowered her head and dragged her feet out of the cellblock, back to wherever she had picked up the keys. Prince Andrian did not know whether to laugh or cry. His daughter needed him, and he could do nothing for her. He sat back down on his cot and waited for his child's return.

A large thump caught Prince Andrian's attention, so he leapt to his feet and leaned on the posts in his cell. Several voices murmured behind one of the doors to his left. He strained his ears to hear what they said to each other, but he could not make out any specific words.

With a creaking *whomp,* the door flew open to the small corridor and in burst not only Sabrina, but also Lord Julian, Sir Idwal, Father Dallan, and Sir Cathaoir.

The men bowed to the prince. Lord Julian, of the five, looked the most disturbed, and Prince Andrian begged them all to rise. "What is all this? Explain yourselves to me."

"Your Majesty, we have most grievous news for you," began Sir Idwal.

Prince Andrian felt his heart swell painfully.

"Queen Mireille has passed this morning . . . I am sorry, my brother." Lord Julian avoided his brother's eyes.

Prince Andrian collapsed on the floor, his hands clutching the prison bars.

Sir Cathaoir sneered at the prince, "Died . . . of a broken heart."

The prince shook his head. *It was not so . . . she was so ill . . . it must have been something else, a fever, a cough . . . anything else.* "Are you certain?" he croaked.

"Quite," insisted Sir Idwal.

Prince Andrian sat in shock. The four men watched him shatter like glass. From Andrian's heart burst forth a howl that echoed his damnation throughout the entire castle.

Father Dallan longed to comfort the young man, but Andrian had curled in a ball with his hands clutching his head as he wailed.

Lord Julian cleared his throat. "We have further news, and again it will be a burden for you to hear. Please try to remain calm."

Prince Andrian looked up at his brother's face. Usually rosy and cheerful, it had grayed, and the line of his mouth twisted into a frown.

"What worse news have you for me, Julian? For I can imagine nothing as terrible as the death of my mother over my sins." Andrian's eyes bled from his heart and Julian struggled to speak.

"In the present circumstances, meaning the passing of the queen, you are not only denied your plea for trial by ordeal, but also your stay of execution has been cancelled. You are to be burned alive tomorrow at dawn." Lord Julian crouched by the prince. "I am so sorry, Brother."

Prince Andrian's stomach did a somersault. "I thought I was to be beheaded. Why such a drastic change?"

Sir Cathaoir smirked. "Your father wanted you to suffer for all you've done. Being burned as a heretic might be much more of a show for the crowd, eh? Didn't want to disappoint all your enemies, did he?" He laughed.

Lord Julian turned and looked up at the knight. "Hold your tongue or you shall share his fate. I know your past as well, sinister knight of desolation."

Sir Cathaoir was silent.

Father Dallan told his friend that he would stay awhile and give him comfort if he wished. Prince Andrian nodded with acceptance.

"Indeed this is news of great sorrow for me. Not only has my mother left this world, but also I shall join her tomorrow." Prince Andrian reached through the bars for his daughter, who through all of the commotion had remained by the bars nearest to her father.

"Papa, Papa, I love you, Papa." Sabrina reached through the bars for her father and began to sob.

The men watched the young child desperately kissing her father through the cold metal, and Lord Julian frowned and waved his hand. "Open the door for her. Let her say goodbye to him."

At once the doors clanged open, and Sabrina ran inside and threw herself into her father's arms. Prince Andrian wept with sorrow and with joy as his baby snuggled into his arms. Sitting on the floor, he rocked Sabrina. Large tears fell from his eyes and wet the princess' jet-black hair. She sucked on her fingers as he sang her another lullaby, a song of lamentation that only Lord Julian could understand:

> *"A ma connaissance, ma vie est hors d'usage. Je vais tentes le sort, parce que j'ai perdu la baile. Je ne peux s'en prendre qu'a moi-même. Mais tu, ma fille, sembles être née sous une bonne étoile. Sabrina, je n'ai pas l'intention d'abandonner tu, parce que je t'adore. Soyez sur que je ferai tout mon possible être avec tu."*

The men were astounded that the prince could sing, and even Sir Cathaoir struggled to contain a single tear that fell from his eyes. Sabrina leaned her small face into her father's neck as he rocked her.

"*Ma belle fille . . . ne pleure pas . . . ne t'en fais pas; je t'adore. Je t'adore.*" Prince Andrian caressed his daughter's hair and kissed her forehead.

When Julian saw fit to take Sabrina from her father, she clung to him, and he could not help but cling to her as well. "Just awhile longer, please," he moaned.

"Your Highness . . . we need to leave soon. I do not wish to be here for your execution with a child of four winters. It would kill her to see her father die that way." Lord Julian broke the grip between his brother and his child.

Both Sabrina and Andrian wailed as they parted. Sabrina reached out for her father and grasped his fingertips. Lord Julian slapped Andrian's hand hard and rushed the child away from him so that she might calm and be ready for the ride to his home in Sussex.

Prince Andrian lay prostrate on the floor as his daughter shrieked for him. "I shall never see her again!" Prince Andrian hollered and pulled his hair.

Father Dallan entered the cell, and Sir Idwal grabbed Sir Cathaoir away from his lord's mournful presence. Father Dallan sat beside Prince Andrian and they prayed for the prince's soul, for his redemption, and for God to grant him peace the following day.

Chapter Eighteen

At dawn, Prince Andrian heard the door to the donjon clang open. The king had sent three soldiers and four servants to ready the prince for his execution. Prince Andrian had stayed awake all night reading the Bible. Earlier that morning, Julian had visited to inform Andrian that no one would defend him, and therefore the death sentence stood.

The servants led the prince to an adjacent cell, where he bathed. Though he did not mind being clean, the water felt like the winter sea. His wounds exposed to all in the chamber, the servants looked upon him with renewed disgust. Each purple mark upon his body was earned after he had murdered so many good men. They scrubbed him as hard as they could to remove his evils. After he had washed with expedience, a servant shaved the prince's face clean, with the solders watching to make sure he did not confiscate the blade. Another servant handed him pure white garments. When his appearance measured up to the king's standards, as read to the prince from a letter given earlier that morning, they brought him back to his cell.

Julian had read the letter aloud for his brother, for Andrian could not concentrate on anything but the hope he might go to heaven after his execution. He told Julian that if God gave him grace he would spend eternity with the woman he loved and his son, and that he would never again feel lonely. Julian frowned at his brother's hope.

Father Dallan came in at dawn to Prince Andrian's cell and gave him his last rites; Andrian confessed his sins, he was anointed with oil, and then, with tears, took his viaticum.

"I pray it is a quick end." Prince Andrian looked out the window at the pink sky, and wondered if it would turn red with his death. He wondered if he would pass into the next life carried by the angels or torn to bits by winged demons. He also wondered if anyone would mourn him when his body rested. He hoped his daughter might wish him peace into the next life.

Father Dallan patted Andrian. "Find strength, for God will ease your suffering." He handed Andrian a comb and leather strap to tie his hair back. "So it'd look less unruly."

Prince Andrian combed his matted hair and fastened it neatly. Prince Andrian felt his smooth face and sighed. "How do I appear?" He paused at Father Dallan's silence. "I am doomed; I know it."

Father Dallan embraced him and said, "Peace be with you," and then made the sign of the cross on his forehead.

The guard insisted the prince get moving, and so he followed them outside, where a few hundred people had shown up to watch him die. Their eyes burned holes in him as guards led him to the platform to await his public sentencing. The sea of enemies bobbed up and down as everyone tried to get a better look of the damned ruthless prince.

King Arundel stood up and the tide of spectators ceased ebbing. "My people, I come to give you peace from my son's tyranny at last as I announce his final sentencing. I hope there are no objections to the verdict, though I hardly think with the terror my boy has caused there will be a man to deny this is fair." The crowd burbled their agreement, and he continued, "I was advised by the *curia regis* that I should not preside over this trial, but I should allow my seneschal to read the verdict. However, I feel it is of utmost importance that I personally denounce my son's behavior and apologize to my subjects for having any faith that my son would ever change."

Prince Andrian's heart sank at his father's words. He had kept faith in his son after all he had done to ruin his father's name. King Arundel had given him repeated chances to redeem himself; he had given him power, he had tried to guide him, and he had punished him when no other options seemed available. By standing before the crowd, accused of so many crimes, Andrian had failed completely. He deserved no more chances.

King Arundel read from a scroll of parchment: "Andrian Gilbert, You stand accused of no less than fifty counts of willful destruction of property, and the council has found you guilty on all counts. You stand accused of 223 counts of rape and have been found guilty of 124, several charges had been dropped due to pregnancy and others were unable to prove harm. You have been accused of seventy-five counts of attempted rape, and have been found guilty of twenty-six. You have been accused of thirty-four counts of aggravated assault. The charges have stood, and on every count you were found guilty. You have been accused of fifty-six counts of attempted murder and have been found guilty of twenty-nine. You have been accused of murder seventy times, and have been found guilty of twenty-five. The charge of heresy has been dropped. Finally, you have been found guilty of high treason to the crown."

Prince Andrian tried to keep track of the charges, and found himself dismayed at all the horror he had caused all of his father's subjects. If he had not hung his head in shame then, it certainly became more apparent after King Arundel read all the charges.

"For the damages my son has caused, a fine of 400,000 crowns has been issued. For the charges beyond mere destruction and bedlam, the sentence is death. Lord Julian Robert de Langeais has met the price for his brother, and it has already been paid in full." The king looked at his son. "Though your brother was kind enough to take it upon himself to beg money from other countries as a ransom for your life in exile, I fear you must still pay for high treason."

Prince Andrian swallowed. The way his father glared, he might as well have been singing a sirvente about the downfall of the ruthless prince.

The king added, "Your request for trial by ordeal has been denied due to personal suffering inflicted upon your king's heart, unless you can conjure an acceptable reason for me to reconsider in your last moments."

Prince Andrian stood transfixed.

The king asked him, "Have you anything to say for yourself before we send you to your death?"

Prince Andrian nodded.

"Let us hear your plea."

Prince Andrian knelt before his father. "Of the crimes which I have been convicted, I am indeed guilty, and I accept the verdict as it is the will of the people and is surely just. I only beg as you watch me burn to ash that you give me the dignity in death you denied me in life."

King Arundel's eyes watered at his son's sorrow, but soon they hardened. Andrian had always been a talented actor. He played upon his feelings even as he stood before the crowd and begged. Evil had no limits with the young man. King Arundel snarled; Andrian had no shame.

Prince Andrian lowered his face. His father despised him even unto death.

King Arundel called to a guard, "Tie the criminal to the post and we shall have a bonfire."

The guards raised Andrian to his feet, and he whispered to his father, "I am so sorry. God have mercy on my soul."

The guards marched the prince to the post and lashed him to it. Andrian looked out at the crowd, and still no one spoke. Justice would finally prevail, and no one wished to miss a moment of it. All eyes in the crowd prodded him in the gut. All those eyes and their faces, their faces bleeding one into the other: victims of the wrath of the ruthless prince.

Within the silent crowd, Prince Andrian heard a tiny voice cry out, "Papa!" The prince's eyes flicked through the mob to see where the voice came from. Surely Sabrina had gone with Julian to Sussex and he had only dreamed of her in sorrow. But no, he heard it again, "Papa!" And then he saw her, squirming through the crowd, wailing, with her hands raised toward him. "Papa!"

Julian tried to grab her, but she slipped through his grasp. Tears fell from Andrian's eyes. "Sabrina!" He moaned, "Sabrina!"

"Papa!"

Julian caught her by the dress and pulled her away, screaming, kicking, and biting, farther from the crowd.

"Sabrina," Andrian wept. He had doomed his child to loneliness because of his own stubborn pride. He had ruined her life twice: once when he kidnapped her from her mother, and the second time by getting himself executed. He did not deserve fatherhood.

The king watched the child taken further away, nodded, and a man with a torch lit the sticks around Andrian's feet.

Sabrina shrieked in horror as fire and smoke hindered her view of her father. "PAPAAAAAA!" Sabrina buried her face in Julian's neck and wailed, "Papa gooone!"

Prince Andrian began to sweat from the overwhelming heat. He coughed on the smoke scorching his lungs. His nostrils burned and itched, and each time he sneezed the soreness intensified. His nose bled and he snorted, for he could not wipe the red oozing muck away though he tried to loosen the rope binding his hands behind the post.

Consciousness slipped further from him, and he saw a woman in the flames. She leapt on the sweltering wood; it looked like she tried to extinguish the flames with her wiggling toes. Prince Andrian's half-shut eyes followed her while she skipped up to him. "Andrian."

His eyes watered with the blackened stinging and he croaked, "Who calls me?"

The image put her hand on his face and she felt as real as the flames around him, though her fingers chilled him against the burning surroundings. "Andrian."

He croaked, "Aye?"

"You called to God and begged for mercy, and He has heard your cries. If you swear to uphold virtue the rest of your life and do His will no matter what burdens He bestows upon you, then you shall not die today."

"I swear it . . ."

"For your sins you shall receive penance until you have repaid your debt. Accept this fate and you have your freedom from the bondage of damnation."

"I accept that fate."

The image kissed Andrian on the mouth, and he felt his lungs clear though he stood in the midst of crackling flames.

"What the devil is going on?" cried King Arundel. One by one the flames extinguished around the doomed prince. Someone had blown out the deadly candelabrum. "Relight the flame!" King Arundel roared.

"I can't!" cried a guard. "It's like they've been wet!"

King Arundel sat dumbstruck for a moment, and then he yelled, "Well, throw more wood on!"

Several corpulent men tossed a mountain of wood on the nearly extinguished pile and rekindled the last of the dying flames.

Prince Andrian felt a dozen hellcats lick his body and he cried out in pain, but the image pirouetted around him and kept most of the flames at bay.

"Won't he just die?" cried the executioner. "It's not natural to burn this long and live!"

"He's a warlock!" cried several people.

When the fire burned down low, everyone could see that Prince Andrian lived, though cataleptic, and the flames had merely scorched his clothing and singed his hair.

King Arundel sent the guard to remove his son. They untied him, and he collapsed on the ground. Andrian had not made an effort to reach out as he fell, so perhaps he had died as the smoke had billowed about him. One guard grabbed the prince's face and forced one of his eyes open. "Sire, he lives!"

Violent words rushed through the crowd.

King Arundel pulled his beard. "My son must be a warlock!" He cried out, "The plea for trial by ordeal has been granted. Now it is up to God to judge this evil man before us." The crowd seemed satisfied.

He continued, "Tomorrow, Andrian Gilbert shall endure ordeal by water since fire could not touch him!"

*   *   *

When Prince Andrian awoke, he lay in his cell and Father Dallan sat beside him. "They put you to death as well? Why, for aiding a criminal?" Andrian whispered.

Father Dallan laughed. "No, my friend. I've come to ask you how it was you were able to survive through that. I don't know if you were aware of it, but it looked as if the fire was putting itself out."

Andrian sat up. "So I was *not* dreaming." Father Dallan's eyebrows twisted with interest. *"Une femme danse . . ."* Andrian hesitated. "A woman danced around me . . . her feet ceased the flames, her white cloak shielded me from the burning. She made me swear an oath to God . . ."

Father Dallan covered his mouth. "You have been protected by an angel. You are *blessed*, Andrian."

The prince swallowed. "But how can that be? For I have the blood of innocent men on my hands, not to mention the number of women I have defiled." He sighed. "God is merciful if he saves me though I am less worthy than a legless horse."

Father Dallan shrugged. "God has plans for you; he is mysterious in his ways. Perhaps your life shall change this kingdom, for the better or the worse."

Prince Andrian nodded. "What is to happen next?"

"Tomorrow you shall face ordeal by water. The public claims you have been proven to be a warlock."

Prince Andrian moaned, "But surely you know I am no such thing. My father cannot believe such lies."

Father Dallan patted his hand. "No matter the opinion of others, God would not spare such evil."

Prince Andrian covered his face. "If I shall endure torture for my soul . . . so . . . so be it."

*   *   *

The jury brought Prince Andrian to the River Thames the following day for judgment. The guard bound the prince with rope, and seven witnesses, including Father Dallan, agreed to stay there to ensure the young man called no assistance.

Before the ordeal, the witnesses introduced themselves as Father Dallan of Selsey, Lorcan of Carrickfergus, Sir Garland of Winchester, Sir Cathaoir of Devon, Sir Idwal of Dornach, and Bromley the executioner. They all shook hands and agreed that if Prince Andrian passed the ordeal he earned a pardon.

Bromley the executioner shoved the bound Andrian into the water, and when he floated, they pulled him out.

Sir Cathaoir cried out, "He's a warlock!"

Father Dallan retorted, "God wanted him to live, so why would he save a warlock?"

Sir Cathaoir shook his fist. "Andrian entered into the devil's inner circle of imps then renounced his baptism. His mortal body now fears water!"

"Foolishness!" cried Father Dallan. "How could you think that unless you have made such a pact yourself? Let us throw you in and see if the same holds true!"

Sir Idwal shoved Sir Cathaoir into the river, and he too floated above the water.

"Warlock indeed." Father Dallan shook his head as Sir Cathaoir struggled to pull himself from the icy Thames.

Sir Idwal grabbed hold of Sir Cathaoir's tunic and yanked him from the water. "If what Father Dallan says is so, then a weight should prove his innocence!"

Prince Andrian watched in horror as two knights dragged a millstone before him.

"That'll sink 'im!" cried Sir Garland.

They tied the millstone around Prince Andrian's neck and heaved him into the water once again. They all hollered out in shock; Andrian still floated! They watched the prince floating face down and struggling to bring his head above water to take a breath of air.

"At least he'll drown." Sir Cathaoir shrugged.

"You'd drown an innocent man?" cried Father Dallan.

Sir Garland jabbed his finger at the prince. "How could you claim he is innocent?"

"God thinks so," Father Dallan said. "The weight of sin does not bear his soul to drown in guilt."

"Oh for goodness' sake." Sir Cathaoir rolled his eyes.

They removed Andrian, and he coughed and sputtered.

Lorcan cleared his throat. "We should grant the prince absolution. I have never seen fire act the way it had yesterday, and my own mother had been burned as a witch unjustly. Even she had not been saved by the inferno as the prince had." He swallowed. "I know that my mother was innocent."

*　　*　　*

Lorcan, the household steward, brought King Arundel his son's outcome. The king called for more ordeals and dually reminded the steward that Andrian the Ruthless earned a guilty verdict at his trial.

Lorcan bowed to the king and later brought forth the king's insistence to the jury that indeed Andrian had not earned clemency and that he would yet endure another ordeal.

Thus, the ordeals intensified: Andrian walked nine paces with a red-hot iron bar in both of his hands. Seven days later, his hands suffered severe scars but had otherwise healed completely.

Andrian walked through nine red-hot ploughshares while blindfolded, and he avoided every one.

The king required Andrian to remove a stone from a pot of boiling oil. King Arundel had paid Sir Cathaoir to make sure that when his son reached in for the stone he could not remove it with his hand. Not only did Andrian remove it, his scalding healed in seven days as the iron bar wounds had.

All of the ordeals wore Prince Andrian down, but in between each ordeal he read the Bible until he fell asleep from exhaustion. Six ordeals he had faced, and he had read the Bible six times.

On the seventh day after the last ordeal, King Arundel spoke with Lord Julian at supper. "What do you make of this whole thing?"

"He's obviously innocent," Lord Julian said while eating a peach.

"But you know his guilt! You were the one who told me of his threats!"

Lord Julian shrugged. "The only problem is that Andrian is found innocent in every trial." He counted on his fingers. "He survived being burned alive. He twice over lived through drowning. Not only did Andrian's wounds heal from the red hot iron, but he also avoided the ploughshares, not to mention he removed the rock from the oil, and I heard a rumor that it was fixed." He held up six fingers. "I'd say that about lets him loose on the kingdom."

King Arundel stroked his beard. "That is indeed the difficulty." He then picked up a peach and gnawed on it. "Andrian had assistance, I am certain." He sighed. "Why would anyone wish for him to live? He has done such evil."

"There are men who say that he was saved by an angel as he burned at the stake. Those men believe it is against God's will to further punish the prince."

"Who are these men who think such foolish things?"

Julian shrugged. "There still are ways to make sure justice is served." He swallowed some of the fruit. "Hang him." He bit hard into the peach. "Or behead him." He wiped juice from his chin and chewed. For a moment he tapped his fingers on the table. "You know, Father, no matter what you do, if God favors him he shall live." He raised a finger. "It might only further prove his innocence if you put him to more tests, which I am sure he will pass. The man is untouchable."

King Arundel nodded. "I am not mistaken to assume you have heard that the witnesses all attest to the fact that Andrian has survived each ordeal unaided. I placed some of my most skeptical men as witnesses, and even they admit it is a bit odd how he survives such ordeals." The king put his peach down and raised his eyebrow at him. "Throngs of onlookers have gathered simply to watch the spectacle. It is like the Roman Empire here. Give them a blood sport to watch and they cheer like mad. I do not think they care who it is that wins."

"This is the work of God." Lord Julian ate the last bite. "Or of the devil." He tossed the peach pit behind his back.

King Arundel placed his hands together. "I know how to make sure the prince shall not survive the next ordeal."

"And how is that?" Julian grabbed another peach.

The king smiled. "*You* will hang him."

Julian dropped the peach on the ground. "You surely do not mean that."

"I do. And if he survives that, I shall consider *you* to be in league with the devil and I shall have you *both* beheaded." He took another bite of his peach.

"But, Father, you know I am an honest Christian man. I would never be in league with the devil. Perhaps it is time to accept God's judgment and release my brother. He is, after all, your *son*."

King Arundel snorted and threw his peach at the wall. "Andrian must pay for his crimes."

Lord Julian sighed. "Has he not been through enough? You wished for him to show mercy. He has wept before the masses and begged your forgiveness. He has paid greatly for his evils. Allow him enough mercy to go free as an outlaw."

"He has not paid the dear price for the pain he has caused me."

Lord Julian cried, "He *has* paid dearly! He has lost everything! He has lost his pride, his dignity, and his honor! Though no one believes a word he says, I can attest that he is an honest man! He lives with the burden of loss so great on his shoulders every moment of the day, and you tell me he had not paid! Surely you must be more lenient!"

King Arundel stood up and pounded his fist on the table. "Hang him at dawn or I shall behead you both for treason!"

* * *

During the time of Prince Andrian's trial by ordeal, Sabrina went to Sussex to stay with Julian's wife, Margrethe. Sabrina did not dislike her aunt or the estate at which she stayed; she did, however, despise her cousins Ferelith and Desmond. More so she hated her cousin Ferelith because she rarely saw Desmond, but she thought he was probably just like her, noisy and mean.

Ferelith threw tantrums and screamed if she did not get her way. She also wanted to play dolls *all* the time. When Margrethe insisted they have fun together, Sabrina always had to play with the evil prince doll.

"Sabrina, this doll's name is Andrian. You can have him, and I'll play with this doll." She held up a golden-haired princess. "Real princesses have gold hair and white skin." She glared at Sabrina. "You've got black hair and skin like a roast."

Sabrina frowned and looked at the Andrian doll.

The girls sat and groomed the dolls and Sabrina looked up at Ferelith. "How come he's Andrian?"

Ferelith sighed and rolled her eyes. "It's the bad prince's name, stupid."

"Who's bad prince?"

The little girl laughed. "He's your Papa!"

Sabrina began to cry and ran outside with the bad prince doll clutched in her arms.

Uproar sounded from the bailey; the shouts and wailing attracted Margrethe's attention. She rushed to see the commotion and found Sabrina weeping as she cradled something in her arms. Her daughter slapped at Sabrina and howled.

"She stole my doll, Mama!" Ferelith pointed with a red face.

When Margrethe saw which doll she clutched, she looked over at her daughter and cried, "Let her have it. Her father never gave her a doll before."

"Twit!" Ferelith seized the doll, ripped its head off, and threw it on the ground. Then she kicked it before running away and screaming at the top of her voice.

Sabrina plucked the Andrian doll from its death on the ground and then tried to put the head back on. She forced the two parts together over and over, but every time they fell apart again. Sabrina clasped it to her chest and cried.

Margrethe reached her hand out. "Here, I can mend it for you."

Sabrina looked up at her and then at the injured effigy. Its face looked sad, so she handed it over.

Margrethe took her inside to repair him. After sewing and clipping, stuffing and re-stuffing, she announced, "Good as new."

Sabrina smiled with tears in her eyes and snuggled next to her doll. She looked up at Margrethe. "Papa no bad. He good. I love Papa." She kissed the toy and rocked it.

Margrethe frowned. "Listen to me; your papa isn't coming here to take you home. You're going to live with us from now on."

Sabrina's eyes widened. "Papa . . . dead?"

Margrethe crouched beside her niece. "Sabrina, when your papa did the things he did, he made a lot of people mad, and even *his* papa was mad."

"Why?"

"Well, he really hurt a lot of people. He hurt your mama too."

Sabrina looked at the doll; someone had drawn an evil grin on its face. "Papa *hate* Mama?"

Margrethe shook her head. "No, sweet child, but sometimes people get hurt even if they love the other person. And sometimes they love them too much and it hurts."

Sabrina kissed the doll. "Papa hurt 'cause he love me." She cried, "Papa . . . dead."

Margrethe embraced Sabrina. "Your papa *is* going to die. It's because he hurt too *many* people."

Sabrina looked up. "Can I go home now?" She patted the doll on the head. "Want see Papa."

Margrethe sighed. "This *will* be your home soon."

"No . . . no, no, no, no, no, no!" She escaped Margrethe's embrace and ran.

Outside, Sabrina sat under a tree and caressed the doll's head. "Love Papa . . . come home . . ."

Ferelith pranced up to Sabrina and sneered, "I heard evil Prince Andrian is going to be hanged tomorrow. He's going to die. Ha-ha.

When he dies, my father will be king after my grandfather goes to his grave." She smirked. "*My* father will be a much better king than *yours*."

Sabrina's lip quivered and she looked down at the doll. For an instant, she saw a tear fall from its face. Then she realized the tears were her own.

Suddenly a little blond boy came marching up to Ferelith and Sabrina. "Are you teasing the princess *again*?"

She crossed her arms. "Sabrina's no princess. Her mama's a commoner."

The little boy frowned. "So was our grandmother." He put his arm around Sabrina. "Want to play dragon slayer? Your doll can be the noble prince who slays the dragon." He held up a worn pair of hose.

Sabrina's face brightened. "Okay."

The boy made a dragon out of the hose and his hand was the mouth.

Sabrina's doll attacked the dragon and said, "For Mama!"

The boy made the dragon gag and wail, and it fell to the ground.

Sabrina liked her cousin Desmond after all.

*   *   *

At dawn, soldiers led Andrian to a peach tree in the castle orchard, where a rope dangled, ready to end his prolonged suffering. He looked up at the rope twisting and swinging in the soft breeze. What a pity to die on a day such as that, for the warm sun called for him to gambol about, laugh, and love everyone.

From the ashen look on his brother's face, Andrian knew that the king had sent him to play the executioner, and he had no chance to survive anymore.

The largest crowd yet had come to watch the prince's execution. It had become somewhat of a curiosity, Andrian's avoidance of death. Many placed bets as to whether or not he would perish at the hand of his brother or if he would survive yet again and go on to some new peril. Prince Andrian watched money pass from one hand to another and felt tears come to his eyes. He stifled them in hope that no one would bet on how long it would take him to bawl like a child.

A witness to every one of Prince Andrian's ordeals, the young red-haired girl hid from sight behind another peach tree. She marveled at his stamina but knew he could not survive a hanging unless he had a little help from the less-than-divine. As she studied the hard features of the doomed prince, she recalled her grandmother's superstitious joke on Saint Faith's Day.

Her grandmother had baked a cake for her. "Rioghnach, you are now thirteen and ought to start thinking of marriage." The girl passed pieces of the cake through a golden ring, which she then hung from her bedstead. "What good'll this do?"

Her grandmother smiled. "Tonight, you'll dream of the man you'll marry."

Rioghnach rolled her eyes. "I don't want to marry an ugly brute. Can't it wait 'til I am thirty instead?"

Her grandmother chortled, "This is your lucky year. Now go to bed and dream of your love." She kissed her on the forehead.

Looking into the dark eyes of the man awaiting execution, Rioghnach knew that if she did not act her future husband would die at the end of a rope that morning. The fate of her kingdom rested upon her shoulders. The ruthless prince *must* live.

Prince Andrian mounted his horse, and Julian tied his hands behind his back. Lord Julian slipped the noose over his head. "Do you want a blindfold?" Lord Julian asked him.

Prince Andrian shook his head.

Julian sighed. "I did not wish for this to endure so for you. I begged Father to cease his vengeance, but he refused to listen to me." Lord Julian whispered, "You have friends here. Sir Idwal switched the pot of oil so you might succeed in retrieving the stone. I knew you had cunning as a soldier and I suggested the ploughshares. You said to me long ago that you have such rough hands that you put ointment on them to soften them for the ladies. I knew that the hot bar would not cause you terrible misery. To help you float, I had the cook bring you bean soup."

Andrian sighed. "How did I survive the fire? For then you could have done nothing."

Julian leaned toward him. "That was *surely* an act of God. After seeing that miracle, many of us knew that Father had done wrong by continuing to make you suffer. We intended to have you pardoned and exiled so you might live in France in peace." Julian patted his arm. "I had not planned to hang you. I hope you can forgive me for doing Father's bidding."

Andrian stared toward the horizon. "Do not ask to be forgiven for doing what is right. I deserve death; it just has not come as quickly as I had hoped."

The little girl crouched low behind the tree, her cloak draped behind her back to conceal a disfiguring lump. She memorized the prince's stoic face. He looked different from the abuse at his arrest. His eyes had dulled; no longer did they burn with his passions. The girl peeked further around the tree and the prince spied her.

Her loyalty would earn her God's grace he hoped. "Kill me already." Prince Andrian closed his eyes and squeezed the girl's message in his fist.

Julian hesitated and then struck the horse's rump. The horse did not budge.

Andrian swallowed and looked down at the black stallion that had been his comrade for years. "It is time to let me go." He kicked the stallion's flanks, and the horse charged with a saddened whinny. The noose of death went from slack to taut. The prince's neck had not snapped on the fall, so Julian condemned him to strangle to death. Julian could not watch his brother choke. He turned away and shut his eyes.

At first the prince struggled while he dangled breathlessly. The *whump-whump* sound of his heart grew loud in his ears. After a moment his mouth sputtered orange froth as he felt the pounding burn into his chest. Andrian could only think about his mistakes during his last seconds. The sound of his heart grew faint as buzzing droned in his ears. He did not want to die yet. He needed to do so much more, and thinking this, his light pulsed into darkness.

Rioghnach watched the prince turn scarlet as he gurgled in silent pain. She looked around, removed a bow and an arrow with a vane removed from under her cloak.

Andrian's eyes rolled back into his head and he started to spasm, his legs twitched involuntarily.

The girl fitted the notch to the cord and aimed. She whispered, "Help him, Bel," and shot it. The fluke broke the rope, and the prince fell to the ground with a thud.

Julian heard the noise and turned around; his brother lay on the ground, heaving, with air whistling into his sore lungs. He wondered who might have cut the rope, and the crowd wondered, looking around with a rising murmur, though no one spied a culprit.

The little girl climbed up into the tree above him to get a better look. She gazed down at the wide-eyed man; though bruised and red with stress, his soul shone through his exterior.

Julian bent down and cut the rope holding his brother's hands together.

Prince Andrian rubbed his neck, amazed that the strange girl who had followed him everywhere smiled down at him. He opened his palm to reveal the deerskin and mouthed, "I will find you." He had survived yet another ordeal, and that time the little red-haired girl had brought him from beginning to end. Julian looked at Andrian, who smiled up into the tree. He tried to find what he gazed after, but saw nothing.

The crowd babbled and Julian took Andrian's hand and helped him to his feet. Andrian wavered and leaned on his brother to keep from falling over. Andrian looked at Julian and smiled. "I have for once found something I am better at than you."

Julian sighed. "What?"

He laughed. "Killing people."

Julian embraced his brother's shoulders. "My God, I never wanted you to die." He turned to the crowd to announce: "It has become apparent to me that Prince Andrian Gilbert has been totally cleared of all charges by the will of God. Therefore, my brother shall be declared innocent and retain his life hereafter until he is called home for eternity due to natural causes."

"Or until I fall short of grace again," Andrian whispered.

*　　*　　*

A herald brought King Arundel news of his son's most recent escape from death. Few approved of the prince's survival, but no one could deny the fact that God gave Andrian Gilbert, the ruthless prince, life. The king found he could do nothing to change the outcome of both the trial and the hanging, so he publically turned his back on his scion. "God wishes for him to live, and I cannot go against God's will," he announced soon after the prince's release, "but he is no longer my son."

*　　*　　*

When Sabrina arrived in Eddington, she asked Julian where her papa was. He told her that he was resting. Sabrina ran toward the prince's apartment in the keep and up to his room. She opened the door with huge eyes. Her father lay asleep in his bed, but she was so glad to see him that she cried, "Papa!" and leapt onto his sleeping form.

Prince Andrian awoke to his daughter kissing his face and snuggling beneath the covers with him. "Sabrina, you are home!"

Sabrina smiled at him and fell asleep curled next to her father.

Chapter Nineteen

Four years had passed since Andrian had come home and had earned clemency through surviving torture. Since King Arundel had denounced Andrian as his son and placed the fate of his kingdom on hiatus, Andrian had made the decision that he would turn his thoughts toward the repayment of his debt to those who had suffered by his hand. He also wished to reward those who had remained loyal to him throughout the ordeals. The only person left that he had been unable to reward had been that red-haired girl.

The girl had not stayed to speak with him after he recovered from his ordeals. In fact, he had watched her walk away with what looked like relief. He had given her his word that he should find her again, and he would not break his oath. He wrote letters to countless lords, "Have you seen this girl?" He offered rewards of money, land, and even rank to anyone who would turn her over to him. The response to his inquiries all made him sound like a lovelorn lunatic. He still carried the deerskin in his pocket as a reminder of the gift of life she had bestowed upon him. He would not give up, even if he must write a thousand letters and knock on every door in every town in every fiefdom.

Four years of days that melted into one another pulled Andrian toward both educating his daughter and grooming her for the life of a noblewoman in between his obsessive letter campaigns for the mystery heroine. Andrian enjoyed listening to his daughter recite poetry while he lay on the grass in the upper bailey.

In the evenings, after her poetry and Latin lessons, Sabrina frequently dined with her grandfather and learned her manners and her place in the household. Sabrina was only eight, but she was a studious child and a hard worker. King Arundel frequently praised her cool head and nobility of character, something her father certainly lacked. Sabrina bit her tongue at the remarks, though she would frequently report them to her father.

Late nights found Andrian walking the halls of the castle with notes he had taken during mass or return letters from those who denied seeing the mystery girl, or even letters from Kieran, who quite enjoyed her life in the convent.

Late in the summer, the air had been warm that day, so Andrian stayed up later than usual to pace the castle. He squinted at his notes, for even the torches around the halls shed little light. He stopped beneath the glow and held the paper further from him, mumbling with irritation at the darkness.

"Milord?" a voice whispered.

He frowned as he read.

"Milord?"

He looked down at a maidservant twisting her hands together. "Is there something the matter?" He folded the notes and shoved them in his belt.

She did not look up at him, as though he would consider eye contact with him a crime.

"Father Dallan wants to see yeh right away. Said 'e needed to speak about somethin' important."

Andrian smiled. "Lead the way."

As they entered the meeting room, Father Dallan sat in a chair by a table. "Andrian, so good of you to see me at this time."

Andrian sat beside the priest. "*Bon soir.* I have been wandering aimlessly again."

"So I heard." The priest turned to the servant. "Will you bring us a drink?'

She curtsied and left them to talk.

"I've some disturbing news for you." Father Dallan pushed a scroll of parchment toward him. "This came from the north. It seems as though you have enemies still in your father's kingdom." He pushed another scroll toward him. "This came from Spain. It seems you have enemies abroad as well."

Andrian read the letters and frowned. "I have to act upon these threats, Father. There is nothing worse than a man who allows such words to go unanswered."

Father Dallan sighed. "I received these from Sir Idwal. Apparently these types of letters have flooded the king for quite some time but he has done nothing."

Andrian glanced up as the maidservant entered with wine and bread. "Thank you."

As she set the food down, she knocked an oil lamp onto the battle plans Andrian had worked on for months. Andrian leapt from his chair, for the flames shot toward the woman and he with a crackling roar. A stream of curses expelled from his mouth as he removed his cloak to smother the flames. "Ahh." He recoiled as the flames singed his hands.

Father Dallan stood back to watch him dance about, careful not to catch himself in the fire.

With the last ember squelched, Andrian wiped his forehead. "That was exciting."

The maiden fell prostrate on the floor and cowered. "Please don't kill me . . . it was an accident."

Andrian reached out for her and she closed her tearful eyes. He placed his hand gently on her shoulder and whispered, "I'm so sorry that I caused you to fear me. Please forgive me."

She looked up with confusion. She placed her hand on his and it trembled, but with sorrow, not anger.

"Please stand up, I beg you."

She stood and he took her hand and squeezed it. "I am only glad you were not injured by the fire."

"But your battle plans . . . they're ruined . . ."

"They can be made again, you cannot be." He tapped the side of his head. "They are all in here."

She turned and ran away, screaming, "My lord prince has been possessed!"

Prince Andrian sighed and sat once again with the threatening letters in hand.

* * *

When Prince Andrian left the castle in the morning for his daily walk with Sabrina, Eddington seemed as it always had. People wandered about their business and flapped their hands in lively conversation. When the prince and his daughter returned from their stroll, the air suddenly felt murky with fear and panic.

Sir Idwal sprinted to the prince from the guard gate. "Milord, King Arundel wants you to go to him right away."

Prince Andrian furrowed his brows and turned to his daughter. "I want you to follow Sir Idwal. He shall take you to your room, and I want you to stay there until I come to talk to you."

Sabrina nodded, and Prince Andrian ran to find out what his father wished of him.

King Arundel paced back and forth in the greater hall before his throne. He looked up at the same time the prince knelt before him.

"You called for me, my liege?"

King Arundel stopped his pacing. "Yes, I did. I only wanted you to know that there is an uprising against me. Several nobles from the north have assembled armies to attack and overthrow me."

"I heard from Father Dallan earlier." Prince Andrian swallowed. "I intend to speak to them. There must be a way to cease the war before it begins."

King Arundel bade him to rise and he placed his hands on his son's face. "You have done this. You have divided my kingdom. Even though you *claim* to have changed your ways, the past still affects all."

Andrian raised his face to his father and looked him in the eyes. "What is it you want me to do?"

"I want you to leave. Perhaps if you go I shall have peace here once again."

Prince Andrian kissed his father's trembling hand. "I wish to stay and defend my king." He leaned his head against his father's robes. "Make me a knight. I swear I shall defend you even if it shall cost my life."

"Utter nonsense." The king yanked his robes away from his son. "I asked you politely to leave, but now I must be hard. I exile you, Andrian."

Andrian stood with a grimace.

"Pack your belongings and leave my country."

Andrian bowed. "As you wish, Your Majesty." He took the coronet from his head and turned it in his hands. "I am sorry I no longer deserve this."

King Arundel turned his back and heard a clang on the floor. Boot steps faded and he turned around. His son had obeyed his command and had not made a fuss. Perhaps the young man had changed. He was, after all, twenty-nine years old. He had a daughter he had raised thus far, and with much pleading on his own behalf, the pope had accepted Andrian back into the church. Still, King Arundel convinced himself that exiling his son remained the best thing he could do for his kingdom. Julian would be a better king than Andrian. He had made his decision.

Andrian rushed to his apartment in the keep. "Sabrina," he said as he flew into her room and shut the door. "*Ma petite ange*, I have come to say goodbye."

"Papa?" Sabrina began to weep. "Are you going to war? I heard people saying that there's a war and that it's your fault, but is it true?"

Prince Andrian nodded. "Indeed." He sighed. "If things go poorly, I shall go to France for a spell. I promise, whatever happens, I shall return for you."

Her eyes welled up and she clutched his robes. "Don't go away. Take me with you."

"I wish I could bring you, but where I go I know not at the moment." He kissed her and pulled her into his arms. "I will not be back for quite a time, but I want you to study what I taught you and read every day. I want you to behave yourself for your *grandpère* and mind your manners until I return."

Sabrina snuggled into his arms. "When you come home, then I can misbehave?"

He smiled and rocked her. "When I return, we shall both misbehave . . . at least a little."

Sabrina nodded and kissed him many times on the nose and cheeks. "Goodbye, Papa. I love you."

He released her and stood up. "*Adieu*, Sabrina." He kissed her once more on the forehead. "*Tu ne pleures pas pour moi. Je t'adore ma petite ange.*"

She grasped his hand and held it.

"I must go now. Try to understand, *ma belle fille*."

She wept and nodded. "Don't forget me, Papa. You promised you'd come home."

"I did." He embraced her and whispered, "I *never* break my word."

*   *   *

King Arundel gave his son five days to leave the borders of his country, but as Andrian packed his belongings into his pack, he realized that leaving his country meant leaving his family and his people unprotected from danger. Even if it meant a second trip to the gallows, he would become an outlaw and fight those who meant his father harm.

Out of his bedside chest Andrian pulled the armor he wore in the Holy Land. Too precious a treasure, he had not worn it since the age of twenty-four. He slipped it on over his tunic. It still fit him, albeit a little snugly around the middle. Four years of peace had fattened him up. He strapped himself into his brigandine, his greaves, his spaulders, and tossed his gauntlets in his pack along with his great helm. His black cloak he threw over his shoulders and clasped to his brigandine. A knight he would be, whether his father wished it or not.

Andrian, now an unknown knight dressed in black, exited the keep in full battle garb. Though many turned their heads at the knight in black rushing to the stables for a horse, none were too surprised. War was upon them, and many such sights were yet to be seen.

The black knight upon a black stallion rode out the portcullis in search of his future.

Weeks of riding it took for the black knight to come upon any sort of organized resistance. Many towns had come together to shore themselves up for the certain doom in the battles ahead, but none had men to spare for defense. Most of the men-at-arms marched under the banner of Lord Julian and his knights, though rumors spread that the king's army had become soft in Prince Andrian's retirement.

In Cricklade, Andrian had years ago fought and found himself near death. In Cricklade, Andrian found the closest thing to a mercenary resistance he could join. He had spied them as he rode down from a high hill. He chuckled to himself, for their inexperience would have killed them had he been his old army sneaking up on their flanks.

Andrian approached the battalion stationed in view of an oncoming wave of rebels led by the knights of the Duke of York. So engrossed were they in their analysis of the enemy across the hillocks that when the black knight and his horse thundered up to them they leaped back and fell upon each other. The black knight waited until they regained their stance. He struggled desperately not to laugh at their mishap under his great helm.

"Friend or foe?" They collected together and pushed toward him.

"I wish to join you." The black knight held up his hands.

The leader of the resistance called himself Daibhidh. His blond hair seemed almost as frightening as the words that spewed from his mouth. Andrian knew that Daibhidh's army had potential if they could pick up more men-at-arms in the area, and if they would pay attention to all their flanks.

"What's your name?" Daibhidh frowned at Andrian. "Who do you give allegiance to?"

Andrian frowned under his helm. "I have no name, and as of this week I have not a country. I am a mercenary as these men."

Daibhidh smiled. "Remove your helmet so I might see who I fight beside."

"Does it matter who you keep your company? I am a seasoned warrior, and I will win battles. That is all you need know." The black knight flexed his fingers and rolled his neck.

"If you fall, I want to know to whose widow I should give my condolences."

Andrian's horse reared as Daibhidh spoke. "Sir, the woman I love is dead. No one will weep for me." He drew his sword and it flashed. "Let me join you. I long to crush the skulls of my enemies in my fists."

Daibhidh shrugged. "If you fight as bravely as you talk, then come with us."

Andrian nodded.

The Duke of Winchester had also sent a formidable army to attack Eddington. Andrian watched the marchers flood into the plains with a thundering *boom-boom-boom*. The men in the black knight's army, mounted and on foot, trembled as the mass of armed rebels darkened the field of dying blooms.

"They outnumber us, sir. We can't win." A young man looked up at Daibhidh.

Daibhidh swallowed as he took in the wriggling masses across from them. "What've we gotten ourselves into?"

Andrian looked over at his pale face and smiled. He rode out in front of the meager army and turned toward them. "We shall win. These men are lazy and fat from lack of battle."

The small battalion turned toward Andrian and dropped their weapons. Some wailed with fear, others urinated on themselves, still others sat on the ground and shook their heads.

Andrian's horse reared. "Get up. We fight like men, not like dogs! Men stand on two feet and carry weapons; dogs crawl on the ground and piss themselves! Now, to your feet or I shall fight them myself and return in victory to shame the lot of you!"

The men looked at each other. "But there are thousands of them and we may have but three hundred."

The black knight chuckled. "Would it be the first time in history that such odds had played upon the fields of battle?" Andrian drew his sword and turned his horse toward the armies of the Duke of York and the Duke of Winchester. He kicked its flanks and charged down the hill, one man against thousands.

"Bloody fool's given away our position." Daibhidh shook his head.

The army saw the lone rider on the dark horse charging down the hill with his sword drawn.

"What kind of idiot runs straight to his death?" a soldier said as the rider flew toward the army.

The pikemen lowered their spears at him and laughed. Archers raised their arrows to him, but a captain hooted. "Don't waste your arrows."

Andrian rode close enough to see their eyes, bloodshot with the stress of a long march, and stopped his horse. The black stallion reared. He swung his sword in the air and howled at them, "Go home or you will die!"

The soldiers shrieked with laughter and several dropped their defenses. Andrian charged them, and as he slipped in and out of their ranks, he destroyed several men without personal injury. Before he left the mass of soldiers, he stole a spear right from the hand of a now open-mouthed pikeman and whirled it above his head in full gallop.

He rode back to the battalion on the hill and tossed the spear into the ground in front of Daibhidh. "It starts, *mon ami.*"

"ARE YOU MAD?"

Andrian pulled off his helmet. "Absolutely."

Several men looked at each other. *"Andrian the Ruthless."*

"We're gonna win," Daibhidh said to himself. "We're gonna win!" He shook his sword in the air. He shouted and the battalion roared as the dark-hearted prince raised his sword.

"What the *hell* was that?" the captain said as a thunderous roar traveled into the valley.

One soldier pointed toward the knoll as a dark figure and his horse appeared. After the figure came three hundred men-at-arms and mounted cavalry.

"It's that buffoon who attacked us alone." The captain squinted.

Another man looked up. "We're doomed."

The captain rolled his eyes. "There are only a couple hundred of them, and thrice as many beside us. You're an idiot."

"Call a retreat."

The captain shoved the soldier. "I give the orders around here, you coward."

The battalion thundered down the hill, beating their shields and howling at the army. The dark rider led them with his black hair streaming behind him.

"Andrian the Ruthless Devil himself," the captain said as the battalion smashed into his flank and broke the ranks.

Blood splattered into the prince's face as he slashed through the men as if shearing wheat.

"Retreat!"

Andrian the Ruthless, cloaked in blood, snarled at the foot soldiers and plowed through them three and four at a time.

"He's gone berserk!"

The antagonizing army dropped back and then began to run as the ruthless prince hacked his way toward the officers.

Screams testifying to the prince's immortality spread and dissipated the armies of the dukes. Andrian and his demon stallion pursued the running soldiers. The black prince howled at them as he swung a sword with his right hand and railed them with a stolen halberd in his left hand. Several battlefield knights followed suit, though Andrian was the only chevalier mad enough to release the reins of his horse to stab at the running and screaming pikemen.

When the last enemy soldier had fallen or run with his hands on his head, weeping, what remained of the defending battalion cheered, "Huzzah!"

Andrian and his stallion returned to rejoin the ranks, his sword, crimson with the blood of his enemies, held triumphantly.

Daibhidh handed the prince a cloak to wipe the stains from his face.

"Brilliant, Milord. Just brilliant."

Prince Andrian wiped his eyes. "There shall be more time to celebrate later. Now we must ride to meet the Count of Devon's army before he crosses into Wessex." The prince licked his lips. "We need at least five hundred more men. Let us move out."

Daibhidh nodded as they headed west.

After Briton had fallen into chaos during the uprising of the duchies, the rightful heir to the throne had been contested. The exile and disgrace of Andrian Gilbert, the ruthless prince, brought war closer to the doors of Briton than ever before. Not only had the duchies marched upon their own king, foreign kings also vied for the crown of Briton. Andrian the Ruthless no longer held his sword firmly in the soil of the crumbling nation.

Long ago, Andrian the Ruthless had come through the towns of Briton and razed them. Long ago, the villeins had screamed in fear at the sight of the shadowy figure upon the hill, his black hair whipping in the wind behind him. Long ago, the prince of darkness had been the most despised warlord in all of Europe. Now every battle ended with victory for the soldiers who rallied behind Andrian the Ruthless. From town to town they marched, and they never failed to snowball dozens of men to their cause. The black figure appearing on the hill above meant the god of war was on their side and their devoted offerings had pleased him.

The people of Briton had spoken, let Andrian drive the dukes back to their castles and let the invaders from the north feel the tear of his sword through their sails. For a time, the peasants forgot the shame the prince had brought upon the country. They only saw that the vile man was not simply winning victories with half to a third of the men of the enemies' armies, but he crushed them like ants under his boot.

As for the ruthless prince, he saw each battle as a defeat. He destroyed the men whom he had sworn to protect. Guilt threatened to sway his decisions, but the look his daughter gave him as he had left her behind in Eddington fueled his desire to vanquish those who put his child in danger. Andrian the Ruthless went from the unknown black knight to a general once again, though this time by the will of the people and not his own. His commanders huddled around Andrian's table and analyzed his battle plans. Knights swore fealty to a man who no longer was welcome in the country by order of the king, and yet not one desired to remove him from power. Briton had needed a philosopher king for so long, but on its knees, Briton begged for their sovereign warrior.

Chapter Twenty

Long battles took bricks out of the castle that was Andrian the Ruthless. Dreams crept into his cracking walls like rats into grain stores and gnawed at his mind and heart. Days and weeks on the back of his steed dragged memories up he had suppressed to strengthen himself. Now as his body wore down, and his soul trembled with the endless siege of battle, the great warrior closed his eyes even during marches.

Forests in his mind loomed with the mists of his past. His sister and her brokenness lying still in her bed, her last breaths drawn as she gazed up at her brother. The pain in his father's eyes as he beat his son mercilessly for his disobedience manifested as haunting visions, the sting of the open wounds revisited his flesh.

Nights in his tent scattered memories between his waking and sleeping moments. The prince in near feverish hallucinations would watch his pain unfold as though a shriveled thorn bush had unfurled in his heart.

*   *   *

"What a lovely day, Jonquille." Andrian looked out the window and then at his sister, bedridden with illness.

Jonquille had paled since last Andrian had seen her. Death shadowed her, and King Arundel locked her away as if she were contagious.

"Andy, will you take me out today?" Jonquille struggled to sit up but collapsed.

Andrian sat on his sister's bed and stroked her broken strands of hair. "Jonquille, you know Father does not wish for your sickness to worsen by being out of bed."

Jonquille swallowed and tears dribbled down her cheeks. She eyed the crystal blue sky and coughed. "I don't want to live like an invalid."

"But you are an invalid." He chuckled and kissed her forehead. "I will see what I can do."

She nodded and watched him leave the room.

Andrian stalked toward his father's chambers and put his ear to the solid wooden door. Hearing nothing inside, he snuck back to Jonquille. "I can sneak you outside." Andrian removed his cloak and laid it on the bed. He pulled his sister out from under her covers. Though only a year younger than he was, she was flesh and bones her illness had stolen the meat from her. "Have you enough strength to hold on to my back?"

"I think so."

Jonquille clutched her brother around the neck, and he threw the cloak over himself.

"Out to the river today? Or perhaps the stables?"

"Andy?"

Andrian hushed her as he exited the room, a hunchbacked prince an unusual sight to behold. Julian, watching the malformed boy of thirteen plodding down the corridor, had become accustomed to watching his younger brother breaking rules concerning Jonquille's well-being.

Julian set his Bible down and followed behind. He cleared his throat as Andrian descended the stairs.

"Lovely day, is it not?" Andrian stammered.

"Quite lovely for you or me, but not so lovely for the ailing of the household." Julian placed his hands on his hips.

Andrian placed his hands together. "I have no idea what you mean. The ailing is where she should be. Go and see."

Julian raised his eyebrow. "So . . . you have grown a repulsive hump since this morning, haven't you?"

Andrian glanced over his shoulder. "Aye. Funny things those humps are. Keep popping out of nowhere to spite."

Julian tapped his foot. "And you do not tell the physician about the hump, as you forget to tell him about your recurring belly, and your need to clothe Bob?"

Andrian put his hands on his hips. "I resent your comment about my dog. Bob enjoys wearing my robe. He thinks he is a person."

"Or he carries one. I do not think you are being wise by letting Jonquille outside. She is very sick, and these forbidden holidays will kill her sooner or later."

Andrian rolled his eyes. "Julian, the darkened room will kill her. She is in a tomb she does not need. The sunlight will do her good, you shall see."

Julian pointed upstairs. "Back to bed, and leave her be. She needs rest."

Jonquille poked Andrian and whispered in his ear. "Run."

Julian's eyes widened, and Andrian laughed at him.

Shooting as an arrow from the bow, Andrian sailed down the stairs and skipped the last three steps. Julian hollered behind him, but he cackled all the way out the door. His cloak fluttered in the breeze as Jonquille lifted it above her head.

Toward the middle bailey, Andrian carried his sister and halting before he died of breathlessness, set her down with gentility.

Jonquille giggled as she lay on the ground, her cheeks glowing with the sunlight.

Andrian laughed, then coughed, and then laughed again. "Why did Julian make such a funny face?"

Jonquille smiled and made a rude gesture.

After guffawing over her impudence, Andrian sat down and wiped his eyes. "You should not have angered him. He has kept our secret for a long time."

Jonquille grabbed her brother's hand and squeezed it. "Thank you."

Andrian shook his head. "To whom else would I have to talk if you did not sneak about with me?"

"You've got lots of friends, don't you?"

Andrian sighed and mutilated the grass.

"Out with it. Why don't you have friends like Julian does?"

He shrugged.

Jonquille sat up with Andrian's help and leaned on him. "Is it because you're so cute? And because you're so charming?"

"Stop it." Andrian blushed.

"I bet I know what it is."

He cocked his head at her and sighed. "What then."

She tickled his chin and giggled. "It's because you walk around with a dirty face."

He wiped his chin. "Hey. I am trying to grow a beard!"

"Looks more like dirt to me."

"That is because you are a little girl."

"Ha! I'm a year younger than you, so that means you're just a little boy. So there."

Andrian stuck his tongue out at her. She returned his gesture.

Placing her fingers on his upper lip, she chuckled. "I can feel that you've got something there."

"See? Soon, I shall have a moustache and beard, and no one will call me boy."

Jonquille's smile broadened.

"What's so funny?"

"Well . . . I think that your voice sounds like Julian's."

Andrian puffed up. "Julian is twenty-one. I sound like a man then."

"Sure you do, until Father calls and you answer 'aye' with a voice like a mouse." She cackled as Andrian crossed his arms and sneered.

"Laugh all you want, Jonquille. Soon I will go to war, and when I come back, I will look like a man and be experienced like one." Andrian looked over at two boys hardly older than himself. "They are squires, and they get to help the knights in battle."

"Father will never let you fight. You're going to go to school."

Andrian smirked. "That is not what I heard Father tell Julian."

"What?"

Andrian sat up straight. "I overheard a conversation. I shall see battle."

Jonquille's eyes widened.

"I think it will make me tough."

Jonquille giggled. "Sure will. After you're hung out to dry in the sun like salted pork, I don't think you would last long."

Andrian gasped. "Why not?"

"All right, when the battle stops because a girl screams in terror, and the men see it's you and your manly voice . . . how embarrassing."

He snorted, "I do not sound like a girl."

"Just now! Didn't you hear it?"

"What?"

Jonquille covered her mouth. "Ha! When you said 'not', your voice went eep!"

"Did not."

"Did too."

"You just want me to be mad. It will never work."

Jonquille chuckled and felt her brother's chin again. "When you grow your beard, don't have one of those ugly braided things those wild men of the north have."

"Why not? They look scary, and I want to look scary."

"No one will find you scary if you try to roar and say 'eep'."

Andrian felt his chin. "Fine. What beard is good to you?"

Jonquille traced Andrian's mouth and chin. "Right around there. That's good. And you have to have everything else shaved."

"That does not sound scary at all."

"It will be scary enough when your enemies hear your name." Jonquille grinned.

"Andrian is not a scary name."

Jonquille shrugged. "Make it scary."

Andrian lay on the grass and pulled his sister beside him to look at the sky. "How do I make my name something to fear?"

"Well . . . you could belch your name. That's scary."

Andrian could not help it, he laughed. "That is disgusting. Although if I have consumed enough onions, I suppose it would be a bit frightening."

"Oh, I'd cry, and I don't cry about anything."

"Hmm . . . scary. Suppose I make up a name for myself that would drive men away for leagues." Andrian grumbled. "Ehhhh, how about Andrian the Gargantuan?"

With that, Jonquille hooted. "You're hardly taller than me! I must be a giant too then!" She looked over at him. "Andrian the Scum Tosser."

"Hey, I like scum."

"You would." She smiled.

"Andrian the Troll."

Jonquille scratched his chin. "Trolls are hairy."

He sighed and looked at the clouds. "There is a storm coming."

"So what?"

"So . . . so you should go inside."

"Not until I want to."

Andrian sighed and sat up. "Come on, Jonquille. Inside we go, come rain or snow."

"Or outside we stay and head inside some other day."

Andrian pointed at her. "That was good."

"Inside if we must."

"Aye, or my lip Father will bust."

"Or he'll burn you to dust."

Andrian laughed and hauled her into his arms. "In bed, Jonquille shall dream until she is well."

"Carried by Andrian, the Ruthless Prince from Hell."

He stopped. "I like that."

"Do you?"

"I do."

His sister's image faded into the depths of his sleep-wary eyes. Andrian placed his hands behind his head. So long ago had it been since Jonquille had succumbed to consumption, that her face now consisted only of her eyes in his mind; Andrian could barely even see her smile. Sabrina resembled his sister and perhaps that was the reason his father had taken to his daughter so greatly.

Prince Andrian lay with his eyes closed, trying to see his child in his mind. Even she had faded away from view. He had spent so long away from her that he may not even matter to her any longer. In the life of a child of the court, it was customary that an heir apparent would be molded according to the expectations of those who would see him or her on the throne. Prince Andrian had not remained home long enough to begin his lessons with her.

War could be months, years, could never end. Would his daughter be a woman when he returned? Would his daughter know him at all? Would Andrian even return home from war? Prince Andrian grimaced in the darkness. In his absence, the king would groom her to be sovereign queen and sow the seeds of enmity of her own father in her soul.

Andrian fell asleep to a vision of his daughter dressed in gold and jewels upon the throne; in one hand she held a scepter, and in the other a sword; her foot resting on the scorched skull of her father.

Chapter Twenty-One

For a year, battles raged in the kingdom of Briton. When the armies relinquished their obsessive chasing and attacking of one another, Prince Andrian fought with himself. Nightmares plagued him night after night. His desire to throw down his sword and accept his fate became stronger. The war would never end as long as he lived. Days bled into nights as his company marched up and down the country in hopes to diminish the threats sent out to his father, the king. Andrian felt himself continue to weaken in his state of exhaustion, his very soul had begun to slump in his body. Andrian's only consolation in his exhaustion became the rare dream Farida now entered.

Like days of old, Andrian slept on a cot in his tent. In the absence of his wife, his only comfort became his favorite tunic and the armor of the desert kings. Slumber had fallen upon him earlier that night, though as he tossed and turned his restlessness kept him from the deep sleep he needed to recover his battle-worn body.

"Go to the sea, Andrian. You need to rest yourself. It's been too long since you've slept." Farida caressed his forehead.

He opened his eyes and looked up at her, the glow around her heavenly. "My love, I beg you to come with me. We can rest together."

She laughed and kissed him. "Not yet. Someday we'll be together again. You've a long time yet on earth."

Andrian frowned. "But you sit with me now."

"Do I?" Farida reached for him, and he felt cold and sad.

He awoke and sat up, tears streaming down his face. He lay back down and looked at the stars through holes in his tent fabric. Andrian decided to gain strength with his last loving memory. Pershore became his last pilgrimage and the most painful one he could imagine a man might go on.

Andrian's battalion had grown from a paltry three hundred men in his first battle to an intimidating 3,500 in a year's time. The prince laid waste to all who crossed his path. Up and down for a thousand miles his men pounded the enemies of the crown until all that remained gave a last desperate strike at Eddington. Unbeknownst to the prince, the scrap of curs belonging to the Duke of Selsey marched east of his military while he took a short respite to sleep in his home for the last time. Andrian rode alone to Pershore and gave his men instructions as to where to meet him for battle.

Andrian and his black stallion flew along the fields that once upon a time had overflowed with wildflowers only Heaven might bear in its soil. Now the grass had browned with the tramping of the boots of thousands of soldiers and iron-shod warhorses. Thrown clots of dirt littered the remaining sprinkles of flowers, yellowing and downhearted. The once ice crystal stream had clogged with mud and refuse from the army camps that repetitively chose the meadow to pitch their tents until it became as foul as the streets of London. The forest around Andrian's hidden cottage felt the sting of the men-at-arms. Branches from trees no longer littered the ground. Stumps gashed through the earth like teeth through gums. Years of growth had been stripped away by the hordes of soldiers looking for fire fuel. Andrian's little home still stood, though the rickety walls had lost much of their mud plaster as the visiting armies had removed rocks from the foundation to make their fire pits.

In ancient history, a simple soldier named Andrian had asked a dark-eyed nomad named Farida to spend her life with him. The warrior never went to battle without his beloved idol, Hathor, on the dunes above, her *kalasiri* majestic turquoise next to the fine white sands. Often she would hold her scarlet shawl up so the wind would billow it as a cloud behind her. Andrian would follow the sight of her floating *haïk* home as the Israelites followed the pillar of fire to freedom. The nine-year war ended and Andrian and his bride made the long journey by sea back to the wet Isle of Briton. For the love of her villainous husband, Farida had abandoned the desert of powdered diamonds and golden tombs that touched the sky.

Andrian had worshipped his Egyptian goddess of love, and in return for his admiration, she had adored him, comforted him, and tormented him. Then just as she had come into his world, she left it.

The great palace walls that she held up disintegrated. The once proud warrior met battle without raising his sword.

Without the shining light of his desert queen, the warrior worshipped murkier entities. Darkness had always been his way, but the inferno now burned brighter than a funeral pyre and hotter than the bowels of Ararat. For her loss the whole world trembled with the wrath of the god of war, and for his pain he felled great kings to their knees with hands to the heavens. Written on the walls of great palisades were the names of the dead who fell as the warrior with the might of the lion-headed Maahes struck his shield with a roar.

Now, at the eve of his last great battle, the warlord made his decision alone. No goddess stood in the distance to welcome him into her arms. No palace had he, and no country. His home decimated, his queen dead, and his soul burning in the rubble, the once great warrior returned to the humble shack in the now forest of kindling to worship the relics of his past.

A temple to his queen, Andrian's hut deteriorated under the delicate touch of his fingertips. Dust obscured the outline of his memories, and the last of the straw upon the floor blew away with the flutter of his cloak. As quietly as he would enter a cemetery, he entered the room where Farida had become a saint, and eased himself upon the bed. The bedding remained, grayed with age, though the brownish stain of blood marred its surface and vermin had stolen the stuffing. He traced the last remnants of his wife. Farida had bled for him, and for a decade his heart had bled for her. He removed his knife from his belt and sliced a small square from the mattress. His artifact would be all he had left of his family. Time had razed everything else.

Andrian exited the house in silence and meandered over to the garden where long ago he buried his wife and son. He knelt before the rock pile that had since grown over with wild grasses and his neglected onions, growing prosperously with his blessing.

He pulled out the smooth white stone from his pocket. "I always told you I would give you the moon." He placed it by her grave. "That I could never really promise, for it never was mine to give." He sighed. "But I gave you my heart, as pathetic as you said it was. I just hope that was good enough." He kissed the white stone, now on the topmost part of the grave, and whispered, *"Requiescat in pace, Farida la vache de mon coeur."* He made the sign of the cross, and tears still streaming down his face, he rose and left the monument.

*　　*　　*

Smoke billowed like a dark stairway to heaven, and from his position from atop the highest tower on the keep King Arundel watched it rise and dissipate. The wraith of an army flowed over the horizon and swallowed up the countryside as it approached the curtain wall. The smoke in the distance now trailed with a glittery red. The forest to the east had been set to burn.

King Arundel wrung his hands as the blackness crept maddeningly close. "Why are my armies not stopping this?"

Sir Idwal, bloodied and bruised, stood by his king's side. "Your Majesty, your armies have fled." He sighed. "Let me find help. I am sure your son will lead the charge to victory."

King Arundel waved his hand. "Julian is nowhere to be found. I have already tried to reach him."

Sir Idwal paused. "Julian was not who I wished to seek."

The king leaned over the embrasure and sighed. "This is madness."

"With your permission," Sir Idwal began, and the king waved him away. The knight bolted down the tower stairs and shouted, "Ready for battle!" as he slammed his gauntlet down the walls with a *clang-clang-clang*.

The offending noblemen's armies attacked King Arundel's castle with trebuchets filled with burning caskets. Rockets flew into the air, fell into the wall, and exploded. Men tumbled from the wall walk with a faint, *"Eaaaah!"*

Up to this point, as far as King Arundel had been concerned, Andrian had accepted his exile and had taken the ship to France, where he was to stay in Langeais, his childhood home. As the king watched the armies outside the great walls chip away at the mortar, he began to hope the rumors were true that the ruthless prince and his army of goblins had remained in Briton. Putting his faith in his nebulous son scared the king more than watching the rogue armies undermine the outer curtain.

For months, Lord Julian had called upon very last soldier in the king's demesne to protect Eddington. Though his father had insisted he lead the army to victory, Julian found it dismal to rally the rag-tag crew. After his own fiefdom fell under siege, he became trapped behind his own wall of stone. His family and he hunkered in the keep, waiting for their demise. Julian heard nothing but the sound of battle in the world below his tower.

Surrounded by the smoky dusk, King Arundel stood alone on the turret. He felt safe on his high perch, though no one could afford to guard the king since he had exiled Andrian the Ruthless. The soldiers had grown useless without their commander; morale had melted away.

King Arundel leaned on a sword beside him, though his old muscles could scarcely lift the blade to his hip, let alone swing it with enough force to scratch a man. King Arundel scanned the fields before his castle for any sign of relief. He bowed his head with a frown.

In the distance, the roll of thunder echoed. King Arundel looked up as thousands of men in Roman order marched toward Eddington. As they drew closer, the king saw that the rhythmic throb came not from a storm but from the beating of the weapons of soldiers upon their shields and breastplates. Before the soldier line, a black horse with a black rider trotted. The army at the gate of Eddington scrambled at the sight of the line coming toward them, and struggled to turn their catapults and trebuchets around.

Andrian raised his sword in the air and shouted, "Death before dishonor!"

A great voice behind Andrian shouted in kind, and as Andrian charged, they screamed like a great dragon, their weapons flailing. Trebuchets flung burning rockets at the flood of men. As the burning oil crashed into the soldiers, screams carried to King Arundel. He leaned over, amused at the scurrying below. The dark rider and his horse twisted and dodged the zooming balls of fire. He ducked a flaming rocket that knocked a man to his death only meters behind him. King Arundel found himself clapping with excitement at the bravado.

With a hurl of his sword, Andrian sliced the head clean off a soldier launching another round of fire at his men. The sword lodged in the wood of the war machine, and as Andrian rode by, he liberated it like the Excalibur. On his way back around, Andrian roared toward the rest of the soldiers and their payloads of doom. Archers released their stingers at the black streak galloping toward them, but they fell from the air splintered. King Arundel cackled aloud.

Andrian's army now fell upon the threat and ripped it apart like a hound with a rabbit. Everywhere the berserk black blur flew, stillness followed. The king found himself shaking his fist in victory from atop his tower.

Behind King Arundel, a man dressed in a friendly soldier's uniform approached. "Good evening, my liege." The king turned around and smiled as the soldier bowed.

"How fares the fight outside the walls?" King Arundel clasped his hands together.

"We'll win, sire." The man pulled a knife from his belt, stabbed the king in the chest several times, and fled down the tower steps.

King Arundel fell to his knees with a cry and slowly sank onto his belly. King Arundel lay on the cold stone with the image of the traitor burned in his mind.

* * *

King Arundel lay pallid in his bed, and at the beckoning of Sir Idwal, Andrian had entered the keep. Lord Julian had found himself rescued after the armies outside his own walls had fled from the strikes of Andrian the Ruthless. With armed guards, Julian had followed the trail of destruction that Andrian left in his stead as he demolished all resistance from Selsey to Eddington. Lord Julian and his guard watched the battle progress with the safety of distance. When no more enemies raised their weapons to the war god on his demon steed, the cry of "Huzzah!" signaled Julian's welcome into the remnants of his brother's glory.

Now, the victory seemed useless as the brothers comforted the king. His face had grown gray and his mouth remained open with each painful breath.

Andrian, reeking of blood and sweat, knelt by his father's side. "I am sorry I have failed you yet again. You lie dying because of me." He began to weep. "Forgive me, Father. All I ever wanted was your favor, and now I have murdered you."

King Arundel weakly shook his head. "I have never had this much excitement in all my life." He raised his hands slightly and tapped his fingers together. "Bravo, my son."

King Arundel beckoned for Julian to approach. Prince Andrian smiled at his brother, for he knew that Julian would undoubtedly make a better king. And though sorrowful more for disappointing his father, he accepted his loss of the crown. He placed one hand on his father's arm and the other on Julian's shoulder.

King Arundel kissed each of Julian's cheeks and his forehead. "Take care of your wife and family and help your brother make wise decisions." He sighed. "You have been a blessing as a son, and I pray you are prosperous and fruitful. The country needs more men with your principles and diplomacy."

Prince Andrian smiled and nodded; his brother had earned his blessing. Andrian felt shame for treating him poorly in his youth, and so he promised himself he would swear fealty to the new king instead of returning home to France.

Before Andrian could say a word, the king removed the signet ring from his trembling hand and placed it in Andrian's fist. "Rule your kingdom with these things in mind: justice, love, and compassion. With these things your line shall flourish, and you shall be able to hold your head high the rest of your days. No longer lower your eyes in shame for your sins, for you *have* been forgiven by me and all who have been wronged."

Andrian quavered.

"Long ago, my son, you asked an important question of me." King Arundel frowned. "I realize now my answer to that question nearly destroyed your life."

Andrian shook his head. "What are you saying?"

"Hush." King Arundel squeezed his hand. "I am sorry for the loss of your *wife*."

"*Merci.*" Andrian kissed his father's hand repeatedly. "*Merci beaucoup.*"

King Arundel pulled his son closer, placed his hands on his face, kissed his forehead gently, and gripped him. "Andrian, I am so very *proud* of you."

As Andrian leaned into his father's embrace, the king's hands slipped from his son's armor and fell to his sides.

"The king is dead," Lord Julian announced.

"Long live the king," the knights in the chamber chanted.

"*Long live the king.*" Lord Julian bowed his head and backed into the shadows.